★

As she stared at the scene before her, she wanted to scream, but no sound came out. The man lay naked in a pool of blood beside the bed, slack-jawed, eyes wide and staring. His hairy chest was soaked in blood— dark, almost black. A telephone, dragged from the bedside table, lay on its side beneath his outflung hand. It, too, was smeared with blood.

Vikki scrambled on all fours in her panic to get away, oblivious to the pain stabbing at her head. She slipped and fell, scrambled to get up and found her hand entangled in some soft material.

Simone's dress! Blood spattered and torn. She didn't understand. How could the dress be...? She looked down.

She, too, was naked and her skin was streaked with blood.

──────────── ★ ────────────

"...a very well-put-together, classic-style British police procedural, and an enjoyable one at that."
—*Mystery News*

FRANK SMITH

THREAD OF EVIDENCE

WORLDWIDE®

TORONTO • NEW YORK • LONDON
AMSTERDAM • PARIS • SYDNEY • HAMBURG
STOCKHOLM • ATHENS • TOKYO • MILAN
MADRID • WARSAW • BUDAPEST • AUCKLAND

For Jeane and her unfailing patience in this special year

THREAD OF EVIDENCE

A Worldwide Mystery/April 2002

First published by St. Martin's Press, Incorporated.

ISBN 0-373-26416-X

THREAD OF EVIDENCE

ONE

Saturday, 23 September

"I WANT THAT MAN out of here. Understand? He's been here the best part of two hours, and I have people waiting. I want him out *now!*"

"But I can't simply *tell* him to leave," the waiter objected. "You know what Mr. Bolen's like. Besides, he just ordered another drink."

Leonardo, maître d' and absolute ruler of the Elizabethan Room, bristled. "I said, get rid of him!" he hissed fiercely. "I don't care how you do it, but do it."

The waiter sighed as he made his way toward the corner table where a well-built, dark-haired man sat hunched over a sheaf of papers and a pocket calculator, seemingly oblivious to his surroundings. "If there is nothing else, Mr. Bolen," he ventured, "perhaps you would like…?"

"Ah! There you are, lad." Jim Bolen didn't look up, but continued to write. "Thought you'd left for the night or gone on your holidays. What do you call this?" He shoved his drink across the table, slopping it on the cloth.

"Irish whiskey, sir. That *is* what you ordered, and—"

"I know what I ordered, and it wasn't this muck. Who's on the bar tonight?"

"Bingham, sir, but—"

Bolen grunted. "Thought as much. Take this back and tell Bingham that when I order Irish, I don't mean water from the bog, and if he tries it on again it will be the last drink he serves in this hotel. Got that?"

"Yes, Mr. Bolen. I'm sorry, Mr. Bolen."

Bolen lifted his head and favoured the waiter with a smile. "And you'll be gone as well," he said pleasantly, "since you no doubt split the take with Bingham."

The waiter opened his mouth to protest, then wisely closed it. No point in digging himself in deeper, especially when the man was right. He removed the offending drink and made for the bar, aware of Leonardo's smouldering eyes boring into his back as he left the room.

Jim Bolen tossed his pencil aside. He leaned back and closed his eyes. It would be tight, damned tight, but if he could bring this off it would be worth it. A grim smile touched the corners of his mouth. Lambert would be as good as finished.

He drew in a long breath and let it out again as he savoured the thought. He'd waited a long time for this.

"You devious bastard!" The words were spoken softly, but there was no mistaking their hostility. "Laura said I'd find you here. Getting everything sorted for Monday's meeting, are you, Jim?"

Jim Bolen stifled a groan. That voice was the last one he'd expected to hear this evening. A welcoming smile spread across his rugged features as he opened his eyes. "Harry!" he said expansively. "I wasn't expecting you back for another week." His expression changed to one of concern. "Nothing wrong, is there? Dee's not ill, is she? The kids all right?"

Harry Bolen pulled a chair away from an adjoining table and sat down facing his brother. Jim was the elder of the two, and heavier set than his brother, but so similar was their appearance that they were often mistaken for twins. Both were six feet tall, broad-shouldered, and both had the same deep-set eyes and unruly hair—except it was Harry, at age fifty, whose hair was beginning to turn grey.

Harry shook his head impatiently. "You know damned well why I'm back," he told his brother, "and it has nothing to do with Dee and the kids. Laura phoned me in Vancouver. Said she'd tried to stop you going through with this nonsense, but you wouldn't listen. She said you were going to be meeting here with the Whitehall crowd on Monday to present the proposal."

He paused, holding his brother's gaze while he lit a cigarette. "She also told me that you had thrown her out," he went on softly. "So would you like to tell me just what the hell is going on?"

Jim Bolen shook his head and sighed heavily. "God knows I didn't want to, Harry," he said, "but Laura's in bed with Lambert. Has been for months, and I couldn't…"

"In bed with—" Harry's voice began to rise before he cut himself off abruptly as diners at the next table turned to look. "I don't believe it! Laura having an affair? With *Lambert?*"

Jim shook his head impatiently. "I didn't mean that literally, for God's sake. I meant she's been talking to him—or I should say listening to him, and taking his side. He's running scared and he's trying to get at me through her. At us. He can't stop us any other way, and he can see the writing on the wall. When this deal goes through, he'll be as good as finished."

Harry's eyes hardened. "And that's what this is all about, isn't it?" he said. "Get Lambert, never mind the cost. Never mind what it's doing to your marriage or to those around you. For Christ's sake, Jim, forget it. We went through all this before I left and you agreed to let it drop."

He reached for an ashtray and ground out his cigarette. "I should have known there was something up when you were so keen for us to go off to Canada to see the kids and our new granddaughter. You thought you'd have it all sewn up by the time we got back, didn't you? Well, in this case, I'm with Laura, and I'm damned glad she rang me and I came back in time."

Harry Bolen leaned across the table. "It won't work, Jim," he went on earnestly. "I won't let you destroy our business. It's taken us too many years to build it up, and I won't be a party to this."

"You already are."

Harry's eyes narrowed. "And what the hell is that supposed to mean?"

Jim shrugged. "It means, little brother, that those papers you signed in such a hurry before you left gave me full signing authority. The deal is as good as done. All I have to do on Monday is present our proposal and our bid and we're in business."

Harry leaned back in his chair and shook his head slowly from side to side. "Oh, no," he said quietly. "I've gone along with you on a lot of things, Jim, but this time you've gone too far. Destroying Lambert is an obsession with you. Leave it alone,

Jim. We have all the business we can handle now. Why go on with this when you know it will ruin us?''

"Why? You have to ask why?'' Jim Bolen stared at his brother as if baffled by the question. "For God's sake, Harry, he killed our father! Isn't that reason enough?''

Harry brushed the words aside. "We don't know that," he said. "The witnesses at the inquest were all—''

"—bought off by Sam Lambert!'' Jim Bolen snarled. "You know it and I know it. And what about our mother?''

"Oh, for God's sake, Jim, she would have died anyway. The doctor made that very plain, so don't try to blame Lambert for that. Besides, it was a long time ago. It's over; let it go.''

"Christ! You're just as soft as Laura. Has Lambert been getting at you as well?''

Harry regarded his brother stonily. There was no reasoning with him on this subject; he'd been foolish even to try. He tried another tack. "Look, Jim, forget Lambert for a minute. Think of the business. Now is not the time to be over-extended, and we'll be in over our heads if you go ahead with this scheme. Let Lambert take this one on. It's too risky for us. Besides, he'll probably outbid you anyway.''

Jim Bolen smiled. "Not a chance,'' he said.

"You don't know that," said Harry irritably. He could barely restrain himself from leaning across the table to wipe the smug look from his brother's face.

"But I do, Harry. I do.''

"How?''

The smile on Jim Bolen's face deepened as he tapped the side of his nose with a forefinger. "Never mind *how* I know, Harry, boy. But you can take my word for it, I *know!*''

"I wouldn't take your word for the time of day, at the moment,'' snapped Harry. "Besides, where's the money coming from? Tell me that.''

"We have the money.''

Harry became very still, and suddenly felt cold. "What do you mean, we have the money?'' he breathed. "What have you done?''

Jim remained silent for a moment. "Mortgaged the house,''

he said at last. Harry frowned. Brookside was worth at least seven hundred thousand, but that was nowhere near enough. "And the Bolen Building," his brother added. "And the banks are prepared to back us."

"Using what for collateral?" Harry scoffed. It would take more than the house and their office building to swing the Ockrington deal.

Jim Bolen leaned back in his chair and smiled again. "Bolen Brothers," he said softly.

Harry could feel the blood draining from his face, and it seemed as if his veins were filled with ice. "You've no right!" he whispered hoarsely. "Damn you, Jim!" His open palm hit the table like a pistol shot, and a woman at an adjoining table jumped and spilled her soup. Leonardo, at his post beside the door, started forward, then thought better of it when he saw the look on Harry's face. He turned away and busied himself with menus.

Harry rose slowly to his feet, his face white with anger. "You're out of your mind," he said contemptuously. "This thing with Lambert has scrambled your brains, and I'm not going to stand by and see you destroy the business we've worked so hard to build. I'm going to stop you, Jim. By God, I'll stop you dead!" Harry thrust the chair back so hard that it fell and spun across the floor. The hum of conversation died, and every eye in the room followed him as he strode toward the door.

TWO

VIKKI LANE HUDDLED in the doorway, arms wrapped around her too-thin frame, trying to keep warm. It had been pleasant enough when she'd first arrived on her small patch, but the temperature had been dropping steadily ever since. And this was only September. What would it be like in winter, standing out here with nothing more than a mini-skirt and top between her and the elements? She jigged up and down and rubbed her arms, but it didn't help.

A dark car drifted along the kerb, one man driving, window down. Vikki stepped out into the pallid glow of the street light and tried to stop shivering as she approached the car.

"Remember, walk slow and loose, shoulders back," Simone had told her. "Bring each foot forward and slightly across the other one. Makes the hips swing. They like that. See?"

She had demonstrated, and Vikki had to admit Simone had a lot to swing. Taller than Vikki by a good four inches—and older by some ten years—Simone was beautifully proportioned, and her ebony skin and jet-black hair shone as if polished. When Simone walked down the street, men and women alike paid attention.

But it was hard when you were freezing to death and you weren't used to high heels and you knew that your pathetic little body couldn't begin to compare with Simone's.

The car stopped. A jacket hung on a hook behind the driver, half covering the near-side rear window. Business man, thought Vikki, as she came closer.

A shadow moved behind the coat.

Panic flared within her as she veered off sharply and walked rapidly away. Her heart thumped wildly as she listened for the slam of the car door and the sound of footsteps thundering down the pavement behind her. She wanted to run, but was afraid to try in her high-heeled shoes.

The engine roared and tyres screeched as the car shot away. Vikki glanced behind to see it turn the corner, and breathed a sigh of relief. Thank God she'd seen the coat move and the woman in the back seat. Police! If Vikki had so much as opened her mouth, they'd have had her.

She stepped into the shelter of a doorway and peered at her watch. It was a cheap little thing that lost ten or fifteen minutes a day, but it was all she could afford. Only eight o'clock. She groaned. Four more hours before she could pack it in.

A car slowed and stopped a few yards down the street, and Vikki drew back instinctively. The door opened and Simone slid out, bent to say something to the driver before she closed the door, then blew a kiss as the car took off again.

Vikki stepped out of the doorway. "Coppers are out," she said breathlessly. "Nearly had me a few minutes ago. Man driving; woman hiding behind a coat in the back."

Simone shrugged. She knew the ploy, but at least the girl was learning. "What's happening, apart from that?" she asked.

Vikki shivered and wrapped her arms around herself. "Sod all," she said bitterly. "And I'm—" She broke off as a car slowly drifted to a stop. "Watch it," she cautioned. "Could be another lot."

Simone turned and looked. "Not unless they've taken to driving Jags," she observed laconically. She patted her hair. "Could be my lucky night, kid."

The near-side window slid down with a soft whirring sound. The driver leaned over and beckoned with a gloved hand. He wore a cap and dark glasses, and his face was in shadow.

Simone started forward, hips moving smoothly, and Vikki felt a stab of envy. What chance did she have with someone like Simone around?

The driver waved his hand impatiently, palm outward, then pointed. Simone hesitated and looked back at Vikki with a puzzled frown. "I think it's you he wants," she said. Her tone implied she couldn't think why.

Vikki moved forward hesitantly. The man drew back as she reached the car and leaned inside.

"What's your name?"

"Vikki."

"Vikki," the man repeated. "I like that. Here, this is for you, Vikki." He held something in his hand. "Fifty pounds," he said crisply. "Take it." He didn't sound local. Educated. Touch of class. Money. He was driving a Jag, wasn't he?

Vikki tried to open the door. "It's locked," she told him.

The man shook his head impatiently. "I said take it. I don't want you now, but there's fifty more if you do as I say."

Vikki eyed him. "What do I have to do for it?" she asked, suspicious.

A smile touched the corners of his mouth. "Nothing out of

the ordinary," he assured her. "But I want you for the night. Come to my hotel room at midnight and there will be another fifty in it for you. All right?"

"And it's straight?"

"Absolutely."

Vikki reached for the money, but instead of releasing it, his other hand shot out and grasped her wrist. "And you'd better not let me down," he said softly. "If you take this money, make sure you're there on the dot or I'll come looking for you. Understand?"

He was hurting her wrist. She tried to pull away, but his grip was firm. "I'll be there," she gasped. "Which hotel? What room?"

"Room 203 at the Tudor."

"The Tudor?"

"Yes. Why? Is that a problem?"

"No! No. It's just that it's a bit off my patch, that's all. I haven't been there before."

"Right, then. Come straight up to the room. Don't stop to talk to anyone on the way. And wear something more than you've got on. Something decent or you'll never make it past the desk. All right?"

Vikki nodded vigorously. "I'll be there," she assured him. The man released her wrist and handed her the money. Still leaning inside the car, she tucked it into the waistband of her skirt. She stepped back and joined Simone as the car pulled away.

"So what was that all about?" Simone demanded.

Vikki grimaced. "Changed his mind," she said dejectedly, and before Simone could ask more questions, she shivered violently. "I'm freezing," she declared. "I'm going up to Lee's to get warm. Want to come?"

Simone shook her head, as Vikki knew she would, and shuddered delicately. "The place is filthy," she said. "I don't know why you go there."

"Because it's the only place round here that's warm," said Vikki as she moved off.

"Better not let Luke catch you," Simone called after her.

"You get back without any money again tonight, and you know what'll happen, don't you?"

Vikki waved her hand without turning round. Her fingers strayed to the waistband of her skirt; she felt the crisp notes tucked safely there and could hardly contain herself. Who cared about Luke when you had fifty quid? She felt like skipping, but she daren't while Simone was watching. Time enough for that later—after she had the other fifty.

"WEAR SOMETHING DECENT," the man had said. Trouble was, she didn't *have* anything decent. At least, nothing that would pass muster at the Tudor. Her face clouded. She'd never been to the Tudor Hotel, but Simone had warned her about the place, so she would have to be careful. But first things first.

She poked half-heartedly through Simone's clothes, and was about to turn away when she spotted the black dress. It would be far too big, of course, but she pulled it off the hanger and eyed it critically. It *might* work if she pinned it at the back and wore her mac over it. After all, it was just to get past the desk.

Twenty minutes and six safety pins later, Vikki stood before the mirror mounted on the back of the door. "Not bad," she told her image in the mirror, "though, God knows what it looks like at the back." The thought of what Simone would say if she could see what had been done to her dress gave Vikki pause, but she thrust the thought from her mind. With any luck at all, Simone would be sleeping by the time Vikki returned, and the dress could be slipped back in the wardrobe without her ever knowing.

She remembered seeing a small evening bag of Simone's on the top shelf of the wardrobe. It would look better than the tatty old thing she had. Vikki hesitated only for a moment, then told herself that if Simone didn't notice that the dress was gone, she was hardly likely to miss an evening bag.

In for a penny, she thought recklessly as she transferred her few bits and pieces to the evening bag. She tucked it beneath her arm and stood before the mirror again, turning this way and that. It would have to do, she decided. There was no way she was going to let that kind of money slip through her fingers.

Besides, if it was anything like the other times, the dress would come off as soon as she got there anyway.

Now, she must do something with her hair.

VIKKI LANE APPROACHED the entrance of the Tudor Hotel with trepidation. She'd walked all the way from Cresswell Street, and her feet were sore. She leaned against a shop window, balancing herself, first on one leg, then on the other, as she took off each shoe, and sighed with relief as her feet were exposed to the cool night air.

Somewhere nearby a clock began to strike the hour. Vikki peered unbelievingly at her watch. Eighteen minutes to twelve and the second hand was still. She shook the watch violently, but it made no difference.

And she'd been congratulating herself on arriving early!

She could see the desk and the lift beyond it through the big glass doors. A man and a woman stood behind the desk, their backs toward her. She sucked in her breath. She hadn't counted on the man being there; if he was the one Simone had told her about, she'd never get past the desk. Hardly daring to breathe, Vikki opened the door and slipped inside, eyes glued to the pair behind the desk. If either one of them turned round, they couldn't help but see her.

She slipped off her shoes and flew barefoot across the marble floor to the safety of the stairs. She didn't stop until she reached the second floor, pausing only long enough at the top of the steps to put on her shoes before moving down the corridor.

Room 203 was at the far end. She raised her hand to knock, but as she did so the door swung inward. It was dark inside. Vikki jumped when someone spoke.

"You're late! I told you midnight on the dot. Come in and shut the door."

She recognized the voice and breathed easier as she stepped inside. "I'm ever so sorry," she said, "but my watch..." A hand rested on her shoulder. "Never mind that," he said impatiently. "Let me take your coat."

"It's all right," she said quickly, fearing he would turn on the light and see the mess she'd made of the back of the dress.

"I can manage." She began to shrug out of the coat, but his hand tightened on her shoulder and she found herself being turned with her back toward him.

"It's no trouble," he said. "No trouble at all."

THREE

AT THE FRONT DESK of the Tudor, Brenda Jones yawned. She wished Quint would stop fussing and let her get on with her work. It was bad enough having to work the night shift without the night manager poking and prying into everything she did.

The muted sound of a buzzer broke the silence. Brenda picked up the phone. "How may I help you?" she asked pleasantly, more for the benefit of Norman Quint than because she was feeling particularly helpful.

"Help me," gasped a hoarse voice. "Please help me. Quickly. Do you hear me?"

"Yes, I hear you, sir, but—"

"For God's sake, come quickly. Room 203. I need..."

There was a crash, then silence. The line was dead. "Hello? Hello, sir? Are you still there?" Brenda listened intently for several seconds, then, frowning, turned to Quint.

"What is it, Mrs. Jones?"

"I'm not sure, Mr. Quint. I think it could be someone playing the fool." The voice had sounded odd. And there was always someone who thought it very funny to have her run up to his room for nothing—or to proposition her. "He said he needed help."

"What room?"

"Room 203."

Bolen! What the hell did he think he was playing at tonight? "Are you sure?" Quint asked sharply. "Did he ask to speak to me?"

"He said he needed help," said Brenda worriedly. "He sounded...odd."

Quint's mouth set in a thin line. He was tempted to tell the woman to forget it, but on the other hand, since it was Bolen... "Go up and check," he ordered brusquely, "but don't take all night about it."

Brenda crossed the floor to the lift, and once inside, pressed 2.

The sound of raised, excited voices grew louder as the lift came level with the first floor and stopped. The doors opened, and she found herself face to face with a crowd of boisterous young men pushing and shoving each other around.

Part of the Rugby crowd.

The thought of that mob crowding into the lift with her was too much. She moved to get off, but was forced back and surrounded as they all pushed into the lift.

"Going up, then, are we, luv?" yelled one lad in her ear. He was fat and sweaty, had long, lank hair, and smelt of beer. "Let's all go for a ride together." The doors closed and the lift began to rise.

"I must get out," said Brenda firmly. "There's an emergency."

"Oh, aye? Well, we've got an emergency as well, haven't we, lads? We're one short for the game, and you'll do nicely in the scrum."

The roar of approval that went up was deafening in the small space. Brenda Jones prided herself on her ability to cope in most situations, but surrounded as she was by this unruly mob, she was suddenly afraid.

The doors opened. She struggled to get through, but no one would give way. "I must get out," she pleaded. "I told you, there's an emergency."

"Oooohhhhhh dear," said Lanky Hair.

"Oooohhhhhh dear," chorused the others, and a voice in the corner began to sing: "Oh, dear, what can the matter be? Oh, dear..." The others joined in, roaring the song at the top of their lungs.

The doors closed and the lift continued upward.

LET ME TAKE YOUR COAT. It's no trouble. Let me take your coat.
It's no trouble...

The words kept running through her brain like an endless tape.
Why wouldn't it stop? Why was it so dark?

Vikki moved her head, and lights exploded behind her eyes.
Her stomach heaved and red-hot fluid spewed from her mouth.
She could feel it running down her chin and neck. She choked,
struggling for breath. She vomited again and forced herself to
roll on her side, gasping, gagging, retching as yet another stream
spewed forth. She struggled to her knees, holding herself up with
shaking arms and praying for the pain inside her head to stop.

Vikki opened her eyes and gazed with horror at the stinking
mess around her. She couldn't think. Her vision blurred every
time she moved, and she didn't know where she was. Her arms
were shaking so hard that she had to force herself to turn and
sit up. Her vision cleared.

As she stared at the scene before her she wanted to scream,
but no sound came out.

The man lay naked in a pool of blood beside the bed, slack-
jawed, eyes wide and staring. His hairy chest was soaked in
blood, dark, almost black. A telephone, dragged from the bedside
table, lay on its side beneath his outflung hand. It, too, was
smeared with blood.

Vikki scrambled on all fours in her panic to get away, oblivious to the pain stabbing at her head. She slipped and fell, scrambled to get up and found her hand entangled in some soft material.

Simone's dress! Blood-spattered and torn. She didn't understand. How could the dress be...? She looked down.

She, too, was naked and her skin was streaked with blood.

"DAMN THAT WOMAN. Where is she, anyway?" muttered Norman Quint. The telephones were ringing and she was nowhere
to be seen. He glanced at his watch. Twelve-thirty and no sign
of her; she'd been gone for at least fifteen minutes.

Annoyed, he threw down his pen and picked up the phone,
only to hold it away from his ear as a woman's voice, shrill with
anger and indignation, demanded to know what he was going to

do about the louts charging up and down the fourth-floor corridor, keeping everyone awake.

Before he could reply, two more calls came in, and then a third, all voicing the same complaint. Swearing beneath his breath, Quint came out from behind the desk and punched the button for the lift. Behind him, the telephones continued to ring. "Come on! Come on!" he muttered as he watched the light above the door.

It had to be that Rugby crowd. The ones who had booked in late when the bus that was supposed to take them home had broken down. They'd all been boozing heavily, but he couldn't afford to turn that many people away. So he had charged them top rate and taken them in.

The lift arrived and Quint got in. Still muttering, he stabbed the button for the fourth floor. The doors had almost closed when a wraithlike figure darted across the open space between the bottom of the stairs and the front door. In a second she was gone and the doors of the lift had closed. Quint frowned. He'd only caught a glimpse of her, but he was sure the girl was barefoot and carrying her shoes.

IT TOOK ALMOST HALF an hour to sort things out and get everyone back to their rooms. Fortunately, by the time Quint arrived, some of the more sober members of the team—who had themselves been trying in vain to sleep—had come to the rescue, and it was they who finally took charge and wrestled their friends into their respective rooms.

Brenda Jones was shaken but physically unharmed. In desperation, she had pretended to enter into the spirit of the game, hoping for a chance to slip away, but Lanky Hair stuck by her side, as did a couple of his mates, and their idea of a contact sport was not one she shared.

She felt unclean, and as she and Quint descended in the lift together, she began to tremble. Even Quint, who was not the most sensitive of men, could see that she was upset, and in a rare moment of compassion told her to go out to the kitchen and make herself a cup of tea. And it was only then, while she was waiting for the kettle to boil, that Brenda remembered the call from 203.

LATER, NO MATTER HOW hard she tried, Vikki couldn't remember how she'd managed to force herself to move. It was all a jumbled blur, with images appearing and disappearing like pictures flashed at random on a screen.

She remembered the clock with its bright-red numerals beside the bed: 12:18 A.M. She couldn't believe it. She was sure she'd been unconscious for hours, yet according to the clock it couldn't have been more than a few minutes. She thought it must have stopped, but even as she watched, the figure changed to 12:19.

And she remembered the sheer terror of the moment when she realized how it would look if someone found her there; remembered, too, trying to wash the blood off her body, and seeing her face for the first time in the mirror and bursting into tears.

There were scratches on her face and neck; one eye was almost closed, her lips were swollen, and a bruise was spreading darkly on her chin. She'd been beaten, yet try as she might, she couldn't remember a thing about it, and *that* scared her more than anything.

She remembered the knife. A knife stained with blood that skittered across the floor to disappear beneath the bed when she'd snatched up the dress. She'd recoiled, sobbing hysterically as she scrabbled about the floor, frantically searching for her knickers and her shoes.

She found her shoes, but her knickers were nowhere to be seen, and she daren't stay any longer. In frantic haste, she scrubbed at the top of the dress in the bathroom basin, and dried it on a towel as best she could before pulling it on. It felt wet and cold against her skin, but it would have to do. She found her mac on the back of a chair, slipped it on and buttoned it to the neck to hide the tattered dress. There was a scarf in the pocket of the mac, and she pulled it tightly round her head to hide as much of her bruised face as possible.

Thank God there had been no one in the corridor. She'd been tempted to go down the back stairs, but she didn't know where they might lead, so, shoes in hand, she'd returned the way she'd come. She hesitated only for a moment at the bottom of the stairs before bolting for the door. Outside, she'd paused just long enough to put on her shoes before walking swiftly through the darkest back streets that she could find.

What was she going to tell Simone? The dress was torn and soaking wet, and… Oh, God, the bag! Simone's evening bag! Vikki groaned aloud. She'd completely forgotten it till now. How was she going to explain that away without telling Simone everything?

She couldn't. She couldn't tell *anyone* what had happened. How could she when she didn't know what had happened herself? Everything was so mixed up in her head. She remembered nothing between the time she'd stepped inside room 203 and when she woke up on the floor.

How could she explain to anyone that she'd killed the man who'd hired her for the night, yet couldn't remember doing it? No one would believe her.

A car cruised slowly past the end of the street. Vikki slipped into the deep shadow of a shop doorway and tried to stop herself from shaking. Coppers! That was all she needed. She leaned her pounding head against the glass. She wanted to curl up and go to sleep—to sleep and wake to find that this was nothing but a nightmare.

But it wasn't, was it? It was all too real and there was nowhere she could go. She thought of turning herself in to the police, then dismissed the thought at once. She'd be charged with a murder. They'd remember her from two weeks ago when she'd spent a night in the cells with Joanna Freeborn. They'd check… *Joanna!*

Vikki held her hands to her head as she tried to think. Joanna had said she lived on a narrow boat at the end of a canal that was no longer used. What was it called? Something or other Arm. Raddington! That was it. "Rhymes with Paddington, like the station in London," Joanna had told her. Vikki had promised herself that she would visit Joanna one day if only to thank her again for helping her through that dreadful night.

Terrified of what might happen in the morning, and unable to sleep, Vikki remembered how Joanna had sat with her for much of the night, talking, soothing, and, more importantly, listening. "I felt as if I'd known her all my life," she told Simone the following day. "I felt safe with her."

In fact, Vikki recalled, she had talked of almost nothing but Joanna for days, until Simone had turned on her and told her bluntly she was sick to death of hearing about this woman who lived on a boat. "Who put good money out to pay your fine?" she demanded. "Who's been watching out for you these past weeks? If this woman is so bloody fabulous, why not go and live off her for a while? Now get your arse out there on the street and start paying some of that money back!"

The words had stung at the time, but thinking about it now, Vikki realized that Simone had every right to be annoyed. If it hadn't been for Simone, she might well be in jail at this very moment, and she *was* grateful. But she didn't want to live like this; tramping the streets at night; trying to avoid the police; shaking with fear every time she got into a car with a stranger, wondering what he would want to do with her, and knowing he could do anything he chose.

In the cold darkness of the cell that night, Joanna had given her a glimpse of another kind of life, a life where she wouldn't have to be afraid, where she could live with normal, decent people, have a normal, decent job, and a life where love meant something other than a one-night stand.

Tears rolled unchecked down Vikki's cheeks as she sank slowly to the ground. Propped with her back against the door, battered, bruised, head pounding with every pulse-beat, she just wanted to sleep, never to wake again. She drew up her knees, wrapped her arms around them, and rested her throbbing head. Her thoughts began to drift and she found herself thinking once more of her erstwhile friend.

Joanna Freeborn was a striking woman. Her arms and legs were tanned deep brown, and her face glowed with the vibrant colour that only long exposure to sun and wind and rain can bring. Her jet-black hair fell almost to her waist in lustrous waves, and there were crow's-foot lines around her eyes that crinkled when she smiled. How old was she? Thirty, thirty-five, perhaps? It was impossible to tell.

She worked, she'd told Vikki, in the local pub, and belonged to a group called The Wanderers. "We do plays," she said. "There are eight of us, although it's not often we can all get away at the same time. We play village halls, mainly, the odd fête, and last winter we did *The Foreigner* for four nights at a theatre in Chester, and they said they'd have us back again this year."

The police had charged Joanna with being drunk in charge of a horse. "But that was a lie for a start," she told Vikki. "That horse had a mind of its own, believe you me! Anyway, I'd have brought it back in the morning."

She'd been to a party in town, missed the last bus, and decided to walk the five miles home. But halfway there she saw a horse grazing on the grass verge. "A big white horse. Friendly old thing. There was no one about; no open gate nearby where he might have come from, so I took it as a sign from heaven that he'd been put there for me to ride."

Her eyes danced. "I tried explaining that to the policeman, but he was an officious little sod, so I ended up in here for the night."

Now, huddled in the doorway, shivering, Vikki remembered other things Joanna had told her that night. The pub where she worked was called the Invisible Man. Joanna had said the sign outside the pub showed a small terrier on the end of a leash, but there was no one holding the other end. The space where the dog's owner should have been was blank. Vikki hadn't known whether to believe her or not.

"Come out and visit me," Joanna told her. "I'm always around in the mornings. Take the Ludlow bus and ask the driver to drop you at Raddington Lane. It's less than half a mile from the main road to where I live. When you get to the pub, go round the back and you'll see a footpath leading off to the left. Follow it and you can't go wrong. It leads to the old tow-path alongside the canal, and I'm just a few yards down from where it comes out. It's the only boat there. It's called *Blythe Spirit*. You can't miss it."

Take the bus, thought Vikki, despairing. Right. In the middle of the night? And with nothing for bus fare even if there had been a bus? Every penny she had was at the flat, including the fifty quid she'd hidden beneath the wardrobe.

She lifted her head. It didn't seem to be throbbing quite as much. Five miles, Joanna had said. Could she walk it? She could but try, and if she had to die somewhere, it might just as well be in some ditch alongside the road as here in this grotty doorway.

FOUR

DETECTIVE CHIEF INSPECTOR Neil Paget was not in the best of humours as he drove into Broadminster at two o'clock in the morning. He had spent some four hours last evening trying to recover files he'd lost on his computer when the power failed in the middle of an entry. He'd found some of them, but where the others were he had no idea, and it had been midnight before he had given up in disgust. So when the phone rang at half past one, he had barely closed his eyes.

In addition to being the newest, the Tudor was considered to be the best hotel in Broadminster. Built a mere eight years ago, it was also one of the tallest buildings in the town. The battle over that had gone on for months, but the promise of attracting more business to the town by means of the Tudor's large convention- and meeting-room facilities, to say nothing of superb dining, had won out over the aesthetics of Broadminster's ancient skyline.

As for dining, Paget could vouch for the excellence of the fare in the Elizabethan Room. He and Andrea McMillan had dined there on more than one occasion last year, when things were going well between them. Not that they weren't going well now—except he hardly ever saw her outside work. To be fair, their jobs were so demanding that it was difficult to make arrangements and keep to them, but on the other hand, they'd managed it before. He dismissed the thought as he crossed the lobby and made his way upstairs.

The scene-of-crimes team, headed by Charlie Dobbs, had already started work. There, also, was Sergeant Tregalles, who lived no more than ten minutes away from the hotel.

"Nasty one," Tregalles told him. "Man by the name of James Bolen. Stabbed five times, as near as I can tell without moving him. It looks as if there was some sort of fight or struggle. Watch your feet, sir; someone's been sick all over the floor."

Paget could smell it as he moved into the room. He moved carefully, stepping over a broken table lamp lying on its side. His stomach stirred uneasily as he stood looking down at the naked body on the floor. There were five ugly-looking stab wounds clustered just below the rib-cage. The blood around them had dried, as had the crusted pool that stained the carpet. Dark blotches marked a blanket that looked as if it had been dragged from the bed by the dying man to try to stanch the flow of blood. He leaned closer. There were scratches on the face, beginning just below the left eye and ending at the chin.

"Bolen," he said ruminatively. "Isn't he the builder?"

"That's right. James Bolen of Bolen Brothers. They built our house, as a matter of fact. There are two brothers. Or there were. The other one is Harry Bolen. He's the younger of the two. I met him when we bought the house. Seemed like a nice bloke. Came round a couple of times after we moved in to make sure that everything was all right."

Paget nodded but still looked puzzled. "Why is he here?" he wondered aloud. "Doesn't he live in that big house just past the bridge on the Clunbridge Road?"

Tregalles nodded. "That's the one," he confirmed, "but according to Mr. Quint—he's the night manager here—Bolen stays here quite often on weekends, and he has a meeting room booked for Monday afternoon and all day Tuesday. It was a Mrs. Jones who found the body. She works the night shift on the desk. I had a word with her, but she's pretty shaken up, so I thought it best to let her go home. Seems like she had some sort of run-in with a bunch of lads earlier on, then finding the body really knocked her for six."

"Anything taken?"

"Doesn't look like it. Certainly not money. There's a wallet with more than two hundred quid in it in the pocket of his coat. That briefcase on the floor is full of papers; I suppose something could have been taken from that.''

The two men moved aside as a photographer moved in and began taking pictures of the body. Paget circled the room. The covers on the bed were in disarray, and one of the pillows lay on the floor. A pair of light-grey slacks with the belt still in the loops had been tossed across the back of a chair beside the bed, and a white shirt, underpants, socks, and knotted tie lay in a heap on the seat. One black slip-on shoe lay on its side beneath the chair, while its mate was just visible beneath the bed.

The briefcase to which Tregalles had referred stood beside a table in the corner of the room. A pen, a pad of paper covered in figures, and a pair of glasses lay on the table. Paget looked at the figures. Some of the numbers were in the millions, but there was nothing to indicate what they meant.

The door of the recessed clothes-closet stood open. Inside, he could see a brown two-piece suit, a grey-green hound's-tooth-check sports jacket, two white shirts, two ties, and a pair of brown brogues. Paget stood on tiptoe to look on the top shelf, but all he found there was a layer of dust that looked as if it hadn't been disturbed for months. An open suitcase on a stand beside the wardrobe contained pyjamas, underpants and socks. Paget left them undisturbed; he'd receive an itemized list soon enough. A quick look at the bathroom revealed a shaver and other toilet articles laid out on either side of the wash-basin.

''Bloody hell!'' The words were spoken softly but with vehemence as the photographer rose to his feet and examined his knee. A spot of blood appeared. The man pulled up the leg of his slacks and began dabbing at his knee with a handkerchief. ''Glass,'' he said, holding up a tiny shard for all to see. ''Must be the bulb from the lamp. I didn't see it there,'' he told Charlie, who had come to take a look. ''Better warn Dr. Starkie to watch it when he comes.''

Charlie glanced at his watch. ''*If* he comes,'' he grumbled. ''He should have been here long since.''

Paget looked thoughtfully at the floor. ''When you take samples from that patch of carpet, I'd like you to mark on the floor plan the area covered by the broken glass," he told Charlie. "I think it might prove useful."

Charlie grunted acknowledgement. He was a taciturn man at best.

Still somewhat preoccupied, Paget turned, and in trying to avoid the glass-covered area, almost fell over a white-clad figure bent over the victim's clothing on the back of a chair. "Sorry," he said as he grabbed at the figure to steady himself. "I didn't see…" He stopped, and snatched his hands away as if he'd been burnt.

The figure straightened and turned to face Paget. "That's quite all right, sir," said Grace Lovett with an impish grin. "I'm used to being overlooked."

"Grace? I—I'm sorry. I didn't realize it was you." He could feel the colour rising in his face.

"It's these new suits and hats," she told him, dead-pan. "They make us all look alike."

"That'll be the day!" Tregalles muttered beneath his breath, but still loud enough for his boss to hear.

"Well…no harm done, I suppose," said Paget gruffly as he moved away. "Sergeant?"

"Sir!" Tregalles replied smartly, and wiped the smile from his face as he followed Paget from the room.

Paget didn't know why he should feel so embarrassed. It was an honest mistake. But he'd clutched hard to save himself, and it was too late to do anything about it by the time he realized that it was not a man he was holding. Fortunately, Grace had taken it in good part, but he'd still felt foolish. And Tregalles hadn't helped.

Paget liked Grace. Charlie had other good people on his team, but Grace Lovett had a talent for analysis that went beyond the obvious. Whether it was a matter of perception or intuition, Paget didn't know, but whatever it was, it had served them both well in the past.

"Right," he said as he and Tregalles moved out into the corridor. "I want a statement from everyone on this floor: What did they see? What did they hear? Anything the slightest bit unusual—you know what we need. Meanwhile, I'll have a word with this man, Quint.''

"You want the statements *now*, sir?'' Tregalles grimaced as he looked at the time. People would not take kindly to being dragged from their beds in the middle of the night.

"Is that a problem, Sergeant?''

"It *is* the middle of the night,'' Tregalles pointed out.

"I'm well aware of the time,'' said Paget testily, "but the job has to be done, and half of them are probably awake by now with all this activity going on, so let's get on with it, shall we?''

"So, IT WAS ABOUT three quarters of an hour before anyone answered Mr. Bolen's call for help,'' said Paget. "Is that right, Mr. Quint?''

The night manager bridled. "Well, yes, if you want to put it that way, Chief Inspector.'' Quint was a short, balding, sharp-featured man of about fifty. He resented the fact that a murder had been committed in what he had come to regard as *his* hotel. He resented, also, that the sergeant, who had spoken to him earlier, had taken it upon himself to send Brenda Jones home, leaving him to answer all the questions.

"I sent Mrs. Jones up as soon as the call came in,'' he continued, "and I thought that's where she was. But those bloody hooligans wouldn't let her get off the lift. Every time she tried to get out, they held her back. They kept riding up and down until they became tired of that game, then piled out on the fourth floor and started throwing a ball about and wouldn't let her go. But I knew nothing about that at the time. It wasn't until some of the guests phoned down to complain about people running up and down the corridor that I knew anything was wrong.''

Quint sniffed. "By the time everything was sorted, I'd forgotten about the call, and so had Mrs. Jones. Later, when she did remember, she went upstairs and found…'' Quint drew in a deep breath and swallowed hard as he remembered the scene. "But you've been up there,'' he went on. "You've seen it for yourself.''

Quint shook his head, trying to rid himself of the image. "When she came back down, I thought she was going to faint, she looked so white. 'Mr. Quint,' she says, 'Mr. Bolen's dead. I think we'd better ring the police.'

"To be honest, I didn't know whether to believe her or not," he went on. "I mean, she was still upset about that run-in with those yobs upstairs, and I thought she must be mistaken. At least about Bolen being dead. So I told her to stay in the office, then went up to have a look for myself."

"The door to Bolen's room was open?"

"No. Mrs. Jones had closed it, so I had to use my passkey. But she told me it was partly open when she first got there, which was why she went inside."

"Did you touch anything?"

"Good God, no. I came straight back here and phoned you lot."

"Did you or Mrs. Jones see anyone go in or out around that time?"

"No. I..." Quint stopped, frowned, and looked off into the distance, as if trying to recall an elusive memory. "There was a girl," he said. "Funny, that. I'd almost forgotten her."

Paget raised an inquiring eyebrow.

"A girl," Quint said slowly. "Not much more than a kid. She came down the stairs and ran across the lobby to the door just as I was getting in the lift to go upstairs to look for Mrs. Jones. I only caught a glimpse of her as the doors were closing, but the odd thing was, she was barefoot and carrying her shoes in her hand."

"Can you describe her?"

"She had a scarf over her head, so I didn't see much of her face. Very young, though; very pale. I'm not sure about her hair. It might have been fair, but the scarf hid most of it, and she was wearing a mac buttoned up to the chin. Not very tall. Not much more than five feet one or two, I shouldn't think. Thin. Bare legs, and as I said, bare feet."

"Colour of the scarf and mac?"

"Dark scarf. Can't say as to colour. And a light-coloured mac. Cream, light brown or grey; I'm not sure."

"And the shoes? You said she was carrying her shoes."

"Fancy ones. You know the sort—high heels, nothing much

but bits of leather straps on top. She was carrying them by the straps.''

''Very good, Mr. Quint. Do you remember what time that would be?''

Quint thought back. ''It was just after half past twelve when the calls about those young tearaways began coming in, so it would be a couple of minutes after that.''

''Had you ever seen the girl before?''

''Don't think so, but as I said, I couldn't see her face.''

''Did Mr. Bolen have any visitors after you came on duty last night?''

''No one asked for him, if that's what you mean. But people come and go all the time, and I have no way of knowing whether they are guests or visitors unless they actually come to the desk. We ask the guests to leave their keys here, but a lot of them don't.''

''You say that Bolen came here quite often. Was he always alone?''

''That's right,'' Quint confirmed. ''Always the same room, if it was available.''

''He was married?''

''That's right.''

''But his wife never accompanied him when he stayed here?''

''No.''

''Did he ever give you any idea why he would stay here rather than go home?''

Quint shook his head. ''I assumed it had something to do with his business. He wasn't the sort to stop and chat. Not like his brother, Harry.'' Quint paused. ''Come to think of it, Harry Bolen was here earlier on. Well, not actually *here*. I saw him in the car-park as I was coming to work. He was standing beside his car, talking to someone inside.''

''What time was this?''

''About quarter to eleven. I start at eleven.''

''Did you see who he was talking to?''

''No. Well, I could tell it was a woman, but all I could see was the back of her head. Mr. Bolen had the door open and the light was on inside the car.''

"What about the colour of her hair? Could you see that?"

Quint pursed his lips. "Fair, I think. Yes, I'm sure it was fair."

"Did you hear anything of their conversation?"

"No."

Paget sensed a growing resistance to his questions. He had the feeling that Quint knew more than he was telling, but there was nothing to be gained by pushing the man at this point. Besides, he was anxious to get back upstairs to hear what Charlie and Reg Starkie had to say.

"WE FOUND THIS UNDER the bed," Charlie Dobbs greeted him, holding up a clear plastic bag containing a short, broad-bladed knife. It had an imitation leather handle; it was the sort of knife favoured by Boy Scouts, and the chances of tracing it would be virtually nil. The handle was stained, and the blade was streaked with what looked like rust. But the edge of the blade looked as if it had been honed recently, and the dark-brown stains had nothing to do with rust.

Charlie nodded in the direction of Reg Starkie, the rotund pathologist, who was kneeling on the floor beside the body, muttering into a microphone attached to his lapel. "Reg won't commit himself until he's done the autopsy, but he did agree that the knife appears to match the shape of the wounds, so chances are this is your murder weapon. If it's not, I don't know what it's doing here. Oh, yes, and somebody used the bathroom to clean himself off before leaving. Or herself, more likely."

"You think a woman did this?" Paget asked.

Charlie shrugged. "Don't know," he said. "But we found a pair of panties—if you can call something the size of a postage stamp panties—in the bed. There were blonde hairs in the bed as well, and more blonde hairs in the wash basin. We also found a black evening bag; it had slipped down between the seat cushion and the side of the chair. Not much in it: lipstick, a compact and some tissues."

Tregalles appeared in the doorway. "Can't say *that* did a lot for public relations," he declared with a cheerfulness that belied his words. "But I have spoken to everyone on this floor, and no one admits to seeing or hearing anything."

"Anyone check the empty rooms?" asked Paget.

"Yes. And there's no sign that they have been disturbed," Tregalles assured him. "As for the rest of the floors, I didn't see the point of getting people up right away, so I've arranged to have some of our people on each floor by six o'clock. They'll knock on doors and ask the usual questions. And," the sergeant concluded, "I have two of our people standing by downstairs to make sure that no one leaves the hotel without being questioned and having their name and address checked."

"Right." Paget looked around the room. "There isn't much more we can do here," he observed, "so once Reg has finished his examination…"

"Which I've done," growled Starkie as he packed the last of his instruments away and closed the box. "But I would like to take a closer look at that blanket." He struggled to get up, then sank back. "I'm getting too old for this sort of thing," he puffed. "Give me a hand up, will you? It's the knees. They don't work as well as they used to."

"I'm not surprised," Charlie muttered as Paget moved to help the doctor to his feet. "What we need is a block and tackle."

"I'll bloody block and tackle you if you don't give me a hand up." Starkie's face, already red, was slowly turning purple and he was wheezing heavily. Even Charlie looked alarmed as he moved in to give Paget a hand.

"One of these days, Reg, you're going to get down there to examine some poor sod, and you're not going to get up," Charlie warned. "What do you weigh, now? It feels like twenty stone."

"None of your damned business," Starkie growled. "I told you, it's my knees!"

"It's not so much the knees as all that weight on top of them," Charlie shot back.

"Damn you, Charlie—" Starkie broke off in a coughing fit. His face turned even redder as he fought for breath.

Paget shot a warning glance at Charlie. What had once been friendly and amusing banter between two friends was no longer funny. In his attempt to make Starkie see what he was doing to himself, Charlie's gibes had become more and more barbed, which only served to infuriate Starkie. The trouble was, Charlie was genuinely concerned about the doctor's deteriorating health, and in his own peculiar way was trying to help.

But Starkie didn't see it that way. He *knew* he had a problem. He *knew* he should do something about it, and he felt guilty enough without having his friend constantly remind him.

"Get Reg a glass of water," Paget told the inspector as he led Starkie to a chair. The doctor sank into it gratefully. He was still wheezing heavily, but the redness in his face was slowly fading.

"Just sit still for a few minutes," Paget told him. Charlie returned with a glass of water and handed it to Starkie without a word. The doctor sipped it slowly.

The wheezing subsided. "Touch of asthma," he told Paget as he set the glass aside. He took an inhaler from his pocket, blew out his breath, put the tube into his mouth and inhaled deeply. The effort started him coughing again, but his breathing gradually returned to normal.

Charlie picked up the glass. "Sorry, Reg," he said gruffly, "but you..." He stopped as he saw Paget's warning look. "Sorry," he muttered again, and abruptly left the room.

Starkie watched him go with smouldering eyes. "Sorry?" he scoffed beneath his breath.

"He's concerned about you, Reg," Paget told him. "We all are. It's just his way. You know what he's like. You should. You've been friends for God knows how long."

"Yes, well, he's got a damned funny way of showing it. Now, do you want to know about this body of ours, or—?"

Starkie gasped as a jolting shudder shook his frame. Colour drained from his face. He clutched feebly at his chest. His head jerked up as he tried to speak but no sound came out. Flecks of spittle formed on lips that stood out like purple slashes against his chalk-white face.

Paget caught him as the pathologist slumped forward in his chair, and lowered him gently to the floor.

FIVE

HARRY BOLEN CAME UP out of a deep sleep. He couldn't remember where he was; his jet-lagged mind refused to function, and it took him several seconds before he realized he was at home in his own bed.

And someone was leaning on the bell.

The house sounded strangely empty as he switched on the light and looked at the time. Ten minutes to five? And the bell was ringing again.

"All right! I'm coming," he bellowed angrily as he grabbed his dressing-gown and staggered down the stairs.

The ringing stopped. Thank God for that, at least.

He paused at the door to rub the sleep from his eyes. Caution asserted itself, and he switched on the outside light and peered through the spyglass in the door.

A tall, broad-shouldered man stood there; rugged features, hair prematurely grey at the temples; thirty-five to forty, perhaps. Dressed neatly in a grey suit and navy tie. Open raincoat. As if he knew he was being scrutinized, he took out a card and held it up.

Harry squinted, but he couldn't make out what it said.

He opened the door.

"Mr. Bolen? Mr. Harry Bolen?"

"Yes?"

"Detective Chief Inspector Paget. I apologize for waking you at this ungodly hour, but I'm afraid it's necessary. May I come in?"

"JIM? DEAD? Murdered?" Harry Bolen stared slack-jawed at Paget, then shook his head as if trying to clear it. "I can't believe it. I was talking to him just a few hours ago. When? What happened?"

When Harry first opened the door, Paget experienced the eerie feeling of seeing a reincarnation of the man he'd just left with five stab wounds in his chest. The resemblance was startling, but now, facing him in full light, he could see that Harry was a somewhat leaner version of his brother.

"As far as we know, it was somewhere around midnight," Paget told him, "but as to exactly what happened, it's really much too early to say. Our people are still on the scene, and all I can tell you is that your brother was stabbed. As yet we don't know by whom or why."

"Stabbed? Good God! What...? I mean, did someone break into his room? Someone trying to rob him? What?"

"Unfortunately, sir, as I said, we don't know the answers to those questions, which brings me to one of the reasons I am here. I realize what a terrible shock this must be for you, but it would be a great help if you feel up to answering a few questions. We have tried to contact Mrs. Bolen, but no one seems to be at home. Would you happen to know where...?"

"God! I still can't believe it," Bolen burst out. "I mean, Jim was fine when I left him." He stopped and flicked a glance toward the stairs as if considering what to do next. "You'd better come through," he said, and turned to lead the way.

The room to which he led Paget was part office, part retreat. A large desk, computer, filing cabinets, and a credenza full of books took up one side of the room, with framed photographs of Bolen Brothers projects, ranging from the New AquaCentre in Clunbridge to a block of flats in Hereford, all but covering one wall. The other half of the room was given over to comfort and relaxation. High-backed leather chairs formed a semicircle around a coffee-table in front of a marble fireplace. Bolen flicked a switch as he entered the room, and realistic-glowing coals instantly sprang to life. One side of the chimney-breast was filled with audio-video equipment, including a huge television screen whose baleful eye, even in sleep, dominated the room.

But it was to the glass-fronted cabinet on the other side of the fireplace that Bolen moved as he waved Paget to one of the chairs. "Would you like a drink?" he asked. "Or isn't that allowed in your job?" He opened the cabinet doors. "I've got most things here," he offered.

The chief inspector sank into the cushioned softness of crushed leather. "Thank you, but no," he said wearily. In fact, he would have loved a drink, a good stiff one. Starkie's collapse had shaken him, and the fact that the doctor was now in the best hands possible did little to make him feel better. Even recognizing that Starkie was, at least for the most part, responsible for what had happened didn't help. Charlie had tried hard enough to warn him, but those warnings had only served to make Starkie all the more stubborn. Now Charlie was feeling bad because he thought it might have been his nagging that had pushed his friend over the edge.

Bolen poured himself a large brandy, and drank deeply. "As you wish," he said. He yawned and shook himself. "But I need something to wake me up. I'm still jet-lagged." He glanced at his watch. "I don't think I've had more than four hours sleep in the last couple of days. Never could sleep on the plane." He closed the cabinet door and brought both drink and bottle with him as he took a seat facing Paget. He set the bottle on the table beside the chair, took another drink, and rested his head against the padded back.

"You are quite certain it *is* Jim, I suppose?" he asked abruptly.

"If there had been any doubt in my mind, I'm afraid it would have been put to rest the moment I saw you, sir," said Paget. "You and your brother look very much alike."

Bolen heaved a sigh. "It's just that, you know, mistakes have been made in the past, and I thought perhaps..." He lifted a hand and let it fall in a helpless gesture.

"You mentioned jet lag," Paget ventured. "You've just returned from where, sir?"

"Canada. My wife, Dee, and I were over there visiting our son and daughter-in-law in Vancouver. They've just had their first child; our first grandchild. Catherine Elizabeth." His face softened, but only for a moment. "Dee is still over there, but I came back early. Business problems. Got in yesterday afternoon, picked up the car, drove straight down here and tracked Jim down at the hotel where he was having dinner."

"Can you tell me what time that was, Mr. Bolen?"

"That I saw Jim? Eight, eight-thirty, somewhere around there."

"You're sure about the time, are you, sir? It could be important." Norman Quint had said he'd seen Harry Bolen in the car-park behind the hotel around eleven.

"As I said, it could have been a few minutes either side, but you don't have to take my word for it. There were plenty of witnesses."

"Witnesses, Mr. Bolen?" Paget leaned back in his chair and waited. Harry looked as if he hadn't slept at all. He was pale and hollow-eyed, and he kept rubbing the back of his neck as if it were stiff.

"That's right, and I'm sure they'll be only too happy to give you their version of the events. They probably found it highly entertaining." Harry eyed Paget thoughtfully over the rim of his glass as if trying to judge the chief inspector's reaction to what he was about to say.

"You see, Jim and I had a row last night, a very public row in the middle of the dining-room in the Tudor Hotel. It was why I flew home early—not to have a row with Jim, but to try to get him to see reason." He grimaced. "But I suppose I knew from the start that it would end up in a row. There was no way Jim was about to change his mind."

"Change his mind about what, Mr. Bolen?"

"This damned Ockrington deal!" Bolen snapped, then immediately looked contrite. "I'm sorry, Chief Inspector," he apologized. "I didn't mean to… It's just that now, with Jim dead, it all seems so…so bloody futile and unimportant."

"And what, exactly, is the Ockrington deal, Mr. Bolen?"

Harry Bolen set his drink aside. "I'm sure you must have read about the Ministry of Defence closing the training camp at Ockrington at the end of this year," he said. Paget nodded. "There are three square miles of land for sale, about one third of which is prime building land. The trouble is, the M.o.D. insists on selling it as a complete package, and between the pressure from the people in Ockrington, who will lose a lot of business when the camp closes down, and the environmental people, who want it returned to its natural state, they have put so many conditions on the sale that it would take years for any buyer to see a return on his investment.

"Quite frankly, Bolen Brothers hasn't got anywhere near that kind of money, at least, not without mortgaging everything to the hilt, but Jim was determined to have that land no matter what the cost."

Harry paused and picked up his glass. "Don't misunderstand me," he continued quietly. "My brother was the driving force behind Bolen Brothers. He was the one with vision; he's the one who made us what we are today. But in recent years he has become obsessed—and believe me, Chief Inspector, I use the word advisedly—with having Bolen Brothers become the biggest developer in the area. He was prepared to do almost anything to accomplish that goal, and he saw the Ockrington project as a way to do it.

"But it was crazy, and everyone except Jim could see that. In this case he was dead wrong. If he had gone ahead with it, we would have been bankrupt within a year, and I told him that. So did John, his son. I *thought* I had his agreement to drop the idea before Dee and I left for Canada—I wouldn't have gone, otherwise—but when Laura phoned me around ten o'clock Friday morning—that's Vancouver time—to tell me that Jim was going ahead with the deal, I knew I had to get back to try to stop him. So I grabbed the first flight I could get on Friday evening and got in, as I said, yesterday afternoon."

"Laura...?" said Paget.

"Jim's wife. She had tried to reason with Jim, but he—" Harry Bolen broke off and remained silent for several seconds, then shrugged. "He wouldn't listen," he ended simply, and drained his glass.

"How did the argument end last night?"

"It didn't. Jim refused to see reason, and I'm afraid I lost my temper. I could see there was no point in trying to continue the argument there in the dining-room, not with everybody listening to every word. It was getting out of hand, and we were making a spectacle of ourselves, so I left."

"And went where?"

Bolen poured more brandy into his glass. "I came home," he

said. "I decided that the best thing for me to do was to get some sleep, then tackle Jim again in the morning."

"About what time did you get home?"

Bolen thought about that. "Around nine or just after, I should think."

"You didn't go out again?"

"No. As I said, I was dead tired, so I went to bed."

Either Quint had been lying about seeing Harry Bolen later in the evening, or Harry was lying now. "Could you give me some idea of what your brother was like?" Paget asked. "A sort of thumbnail sketch, if you will. It's very hard for us to put things in perspective if we don't know something of the victim."

Bolen stared into the middle distance. "Jim was a very dynamic man," he said slowly. "He had a quick mind and was never happier than when he was in the thick of things—estimates, costing, scheduling, dealing with suppliers and sub-trades. He could tell you to the penny how much things cost, and he had a talent for estimating what others would be bidding on major projects, then sliding our bid in a few thousand under. Me, I'm more of a hands-on type. I prefer to be out on the job, supervising and watching the projects take shape. Jim preferred the office."

"What was he like away from work?" asked Paget. "He was married, of course. Happily, would you say?"

"Well…Jim could be a bit difficult to live with at times," said Harry. "He and Laura had their differences, but then, who doesn't?"

"Children? You mentioned a son named John."

"Yes. John is the eldest. He works for us in the office. First came to work for us in the summer holidays when he was sixteen." Harry smiled. "Dragged in kicking and screaming, as I recall. All he wanted to do was play tennis and become a pro, but Jim wasn't having any of that. John went to university, did quite well and came into the firm full-time. Jim was planning on having him take over the accounting department at some point, but I don't know what will happen now.

"Then there's Prudence. She's a bit of a handful, I can tell you. I can see a lot of her father in Pru. She's twenty. She's just gone back to university after the summer holidays. Good thing, too."

"Why do you say that?"

Harry Bolen allowed a wry smile to cross his face. "Jim insisted that Pru take a course in self-defence while she was at home this summer. As I'm sure you know only too well, there have been a number of attacks on young women recently, and Jim wanted Pru to learn how to defend herself. Trouble was, Pru was only half-way into the course when she brought the instructor home and announced that she intended to marry him. God! You should have heard Jim! The chap's name is Malone. Mark Malone. He owns or manages that garden centre on the Ludlow Road, but he runs the self-defence course in the evenings. He's about ten years older than Pru."

"What was your brother's objection?"

Bolen shrugged. "He dismissed Malone out of hand as an opportunist who saw a way to get to his money through Pru. Mind you, I don't think anyone who wanted to marry Pru would have gained Jim's approval. I think—"

Whatever Harry Bolen thought, Paget was never to find out because he stopped in mid-sentence, eyes fixed on something— or *someone*, as it turned out—behind the chief inspector's chair.

"Harry? What are you doing up? Do you know what time it is? I thought I heard you talking to someone."

Paget, hidden from the speaker's view by the high-backed chair, rose to his feet, as did Bolen.

The woman advancing into the room looked and sounded half-asleep. Wrapped tightly in a full-length quilted dressing-gown, she was tall and slim and very pale. Her light-auburn hair had been pinned up, but now it hung in ragged strands around her shoulders. As she turned her head, Paget could see that the flesh around her left eye was bruised and swollen, and by the way she peered at him, that she was having trouble with her vision.

"I—I'm sorry," she stammered, brushing her hair away from her face. "I heard noises. I didn't realize...I left my contacts upstairs. I didn't know you had someone with you."

Bolen avoided Paget's eyes as he brushed past and moved to the woman's side. "It's all right, Laura," he told her soothingly.

"I had hoped you would sleep right through, but now that you're here, you had better sit down. This is Detective Chief Inspector Paget, and I'm afraid he's the bearer of bad news."

SIX

LAURA BOLEN MUST have been a beauty when she was young, thought Paget. Even now, in her middle years, she was a very attractive woman. But at five-thirty in the morning and without benefit of make-up, she could hardly be expected to be at her best. Her face was pale and drawn, and as Bolen led her to a chair, Paget could see more clearly the large, crescent-shaped bruise and swelling on her cheek.

He sat down again. He had been about to leave, but this latest development required an explanation. Bolen had avoided the question when asked if he knew where his sister-in-law might be, and Paget had put it down to the fact that he was upset over his brother's death. But now it seemed that Harry had side-stepped the question deliberately.

Laura clutched the collar of her dressing-gown beneath her chin. She held herself stiffly as she turned anxious eyes on Harry. "There's been an accident, hasn't there?" she said huskily. "Is it one of the children?"

"I'm afraid it's Jim," he told her. "I'm sorry, Laura, but Jim was…he was killed last night."

Laura sucked in her breath and stared at her brother-in-law. "Killed? How? Where?" She swung round to face Paget. "What happened?" she demanded.

Briefly, and choosing his words carefully, Paget repeated what he had told Harry Bolen. Laura's eyes never left his face throughout the narrative, and when, in answer to her question, he told her how her husband had died, she shuddered.

"What a horrible way to die," she breathed. "Do you know who did it?"

Paget shook his head. "No, which is why we are trying to trace Mr. Bolen's movements throughout the evening."

Paget leaned forward in his chair. "I know this must come as a terrible shock to you," he said gently, "and I will understand if you don't feel up to answering questions at this time. But the sooner we know about events leading up to your husband's death, the better chance we have of finding the person responsible. Mr. Bolen, here, has been most co-operative as it is, but I'm sure there are some things with which only you can help me."

Laura Bolen was silent for a moment, then nodded slowly. "I want to help in any way I can," she told him, "but..." She blinked rapidly several times and rose to her feet, wincing as she did so. "Do you mind waiting while I go back upstairs and put my contacts in? Everything is so blurred without them, and I find it hard to concentra—" The word caught in her throat and her eyes were moist as she fought for control. She tried to speak again, then gave up and almost ran from the room.

"Is it really necessary to question Laura now?" Harry demanded. "I mean, good God, man, she's just this moment learned that her husband has been killed, and you can see she's upset. Can't you leave her alone for at least a few hours?"

"I did offer Mrs. Bolen a choice," Paget reminded him, "and she can still refuse if she wishes. But as I told you in the beginning, the sooner we can talk to people while things are still fresh in their minds, the better."

Harry snorted. "Some choice!" he muttered, and lapsed into a moody silence.

"Why did you avoid telling me that Mrs. Bolen was here in the house when I told you we had been trying to contact her?" asked Paget.

Harry eyed Paget stonily. "Because you would have jumped to the conclusion that there was something going on between us," he growled. "Isn't that what you're thinking now?"

There was no denying that the thought had crossed Paget's mind. "I'd prefer to hear your explanation," he said.

Bolen picked up his glass, looked at it for a moment, then set it aside again. "Look," he said, keeping his voice low, "the only reason I'm going to tell you this is because I don't want you badgering Laura. She's been through enough already, and I'd like your word that what I do tell you will remain confidential. Understand?"

"I understand," Paget told him, "but you must understand my position as well. Whatever you tell me will remain confidential only if it has no direct bearing on the investigation. If it does, I make no promises."

"It's got nothing to do with what happened to Jim," said Bolen angrily. "I just want to make sure you don't go away with the wrong impression." He sighed heavily. "This isn't easy for me to say, but when I spoke of my brother being obsessed with beating the competition, what I should have said is that his obsession was directed at one particular competitor, Keith Lambert. It's a long story—it was a personal thing with Jim. It goes back a long time, and to say that it had affected his judgement would be an understatement."

Lambert. Paget knew the name. It would be hard not to in an area where it sometimes seemed as if the only two builders were Bolen Brothers and Lambert, so ubiquitous were their signs.

Harry glanced at the door before continuing in a low tone. "Laura was very much aware of what it would do to the firm if Jim went ahead with the Ockrington project, so when she realized that Jim intended to rush through a deal with the M.o.D. while I was out of the country, she tried to stop him. They argued…" Harry moved uneasily in his chair. "I don't know what happened, exactly, but it seems that Jim lost control. Laura said he accused her of interfering, of going behind his back, of being disloyal, and God knows what else. When she tried to reason with him, he hit her. You saw the bruise yourself.

"When Laura telephoned me in Vancouver, she did so from here. You see, when we left, she offered to look in on the house from time to time—you know, water the plants and make sure that everything was all right. So when Jim threw her out, the only place she could think of to go was here. John would have taken her in, but his is a small bachelor flat, so I told Laura she was welcome to stay here as long as she liked."

Paget frowned. "Was your brother normally a violent man, Mr. Bolen? Had anything like this ever happened before?"

"No. That is…" Harry looked trouble. "To be honest, I don't know," he confessed. "Laura never said anything, but then, she wouldn't. I've never seen her bruised before, but on the other hand, nothing quite like this has ever happened before. It was only when Keith Lambert—"

He broke off as the door opened and Laura Bolen entered the room.

The change was quite remarkable. She was more self-assured as she walked across the room and took her seat. She was still pale and the rims of her eyes were red, but she'd taken the time to comb her hair, apply a touch of make-up, and put on some slippers. The bruise and swelling were still visible, although not as obvious, and he could see now that his original assessment was confirmed. Laura Bolen was indeed a very handsome woman.

"Sorry if I interrupted," she told Harry, "but I couldn't help overhearing Keith's name as I came in. Surely, you're not going through all *that* again?"

Harry shrugged guiltily. "I was explaining to the chief inspector what happened when Keith came round on Friday, and why you were staying here," he told her. He studied her face for a moment. "You don't have to do this, you know," he told her. "It can be left till later."

Laura shook her head. "It's all right, Harry," she assured him. "It *is* a shock—in fact I don't think I've taken it in yet—but I want to help if I can. It's the least I can do."

"Thank you, Mrs. Bolen," said Paget as Harry slumped back in his seat. He paused for a moment, then began with a question that had puzzled him from the beginning. "Can you tell me *why* your husband was at the Tudor Hotel last night?"

"He had meetings scheduled there with some ministry officials from London."

"I understand that, but the meetings aren't scheduled to begin until tomorrow afternoon, so why did your husband book into the hotel two days before, when he lives not ten minutes' drive from town? Was he meeting someone else there on the week-end?''

Laura Bolen continued to look at him, but it seemed to Paget that her features had become set. ''Jim rarely discussed his business arrangements with me,'' she told him. ''He stayed at the Tudor occasionally to get away from interruptions; usually when he had some new project he wanted to work on. He said there was never enough time during the week, and there were too many distractions at home.''

Paget frowned. ''But with you no longer there, the house would be empty, would it not? Was that the only reason, Mrs. Bolen? I'm told that Mr. Bolen stayed there quite regularly on the weekends.''

Laura Bolen half closed her eyes and brushed a strand of hair away from her face. ''I'm sorry, Chief Inspector, but I really can't help you,'' she said firmly. There was a hint of defiance in the tilt of her chin as she met his gaze.

''When was the last time you saw your husband?''

''Friday afternoon. About three o'clock. Which was when I left the house.''

''And you came straight here.''

''After a brief stop at the hospital. I had nowhere else to go.''

''And you were here yesterday when Mr. Bolen''—Paget indicated Harry—''arrived here from Canada?''

''Yes.''

''But you didn't accompany him when he went off to see your husband at the Tudor?''

''No.''

''Which time was that, Mrs. Bolen? The first time, when Mr. Bolen confronted your husband in the dining-room? Or later, around eleven o'clock, when he returned to the hotel?''

''The first time I...'' Laura stopped and looked puzzled as she saw the look on Harry's face. He opened his mouth to say something, then thought better of it and closed it again. ''What is it, Harry?'' she demanded. ''What's wrong?''

''Mr. Bolen told me that when he returned after having the argument with your husband, he went straight to bed,'' Paget explained.

Laura Bolen looked perplexed. "What on earth made you say that?" she asked Harry. "We both went the second time; you know we did."

The colour that had been rising in Harry's face grew deeper. "I was trying to avoid telling the chief inspector about your being here," he said, defensively. "And when he said that Jim was killed around midnight, I thought... Well, I thought it would be best if I didn't mention that we'd been back to the hotel. Not that it really changes anything," he added hurriedly, "because we were both back here well before midnight."

Laura pursed her lips and slowly shook her head from side to side. "Really, Harry," she chided gently, "I suppose you thought you were doing it for the best, but now the chief inspector is going to wonder, isn't he?"

She turned back to Paget. "But the truth of the matter is that, when Harry came back and told me what had happened in the dining-room, and the lengths to which Jim was prepared to go, I felt we couldn't let matters rest there. There had to be *some* way to make Jim see reason. I felt so guilty about bringing all this to a head by allowing Keith to come to the house to talk to Jim directly, but *something* had to be done. But when Keith left the house, it was as if a dam had burst. I've never seen Jim in such a rage." Tears glistened in her eyes. "He accused me of selling out to Keith, of going behind his back, of..."—Laura swallowed hard—"of all sorts of things," she ended in a whisper.

Paget straightened in his chair. "This is Keith *Lambert* you are talking about, Mrs. Bolen?" he said.

"Why, yes." Laura looked puzzled. "Didn't Harry tell you?"

Paget looked at Harry Bolen. "He may have been about to when you came in," he said, "but perhaps you can tell me now."

Harry groaned. "It's five-thirty in the morning, for God's sake. Can't you let it alone?" He picked up his drink. "You don't have to do this, you know, Laura," he reminded her again.

The chief inspector looked to Laura Bolen. She did look tired, desperately tired, but she brushed her brother-in-law's objections aside with a wave of her hand. "It's all right, Harry," she told him. "It's straightforward enough."

She turned back to Paget. "Keith Lambert approached me a short time ago and asked me to try to persuade Jim to drop this ridiculous feud that's been going on for so many years. He told me that if Jim kept on the way he was going, both firms would suffer, but Bolen Brothers would suffer the most." Laura paused and looked at Harry. "In fact," she went on, "both Harry and I knew that. If Jim had been allowed to have his way, the firm would have gone bankrupt.

"Keith suggested splitting the Ockrington project between the two firms. That way the initial investment would be halved and both firms could make a tidy profit in the long run. But when I tried to point that out to Jim, and he learned that I had been talking to Keith, he went straight up the wall and told me I was never to speak to Keith again.

"But I couldn't simply leave it there, so I did speak to Keith again, and that's when he offered to come to the house and make the proposition to Jim himself. Which he did, and I've already told you what a fiasco that turned out to be."

Paget would have liked to pursue the subject further. Why, for example, if everyone but Jim Bolen was convinced that this Ockrington project would bankrupt the company, would Lambert come along with an offer to save it? Surely it would have been to his advantage to have his biggest rival fold. What could possibly be in it for him? And what was it that lay behind Bolen's obsessive behaviour?

But despite her brave face, Laura Bolen looked to be on the point of collapse, and questions such as those could wait till later.

"So you and Mr. Bolen, here, decided to give it one more try last night," he prompted. "Will you tell me what happened?"

"Initially, I intended to go with Harry to Jim's room," said Laura. "But we talked about it on the way, and I realized that my presence there might make matters even worse. Jim was convinced that I had gone over to Keith's side, and nothing I could say would convince him otherwise. So I stayed in the car. Not that it made much difference, because Jim wasn't in his room. His car was there in the car-park, but he wasn't in the hotel. Harry searched all over, but there was no sign of him.''

Harry took up the story. ''I should have told you earlier,'' he admitted sheepishly, ''but after having that fight with Jim in the dining-room, I was afraid of what you might think if I told you I'd gone back again. But as Laura said, Jim wasn't in his room. I checked the bar, which was just closing, but they hadn't seen him, and neither had the girl at the desk. You can check with her if you like. Her name is Rita. She offered to try to find him for me, but she was just going off shift, so I told her not to bother.

''Anyway, I went out to the car and told Laura that Jim didn't seem to be in the hotel. Laura and I talked about it for a few minutes, then decided there was nothing we could do until morning. So we came back here. And that's it.''

''What time was this, exactly?'' Paget asked.

''Somewhere between ten-thirty and eleven. We were back here shortly after eleven.''

''And then?''

''I went to bed. I was dead tired and couldn't keep my eyes open.'' He looked at his sister-in-law.

''I was exhausted,'' she told Paget, ''but I knew it would be impossible to sleep unless I took a sleeping pill. Unfortunately, I was in such a state that I took two before I realized it, which is why I feel so groggy now.''

Paget rose to his feet. ''Thank you both for your help,'' he told them, ''but just one more question before I go. Can either of you think of anyone who might have hated Mr. Bolen enough to kill him?''

They looked at one another, then shook their heads. Harry Bolen clambered to his feet. ''I'll see you out,'' he said as he moved toward the door.

Paget followed, then paused. ''We will need to have a member of the family make a formal identification of the body as soon as possible,'' he said. He looked inquiringly from one to the other.

''I'll go,'' said Harry. ''When and where?''

''Shall we say ten o'clock this morning at the hospital? Identify yourself at the desk, and I'll arrange for the coroner's officer to meet you there.''

There was a nip in the air as Paget stepped outside, and there was heavy dew on the car. As he wiped off the windows, he thought about the two people he'd just left. He was inclined to believe much of what they'd told him, but he had reservations about their relationship. The evidence suggested that Jim Bolen had been killed by a woman he'd been entertaining in his room, but should that prove not to be the case, both Harry and Laura Bolen would be at the top of his list of suspects.

SEVEN

SHE WAS COLD. Not just cold, but *freezing!* She couldn't feel her feet at all, and her fingers felt like lumps of ice as she tried to draw the bedclothes tighter. She could hear someone from far away, but she didn't want to get up. She just wanted to snuggle down and get warm.

Vikki burrowed deeper, and felt the pain. Her arms, her legs, her head... The bed was uncomfortable, hard and lumpy. The eiderdown was stiff beneath her frozen fingers; it crackled when she moved. It felt like...canvas?

Slowly, painfully, memory returned, and she felt again the fear of being hunted. She recalled how vulnerable she'd felt, alone on the moonlit road that seemed to go on forever. And she remembered scrambling into the ditch and crouching low against the hedge each time a car went by, wishing she had the courage to ask for a lift. She remembered, too, sitting on the roadside, tears streaming down her face as she tore the scarf in half to bind her swollen feet, and forcing the shoes back on again.

Vikki couldn't remember turning off the main road, but she must have done because her next memory was of seeing the pub and the sign with a dog on it and the blank space where there should have been a man. The Invisible Man. So, Joanna hadn't been pulling her leg after all.

The path behind the pub was easy enough to follow through the trees, dappled as it was by moonlight, and Vikki remembered the overwhelming wave of relief she'd felt when she saw the narrow boat tied up beside the abandoned locks. But from that point on, her memory failed, and she had no recollection of coming aboard.

But there was something else tugging at her memory. Lurking there in the dark recesses of her mind; something evil, something…

Suddenly, the events of the night before came rushing back, and she cried aloud.

"I think she's waking up."

The cover was being pulled away. Canvas crackled. Vikki tried to cover her eyes, but her arms wouldn't move and no matter how hard she squeezed her eyelids shut light kept exploding inside her head.

"Oh, my God!"

Vikki didn't recognize the voice. Didn't want to open her eyes to see who was speaking, afraid that it would be a policewoman waiting to arrest her.

It had all been for nothing, she thought bitterly, and began to cry.

"Let's have this tarp off her and get her inside. Put her in my bunk, but be careful." Hands, gentle hands, moved over her body. Vikki felt herself being lifted. Was that Joanna's voice she'd heard? Or was she dreaming?

The voices began to fade, and she could feel herself slipping away again.

"She should be in hospital."

"You're right," agreed a second voice. "I'll ring for an ambulance from the call-box outside the pub. I'll stay there to show them the way in."

"No! Please, not hospital. I'll be all right." Vikki opened her eyes and struggled to sit up, but cool hands gently held her down, and she found herself looking up into the face of Joanna Freeborn. Vikki clutched the woman's hand.

"Please, Joanna," she pleaded. "I don't want an ambulance. I'll be all right. It's just a few bruises."

Joanna snorted. "Just a few bruises?" she scoffed. "You should see the size of the lump on the back of your head, for a start. Your face, your chest, your stomach... Who did this to you? What was it? Some sort of free-for-all?"

Vikki had prepared herself for the questions during her long walk from town. She eased herself into a sitting position to give herself time to collect her wits, and to avoid Joanna's eyes as she lied to her.

"I went with this bloke," she said. "He looked all right, but once he got me in the car, he drove out into the country and pulled off the road. Then he dragged me out of the car and started knocking me about. He was shouting at me all the while. Something about being on his patch, and he said if I came back again, he'd finish me for good."

Vikki looked up at Joanna. "That's the last thing I remember until I woke up in a ditch. I didn't know what to do. I couldn't go back. Then I thought of you. I'm sorry, Joanna, but I didn't know where else to go."

Joanna put her arm around the girl and hugged her gently. "You're safe here with me," she told her.

Tears welled in Vikki's eyes. "But please, Joanna," she whispered, "don't make me go to hospital."

Joanna sighed. "Very well," she said with obvious reluctance, "but I want you to promise me that you'll tell me if you have trouble with your eyes—double vision, blurring, anything like that. Promise?"

"I will. Honestly."

"Hmm!" Joanna looked sceptical. Without taking her eyes off Vikki, she lifted her head and spoke to someone behind her. "I think the first thing we need to do is strip her off, clean her up, and do what we can for those cuts and bruises," she said.

"I'll do it." The voice was low and curiously melodious; the same voice Vikki had heard when she first woke up, and she was suddenly afraid. She'd never considered the possibility that someone else might be there on Joanna's boat. "We need some Elastoplast. Do we have any?"

"I think so. I'll see." Joanna rose to her feet, careful to avoid spilling the bowl of steaming water the second woman carried as they manoeuvred around each other in the confines of the narrow boat. She disappeared, and the young woman set the bowl down beside the bunk and, with gentle fingers, began to undress Vikki.

"Careful now," she warned as Vikki tried to help. "Just lie still. I can manage. And don't be afraid to tell me if I'm hurting you." She smiled. Unthinking, Vikki returned the smile...and winced.

The young woman winced in sympathy and shook her head. "Lie still," she admonished once again. "Just relax; you're very tense." She had a pleasant, soothing voice, and the water was lovely and warm. Vikki closed her eyes and began to drift.

THE WOMAN WASN'T much more than a girl herself. Fair-haired and slim, her features were small and regular, but her eyes were large and soft and brown and ever so slightly bulbous. Like those of a rabbit, Joanna had thought when first they'd met.

Where she had come from, Joanna didn't know. Neither had the girl volunteered her name. She had just appeared one night when they were packing up after a show. She wore a long print dress with little if anything beneath it, and sandals. Nothing else. Her worldly possessions were contained in a rucksack that she carried by the straps rather than slung across her shoulders. That position was reserved for her guitar.

She said simply that she'd like to join them. She wouldn't be any trouble. She'd done a little acting but she liked singing best, and when members of the group tried to put her off, she sat cross-legged on the floor and began to play.

Her voice was thin, but there was a haunting quality about it that caught and held them. Her slender fingers caressed the strings to draw forth sounds that flowed like water from a bubbling spring. The notes grew stronger, surging like a mighty river, then faded once again to the murmur of a placid stream.

It was late and most of them had to work the following day, but for twenty minutes this thin, pale girl held them spellbound with her magic. And when the last note faded, a sigh went round the room, more eloquent than thunderous applause. The girl rose to her feet and slung the guitar over her shoulder. She didn't speak; just stood there quietly, looking from one to the other with those enormous soft brown eyes.

"What's your name?" It was Joanna who spoke first.

"I am whoever you say I am," the girl replied.

"Then I shall call you Bunny. Where do you live?" The girl pointed to the rucksack and shrugged. "Then you'd better come home with me," Joanna told her, and Bunny had been with her ever since.

Bunny never talked about herself. But she was no stranger to work. Less than a week after she came, she landed a job cleaning rooms at the Invisible Man, where Joanna worked behind the bar. And she went through the narrow boat from stem to stern, cleaning, polishing, and doing all the things Joanna had promised herself she would get around to doing one day but never did.

Joanna returned. "What do you think?" she asked in a low voice. Vikki lay with her head on one side, eyes closed, breathing regularly.

Bunny paused and eyed the girl critically. "Somebody has certainly beaten the shit out of her," she said matter-of-factly, "but she's young, and apart from that lump on the back of the head, I don't think there's any permanent damage."

"She must have walked all the way out here, poor kid. And in those shoes!" Joanna lifted one of Vikki's feet. The heels were rubbed raw, and broken blisters covered much of the ball of the foot. "Funny, but I never thought I would see her again."

"This is the girl you told me about? The one in the cells?"

"That's right." Joanna sighed. "She says she was beaten up because she was operating on someone else's patch, but I don't know. The thing I can't understand is why she's so terrified of going into hospital."

"You think whoever did this might be looking for her?"

"Could be," said Joanna slowly. "But perhaps it's better not to ask. At least for now."

EIGHT

"No one admits to seeing or hearing anything unusual, apart from those who were disturbed by that Rugby crowd tearing up and down the corridor on the fourth floor."

Tregalles rubbed his eyes and squinted at his notebook. "Except for one thing," he continued, "and I don't know whether it means anything or not. A Mr. and Mrs. Lyon say they were returning to the hotel around midnight when they saw a girl sneaking into the hotel. They thought it a bit odd at the time, but decided it was none of their business, so they didn't mention it to anyone until they were questioned this morning."

"Did you get a description?"

Paget, Tregalles, and Superintendent Alcott were seated around a table in a vacant room on the first floor of the Tudor Hotel. Tregalles had commandeered the room as a temporary office from which to co-ordinate the enquiries in the hotel. The room was stuffy; both Paget and Tregalles were having trouble keeping their eyes open, and Alcott's chain-smoking didn't help. Alcott himself had, for the most part, remained silent, his sharp eyes flicking from one to the other as he listened carefully.

Tregalles wrinkled his nose. "Not much of a one, I'm afraid. Young, fair-haired, slight build—that's as much as they could remember. They said they only saw her for a few seconds, and for most of that time she had her back to them. The odd thing was, they say she had—"

"—Bare feet?" Paget finished for him.

Tregalles stared at him. "How did you know that?" he demanded. "Did someone else see her, too?"

"Perhaps. Go on. What did this couple mean when they said they saw her 'sneaking in'?"

"She went in ahead of them, but stopped just inside the door as if undecided about going further. According to Mrs. Lyon, she and her husband stopped and waited outside the door because they half expected the girl to turn round and come out again, but she didn't. Instead, she took off her shoes and ran across to the stairs."

"Go on."

"That's it. They discussed it on their way up in the lift, but decided that the girl had simply seen someone inside she didn't want to meet, and had skipped up the stairs in order to avoid them."

"Was anyone else in the lobby when they went through to the lift?"

"Just Quint, and Mrs. Jones."

"You said it was around midnight. Before or after?"

"Within five minutes, either way, they told me. They seemed quite sure about that."

"Sounds like the same girl Quint claims he saw leaving the hotel at about twenty-five minutes to one," Paget observed.

"Which ties in with the time of death and the evidence that there was a young woman in the room with Bolen," said Alcott. "Looks straightforward enough to me. Bolen was having it off with this girl, things got rough and she stabbed him." The superintendent butted his cigarette and lit another.

"It ties in with the time the phone call came from Bolen's room," Paget agreed, "but we don't know that this particular girl was ever in Bolen's room, so I think we had better keep our options open. And time of death is still open until we can get medical confirmation. Unfortunately, Reg didn't have a chance to give us any details before he had his heart attack, and when Charlie played Reg's tape, he said he couldn't make out the words because Reg was wheezing so heavily. He's going to try to get it cleaned up electronically, but it may take some time. Meanwhile, we need another pathologist to do the autopsy as soon as possible."

Alcott drummed stained fingers on the table. "I'll talk to Worcester," he said, "but let's concentrate on finding this girl."

"Those knickers in Bolen's bed were small," said Tregalles thoughtfully. "And the Lyons say the girl they saw was very young. She could be some schoolgirl who was making a bit on the side. Might be worth checking into; find out if Bolen was partial to youngsters. It would explain her sneaking in and out of the hotel like that."

"Did Bolen make any phone calls?" Paget asked.

"Yes, he did, as a matter of fact." Tregalles flipped the pages.

"One. A Broadminster number at nine thirty-two P.M. I haven't had a chance to follow it up yet, but the cross-reference listing shows it belongs to a Douglas Underwood, 54 Stirling Crescent."

Alcott grunted. "That's just down the road," he observed. "Better talk to Underwood and find out what the call was about. Anything else?"

"Bolen's car was in the car-park," Tregalles told him. "Charlie had it taken away for further examination. And that's about it, I'm afraid, sir."

"Any further news on Reg's condition?" asked Paget.

Tregalles grimaced. "Not good," he said. "Charlie says they're talking about an operation either later today or first thing tomorrow morning."

Alcott shot an inquiring glance at Paget. "Anything else?" he demanded.

"It's just that it seems to me Bolen's death came at a very convenient time for his family," Paget said slowly. "I don't think we should overlook that possibility as a motive. If Bolen had been allowed to push this deal through at Ockrington, it could have ruined the lot of them."

Alcott lumbered to his feet, scattering ash as he did so. "That's as may be," he said brusquely, "but let's not go off on some wild-goose chase. Concentrate on finding the girl."

As they left the room, Paget told Tregalles to remain in the hotel and interview the day staff. "And get some people around to the homes of everyone who has the day off. I want to know everything they can tell us about Bolen, and why he spent so many weekends here in the hotel. Find out what went on in the Elizabethan Room last night, and if we can get the names of diners who were seated near Jim Bolen, let's have them interviewed as well."

Tregalles nodded. "And you will be...?"

"Having a word with Douglas Underwood."

LEAVING HIS CAR at the hotel, Paget walked the short distance to Stirling Crescent. It was a pleasant little backwater of semi-detached houses with small front lawns bordered by neatly trimmed hedges and low brick walls. Mature shrubs and bushes vied for space, with hydrangeas seemingly a particular favourite, and number fifty-four was no exception. Blooms the size of dinner plates grew in profusion beside the short driveway leading to the garage.

A plump middle-aged man, wearing a grey track suit and a pair of wellingtons, was stretched across the bonnet of a Granada Scorpio Estate, applying polish with sweeping strokes. What little hair he had was light and sandy, and the skin beneath it glowed pink in the morning sun.

"Good morning, sir. Nice car," said Paget admiringly. "Lovely colour."

The man straightened up and beamed at Paget through rimless glasses. "That's tourmaline metallic green, that is," he said proudly. "Comes up a treat, doesn't she?"

"She does indeed. Are you by any chance Mr. Underwood? Mr. Douglas Underwood?"

The man's smile faded. "I am," he said neutrally. "And you are…?"

"Detective Chief Inspector Paget. I wonder if I could have a few minutes of your time?"

Underwood's face took on a guarded look. "Chief Inspector?" he repeated. He glanced at the car as if trying to think of an infraction serious enough to warrant the time of a chief inspector on a Sunday morning. "What's this all about?" he asked cautiously.

"Routine enquiries," said Paget vaguely. "I'd just like to ask you a few questions. We can do that here, or we could go into the house if you prefer."

"No. No, this will be fine." Underwood picked up the bottle of liquid polish, screwed the cap on carefully, and wiped his hands on a piece of cloth. "What's it about?" he asked again.

"Tell me, were you at home last evening, sir?"

Underwood hesitated. "Y-e-e-s," he answered cautiously.

"Did you receive a telephone call from a Mr. James Bolen?"

Underwood opened his mouth, closed it again and said, "Aahhh!"

"Was that a yes or a no, sir?"

"Well, yes, I did, now that you mention it." Underwood looked down at the bottle in his hand, unscrewed the cap, then screwed it back on again.

"Would you mind telling me the substance of that conversation, sir?"

"It was... It was a private matter," the man said stiffly.

Paget shook his head. "Not any longer, I'm afraid. Mr. Bolen died shortly after making that telephone call to you, which is why I'm here."

Underwood looked stunned. "He *died?* What happened?"

"The telephone call?" Paget prompted.

"Ah, yes, well... He-umm..." Underwood swallowed hard and looked down at the bottle in his hand. "He offered me—aahh—a job," he said in a low voice.

"I see. You are unemployed at the moment, are you, Mr. Underwood?"

The man looked up sharply. "No, of course not. I have a good job."

"Working for Lambert?"

Colour flared in Underwood's face. "How...?" he began, then compressed his lips as if to prevent himself from saying more.

"How did I know you worked for Lambert? I didn't until I saw the Lambert logo on your car," said Paget. His voice hardened. "Now, you say Bolen offered you a job. What sort of job? And why did he wait until late on a Saturday evening to make you that offer?"

Underwood looked down at his hands, brows drawn together as if studying them. "The job was...well, it was just part of it," he said in a low voice. "What he really wanted was information about the bid we are putting in on a job. He said he was prepared to pay for the information, but of course I turned him down."

"I see. Was that job, by any chance, the one at Ockrington?"

Underwood looked startled. Sweat glistened on his brow as he nodded confirmation.

"And you say you turned him down?"

Underwood looked offended by the question. "Well, it wouldn't have been right, would it? I mean, I'm not saying I couldn't have used the money; I could, but there's such a thing as loyalty, isn't there?''

"Very commendable, I'm sure," said Paget. "Tell me, was this the first time Bolen had approached you?"

Underwood shifted from one foot to the other, then shook his head. "He has approached me a couple of times in the past, but I turned him down each time."

"No doubt you informed your employer of these approaches by Bolen?"

"Well, no. I mean, what would have been the point? As I said, I turned Bolen down, so there was no harm done."

"Was that the only reason, sir? Or were you, perhaps, waiting for a better offer?"

"Of course not!"

Paget left it for the moment as another thought occurred to him. Harry Bolen had said that his brother was not in his room, nor was he anywhere in the hotel as far as he could tell, and Underwood's house was only a short distance away. "Did Mr. Bolen come to see you after you turned him down?" he asked.

"Certainly not."

"Did you go to see him or meet him somewhere?"

"No." The answer came swiftly—a bit too swiftly, Paget thought.

"Did he say anything that might indicate he intended to go out, or that he was expecting anyone?"

"No."

"How did he react when you turned him down?"

"He offered me more money, tried to talk me round, but I kept telling him I wasn't interested, so he finally gave up." Underwood shot a questioning glance at Paget. "What was it?" he asked. "Heart attack? Something like that?"

"Oh, didn't I say, Mr. Underwood? He was assaulted and killed in his room."

Underwood's eyes widened and his jaw went slack as he stared at Paget. He made as if to say something, but couldn't seem to get the words out. "When?" he croaked.

Paget regarded him with an air of surprise. "Now, why do you ask that?" he said. "Is the time of particular significance?"

Underwood shook his head violently. "No! No, it was just that...I mean, I was speaking to him on the phone... Well, as you say, it must have happened after that. That's all I meant."

"I see. Tell me, is there anyone who can confirm where you were last evening, Mr. Underwood?"

Underwood shook his head. "I live alone," he said, "but I can assure you I never left the house last night. You'll just have to take my word for it."

"And so I shall," said Paget agreeably. "At least for now. But someone will call you to arrange a time for your written statement. Thank you for your help."

SIMONE SLEPT LATE. It was almost three o'clock on Sunday afternoon when she finally opened her eyes. She reached blindly for her cigarettes and lit one, then propped herself up in bed so she wouldn't go back to sleep and set the place on fire.

The taste in her mouth was foul. She'd been picked up just after midnight by a very young man who had taken her to a house where a stag party was in progress. She was to be a present, he said, to his friend, who was getting married the following week. "He's a virgin," he explained seriously, "so we thought he should have a sort of trial run so he doesn't make a fool of himself on the big night."

Virgin be damned! If that guy was a virgin, then she was a Sister of Charity. She pitied the poor girl he was marrying.

She listened. Not a sound came from the other room. Vikki must have come in late and still be sleeping. Which meant she must have been working. And a good thing, too! It was about time she started paying her way.

Simone finished her cigarette. She was tempted to snuggle down again, but if she wasn't on the street again by seven, Luke would be round to find out why, and she had some washing and ironing to do before then.

"Vikki?" she called as she got out of bed. "Come on, luv. Your turn to get dinner." But when she went into the living-room, there was no sign of the girl. The sheets and blankets were still neatly folded at the end of the sofa, exactly as they had been when Simone had gone to bed.

Simone frowned. The last time she had seen Vikki was when she'd said she was going to Lee's to get warm, but that had been around eight o'clock last night.

"Oh, no!" Simone groaned aloud. "Not again!"

The coppers had been on the prowl again last night. Vikki had mentioned it herself. Sure as hell, she'd been picked up. Simone sighed. The girl wasn't cut out for this at all. She simply didn't have it.

Simone cleaned her teeth while waiting for the bathtub to fill. She wasn't going to bail the kid out again, she told herself. Vikki could stay there. Perhaps it would teach her to be more careful next time. If there was a next time.

It was only later, when Simone was preparing to go out again, that she discovered Vikki's clothes rolled up inside the wardrobe. The same clothes she'd been wearing when she'd gone to Lee's. So what was she wearing now? Swiftly, Simone went through the clothing in the wardrobe and the drawers. Her black dress was missing; so was her evening bag. What else had the thieving little bitch made off with?

Simone lit another cigarette and stood there in the middle of the room, trying to make sense of it all. Why, of all things, her black dress? It would look like a sack on Vikki. So why had she taken it? And where had she gone dressed like that?

NINE

"MRS. JONES? Mrs. Brenda Jones? My name is Paget." He held up his card. "Detective Chief Inspector Paget. May I come in and talk to you?"

"Oh, yes, of course. Sorry about that, but..." She closed the door part-way and fumbled with the chain. "It's just that my husband's away—he's a long-distance lorry driver—and I always keep the chain on when he's gone." She moved aside to let him in, then slipped the chain back on before leading him inside.

The house was small but tastefully furnished. Apart from a newspaper spread out beside a comfortable-looking chair, everything was neat and in its place. The woman gathered up the paper, folded it tidily, and offered Paget a seat. "Would you like a cup of tea?" she asked. "It's no trouble."

"That's very kind of you, Mrs. Jones," he said, "but I shan't be staying long. Just long enough to ask you a few questions."

Brenda Jones folded her hands in her lap and settled herself more securely in her chair and eyed him apprehensively.

She was dressed neatly in a skirt and jumper; her legs were bare and she wore leather sandals on her feet. Probably somewhere in her middle thirties, he decided. A plumpish face beneath a halo of blonde hair made her look younger than she was.

"What can you tell me about Mr. Bolen?" said Paget. "I must admit I'm puzzled. He had meetings scheduled for Monday afternoon and Tuesday, and yet he booked into the hotel on Saturday, and I'm told he often stayed at the hotel on weekends. Do you have any idea why?"

Brenda looked down at her hands. "I'm not sure that I can tell you that," she said. "I mean, they're very strict about our talking about the guests, even among ourselves."

"I don't think you have to worry about that in this case," Paget told her. "If we are to find the person who killed Mr. Bolen, we need to know as much about him as possible, good or bad."

The woman looked up sharply. "Then you *do* know..." she began, then stopped.

"Know what, Mrs. Jones?"

"You said 'good or bad.'"

Paget nodded, wondering exactly what was going through the woman's mind. "Is there something you'd like to tell me?"

Brenda Jones moved uncomfortably in her chair. "It's a bit like telling tales out of school," she said hesitantly, "but then he is dead, isn't he?"

Paget nodded encouragingly.

"Mr. Bolen...well, he's been what you might call a regular," she said slowly. "He usually comes on a Saturday. Sometimes he'd stay for just the one night; sometimes he would stay for two. Everyone in the hotel knew him and knew why…'' Brenda Jones stumbled to a stop, and Paget thought he knew the reason.

"He had women in his room,'' he said. "Prostitutes. Is that not right?''

"I didn't like it, Mr. Paget,'' the woman said earnestly. "You must believe me. I don't like working with the man—not that he's ever bothered me personally,'' she added hastily, "but as long as I didn't have to have anything to do with his…well, his other business, so to speak''—she looked guiltily at Paget—"I put up with it and said nothing.''

"Are you telling me that Quint supplied girls to Bolen?''

"Not just Mr. Bolen. It's a sort of business on the side, you might say.''

"Does everyone in the hotel know this?''

"Some of them do, but not people like the manager, Mr. Landau. He'd go spare if he knew.''

"I see. Did Quint supply a girl to Bolen last night?''

Brenda frowned. "I'm not sure,'' she said. "But something odd happened shortly after I started work at eleven. This girl—her name's Stella; I don't know her last name—came down in the lift and demanded to see Mr. Quint. She was upset about something, and when Mr. Quint came out of his office, she started going on at him about sending her up there and being told to—pardon my French, but it's what she said—'piss off' by Mr. Bolen. Mr. Quint got her into his office straightaway, and they went at it for quite a while before Stella came out again.''

"Was she still upset?''

"I think she was, but not as much as when she went in. I can't be sure, but I think Mr. Quint may have given her some money.''

"Did you see him give her money?''

"No, but she was putting money into her bag as she came out of the office, so I assumed Mr. Quint had given it to her.''

"I see. Can you describe this girl, Stella?''

"Oh, yes. She's a regular at the hotel. She's a big girl, quite tall, dark hair, plumpish face, and she wears a lot of red. I shouldn't think she'd be hard to find. She's been working the hotel for as long as I've been there.''

"Always with Bolen?"

"Oh, no. She goes with others as well."

"So you've seen others going up to Mr. Bolen's room as well?"

Brenda Jones nodded.

"Just one more question, Mrs. Jones, and I'll be on my way. You say that Stella was a big girl. In your experience, did Mr. Bolen prefer smaller girls? Is that, perhaps, why he rejected Stella that night?"

"Oh, no, Mr. Paget. I don't know why Mr. Bolen turned Stella away last night, but it wouldn't be because of that. He liked the big ones. All the girls who went up to his room, at least while I've been working there, were a good size."

BEFORE CALLING IT A DAY, Paget returned to Charter Lane, where he, Tregalles and Len Ormside, who had come in to begin the task of setting up an Incident Room, sat down to pool their information.

"If this girl, Stella, is a regular at the hotel, she's probably in our records already," Ormside observed. "Even if she isn't, chances are that some of our people will recognize the name and description. I'll get on it first thing in the morning. Or we could ask Quint. He must know where to find her."

Paget shook his head. "For one thing, I don't want to jeopardize Mrs. Jones's position if I can help it, and for another, if we alert Quint, he may stonewall us long enough to have Stella do a runner. But I'm curious about this other girl as well. Obviously, she's not one of Quint's regulars or he would never have mentioned her to me. And according to Brenda Jones, she wasn't Bolen's type. But whoever she is, I want her found."

Tregalles nodded. "I can have another go at the hotel staff," he said, "but so far they're all sticking together and deny any knowledge of Bolen or anyone else having girls in their rooms. One of the maids, a part-timer who works weekends, did mention a *man* who came to see Bolen fairly regularly, but she said that was usually on Sunday mornings. She didn't know his name, but she described him as middle-aged, clean-shaven, with sandy hair, but not much of it, and quite fat. Oh, yes, and he wore spectacles.''

Paget was suddenly alert. "Douglas Underwood," he said, "and when I spoke to him this morning, he did his damnedest to distance himself from Bolen. I'd better have another chat with him. Anything else?"

"Reservations are required in the Elizabethan Room," Tregalles said, "so I have the names and telephone numbers of everyone who was there last night, and we'll be talking to them tomorrow."

Paget stifled a yawn. "Any news on when the post-mortem will be?"

"Coroner's office rang to say it's been delayed until tomorrow," said Ormside. "No one available."

Which meant, thought Paget, that the chances of getting an accurate time of death were diminishing by the hour. "Has anyone inquired about Starkie?" he asked. He'd meant to phone the hospital himself, but it had slipped his mind till now.

"I spoke to Charlie this afternoon, and he tells me they'll be operating tomorrow morning," Tregalles said. "He was talking to Reg's wife, and she told him the doctors are quite optimistic about his chances."

"Thank God for that," said Paget. He hoped the doctors were right. After seeing the pathologist, grey-faced and gasping for air as he slumped to the floor that morning, he had wondered whether Starkie would make it at all. Obviously he had, and they must think he had a decent chance if they weren't planning to operate until tomorrow.

He rose to his feet. "Right," he said, "then I suggest we all get a good night's sleep, because tomorrow is going to be a very busy day."

SOMETHING WAS PLUCKING at her clothes, tearing at her skin. She fell against a hard surface; she couldn't breathe. She tried to get up but she was being trampled by a herd of animals she couldn't see. Hooves thudded into her chest, her face...

A blurred image appeared in front of her. A pair of eyes, a

face... It was gone. She felt something pulling on her hair. It was being pulled out by the roots!

It was dark. Pitch-black.

"Feeling a bit better, then?"

Vikki opened her eyes and let out a long sigh of relief as she realized she'd been dreaming. Or was it a dream? That face... There was something about that face.

Joanna was there, holding her hand. "You're looking better," she said. "That sleep did you good. Feel like something to eat?"

Vikki nodded. She *was* hungry. In fact, she was famished. "What time is it?" she asked, and winced. Her whole face felt stiff and sore, and her chest felt as if it had been hammered by...what? She tried to capture the image from her dream, but the harder she tried, the faster it seemed to fade.

"Five o'clock."

"Five...?"

Joanna smiled. "Sunday afternoon. You've been asleep for almost eight hours. Best thing for you, considering the condition you were in. Think you can manage a wash by yourself, or would you like Bunny to help you while I make something to eat? It will have to be a sponge bath, I'm afraid. Bunny and I work at the pub, so they let us use the shower there, but I don't think it would be a good idea for you to go over there in your present condition."

Vikki eased herself off the bunk and stood up. "I'll be all right," she assured Joanna. "And thank you ever so much. I don't know what I'd have done if you..." She blinked hard, fighting back tears. "I'll pay you back, I promise."

"Nonsense! Now, let's see about that bath, and then we'll look for something that fits you better than that awful dress you were wearing."

TEN

Monday, 25 September

MONDAY MORNING was a madhouse in the Incident Room. Detectives, clerks, technicians and their helpers all stumbling over each other as equipment was set up and put in place, while those who had been called out on Sunday brought the regular shift up to speed. Superintendent Alcott arrived in time for the morning briefing, then spent another fifteen minutes asking questions as he prepared his own report for Chief Superintendent Brock.

The Force press officer came looking for a statement he could give to the media, and was told what he could say—which wasn't very much—but more importantly, what he could *not* say. Even the cause of death would be withheld until it could be confirmed by the post-mortem results later in the day. "In other words, the usual blah, blah, blah," he sighed unhappily as he put his pen away and departed from the room.

Paget looked at the time. Nine-fifteen, and things were settling down. Len Ormside had stayed late last night, entering on white-boards the salient features of the crime and results of the investigation so far. He had even managed to lay out tentative assignments for the day. Which was why, despite the appearance of mass confusion, things had gone as smoothly as they had.

"Well done, Len," he told the sergeant as he put on his coat. "If you need to contact me, I'll be in Keith Lambert's office. I have an appointment with him at ten."

KEITH LAMBERT was a stocky, broad-shouldered man of about fifty. He had short, dark, wiry hair, and deep-set eyes beneath a tangle of bushy eyebrows. He came out from behind an old-fashioned wooden desk strewn with folders as Paget was ushered into his office by Lambert's secretary.

"Chief Inspector Paget," he said as he thrust out a hand. His grip was firm and brief. "Sorry to hear about Bolen. Not that we ever got on, but no one deserves to die like that. Please, have a seat." He moved back to his own chair behind the desk. "Do you prefer coffee or tea?"

"Tea, thank you," said Paget. "No milk or sugar."

"Right. Same for me, please, Myrtle," he told the woman who had ushered Paget in.

Lambert toyed with a letter-opener. "Paget..." he said ruminatively. "I used to know a Paget once. He was my dentist. Died suddenly, poor chap, three or four years ago. Good man."

"He was my father."

Lambert sat forward. "Was he, now? If memory serves, he used to live in Ashton Prior in a house my father built."

"Absolutely right," said Paget. "I live there now."

The door opened, and Myrtle returned with a tray containing biscuits, cups and saucers, matching plates, and a teapot. Not everyday china, Paget noted as the woman poured the tea and silently withdrew.

Paget sipped his tea, then set his cup carefully in its saucer. "I know you must be a busy man, Mr. Lambert," he said, "so I'll come straight to the point. I've been given to understand that there has been some sort of feud going on between you and the Bolens for a good many years. Something beyond the normal business rivalry. What was it about?"

Keith Lambert sipped his tea thoughtfully. "Are you suggesting there is a connection between Jim Bolen's death and this 'feud', as you call it?"

"Quite frankly, I don't know," Paget told him. "But if what I've been told is correct, it does seem that your visit to the Bolen house triggered a series of events that ended with Bolen's death. Not that the two are necessarily connected," he added carefully, "but I'm sure you will appreciate that we do have to explore every possibility."

Lambert nodded. "I can see that," he conceded. He took another sip from the cup, then set it down on the saucer and leaned forward, arms folded on the desk before him.

"First of all, it was not a feud in the true sense of the word. It was an obsession on the part of Jim Bolen, and I can tell you almost to the minute when it started. It was in 1964, the fourteenth of July, to be exact, about ten o'clock in the morning. We were working on the top floor of what was then the new town hall. I was just sixteen, and working as a labourer on the job during the summer holidays, and my uncle, Jack Bolen, was working as a carpenter. He was a joiner by trade and had worked with his father in his cabinet-making shop before coming to work for my father as a—"

Paget held up a hand and stopped Lambert in mid-sentence. "Hold on there for a minute," he told him. "What was that about your *uncle?*"

"Jack Bolen. You asked about—"

"You mean that you and the Bolens are related?"

Keith Lambert sat back and looked at him. "You didn't know that?" he said.

"No one thought to mention it to me."

"I see. Well, then, I'd better explain. Jim Bolen and I are—were—cousins. Jim's father, Jack Bolen, was my mother's brother. My father, who died some years ago, was Sam Lambert. He started this firm in the late thirties, built it up from scratch, and did very well. Jack Bolen apprenticed as a cabinet-maker under his father, our mutual grandfather, but with the advent of assembly-line furniture, cabinet-making was a dying business in the fifties, so Jack came to work for my father as a carpenter."

Lambert sipped his tea. "Jack resented the fact that my father had done so well during and after the war. You see, Dad lost a foot in an accident when he was young, so he was unfit for military service. But he was a hard worker, and he had a lot of drive. So by the time the building boom came along at the beginning of the fifties, he was well positioned to expand. He made a lot of money, and that did not sit well with my Uncle Jack.

"Jack was a chronic whiner, always complaining about the job, the equipment, anything and everything. The truth is, he was bone-idle, but he seemed to think that because he was my mother's brother, he should be given preferential treatment. In fact, it was only because he *was* my mother's brother that Dad kept him on at all.

"Anyway, all that is somewhat beside the point. On this particular day, as I said, we were working on the scaffold on the top floor of the new town hall. I was new to the job at the time and I was afraid of heights, still am, for that matter, and my Uncle Jack knew that. He used to taunt me with it and call me a sissy. He'd wait until I stepped off the ladder and was walking along the planks, then jump up and down on them to make them bounce. I'll admit I was terrified. I used to dread working with him."

There was a grim set to Lambert's mouth as he continued.

"He'd dare me to do things. Like swinging out around one of the uprights on the scaffold four stories up, holding on with just one hand, and dare me to prove I wasn't a sissy by doing the same."

Lambert grimaced. "There were days when I was physically sick," he said quietly. "God, it was awful." He passed a hand across his brow. "Unfortunately for Jack, he did it once too often, lost his grip and fell. Broke his back on a pile of bricks in the yard below."

Lambert drained his cup and refilled it, then topped up Paget's cup as well without asking if he wanted more.

"My cousin Jim was fifteen at the time. He'd just started working for us the month before, and he was devastated. He'd always doted on his father, and he believed everything Jack had told him, including what a thoroughly bad lot the Lamberts were. Jack told him my father had stayed behind and profited from the war, while he was away fighting for King and Country, the implication being that Dad had somehow wangled his way out of being called up rather than being declared medically unfit because of the loss of his foot. In fact, Jack was in the Royal Corps of Signals and the farthest he ever got from home was Brora in Scotland. Jack also claimed the reason he wasn't made a foreman was because my father had it in for him, while in fact he would use every excuse in the book to avoid work; the scaffold was unsafe, the hoist wasn't working properly, he'd strained his back. Dad threatened to sack him on a number of occasions, but my mother always intervened and persuaded Dad to keep him on."

"But why would Jim Bolen come to work for a firm that his father was always running down?"

Lambert shrugged. "It was the sixties. The first boom was over, and the truth of the matter is we were the only firm in town even considering taking anyone on."

"So you and young Jim were virtually the same age," said Paget. "How did you get on?"

"We didn't; at least, not then. Jim happened to be on another job when the accident happened, but as I said, he believed everything his father told him. So, when Jack was killed, Jim had to find someone to blame. He blamed me and my father, but especially me. I was the only one on the scaffold when it happened, and apparently Jack used to make fun of me at home, saying that I was always stumbling about on the scaffold, that I was scared stiff—which was true—and that I'd nearly had him off several times due to my clumsiness—which wasn't true.''

"You must have given evidence at the coroner's inquest,'' Paget said. "Wasn't what happened made clear?''

Keith Lambert looked down at the desk. "I told them he fell,'' he said quietly. "I said he tripped and fell.'' He looked up at Paget again. "In spite of everything, my mother did not want Jack's family to have to face the truth about him. She said they wouldn't believe it for a start, and they would think that I had invented the story out of vindictiveness. So I said he tripped and fell.''

Paget shook his head in disbelief. "Are you telling me that Jim Bolen actually carried those grievances forward to this day?'' he said.

Lambert leaned forward across the desk. "Let me tell you exactly what Jim Bolen did,'' he said earnestly. He paused for a moment, eyes fixed on a distant point as if peering into the past. "After the inquest, Jim was very bitter. He accused my father of using his influence at the inquest to have a verdict of accidental death brought in; he claimed that his father had complained for weeks about the scaffold being unsafe, and nothing had been done about it. But the site was inspected immediately following the accident, and no fault was found with the safety aspects of the scaffold.

"Jim quit his job, of course, and we heard no more about him until a couple of months later, when he came to the house one evening and asked to see my father. He was a different person. He said that he'd had time to think, that he realized how wrong he'd been, and he asked if he could have his job back. My father wanted nothing to do with him, but my mother persuaded him to give Jim another chance.

"So he did. And Jim worked like a Trojan. As I said earlier, he was clever and quick to learn and, unlike his father, never afraid of work. Even Dad was forced to admit that Jim was one of the best apprentices he'd ever had. He went into a bit of a slump when his mother died a year later, but that only lasted about a month and he was right back at it again, working as hard as ever. He wanted to know everything and work on every aspect of the job.'' Lambert smiled ruefully. ''It's funny, but it was only the other day that he told me why he came back all those years ago. He was planning even then to destroy me and this company, and he didn't care if it took him a lifetime to do it.

''But back then, Jim was a very likeable person, quite unlike his father, and I admired him. I didn't have much confidence in my own abilities in those days, but he did. He'd tackle anything. He was well liked, especially by the girls. He was always the centre of attention. I envied him. Really, I did.

''He left the firm when he was twenty-one. Dad tried to get him to stay on, but Jim said he wanted to start up on his own. He said he'd scraped some money together, and he and his brother were going jobbing. Harry had been working at the cement works at Thurling until then, but he left his job and went to work with Jim.''

Lambert picked up his cup, tasted it, but the tea had gone cold, and he set it aside.

Bitterness entered his voice as he continued. ''They did well right from the start, and I for one wished them well. It never occurred to me then that Jim harboured any ill feeling toward me, even when he took Laura away from me. It never dawned on me that it was all part of his master plan. As a matter of fact, I didn't know *that* until the other day either, when Laura told me herself.''

''Mrs. Bolen?''

Lambert nodded. ''That's right. We were engaged. Had been for more than a year when she met Jim.'' He gave a shrug of resignation. ''I suppose I'm as much to blame as he was for what happened. I was cautious, serious and…well, dull, I suppose, whereas Jim was like a breath of fresh air. I know it's trite to say, but he swept her off her feet. Within three months of their meeting, they were married.'' Lambert's mouth twisted into a grim smile. ''They were married in May, and John, their eldest, was born in December, so that may have had something to do with it.''

"You're saying that he deliberately set out to take your fiancée away from you as part of some grand design to destroy you, Mr. Lambert?"

Lambert smiled. "Sounds incredible, doesn't it," he said, "and I wouldn't have believed it myself if Laura hadn't told me. Even she didn't know until he threw it in her face the other day." Lambert shook his head as if he still couldn't believe it. "All those wasted years," he said softly. "Can you imagine what that's done to Laura? How she must feel, knowing that the only reason Jim married her was to score off me? And the damnable thing is, I think she loved him. In spite of everything she's had to put up with from him over the years, she still loved him. God!"

Lambert's eyes blazed.

"You kept in touch with Mrs. Bolen, then, during this time?"

"No, well, not really. This is not a large town, so it was inevitable that we should run into each other from time to time, but for the most part we avoided each other. Because of the business we were in, Jim and I sometimes found ourselves at the same table, and we were civil to each other, but even that wore thin as time went by and it became obvious that Jim was playing a cutthroat game."

Lambert sat back in his chair and locked his hands behind his head. "And he was winning," he said frankly. "These past two or three years have not been good. He's underbid us on almost every major job—not by much, but just enough to tilt the scales in his favour, and I don't mind admitting it has hurt us. I've had to lay people off."

"I'm told you approached Mrs. Bolen with a proposal that the two firms should go into this Ockrington project together. Is that right, Mr. Lambert?"

Lambert sat back and regarded Paget with thoughtful eyes. "So you've heard about Ockrington," he said. "Did Laura tell you?"

"I'd like to hear what you have to say."

Lambert nodded. "Fair enough," he said equably. "Actually,

it was a spur-of-the-moment thing on my part. I happened to go into a tea-shop in Shrewsbury one afternoon, and Laura was sitting there alone. I'm not sure what prompted me to do it, but I asked her if I could talk to her, and she invited me to sit down. I wasn't even sure what I was going to say when I sat down, but once I'd started, I simply told her the truth as I saw it. I told her that if Jim continued on the way he was going, he would certainly create problems for us, land being as hard to come by as it is, but he would utterly destroy Bolen Brothers in the process. Whereas, if we went into the project together, we could both do very well out of it.''

"What was her response?"

"Frankly, I was surprised," said Lambert. "Laura agreed with me. She said that she and John and Harry had all tried to talk Jim out of the Ockrington deal, because the firm simply did not have the financing to carry it through to the point where they would begin to see a decent return on investment. She was intrigued by the idea of joining forces, and she promised to try to get Jim to see reason.''

"But he wasn't to be persuaded."

"He went crazy! He told her if she ever spoke to me again, she could forget about coming back."

"Obviously, she did speak to you again."

"Yes. Laura and I met several times. She didn't know what to do. She said there was no reasoning with Jim, that destroying me was the only thing he talked about, and he seemed oblivious to the consequences. For example, he had assured Harry that he would do nothing without Harry's approval, then packed him off to Canada to see his new grandchild and went full steam ahead.

"I couldn't ask Laura to do more, so I decided to tackle Jim myself. And that," Lambert concluded bitterly, "was a big mistake."

"This was last Friday?"

"That's right. Laura told me that Jim would be working at the house that day, so I went round just after lunch. Laura was there and she answered the door and let me in. She took me along to Jim's study where he was working, then left the room.

I half expected him to throw me out as soon as he saw me, and I was surprised when he invited me to sit down.''

"He didn't know you were coming?"

"No. I might never have made it inside the door if he had. But he surprised me. He was very civil. He let me have my say, and I actually believed that I was getting through to him. When I'd finished, he sat back in his chair and asked me if I knew why he had come back to work for my father all those years ago. I said I wasn't sure what he was driving at, so he told me. 'I came back,' he said, 'to learn everything I could about the building trade so that I could destroy you and your firm for killing my father, even if it took me the rest of my life. And that's exactly what I intend to do. Now get out of my house and stay out!'''

"What happened after that?"

Lambert's lips compressed into a thin line and his face grew dark. "I didn't know until later, when Laura telephoned after she left the hospital," he said. "If I'd only realized at the time…" He fell silent, brooding.

"Realized what?" Paget prompted.

"What the bastard was capable of," said Lambert hotly. "He didn't have the guts to tackle me, so he took it out on Laura. She tried to reason with him, but it was useless. That's when he told her he'd only married her because she'd been engaged to me. Told her he'd never loved her, that all she was to him was—" Lambert broke off and took a deep breath. "Let's just say it's something I don't care to repeat. Then he hit her. Knocked her down and told her to get out.

"Laura telephone me from Harry's house and told me what had happened," he continued. "I wanted her to call the police and bring charges against Bolen, but she refused. But she did say she had telephoned Harry in Vancouver to tell him what was going on, and he was flying back as soon as he could get a flight out.''

He shook his head sadly and regarded Paget with troubled eyes. "I went round to see her that evening. I told her I felt responsible for what had happened, but Laura said I'd only been the trigger, that it had been building up for a long time. She said she'd known for years that Jim didn't love her, and she'd blamed herself for not trying hard enough to be a good wife to him, because, in spite of everything, she still loved him.

"What she hadn't known, of course, was his real reason for marrying her in the first place, and when he flung that in her face it really hurt."

And Keith Lambert, thought Paget, was still in love with Laura. It was there in the man's voice and in his eyes. He'd said that Laura still loved her husband, but wasn't it more likely that Laura Bolen would hate her husband? Perhaps even enough to kill him? And what about Lambert himself? Paget put that question to him.

Keith Lambert regarded Paget steadily. "Of course I hated the man," he said. "Hated him for what he'd done to Laura, hated him for what he'd done to me and the firm. But I didn't kill him."

"But you must admit that his death makes things much easier for you. I assume Bolen Brothers will be withdrawing their bid, leaving only yours to be considered."

"Quite right," said Lambert. He didn't seem particularly perturbed by the thrust of Paget's questions.

"So, where were you on Saturday evening, Mr. Lambert? Let's say between the hours of ten and midnight?"

"I was here in this office, as a matter of fact. I can't prove it, but this is where I was. Thinking about the Ockrington project and going over all the figures—and trying to decide which of my staff was feeding Bolen the details of our bid."

"You believe someone is doing that?"

"I'm sure of it," Lambert said. "At first, I thought that they were just that much sharper than we were, but when it started happening on every major bid, I realized something was wrong. Bidding on large jobs is difficult and complicated at the best of times, and many times estimates have to be based on guesswork. Trying to decide whether the price of cement, steel, timber, and everything else that goes into a project will remain stable over the next year is extremely difficult, to say nothing of labour costs, so you do the best you can and hope you've left enough of a cushion to make a profit.

"But when your main competitor brings in a bid that is consistently two or three percent lower than yours, you begin to wonder how he is arriving at his estimates. The answer, of course, is that he knows ahead of time what your bid is going to be."

"I see." Paget thought of Douglas Underwood. It would explain his Sunday-morning visits to Bolen's hotel room. And if Underwood had been supplying Bolen with information on a regular basis, Bolen might well have been calling Underwood for some sort of clarification.

"And did you come to a conclusion?" he asked.

Lambert scowled. "It has to be coming from someone involved in the estimating process itself," he said, "and someone fairly senior at that, because they are the only ones who see the final submission. As for who it is... Let's just say I have my suspicions."

ELEVEN

STELLA GREEN PULLED the covers over her head and tried to shut out the sound of banging on her door. It couldn't be the rent; that wasn't due until the end of the week. It couldn't be Leo, either. He was away on a job. So who the hell was banging on her door at ten o'clock of a Monday morning?

She pulled the covers away from her face, half raised herself in bed and yelled, "Sod off!" then buried herself once again beneath the covers.

But the banging continued. Stella tried to ignore it, but she knew that if she allowed it to go on, it could get her thrown out. It wasn't much of a place, but she wouldn't find anything as cheap anywhere else. She flung the covers back.

"All right! All right! I'm coming," she shouted. "No need to knock the bloody door down." The banging stopped. Stella pulled on a faded dressing-gown and padded to the door. "Who is it?" she demanded.

"Police! Open the door!"

Stella groaned. Police. What the hell did they want now?

The pounding began again.

Stella turned the key and opened the door. A dark-haired man with a pleasant but oddly crumpled face smiled at her. "Morning," he said cheerfully. "Stella Green, is it? Sorry if I woke you up. Mind if I come in?" He didn't wait for a reply but moved inside and closed the door. "Tregalles," he said as he looked around. "Detective Sergeant Tregalles."

Stella moved to the bedside table, found her cigarettes and lit one. "So what do you want?" she demanded. "Haven't you got anything better to do than go round waking people up?" The smoke caught in the back of her throat and she began to cough.

"Those cancer sticks'll kill you," he told her solemnly as he dropped into a chair beside the door. "You should take better care of yourself, Stella."

The woman sat down on the bed and squinted at him through a haze of smoke. "So whadyawant?" she asked wearily.

But Tregalles was in no hurry. "I could murder a cup of tea," he told her. "Why not pop the kettle on while we have a little chat?"

Stella remained where she was. "You want tea, go down the caff on the corner and pay for it," she told him.

He looked hurt. "Don't be like that, Stella. I come as a friend."

Stella snorted, but her eyes were watchful. What was all this leading up to? Try as she might, she couldn't think of anything she'd done that would bring a copper to her door.

"Seen the paper this morning?" he asked as he pulled a copy from his coat pocket. He tossed it across the floor to land folded at Stella's feet.

Stella inhaled deeply and blew out a stream of smoke. She made no move to pick it up.

"Better read it," he advised. "Front page, you can't miss it. About a friend of yours."

She didn't want to pick it up. She had the feeling that she wasn't going to like what she saw.

He rose to his feet. "I think I will have that cuppa," he said.

He made his way into the alcove that served as a kitchen, found the kettle and filled it at the sink.

Stella picked up the paper, opened it and looked at the headlines: *PROMINENT BUSINESS MAN STABBED TO DEATH*. She stared at the picture of Jim Bolen below, and suddenly felt cold. A smaller picture of the Tudor Hotel, with an arrow pointing to the window of room 203, filled the lower corner of the page. She read the article swiftly. Saturday night! The words seemed to leap from the paper, and she knew now why Tregalles was there. Stella tossed the paper aside and sat there drawing hard on her cigarette.

A low-pitched whistle, rising to a fingernails-across-the-blackboard screech, came from the kettle. Tregalles, who had busied himself preparing the teapot and mugs, unplugged the kettle and filled the pot.

"I think you're going to need that when it's ready," he said as he stood in the doorway. He was no longer smiling.

Stella reached for an ashtray and butted the cigarette. "Dunno what that's go to do with me," she said with a careless wave at the paper.

Tregalles shook his head sorrowfully. "And you the last person to see him alive." He sighed. "What was it, Stella? Crime of passion? Or wouldn't he pay the services rendered?"

The chill that had entered the pit of her stomach grew colder. "I don't know what you're talking about," she said, but her words lacked conviction.

Tregalles sighed heavily. "It's no good, Stella," he said. "We know you were with him that night. Quint sent you up there, didn't he? Then you came down with some story about Bolen kicking you out and not paying you. So Quint, being the generous fellow he is, paid you off. Never occurred to him to go up and see what you'd done to Bolen, did it? I mean, why should it? He believed you, didn't he? One of his regulars. You've been keeping his clients happy for a long time, haven't you, Stella?"

Tregalles lifted the lid of the teapot and used a spoon to fish out the tea-bag. "Milk in first?" he inquired.

Stella reached for another cigarette and lit it. The taste in her mouth was foul, and much as she hated to accept anything from this man, she needed something to take the taste away. "Lemon," she said tightly. "Bottom of the fridge."

Tregalles raised an eyebrow in mock surprise. "Fancy," he said, but he opened the tiny fridge, found the half-dried lemon, and squeezed it into the mug. "There you are, Stel," he said as he handed her the hot tea. "Don't say I never do anything for you. Now, then, why did you kill Bolen?"

He poured his own tea and sat down beside the door once more.

Stella drank greedily. The tea was scalding hot. It burned the back of her throat and brought tears to her eyes. "I never..." she began, but stopped when Tregalles began to shake his head.

"We've got witnesses, Stella," he warned softly. "You were there in Bolen's room."

"No! No, I wasn't," she protested. Quint! She thought disgustedly. This was his doing, the slimy little toe-rag! And that prissy woman who worked nights with him. But there was nothing to be gained by denying that she had an arrangement with the man. She was sure that Tregalles already knew that or he wouldn't be here. "I was *not* in his room that night," she declared again. "He wouldn't let me in."

Tregalles looked unconvinced.

"Look," she said earnestly, "I've been with Bolen in the past; I admit that, but when Quint sent me up there Saturday night, Bolen wouldn't let me in. Usually, when I knock—we have this sort of signal, you see, like I'd knock once ever so softly, then knock four times fast, like this"—Stella demonstrated on the bedside table—"he would open the door straightaway because he didn't want anyone to see me outside his room. But not last Saturday. I knocked as usual, but he didn't open the door. I thought perhaps he was in the loo or something like that, so I waited a couple of minutes, then knocked again."

Stella pulled on her cigarette. "There was no one about in the corridor, so I knocked harder, and I heard him come to the door. I said, 'It's Stella, Jim,' but instead of letting me in, he told me to go away."

"He opened the door?"

"No. The door was locked. I tried the handle several times.

He told me to go away through the door. I couldn't believe it. Usually, he'd have the door open and pull me inside quick as a wink. I thought he hadn't heard me, so I told him again who I was, but then he got really angry. He said, 'Piss off, Stella, I'm busy! And you can tell Quint not to send anyone else up, either!''

Smoke trickled from Stella's nostrils. "So I went straight down to see Quint and asked him what he thought he was playing at, sending me up there when Bolen didn't want me. He didn't like that, specially with that Brenda woman being there. I told him I didn't give a shit what he liked, I didn't like being messed about when I could have been making good money. He said he couldn't understand it, that Bolen had asked for me specially. But he would say that, wouldn't he? I think he just sent me up there on spec. He probably reckoned that Bolen would let me in and he'd get his cut as usual.'' She snorted with disgust. "He gave me a lousy twenty quid, and he only gave me that to shut me up and get me out of there.''

Tregalles eyed her thoughtfully. He had, of course, not spoken to Quint at all. Paget was keeping that bit of information about the man's extra-curricular activities for later. Neither did Tregalles believe for a moment that Stella Green had been involved in Bolen's murder. The timing was all wrong, for a start. Brenda Jones had said that Stella had come down shortly after she came on shift at eleven, and it had been after twelve when Bolen called down from his room. But there was no need to tell Stella that.

"Assuming—and I say *assuming*—for the sake of argument that what you're telling me is true, has Bolen ever done this before?''

"Never! Like I said, he couldn't get the door open quick enough.''

"So what was he doing with this other bird, then? The skinny kid, fair hair, pale, about sixteen years old?''

"Bolen? You must be joking. He likes his pound of flesh, does Bolen. That's what he used to say, 'I'll have my pound of flesh, Stel—a pound in each hand,' and he'd laugh.'' Stella looked down at the newspaper, and Tregalles was surprised to see that her eyes were moist.

"So why do you think he sent you packing that night?''

Stella looked off into the distance and frowned. "I don't know," she said. She seemed genuinely puzzled.

"Unless somebody else was already in there with him," Tregalles suggested. "Another girl."

"If he did have somebody in there, it wouldn't be any sixteen-year-old!" she snapped. "He didn't go in for kids."

"So who is this kid, then? She was seen by more than one person. You've been around long enough to know who's working the patch."

Stella shrugged. Broadminster wasn't all that big, and the man was right; she had been around a long time, and she knew every...Stella took a quick drag at her cigarette and stubbed it out.

Tregalles was watching her closely. "What?" he demanded. "You've thought of somebody. Who is she?"

Stella shook her head. "No, no..." she began, but the image in her mind grew stronger. But why would the kid be at the Tudor, of all places?

"I need a name, Stella," he said. "Give me a name. Because if you don't, then yours will do just as well. You *admit* you went up to Bolen's room; you *claim* you never went inside, but can you prove it? And it was a woman who killed him, Stella. Take my word. A name, Stella."

She knew he didn't *really* believe that she'd had anything to do with Bolen's death, but on the other hand, she knew that he could make life very difficult for her if he chose. And if they failed to find the real killer, they might just fit her up for the job. Stella sighed inwardly. To Jim Bolen, she had been a woman he'd paid to have sex with him, but they'd had a lot of laughs together, and she'd like to think that she had meant more to him than just another bed partner. She wanted to see his killer caught, and if that little tart had been involved in his death...

"Talk to Simone," she said. "She's had a kid like that staying with her. Goes by the name of Vikki Lane. But for Christ's sake don't tell Simone it was me who told you!"

HE *READ THE STORY* beneath the headline once again. Not a word about the girl! They had to have her in custody, yet there was *no mention of a suspect or even the usual euphemistic phrase of someone "helping them with their enquiries." It wasn't like the police to keep silent when they'd caught a killer red-handed at the scene of the crime, yet they'd said nothing. So why weren't they letting on they had her? Why?*

The question refused to go away as he sat there, fingers drumming softly on the table.

Unless…? But no, it simply wasn't possible! She couldn't have been feigning unconsciousness. She'd been completely out of it when he left the room. He'd checked. And yet he felt a nagging twinge of doubt. Had there been a flicker of recognition in those pale-blue eyes when he'd pulled the eyelids back? Was it possible that she'd seen his face?

Even if she had, he assured himself, she'd been so far gone that she would never remember it, at least, not well enough to point the finger at him.

But what if she did? He felt the prickle of sweat across his brow. He couldn't allow that. He'd spent too long planning this; he'd left nothing to chance. And yet things had gone wrong— little things, stupid things that never should have happened, and he'd had to improvise. He didn't like that; and he didn't like the fact that there had been no mention of the girl.

TWELVE

THE BOLEN HOUSE was set well back from the road behind a stand of trees. It was quite large compared to others in the neighbourhood, but very plain, functional, almost utilitarian, and Paget wondered if it was a reflection of Jim Bolen himself. Two cars were parked near the front door, and Paget pulled in beside them. One was a white, top-of-the-range VW Passat, complete with sun-roof and all the bells and whistles, while the other was a red low-slung MG with a dog-eared Paddington bear hanging from the rear-view mirror.

He mounted the shallow steps and rang the bell.

The door was opened immediately by a young woman wearing a faded blue shirt and form-fitting jeans. She was tall and slim, and had predatory eyes.

"Saw you coming up the drive," she said, her gaze frankly appraising. "You must be the policeman. John said he'd asked you to come."

He introduced himself. "And you are Miss Bolen?"

"That's right." Prudence Bolen opened the door wider. "I'll tell John you're here," she said, and left him standing in the entrance hall as she disappeared toward the back of the house.

Moments later a young, bespectacled, bookish-looking man, but obviously a Bolen, appeared. He hurried forward, hand outstretched. "Chief Inspector Paget? John Bolen," he said. His handshake was brisk and firm. "I must apologize for my sister; I did ask her to show you through, but I don't think she listens to half the things I say. Please, come with me."

John Bolen led the way to a large, well-appointed office at the back of the house. Paget paused to look out of the French window at the manicured lawn almost completely surrounded by a box hedge and a variety of trees. A white-painted gazebo marked the far end of the garden, and sunlight shimmered on the surface of a small pond beside it.

"Very nice," Paget observed, more to himself than to Bolen, but the man picked up on the comment immediately.

"We can talk in the garden if you wish," he suggested. "To tell you the truth, I've been penned up in here most of the day, and I could do with some fresh air." Without waiting for an answer, he opened the doors and stepped out.

The sun was bright, but there was a hint of autumn in the air, and the grass was still wet from the morning dew in the shadow of the trees. "Sorry to drag you all the way out here," he apologized. "Ordinarily, I would have come to you, but my mother wanted me here. She asked me to go through my father's papers to make sure that there was nothing outstanding. Harry—that is my Uncle Harry, whom I believe you met yesterday—intended to be here as well, but Aunt Dee is flying into Manchester this afternoon, and he's gone to meet her."

"No problem," Paget told him, falling into step beside Bolen.

"You mentioned on the phone that there was a matter you wished to discuss?"

"Yes. Well, to be truthful, it was my mother's idea to ring you. She feels…" John Bolen spread his hands and sighed. Clearly Bolen was not entirely in agreement with his mother on the matter. "She feels that she wasn't quite frank with you yesterday morning, and there are certain things you should know about my father if you are to find the person responsible for his death."

He hesitated before going on, making it clear that he was uncomfortable with what he'd been asked to do.

"You see, for some time, now, he and my mother have been what you might call estranged. They've been living in the same house but more or less separate lives, if you see what I mean."

Paget frowned. "I'm not sure that I do," he said.

Bolen clasped his hands behind him and walked with his eyes fixed firmly on the ground. "Look, Chief Inspector," he said stiffly, "I'd rather not be telling you this at all. I know my father had his faults, but… Well, the point is, my mother seems to think that it may help you with your investigation into his death. You see, Dad sometimes went with other women. I mean, well, you know…"

Paget took pity on him. "Prostitutes," he said matter-of-factly. "If you are trying to tell me that your father was in the habit of staying at the Tudor Hotel most weekends for that purpose, Mr. Bolen, I should tell you that we have come to much the same conclusion."

"Ah!" The man looked both surprised and relieved, but only momentarily. A furrow of concern creased his brow. "Do you mean to tell me it was common knowledge?" he asked in hushed tones.

Paget nodded. "Within certain circles, yes, I believe it was."

"I see." John Bolen looked deflated. "Then perhaps I've just been wasting your time, Chief Inspector. I'm sorry."

"Not at all," said Paget, "because there are a number of questions I would like to ask you, if you don't mind."

"Please, go ahead. If there is any way I can help, feel free to ask anything you like."

"Thank you. To begin with, I would like to know more about this project at Ockrington. I've been led to believe that if your father had gone ahead with it as he planned to do, it could have had devastating consequences for Bolen Brothers. Is that true?"

Bolen looked puzzled. "I'm not at all sure that I see the connection," he said. "With my father's death, I mean. From what my mother told me, I was under the impression it was more like a random act of violence."

"Oh, I'm not saying we've ruled that out," Paget assured him, "but it seems there were a number of people opposed to the course he was taking, a lot of people who tried to talk him out of it, so it has to be considered as a possible motive for his murder."

Bolen flinched at the word *murder*, and it was clear that the idea of being included among the suspects did not sit well with him. He fell silent, and Paget had to ask the question again.

"Yes, well, to be honest, we'd have been lucky to last a year with that millstone around our neck," said John. "My father has mortgaged this house, the building in Broadminster, and other properties as well. The combined payments on those mortgages alone will impact heavily on our ability to carry on our day-to-day business. So the sooner we can get out from under those debts, the better."

"What, exactly, is your position in the company, Mr. Bolen?"

"Cost accountant. Actually, I spend most of my time doing cost analysis and projections, and frankly I was appalled at what my father was about to do. God knows how many hours I spent working up charts and graphs to try to convince him that Ockrington was a bad investment. The M.o.D. has put far too many conditions on the sale for it to be viable, but he wouldn't listen." Bolen smiled ruefully. "Ask my fiancée. She'll tell you how much time I've spent in the office these past few weeks.

"Mind you," he continued, "it was always difficult working with him when we were bidding directly against Lambert. I would spend weeks, sometimes months, costing out large jobs, and I'd cut it as fine as I dared, because I knew Dad would accept nothing less. And then he would come along at the last moment and cut it further.

"At first, I made the mistake of arguing with him. I told him we couldn't possibly make a profit if we used his figures. But he was adamant, and I finally realized that it wouldn't matter what I or anyone else said, so I learned to live with it. We made money on other jobs, but we barely scraped by on some of the big ones. If Dad had only…" He lifted his hands and let them fall again. "But that's water under the bridge," he said firmly. "It makes no difference now."

"Do you have any idea how he arrived at the figures he told you to submit instead of your own?"

"No. And he would never explain. Sometimes they would be just a couple of thousand under, but in some cases it could be as much as twenty or thirty thousand."

"Did you always win the contract based on your father's figures?"

John Bolen's sudden laugh sounded harsh in the tranquil garden. "Clients jumped at it," he said. "Why wouldn't they? They were getting a bargain."

He paused at the edge of the pond, then turned and began to walk back toward the house. He walked, thought Paget, at the sedate pace of a much older man, hands clasped behind his back, eyes on the ground as if in deep thought.

"As a matter of fact," he said, "that was the last thing we talked about when I went up to his room in the hotel on Saturday evening. I thought I would give it one last try before the meeting on Monday, but he refused to listen. Kept insisting it could be done."

"You went to see him Saturday evening?" said Paget sharply.

Bolen nodded. "I did indeed. He'd just come up from dinner; in fact, I arrived just as he was letting himself in."

"What time was that?"

Bolen thought. "Shortly after nine. Say ten past."

"Was anyone with him?"

Bolen looked puzzled. "No. Why?"

"Did you see anyone you knew while you were there?"

"No."

"How long were you with your father?"

"Fifteen, twenty minutes at the most. Not that it did any good.

He became quite belligerent. Kept telling me to get out, said that he'd made up his mind, and that was that. I tried, believe me, Chief Inspector, I really tried, but I had to throw in the towel in the end. There was simply no point in talking to him when he was like that, so I gave up and left.''

"Did anyone see you leave?"

"I stopped at the desk. After almost shoving me out of the door, Dad told me to stop and tell them he wanted to be called at seven-thirty the following morning, and I was to tell them they'd better not forget!'' A faint smile hovered around John Bolen's mouth. "I relayed the message as it was given to me to the woman at the desk, and I remember she smiled and assured me it would be taken care of. She had obviously dealt with my father before.''

"Where did you go when you left the hotel?"

"Home. Well, that's not strictly true. I didn't go straight home. I drove out onto Riverview Road and parked the car overlooking the bridge and just sat there trying to decide what to do next. Unfortunately, there wasn't a damned thing I *could* do, so I went home and tried my best to stop worrying about it. Of course, I couldn't.''

"What time did you get home?"

"Ten-fifteen, ten-thirty. I'm afraid I can't be more precise.''

"What was your father doing when you left him?"

"Muttering a lot. He had his papers spread out on the table, and he was upset about something. He wasn't listening to me, and finally he told me to get out because he had a phone call to make. I was pretty angry myself by that time, so I asked him what was so damned important about a phone call that he couldn't listen to me. But all he kept saying was, 'He's given me the wrong figures. The bastard's given me the wrong figures!' That's when I gave up and left him to it.''

A shadow crossed John Bolen's face. "And that's the last time I saw my father alive,'' he ended quietly.

Paget waited a moment before asking the next question. "Do you have any idea who he was talking about?"

"No. Why? Do you think it might be important?"

Paget side-stepped the question. "Just one more question, Mr.

Bolen, if you don't mind, and then I shall leave you alone. Are you familiar with the terms of your father's will? And if so, would you mind telling me who is the main beneficiary?"

John Bolen's face darkened as he turned to face Paget squarely. "I'm not sure I like the implication of that question," he said harshly.

"There is no implication, Mr. Bolen," Paget told him. "It is simply a question that must be asked in a case such as this. If I don't ask it, someone else will."

John's expression didn't change as he considered Paget's answer. "My mother," he said curtly. "Not that it has any relevance in this case, but my mother will inherit everything."

THE MG WAS GONE when Paget left the house. He was in a thoughtful mood as he drove back into town. The evidence suggested that Jim Bolen had died as a result of a fight with a prostitute, and he was probably wasting his time looking in other directions for a motive. But he couldn't escape the thought that the timing of Bolen's death was extremely fortuitous for a number of people, not the least of whom was Bolen's wife.

Laura Bolen had been assaulted by her husband and thrown out of her own house. No matter how separate their lives might have been up to that point, they had maintained the façade of a united family, and she must have felt utterly humiliated.

Harry Bolen had flown back from Canada in a desperate last-ditch attempt to persuade his brother to drop the project, because he had a lot to lose if Bolen Brothers failed. As did John. But then, so did Keith Lambert if Bolen should be successful in his bid. His business had to be suffering for him to have approached Laura as he had. In effect, he was admitting that Bolen was winning, and that must have been hard for him to swallow.

Still deep in thought, he passed the entrance to a narrow lane when a flash of red caught his eye. He glanced round just in time to see a red MG and a truck parked side by side. Their drivers stood between the two vehicles, heads together, arms around each other. He'd never seen the man before, but in the split second before they disappeared from view, he recognized the girl.

THIRTEEN

PAGET STEPPED OUT of the lift into the fourth-floor corridor of the Royal Broadminster Hospital and made his way along to the office of Andrea McMillan. He knocked and heard her call, "Come in."

He opened the door and stepped inside.

Andrea sat hunched over a stack of forms on which she was scribbling furiously. Before he had a chance to speak, she said, "Be with you in just a second. Take a pew."

Paget sat down and looked around the small office. It looked exactly the same as the first time he had come here to seek an explanation from Andrea about the death of her former husband, and things had gone so terribly wrong. Same overflowing desk; same bookcase with books and magazines piled high on top of it; same narrow window overlooking the car-park.

But was it the same Andrea? he wondered. They had seen each other only briefly in the past few months, and those encounters had been almost entirely professional. Formal, polite, not at all the way it used to be before that business at Glenacres had come between them. Yet he sometimes had the feeling that Andrea herself wished things to be the way they had been in the past. It was nothing he could put his finger on—a fleeting expression in her eyes, something in her voice... He shrugged the thought away. Probably just wishful thinking on his part.

"There!" Andrea McMillan signed her name with a flourish. "Thank goodness that's done at last," she breathed. "And thank you for being so patient, Nurse."

Her eyes widened with surprise as she looked up and realized he was not the nurse she'd been expecting. She felt a little foolish, annoyed that he had not said something. Paradoxically, she was pleased to see him.

Paget shrugged apologetically. "You seemed so absorbed in

what you were doing, I didn't like to interrupt. If you are expecting someone else, I can come back later."

"No. No, it's all right." Now that he was here, Andrea didn't want him to go. "It's just that one of the nurses said she'd pop into the office later, and I assumed…" She smiled and made her own apologetic gesture with her hands.

He looked well. A bit tired, perhaps, but well. And when he looked at her like that she found herself questioning why she'd been so determined to keep him at a distance all this time. But once bitten… She put on her consultant's smile. "What can I do for you, Neil?" she asked. "Is this a social or professional visit?"

"I'm looking for help," he confessed. "I've been trying to find out how Reg Starkie is doing after his operation, but not being a relative, I could barely get anyone to admit he'd *had* an operation, let alone tell me how he is now. Do you think you could find out for me?"

Andrea rolled her eyes heavenward. "Rules," she said, and shook her head. "You must have run into a nurse or a doctor who's had a particularly bad day. Almost anyone in the hospital could have told you how he is. We've all been concerned about poor old Reg."

"Is he going to be all right?"

Andrea hesitated. "Considering the condition he was in, he came through the operation very well," she said slowly. "But he's grossly overweight and he smokes like a chimney. If he hopes to avoid another attack, he's going to have to shed a lot of weight, stop smoking and drinking, and exercise regularly."

Paget grimaced. They both remained silent for several seconds. It would mean a complete change of lifestyle for Starkie, assuming he could be persuaded to stick to it. "He doesn't know this yet, I take it?" he said.

Andrea shook her head. "He's still out of it, and will be for another forty-eight hours, more or less. We're all pulling for him, of course, but…" The doubt in her eyes was plain to see.

Paget silently agreed. He couldn't see Starkie taking kindly to that sort of advice, nor could he see the man following it.

Andrea glanced at her watch. "Look," she said as she stood

up and pushed her chair away. "It's three-thirty, and I haven't had any lunch, so I was about to go downstairs for a cup of tea and a bun. Why don't you join me? After that we can check on Reg again before you leave."

"What about the nurse you were expecting?"

"She can come back later," Andrea said carelessly.

"You're on if you'll allow me to buy."

Andrea smiled. "In that case," she told him as she preceded him through the door, "I shall have a very large bun."

In the event, Andrea had to make do with a very small jam tart, as there was little left from which to choose. She sighed as she poked dejectedly at the sad confection on her plate. "And I was so looking forward to something nice and gooey and horribly unhealthy," she said. She tilted her head back and closed her eyes.

Paget sipped his coffee. "Hard day?" he asked.

Andrea opened her eyes. "Not really. Just trying to juggle too many things at once. Not that I should be complaining; it's my own fault for becoming involved in the first place."

"In…?"

"This parade on Saturday, for one thing," she told him. "That's what I was doing when you came in. I'm on the committee charged with sorting out the placement of each group in the procession. It doesn't sound like much, but you wouldn't believe the things people will do to have their particular entry placed ahead of someone else's."

Paget frowned. "How did you become involved with that?" he asked.

The parade on Saturday morning was an annual event, signalling the beginning of Broadminster's Festival Days. Saturday afternoon was given over to sports events, a fête and garden walk in the grounds of Redford Grange, and there was a concert in the evening. Sunday featured a display of local arts and crafts at the Civic Centre, followed by a series of short one-act plays put on by the local schools in the evening. A series of concerts continued throughout the rest of the week, while the following Saturday would feature the annual traction-engine fair, always a popular event, ending with a fireworks display in the evening.

"Through the riding club," she told him. "I spoke up at the wrong time and found myself on a committee. Some of the juniors will be riding in the parade, including Sarah." Her voice softened. "It's the first time for her, and she's terribly excited about it."

"Sarah would be, what...? Six, now."

"That's right."

"And she's riding already? Isn't she awfully young?"

Paget had never met Andrea's daughter, but he had seen a picture of the fair-haired girl with laughing eyes and cheeky grin. She was sitting astride the top rail of a wooden gate, her long hair blowing in the wind, and her mother was standing beside her, hands ready in case she fell. He remembered all too clearly where and when he'd found the picture—and the countless times he'd wished he hadn't.

Andrea smiled indulgently. "Sarah's been riding since she was four," she told him. "At least," she amended, "she's been learning since she was four, and she's coming along very nicely."

"At Glenacres?" The words came unbidden and he could have bitten his tongue as soon as they were out. It was the last thing he wanted to bring up right now, and his heart sank as he saw the bleak look in Andrea's eyes as she shook her head.

"No, of course not," she said sharply. "I haven't been back there since...well, not since last winter. We use Fairfield now." Andrea pushed her plate aside and picked up her coffee.

Paget searched for something to say. "You'll be riding with Sarah, I suppose?"

"No, she'll be riding her own pony, Pixie. Lovely little mare. I'm not riding at all, but I shall be right behind her with..." Andrea paused and eyed him speculatively. "What are you doing next Saturday morning?" she asked.

Paget shrugged. "A lot depends on how we are doing with this Bolen murder," he told her. "Why? What did you have in mind?"

"But you could probably get a couple of hours off if necessary?"

"Oh, yes. It shouldn't be a problem."

"Good! How would you like to come along and give me a hand, then?"

"I'd be happy to," he told her. There was nothing he would like better than to spend some time with Andrea, and he didn't much care what it was she wanted him to do.

"Helping you with what, exactly?"

"We have a young woman in our club who has MS," she said. "She's riding in the parade. She used to be an excellent rider, but now she has trouble with her balance, and her legs are very weak, so someone has to walk alongside in case she starts to slip. It's best if there are two people, one on either side. You don't actually have to do anything at all except be there just in case. Her condition is getting worse, and this may be the last chance she has to ride in the parade. She's only twenty-three. Will you do it, Neil?"

"It will be my pleasure," he told her. "Just tell me when and where, and I'll be there."

Paget was in a buoyant mood as he drove back to Charter Lane. He had used the excuse of not being able to find out how Starkie was progressing to seek out Andrea, and he was glad now that he had. For whatever reason, Andrea had been more relaxed and easier to talk to than on previous occasions. It was as if some invisible barrier between them had been removed, and the prospect of spending time with her on the weekend was one he looked forward to with pleasure.

He found Ormside and Tregalles with their heads together as they studied the autopsy report on Bolen. "It came in a few minutes ago," Ormside told him, "and we also have a name for our phantom female. Which would you like first, sir?"

"Let's have the post-mortem results," said Paget.

Ormside grunted. "In that case, I'll give you the bad news at the start. The PM was done by a man named Martindale, and the best he can do on time of death is somewhere between nine o'clock Saturday night and one o'clock Sunday morning. Unfortunately, the lab can't do anything with the tape that Starkie made, so we don't know what his conclusion was. Two of the five stab wounds pierced the heart. The others did a lot of damage, but might not have been fatal by themselves. However, Martindale did say that all of the thrusts were very deep, powerful thrusts. His impression is that whoever killed Bolen really wanted him dead.

"So," Ormside concluded, "I asked him about the call for help Bolen is supposed to have made to the desk, and he said it is extremely unlikely that Bolen could have made that call himself."

Which merely confirmed what Paget had begun to suspect. "Anything else?" he asked.

"Yes. The knife found at the scene matches the wounds perfectly, but the interesting thing is this: several pieces of white thread were found *inside* the wounds, which suggests that the victim was wearing a shirt or possibly pyjamas when he was stabbed. The fibres have been sent on for further examination, but he seems pretty sure they come from a shirt."

Tregalles and Paget exchanged glances. No blood-stained clothing had been found in the room, which meant that if Bolen was dressed when he was stabbed, the killer must have removed the evidence.

Paget nodded slowly. "Better check the clothing inventory with Charlie," he told Tregalles. "And find out from Harry Bolen what his brother was wearing at dinner. Also, have someone ask John Bolen what his father was wearing when he went to see him in his room around nine o'clock Saturday evening."

Tregalles frowned. "What was he doing there?"

"The same thing as everyone else, apparently. Trying to persuade his father not to go through with the Ockrington project. And he told me something else. He said his father was in a belligerent mood and couldn't wait to get him out of the room because he wanted to telephone someone. He kept saying that he—whoever *he* is—had given him the wrong figures."

"And Bolen did make a call at nine thirty-two to Underwood," Tregalles observed.

Paget nodded. "I think Underwood has been supplying Bolen with the Lambert bids, and either by accident or design, gave Bolen the wrong figures. If Bolen insisted on Underwood bringing him the right set of figures that night, we could have ourselves another suspect. Anything else of significance in the autopsy report?''

"Yes, there is," said Ormside. "The scratches on the victim's face were made *after* the man was dead, not during a fight or struggle. And there was no indication of recent sexual activity." The sergeant set the report aside. "There's more, but those were the main points."

"Anything in there about cuts by glass in Bolen's feet?"

"No."

"I thought not." Paget crossed the room to stand before a row of photographs from the crime scene taped to a board, and the others followed. "Take a look at the glass around the body," he said. "If that glass was on the floor *before* Bolen died, he couldn't help but tread on it, yet his feet are unmarked." He picked up another photograph taken from a similar angle after the body had been removed. "You see that? No glass under the body, either. That lamp was smashed deliberately after Bolen was killed."

Tregalles nodded. "So the whole scene was a set-up," he said thoughtfully. "Trouble is, who did what? You say that Brenda Jones told you it was a man who rang down for help that night, but we have all this evidence of a girl being in the room, possibly the same one Stella Green told me about."

"Which brings me to my contribution," said Ormside. "We've identified the person whose prints were found all over the crime scene, as well as on the weapon." He returned to his desk and picked up a printed sheet.

"Julia Rutledge. Age seventeen. Twenty-one Crabbe Lane, Tupton, Northamptonshire," he read out. "Convicted on nine separate charges of theft. Failed to return home after leaving the detention centre two months ago. No outstanding warrant. We have pictures." He passed them across the desk.

Paget and Tregalles studied them. The first one, presumably provided by the girl's parents, showed a slight, fair-haired girl dressed in shorts and T-shirt, posing self-consciously against a garden wall. She was very thin and gangly, and looked to be about fourteen. The second photograph was a close-up head-and-shoulders shot against an off-white background. A police photograph. Her face had filled out a little, but her eyes looked enormous as they stared blankly into the camera. The third and fourth shots showed her face in profile. She looked very young and vulnerable, and yet there was a hint of defiance in the tilt of her chin.

Paget flipped through the information sheets. There was not even a suggestion of violence in any of the charges, but apparently the magistrate had thought them serious enough to send her to a youth detention centre for three months. Paget checked the dates. Nothing prior to a year ago.

"What's this note?" asked Paget. "Review pending. Reference Section 79, Sub-section R49223-854, Case Number 7046-32." He handed the sheet back to Ormside. "What's that all about?"

The sergeant frowned. "To tell you the truth, I didn't pay much attention to it," he confessed. "Would you like it followed up?"

"It may not be important, but we might as well have as much information as possible on the girl. She has no record locally, I suppose?"

"Not under that name, no."

Paget continued to study the picture. It was hard to imagine a kid like that mixed up in a brutal murder, but you could never tell by appearances. He turned to Tregalles. "You say you may have a lead on this girl?"

"That's right. Assuming it's the same girl, and I think there's a good chance it is. Stella Green told me about a girl who calls herself Vikki Lane. She described her as a skinny kid who's been staying with another prostitute by the name of Simone Giraud.

"I went round to the address she gave me, but neither of them were there. I spoke to another girl there, and she told me that Simone had gone to Shrewsbury on the bus this morning to do some shopping, but Vikki wasn't with her. In fact, no one I spoke to admits to seeing Vikki since Saturday evening. Could be a coincidence that she disappeared about the same time that Bolen was killed, but I doubt it. I think we're talking about the same kid."

"So when will this Simone be back?" asked Paget.

"Don't know for sure, but I have a policewoman waiting to pick her up as soon as she steps off the bus in Market Square."

Paget nodded his approval. "Run the name 'Vikki Lane' through the computer first thing tomorrow morning," he told Ormside, "and see if there's a record of any charges under that name." He looked at the clock and rose to his feet. "I'll be in my office," he continued, "but let me know when this woman is brought in. I'd like to hear what she has to say, myself."

FOURTEEN

KEITH LAMBERT LOOKED pleased as he emerged from the conference room. The meeting with the dark-suited men had gone rather well, he thought. There had been some concern at the beginning when John Bolen arrived bearing a letter, signed by Harry and Laura, withdrawing the Bolen Brothers bid, but after a hurried consultation among themselves, it was decided to carry on and listen to what Lambert had to say.

But as soon as it became apparent Lambert was not buying the "complete package" concept, the chairman, a plump, red-faced man by the name of Bollinger, objected immediately.

"Completely unacceptable," he declared. "It was made quite clear from the beginning that the land is not divisible. It is either all or nothing, and if this is your position, then we have wasted our time in coming here." He began to straighten papers in front of him as if preparing to leave.

Heads nodded around the table. There were fourteen of them in all. Cardboard name-plates identified each by name and the areas of expertise: "Min. of Def."; "Min. of Ag."; "Min. of Env."; "Housing and Planning"; "Lands and Surveys"; "Regional Planning"; "Rural Dev."; tapering off at the lower end of the table to such cryptic captions as "Eng. S.L. Div." and "Eng. P.V.D.," whatever they were.

But one head remained still. Seated directly opposite Lambert was a thin-faced, mild-looking man whose name-plate read simply: "A. V. Vernon," and his role there had remained unexplained when Bollinger made cursory introductions. Vernon sat back in his chair, fingers steepled beneath his chin, eyes half closed, and it seemed to Lambert as if the man had deliberately detached himself from the rest of his colleagues.

But now he stirred himself and spoke. "On the other hand, Mr. Chairman, since we *are* here," he said mildly, "might I suggest that we hear Mr. Lambert out?"

Bollinger fussed with his papers. "Do you really...?" he began, then stopped as heads began once more to nod, and he realized that all eyes had turned to Vernon. "Well, I suppose we *could*," he conceded, "that is, if everyone is in agreement?" He looked around hopefully for a sign of disagreement, and found none.

"Thank you, Mr. Chairman," said Lambert formally. "I do appreciate the opportunity, and perhaps I should begin by saying that I understand the enormous pressures that have been brought to bear on your respective ministries when it was decided to close the training centre. Pressure from the businessmen and -women who depend on the Centre for their livelihood, pressure from environmentalists, who wish to see the land returned to its original state, and pressure from the farmers in the area, as well as others. So, I have tried to take that into consideration in my proposal."

Bollinger bristled. "If you are suggesting that we are under pressure to be rid of this land at any price, Mr. Lambert, you are very much mistaken. What we are talking about here is prime building land."

"One-*third* of it is *potentially* prime building land, I grant you," Lambert agreed, "but I feel bound to point out that it will be years before a buyer sees a significant return on such an investment. This land has been on offer now for almost six months, and yet you have had only two serious bids, both of which were from local builders. And the reason for that is its location. When it first came on the market, a number of firms were interested, but when they began to add up the costs of transportation of goods and materials to the site, the need to work closely with local authorities, and the added burden of maintaining and developing the other two-thirds over a long period of time, they decided it wasn't worth it. Which is why, until this morning, you've had only two bids. Now all you have is one.''

Bollinger shrugged. ''I repeat: If you think for one moment, Mr. Lambert, that we intend to give the land away, you are very much mistaken. My instruction from the—''

''I'm sure that Mr. Lambert is well aware that he cannot expect to take over the land by default, Mr. Chairman,'' Vernon broke in quietly. He leaned forward, eyes fixed intently on Lambert's face. ''Please continue. What exactly is your proposal?''

Beside him, Douglas Underwood stirred and began to riffle through the papers in front of him. But Lambert touched his arm and shook his head. Instead, he lifted his own briefcase from beside his chair and set it on the table in front of him. ''I have here copies of a proposal which I feel could be beneficial to us all,'' he said as he took a stack of slim folders from his briefcase. ''If you would be so good as to pass them around.'' He distributed them to his right and left, and across the table, then waited until he was satisfied that everyone had a copy.

Bewildered, Underwood scanned his copy and began to feel uneasy.

''In essence,'' Lambert continued, ''what I am proposing is this: that we deal with the prime land, outlined in red on the fold-out map, as a separate issue. Determine a fair price, bearing in mind the length of time it will take to see a return on investment, then look at the development of the remaining land as a joint venture spread over a period of fifteen years. One immediate advantage is that you will have the hard-line environmentalists off your back, because I propose to begin immediately a reforestation project, including the ongoing management required until the trees are well established in the area marked on your map in green. I've had soil samples taken, and I'm assured that not only can it be done, but it would greatly improve and protect the other areas on your maps. I am prepared to underwrite this project completely, provided the land is turned over to me at the end of that time at a nominal fee of one pound.''

There was a glint of amusement in Vernon's eyes as he sat

back in his seat. "And what do you propose to do with the rest of the land and the administrative buildings, Mr. Lambert?" he asked quietly. "Do you expect to pay only one pound for those, also?"

Lambert smiled. "Not quite," he said. "What I am proposing is that I lease the land and buildings for the next fifteen years, and be allowed tax concessions for the first five years, during which time I would upgrade the existing buildings and the facilities around them. At the end of the fifteen years, I would receive full title, again for a nominal sum."

"And what would you do with the buildings during that time?" asked Vernon. "If—and I say that reservedly—*if* we were to consider your proposal, we would insist on retaining the right of approval of any development you might wish to undertake."

"Of course. But I don't anticipate opposition to what I have in mind," Lambert told him soberly. "I propose to bring together a number of small, independent software companies, who are currently scattered around this and adjoining counties. Many of them deal with each other on a regular basis, and while they *can* conduct business from almost anywhere on the globe, they agree it would be beneficial to be closer together in a quiet environment where the overhead costs are low. I believe I can provide that environment."

Vernon raised an eyebrow. "Do you see this as another Silicon Valley, Mr. Lambert?" he asked laconically.

Lambert laughed. "Hardly," he said, "but on the other hand, we are talking about an industry that has grown exponentially, so who knows?"

"Interesting," said Vernon. He turned toward the chairman, "Perhaps this would be a good time to have the tea brought in," he suggested, "after which we can examine some of the details of Mr. Lambert's proposal."

"I THINK IT WENT off rather well, don't you, Douglas?" Lambert observed. "I suspect there will be a great deal of discussion between the delegation here and their masters in Whitehall this evening, but it's a promising sign that we are to meet again tomorrow. In fact, I don't think they have much option. I have no idea who this man Vernon is, but it's clear to me that he is the power in the room, and if we can convince him, the rest of it will be a piece of cake. They want to be rid of that land, and I think we can take advantage of that.''

Douglas Underwood had remained silent throughout the meeting, but now he could contain himself no longer. ''You might have at least *told* me,'' he burst out. ''I spent three months sweating my guts out preparing those figures, and it was all for nothing! I felt like an idiot in there. Where did you get all that stuff, anyway? I'd never seen it before.''

Lambert laid a soothing hand on Underwood's arm. ''Let's just say it was a contingency plan,'' he said. ''Had we been in a serious bidding war with Bolen, we might have used your figures, but when the Bolens decided to withdraw, I thought it worthwhile to try this on for size. But in all honesty, Douglas, if Bolen had not been killed, and had somehow convinced his brother to go along with him, I would have withdrawn our bid and let him take it. We don't need Ockrington at the price they are asking, but if we can get it on our terms, then we should do very well indeed a few years down the road.''

FIFTEEN

SIMONE WAS BONE-WEARY. It had been hot in Shrewsbury, and she'd spent the best part of the day going from shop to shop looking, without success, for a comfortable pair of shoes. Tired and discouraged, she had made her way to the bus, only to be told that the three-o'clock bus no longer ran on Mondays, Wednesdays, and Fridays. She would have to wait for the four-fifteen.

And now, instead of going straight home and putting her feet up for an hour before going out on the street again, she was sitting on a hard chair in an interview room, facing a detective sergeant and a detective chief inspector, and wondering what the hell it was all about.

"Thank you for coming in, Miss Giraud," said Paget once the preliminary information had been entered on the tapes. "We'll try not to take up too much of your time."

Simone leaned back in her chair. "I didn't know I had a choice," she said. "Does that mean I can leave?"

Paget nodded. "You are free to go if you choose," he told her. "We cannot make you stay, but I believe you may be in a position to help us with our enquiries, and I'd very much appreciate your co-operation."

Simone eyed the chief inspector suspiciously. Was this some kind of "good cop, bad cop" routine, or what? she wondered. But the man intrigued her, and it had been a long time since anyone had bothered to call her "Miss Giraud." She nodded cautiously. At least she'd stay until she found out what it was all about.

"Thank you," said Paget as he placed the photographs of Julia Rutledge on the table in front of Simone. "I believe you know this girl. I'm told she has been staying with you. Can you tell us where she is now?"

Simone glanced at the picture. Julia Rutledge? So that was Vikki's real name. Not that she was surprised. Most of the girls had used other names at one time or another, but what did surprise her was that Vikki had been inside. That was evident by the pictures. But it did explain why the kid had been so scared when she'd been picked up the other week. She'd been afraid they'd find out who she was. But she'd been lucky; they'd just held her overnight and hadn't bothered to take her prints or run a check on her.

She shrugged and shook her head. "Doesn't look like anyone I know," she said.

"I think you should take a closer look," Paget suggested. "Bearing in mind that the penalties for obstruction, harbouring a person suspected of having committed a criminal act, and being an accessory to a crime are considerably harsher than those for soliciting."

She didn't like the sound of that, and she didn't think the man was bluffing. What the hell had the kid got herself into? Criminal act? Accessory to a crime? What crime? It went against the grain to help the police with anything, but on the other hand it wasn't as if she owed the kid anything, especially since Vikki had taken off with some of her stuff.

Simone tapped one of the prints with a blood-red fingernail. "So what's she done?" she asked.

"We think she may be able to help us with our investigation into the murder of James Bolen, last Saturday night," said Paget, "and we are anxious to talk to her."

Simone sucked in her breath. The Bolen killing! It had been all over the papers that morning. A chill ran through her. Surely to God the kid hadn't been involved in that! Suddenly, the image of a red Jaguar and a driver wearing sunglasses stirred in her mind, and she remembered watching Vikki as she leaned inside the car, all splindly arms and legs, and wondering why the man would prefer Vikki when he could have had her. And then the man had driven off, and Vikki had told her he'd changed his mind.

And that was the last she had seen of Vikki Lane.

The thoughts flashed through her mind in an instant, but Paget had been watching her closely. "So you do recognize her," he prompted. It wasn't a question.

"I don't know anything about a Julia Rutledge," she said slowly, "but this does look a bit like a kid I've seen around. Goes by the name of Vikki. Vikki Lane."

"I'm told she was staying with you," said Tregalles.

Simone shrugged. "I gave her a place to sleep for a couple of nights, that's all," she admitted. "But she left sometime last week."

"When last week?"

"Thursday, Friday, I'm not sure."

Tregalles shook his head. "She was with you for the best part of a month," he said, "and we have witnesses who saw you with her as late as Saturday night."

"So it was Saturday. What difference does it make?"

"Where is she now?" It was Paget who asked the question.

Simone tilted her head and met the chief inspector's steady gaze. "I don't know," she told him. "And that's the truth. I haven't seen or heard from her since she left."

"But she was living with you; she must have told you *something* about herself," he insisted. "What brought her to Broadminster? Had you known her before? Is that why she came?"

Simone shook her head. "No. The first time I saw her was three or four weeks ago, when some bastard threw her out of a van right in front of me. She told me he'd picked her up on the road and said he was going as far as Hereford, but when he got into Broadminster, he turned off, stopped the van, then dragged her into the park and raped her. Took her knapsack and everything she had in it—not that she had much to start with, but he took it just the same, then pitched her out onto the street and drove off."

"Did she report it? Go to hospital?" asked Tregalles.

"I offered to take her to hospital, but she wouldn't have it. As for reporting it"—Simone shrugged contemptuously—"who would have believed her? Or me, for that matter? Not your lot, for a start. Besides, it was dark, it was raining, and I never thought to look at the number plate until it was too late."

"You said the driver told her he was going as far as Hereford," said Paget. "Was that her destination, or did she intend to go on from there?"

"I don't know. I didn't ask, and Vikki never said."

"Did she ever talk to you of relatives or friends or anywhere she might go? She must have said *something* during the course of her stay. Please try to think, Miss Giraud. It's extremely important that we talk to this girl."

"So you can fit her up for murder?" said Simone contemptuously. She stood up and placed her hands on the table, her dark eyes flashing as she looked down at the two men. "Look, I told you, the kid had just been raped, thrown out of a van, and she was down to skin and bones. I don't think she'd had a decent meal in God knows how long. So I took her in and tried to help her. All right? I don't know where she came from; I don't know where she was going; and I don't know where she is now. And I don't believe she had anything to do with any murder!"

Simone snatched up her handbag, slung the strap over her shoulder. "I'm tired and I'm hungry," she said, "and I've had a sodding lousy day, so unless you intend to arrest me, I'm going home.''

Tregalles moved to intercept her, but Paget remained seated. "If you wish to leave, then you are free to do so," he told her, "but we do have hard evidence that places Julia Rutledge, or Vikki Lane, if you prefer, at the murder scene, and the sooner we can talk to her, the better.''

Simone started to speak, but Paget raised his hand. "That doesn't mean that we believe Julia Rutledge *committed* the murder," he said. "In fact, I don't believe she did, but we do know that she was there in the room at or about the time it occurred. Which is why I would like you to stay and try to think of anything that will help us find her.''

Simone hesitated. There had been something appealing about Vikki, something forlorn and waiflike, and she didn't want to drop the kid in it. But on the other hand, she knew nothing about her. And for some reason she could not explain, she believed this man when he said he didn't think that Vikki was guilty of murder. Besides, on a more practical level, they could make life bloody miserable for her on the street if she didn't at least appear to be co-operating, and she didn't need the hassle.

Simone sighed and sat down again. Might as well get it over with now as later, she decided.

THEY WERE BOTH DEAD-TIRED. Dee Bolen's plane was two hours late arriving in Manchester and traffic was heavy on the roads, so it was after eight o'clock in the evening by the time she and Harry arrived home. Harry carried the suitcases into the house and set them in the hall.

"I'll take the small case up, but everything else can wait," said Dee as she moved toward the stairs. "I know it's early, but I think I'll go straight to bed.''

"I'll see if there are any messages," said Harry, "and then I'll join you. I could use an early night myself. It's good to have you back, Dee.''

His wife mounted the stairs and entered the bedroom. She set the case down beside the dressing-table and sat down on the bed. She felt as if she hadn't slept for weeks. She tried hard to talk herself out of having a shower, but she felt so grubby after sitting all that time on the plane, and then again in the car, that she couldn't go to bed feeling as she did.

Harry came in as she started to undress. "There was a message from Laura on the machine," he told her, "so I rang her back. She sounds upset. She wants me to go over. Says it's important."

"What, now?"

Harry gestured helplessly. "What could I say? She sounds really upset."

"Have the police...?"

"No. There's been no word from the police. It's just... To tell you the truth, I don't know what it is except it's something to do with the business. I'd better go."

Dee began to dress again. "I'll come with you," she said. "I was going to go over first thing tomorrow, but I might as well go with you now."

"No." Harry put a hand on her shoulder and shook his head. "I don't know what it's all about," he said, "but she was quite insistent that I come alone. Besides, you're tired. You should get some sleep."

Dee stared at him. "And you're not? Look at you; you can hardly keep your eyes open. Did you tell her we've only just got in?"

He nodded. "She knows that. She said she's been trying to ring me all evening. I think it might be best if I go alone. I'll be back as soon as I can. It sounds as if she's been stewing about something all day and needs to talk about it."

"What about John? Can't he go over?"

Harry shrugged. "She says it's me she wants to talk to," he said wearily. He kissed Dee quickly on the cheek and turned on his heel. "I'll make sure the door is locked," he called as he started down the stairs.

Dee heard the front door slam and began once more to get undressed. She couldn't understand why Laura was so insistent on seeing Harry now. Couldn't it wait till morning? She took off her earrings, opened the little trinket box, and was about to drop them in when something caught her eye. Dee moved the box aside and looked blankly at the tear-drop earrings made of onyx. Earrings she knew belonged to Laura.

Tuesday, 26 September

SIMONE WASN'T ASLEEP when the phone rang, but she was loath to answer it. She didn't feel like talking to anyone, especially at two-thirty in the morning. She buried her head in the pillow, but the phone kept on ringing.

"What?" she snapped as she picked it up. "Don't you know what time it...Vikki?" Simone struggled to sit up in bed. "Where the bloody hell are you?" she demanded angrily. "The police have had me in half the evening, asking questions about you. What the hell have you been up to? They say you were involved in this murder last Saturday. And what have you done with my dress and evening bag?"

Standing there in the box beside the road, Vikki shivered at the mention of the police. Simone sounded so angry. "What did they say?" she asked timidly. "The police, I mean."

"They've got your picture. They know you've been inside, and your real name is Julia Rutledge, and they say they know you were in the room where this guy, Bolen, was killed. They didn't come right out and say so, but they think you did it. Did you?"

Vikki's legs turned to water. "I—I don't know," she said weakly. "Really, Simone, I don't know. I might have done; it's hard to explain." She rushed on before Simone could speak again. "I'm sorry I took your dress and bag, but that's why I phoned. I hid fifty quid under the wardrobe, and I want you to have it. I know it's not enough, but it's all I've got. I'm sorry, Simone. Really I am."

Simone brushed the apology aside, but at the same time her resolve began to weaken. The police had told her to inform them immediately if Vikki contacted her, and by the time they let her go she'd made up her mind to do exactly that. But now, hearing the kid on the phone, she wasn't quite so sure.

"What do you mean when you say you don't know?" she demanded harshly. "Either you killed him or you didn't."

Vikki gripped the phone and relived once more the scene that had rarely left her mind since she'd fled the Tudor. She'd expected Simone to be angry with her, but she hadn't expected to hear such cold, accusing tones.

"I *don't* know!" she said tearfully. "And that's the God's truth, Simone." Quickly, before Simone could speak, Vikki poured out her story. "Please believe me, Simone," she pleaded, "that's exactly the way it happened, and I don't know what to do. Joanna's been awfully good, but if I stay here much longer, she's bound to find out, and…"

There was a sharp series of sounds and the phone went dead. "Vikki?" Simone held on, listening hard, but the line remained dead. "Shit!" She put the phone down. Call-box. Time had run out. She sat there on the side of the bed, waiting for it to ring again.

Inside the kiosk, Vikki crammed the remaining coins into the slot, coins she'd stolen from Bunny's rucksack while she and Joanna were at the pub. But nothing happened. She pounded the box with her fist; there was a click, and the mechanical sound of dialling tone grated in her ear. Vikki put the phone down, rested her head against the side of the box as tears streamed down her face.

When the phone failed to ring again, Simone's first thought was to tell the police, tell them what Vikki had told her, because if what the kid had said was true, there was a killer loose out there. On the other hand, they weren't going to be too impressed with some bizarre tale about her being knocked out and not remembering what happened. Come to that, Simone wasn't sure she believed it herself.

She got back into bed. Best to stay out of it, she told herself. She'd done her best for the kid and there was nothing more she could do. She began to make herself comfortable when a thought occurred to her. She climbed out of bed again.

Simone got down on her hands and knees and slid her hand beneath the wardrobe. Her fingers touched something, and she slowly drew it out. An envelope, folded once, and inside was fifty pounds.

SIXTEEN

DEE WAS VERY QUIET when Harry came down for breakfast. She'd been asleep when he returned last night, and after what he'd been through with Laura, he didn't want to wake her and have her asking all sorts of questions.

"Have a good sleep, then?" he asked as he sat down. Dee didn't reply. She seemed preoccupied, and she didn't look at him as she set the toast on the table. Probably still a bit jet-lagged, he thought as he opened the paper and scanned the front page.

"Oh, no!" he groaned aloud. "It says here the police are looking for a girl they believe can help with their enquiries. God! I hope she wasn't one of Jim's; she's just a kid! Have you seen this picture?"

Dee didn't answer. Instead she sat down facing him and raised her teacup. "What did Laura want last night?" she asked.

Harry shrugged. "Oh, she was concerned about a lot of things: how the business would carry on, who would look after all the things that Jim used to take care of. You know the sort of thing."

"And it took till after midnight to discuss that?" Dee's voice was flat and cold.

So, Dee had simply been pretending to be asleep when he came in. But why the chill this morning?

Harry set the paper aside. "I suppose it's a sort of delayed reaction," he said. "John was over earlier to help sort out the things that have to be done with regard to insurance claims, inland revenue and the like, but she wanted to talk to me about the future of the business."

Dee set her cup down and took something from the pocket of her apron. "What were these doing on the dressing-table?" she asked as she dropped Laura's earrings on the table.

"Oh, them. I found them when I was clearing up in the spare room," he told her. "Laura left them behind, so I put them on the dressing-table so I'd remember to take them round sometime. They were by your trinket box. Why? You didn't think that Laura had been in our—''

Harry broke off and stared at Dee. ''You *did*, didn't you?'' he accused. ''Oh, come on, Dee, you know better than that. Laura stayed here Friday and Saturday. You knew she was staying here. She was in the spare bedroom and I was in ours.''

Dee's eyes filled with tears. ''It's just that I found those earrings in our bedroom, and you told me on the way home that you hadn't told the inspector that Laura was in the house in case he got the wrong impression, and how she came down in her dressing-gown. And then last night, when she wanted you to go over, I couldn't help wondering…''

Harry came round the table and put his arms around her. ''It's all right, Dee,'' he said soothingly. ''You were tired after that long flight, and your imagination was working overtime. But you know there is nothing going on between Laura and me. I love you, Dee, and I always will. I like Laura the same way you do, but that's all. She was alone in the house last night, and she needed someone to talk to, and that's all there is to it, believe me.''

Dee buried her face in Harry's shoulder. ''I'm sorry, Harry,'' she whispered. ''I don't know what got into me. Hold me, please.''

Later, as Harry drove to the office, he wondered if he had made a grave mistake last night in promising to keep silent. Hopefully, it wouldn't be for long, but he would have to watch everything he said to Dee or he would *really* have a problem.

''FUNNY YOU SHOULD ask about Mr. Bolen's clothing,'' said Grace Lovett, ''because I've been doing some checking on that myself.''

She leaned back in her chair and crossed her long, slim legs. Belatedly, Tregalles realized that he'd been following the movement with more than passing interest, and forced himself to look away. There was a hint of amusement in Grace's eyes as she continued.

''I felt from the beginning that there was something odd about the clothes," she said, "so I did some checking with Sergeant Ormside. According to several people in the dining-room that night, Bolen was wearing a sports coat, white shirt, dark tie, and charcoal-grey slacks, yet we found no slacks of that colour in his room. The clothing we found on the chair and on the floor, which one would assume he had taken off, consisted of"—Grace consulted a list—"a white shirt, *light*-grey slacks, black belt still in the loops, blue underpants, grey socks and black shoes."

She set the list aside. "The sports jacket and a brown suit were hanging in the clothes closet, and there was a brown belt in his suitcase. But when I was bagging the slacks from the chair, it seemed to me that the belt looked short, so I checked it against the belt in his suitcase, and guess what I found?"

Tregalles shook his head.

"The black belt was shorter than the other belt by a good two inches, and the marks made by the buckle were in a different place. In other words, that belt did not belong to Bolen because he couldn't have done it up—at least not without a struggle. It belonged to a slimmer man.

"And then there were the number of shirts we found. Bolen was supposed to be there in the hotel for four days, yet we found only three shirts." Grace shrugged. "Mind you, many men wear their shirts for more than one day, but I spoke to Ms. Bolen on the phone, and she told me that her husband invariably wore a clean shirt every day, sometimes more than one. So I took a good look at the collar of the shirt we found on the chair beside the bed. It was perfectly clean; not a hair, not a dark spot on it, and when I took a closer look, I found it had simply been crumpled to make it look as if it had been worn, and there were no marks around the waist where a shirt creases naturally beneath the pressure of a belt."

Grace rocked gently back and forth in her chair. "Conclusion," she said, bringing her steepled hands together beneath her chin, "somebody wants us to believe that Bolen was naked when he was killed, when in fact he was at least partly dressed. The autopsy report confirms that. The threads they found inside the wounds will be compared with threads taken from Bolen's other shirts to see if they match, or at least are similar, and I have no doubt they will be. All his shirts have the same label.''

"Which means," said Tregalles, "that the killer took away Bolen's clothes because they were blood-stained, including the belt. He screwed up a clean shirt to make it look as if it had been worn and put another pair of Bolen's own trousers on the chair. But he needed to find another belt from somewhere." His eyes met those of Grace Lovett, who was nodding agreement.

"So he used his own," she finished for him.

Tregalles was silent for a moment. "Which strengthens our theory that there was a man other than Bolen inside the room when Stella Green showed up at eleven, and that means Bolen could have died a lot earlier than midnight.''

"What about Bolen's brother? He was up there about the right time, wasn't he?''

"Yes, he was. Harry Bolen claims his brother was out when he knocked, but he could be lying.''

"On the other hand," he went on, "it wouldn't be hard for someone to come up the back stairs without being seen. At the bottom of the stairs there are two doors: one leads into the kitchen, but the other leads directly out to the car-park. The door to the car-park is supposed to be a one-way exit door, and kept closed, but it was unlocked when I looked at it, and some of the staff admitted they come and go that way all the time.''

"And the corridor exit door is no more than ten feet from Bolen's room," Grace mused. "Very handy for someone who doesn't wish to be seen.''

Tregalles rose to his feet. "I'd better get back," he said. "Thanks, Grace. You've been a great help." He moved toward the door, but Grace stopped him.

"One thing more. In going through Bolen's briefcase, we found a copy of what looks like Lambert's bid on this Ockrington project we've heard so much about. You might like to pass that on to Mr. Paget. I believe he was asking Charlie about it, but Charlie isn't here today.''

But Tregalles shook his head. "I shan't be seeing him until later," he told her, "so why don't you phone him yourself? Give

it that personal touch." He winked knowingly. "I'm sure he'd
like that."

SEVENTEEN

IT WAS LATE IN THE AFTERNOON when Tregalles knocked on the
door of Norman Quint's house in Trinity Street in the Old Town.

The woman who answered the door was small, trim, dark-
haired, pretty, and at least ten years younger than Quint. "Mrs.
Quint?" he ventured, and was mildly surprised when she nodded
and said, "Yes, that's right. I'm Kathleen Quint."

"Detective Sergeant Tregalles," he told her. "Is Mr. Quint at
home?"

"Norman's gone to the shops," she said, "but he should be
back any minute. You can come in and wait for him if you like."
She stepped aside and shut the door behind him as he entered.

The house was old, and the front door opened directly into a
small sitting-room. The woman directed Tregalles to a chair from
which she scooped an armful of socks, turned off the television,
then sat down on the sofa.

"Just doing a bit of mending before tea," she explained. She
kicked off her shoes and tucked her legs beneath her. "I expect
you'll want to talk to Norman about that awful business at the
hotel. Such a shame. Norman thought a lot of Mr. Bolen. He
was one of his regulars."

"Regulars?"

"Oh, yes. Norman has quite a few regulars. Some come every
week, others come every three or four weeks, but they all want
Norman to book them in."

Tregalles frowned. "Do you mean they call him at the hotel
at night?"

"Oh, no. They call him here. They used to call at all hours,
but I soon put a stop to that. I told them straight that Norman
needs his sleep, and they were not to call until after four. That's
when Norman gets up. It's hard enough working nights all the

time, without someone ringing up during the day. They were very good about it, I must say, but then I expect they like the personal service Norman gives them. They always ring him a day or two before, and he makes sure they're taken care of. Books them in himself when he goes to work, and all that sort of thing.''

The corners of her mouth turned down. ''Not that *they* appreciate all the extra things he does, nor the time he puts in.'' She sniffed as she flicked her head in the general direction of the hotel. ''Still, it's a job, isn't it? And to be fair, the money's good. Mind you, I don't like Norman working the night shift all the time. It's a bit lonely being here all by myself every night, with nobody to warm the bed, if you know what I mean.''

The front door suddenly opened, and Quint came in carrying a bag containing two French loaves. He stopped dead when he saw Tregalles. ''What's all this?'' he asked suspiciously.

Kathleen Quint darted to the door and took the bag from her husband. She smelt the bread. ''Lovely,'' she breathed. ''And it's still warm. I'll just put it away. Oh, and this is Sergeant... Sorry, what was the name again?''

''Tregalles,'' the sergeant supplied as he rose to his feet.

''I know *who* he is,'' said Quint. ''What I want to know is: What's he doing in the house?''

''I called round to ask you a few questions, Mr. Quint, and your wife was kind enough to invite me in to wait for you.''

''Was she, now?'' Quint looked anything but pleased. He waited until his wife had left the room before he spoke again. ''What is it this time?'' he demanded. ''I've told you and that chief inspector everything I know.''

Tregalles raised a questioning eyebrow. ''Everything?'' he said. ''I don't recall you mentioning Stella Green, nor these bookings you take over the phone at home.'' He made as if to sit down again, but Quint stopped him.

''Not here!'' he hissed, glancing toward the door through which his wife had disappeared. ''Look, I'll tell her I have to go out again. All right?'' He left the room, returning after a few minutes to lead the way out of the house. ''I told her you wanted to go over a few things at the hotel,'' he said as they got into

Tregalles's car, "so let's at least drive around the corner out of sight."

Tregalles pulled away from the kerb and drove down to the market square, where he pulled into an open parking space and stopped. "Now, tell me what happened when Stella Green went up to Bolen's room on Saturday night," he said.

Quint remained silent for some time. "Look, it's not what you think," he said. "Stella was a one off with Jim Bolen. I didn't have any choice. He asked me to find a girl for him, and when I said I couldn't do that, he made it clear that if I didn't do as he asked, he'd make sure I lost my job. So I went along with it the odd time. I happened to know Stella, so I introduced them and it became a sort of regular thing." He spread his hands. "I mean, what could I do? I was caught in the middle."

Tregalles sighed. "Don't come the innocent with me," he said. "You've been rumbled, Quint, so let's stop playing games. You've been running a string of girls in that hotel for years, and Stella Green is only one of them. When this case is over, we'll have to have another chat about that, but right now I want to know why you sent Stella up to Bolen's room that night. According to her, Bolen told her to piss off, and she reckons you were just trying it on."

Quint was shaking his head violently from side to side. "He *did* want her," he insisted. "Jim Bolen phoned me last Thursday and told me to have Stella there at eleven o'clock on Saturday night. So I sent her up. I don't know why he sent her away again."

"So why did you give her money if it wasn't your fault?"

"She was making such a fuss that I had to do something to get her out of there. I didn't want Stella making more of a scene than she already had, not with Brenda Jones out there at the desk. I thought I would straighten the whole thing out later with Bolen, but then he turned up dead."

"You didn't go up to his room to ask him for an explanation?"

"What, then?" Quint looked alarmed. "I never left the desk," he protested. "Ask Brenda; she was there; she'll tell you."

"Is the manager, Mr. Landau, in on this business of yours?"

Quint looked horrified. "Good God, no!"

"You're quite sure it was Bolen who phoned you on Thursday? You recognized his voice?"

Quint nodded. "It was him all right."

"So why do you think he sent Stella away? Did he have another woman in there with him at the time?"

Quint thought about that. "No," he said at last. "No, I don't think so."

"What about the girl you saw sneaking out of the hotel when you were getting into the lift? Could she have been in Bolen's room?"

"No." Quint was emphatic. "Bolen wouldn't have had her. He liked them older, and he couldn't abide skinny ones. He liked them more on the meaty side, like Stella."

"Could Stella have gone back upstairs after she left you?"

"No. I saw her leave the hotel."

"But she could have gone round the corner, through the car-park, and up the back stairs."

"No. Besides, that door is a one-way door. It's a fire exit. You can't get in from the outside."

Tregalles snorted. "You know as well as I do that it's used all the time as a short cut by your staff, and probably by others when it suits them," he said. "Isn't that the way some of your girls come and go in order to avoid the lobby?"

Quint didn't answer the question directly. "Stella was too pissed off to try going back upstairs again," he said slowly, "but Harry Bolen was in the car-park that night. He could have come in that way. I mean, who would know their way around better than he and his brother? After all, they built the place."

STRIPPED TO THE WAIST, Mark Malone bent his knees, straightened his back, and lifted the heavy tub containing a Blue Spruce into the back of his truck. Prudence Bolen, her slim body propped against the side of her car, shivered with anticipation as her smoke-grey eyes caressed his rippling muscles, browned by the sun and glistening beneath a sheen of sweat.

"There, that's the lot," he said. "Time to go, I'm afraid. I

promised I'd have these out tonight. Shall I see you tomorrow?''
He pulled her toward him.

Malone was a head taller than Prudence. His hair was dark,
curling naturally above finely chiselled features that could be
traced directly to his Italian mother, as could the colour of his
skin. But he had his Irish father to thank for his broad shoulders,
slim waist and sturdy legs.

Prudence slipped her arms around him and pressed her cheek
against his naked chest. She wished that they could stay like this
forever. ''Do you have to?'' she murmured. She opened her
mouth, and her small pink tongue moved sensuously against his
skin. She could taste the salt. His broad hands slid down her
body, curving beneath her buttocks as he pulled her to him. She
lifted her head, straining upward as he bent to kiss her. Her
tongue sought his open mouth; she wanted to immerse herself
in him; become part of him. Her slender fingers sought his trousers, searching for the zip.

Malone pulled away. ''For God's sake, Pru!'' He laughed.
''You want it out here in the yard?''

''I don't care where it is,'' she panted. ''I want you now!''

He grasped her fumbling hands. ''I have to go,'' he told her
gently. He spoke to her as he might a child. ''And you should
be at home with your mother at a time like this.''

Prudence tossed her head. ''She doesn't need me. Besides,
I'm sure good old John will be there to hold her hand.'' The
girl began to pull Malone toward an open shed. ''You don't have
to go for a few minutes,'' she pleaded. ''We've got time.''

But Malone remained firm. ''I mean it, Pru. You should be
with your mother.''

Pru pouted. ''If you really loved me, you wouldn't want me
to go. Please, Mark?'' She took his hand and tried once more
to pull him toward the shed.

''No, Pru.'' His voice was sharp. ''I have to deliver these trees
tonight, and you should go home.'' He turned as if to get in the
truck, then paused. ''Have they fixed a time for the funeral?''

''Saturday. Someone rang today to say that Daddy's body
would be released, so the funeral will be on Saturday. John and
Uncle Harry are arranging everything. Why?''

"Because I need to be there," he said, then held up his hand as Pru's face lit up. "In the background," he went on. "I know your father didn't like me, but I should pay my respects."

Prudence sighed. "I wish all this could be over," she said petulantly. She put her arms around him again. "I want to be with you all the time, Mark. Not sneaking around like this."

Malone caressed her hair. "I don't suppose you've heard anything more from the police?" he said off-handedly. "Do they have any idea yet who killed your father?"

Prudence shrugged. "Not as far as I know," she said, "but then, I don't suppose they would tell us even if they did, would they?"

Malone rested his chin on her head, his eyes focused on some distant point. "No," he said thoughtfully, "you're probably right; I don't suppose they would."

EVERYONE HAD GONE home by the time Keith Lambert returned to the office, but that was good; he needed time to think. He took everything out of his briefcase, sorted it into piles, and left them for Myrtle to file in the morning.

He was pleased with the way things had gone this second day of negotiations. Nothing had been settled, but even the chairman had been more amiable toward the end of the day. He was even more certain now that they wished to be done with Ockrington once and for all, and he was offering them a way out. They might balk a bit, and no doubt there would be some hard bargaining over price and tax concessions, but he couldn't see them going back to square one and starting over again in the hopes that they could get a better deal.

As for Underwood, Lambert was almost certain that it was he who had been supplying Bolen with information, but first things first. With Bolen out of the way, a lot of things would change, and Underwood could be dealt with later.

Lambert unlocked the bottom drawer of his desk and took out a framed photograph of Laura Bolen when she was eighteen. Laura Preston, then, he reminded himself as he studied the contours of her face for perhaps the thousandth time. So young. So beautiful. He set the picture on the desk, leaned back in his chair and thought of what might have been if it hadn't been for Jim Bolen.

"And might still be," he said softly to himself.

The phone rang. He picked it up, wondering who would be calling him here at this time. "Lambert," he said.

"Ah, Mr. Lambert, DCI Paget here. I was told you might still be at the office. I wonder if I could come round?"

"What, now?"

"Yes. It is important."

"Well, yes, I suppose…"

"Good. Ten minutes, then. I won't keep you long."

"UNCLE GORDON HAS AGREED to be a pall-bearer," said John Bolen as his mother came into the room. "I asked him about Uncle Albert, but he says he hasn't heard of him in years, and doesn't know where he is. I gather they never got on." John put a tick beside the name of Gordon Cox, his late father's cousin on his mother's side. "So that makes three," he said. "Harry, Uncle Gordon, and myself. What about Bob Newman? He's been with the firm for more than twenty years, and he and Dad always got on well. I think he would like to be asked."

Laura sat down at the table and looked blankly at her son. Was she doing the right thing? she wondered. Was she being fair to John?

"Mother?"

"Yes. Sorry, dear; I was thinking of something else. Yes, I suppose that would be all right," she said. "Whatever you think, John." She made a conscious effort to bring her mind to bear on the matter at hand. "And what about Terry Gardener and Bill Strickland? They were friends of your father's. I think they might like to be asked."

"I'll give them a ring," he said as she glanced at the time. "Didn't Harry say he would be over to give us a hand? I wonder what's happened to him?"

"Oh, dear! I'm sorry; I forgot to tell you." Laura rose from the table to avoid looking directly at her son. "He telephoned. Said he was sorry, but something had come up, and he wouldn't be able to make it this evening."

"Funny, he didn't say anything to me about it at work today," John said as he began to punch in a number.

"No? Well, I expect it came up later." Laura moved restlessly around the room, wishing that this could all be over. She was so utterly *weary,* and so tired of telling lies.

IT WAS COLD AGAIN TONIGHT. The sky was clear and there was a cool breeze from the north, and business was slack. Tuesdays were always slack, and tonight Simone was on her own.

The rest of the girls had gone down to the Green Man to see if they could drum up some business there. But as far as Simone was concerned, the Green Man was nothing more than a hangout for drunks and yobs, and you'd be lucky if you didn't get beaten up, and even luckier if you got paid.

Cresswell Street was a quiet patch, unlike that at the bottom end of Bridge Street where the druggies hung out. Stoned out of their minds, half of them, and you never knew when someone would come at you with a blade, or worse still, a needle. The police were there at least once or twice a week to break up a fight or haul someone away. Up here, they tended to adopt a more liberal attitude of live and let live, although every now and again they would make a token sweep. Simone could live with that. It was the price of doing business.

She walked slowly down the length of Cresswell Street, then started back again. Ten-fifteen. If there wasn't any action by eleven, she decided, she would pack it in.

A car slid into the kerb and stopped some twenty yards ahead, facing her with its headlights on. She continued walking at the same pace, hips swaying provocatively as she approached the car. No need to appear too keen.

It was hard to see past the headlights until she was abreast of the car. The driver sat there, motionless behind the wheel, watching her approach.

The window was open. Simone bent down and leaned inside. Perhaps this would be her lucky day after all.

"Can I help you?" she asked impudently.

The man smiled. "I think perhaps you can," he said. "But

you look cold. Why don't you get in and we'll discuss it further?''

EIGHTEEN

Wednesday, 27 September

JOANNA FREEBORN LOOKED at the time. Ten past six. No need to get up just yet. Besides, she wanted to think about the picture she'd seen in the paper last night at the pub. Vikki's picture, except the two short paragraphs below the picture said her real name was Julia Rutledge, and the police wanted to talk to her about the murder of James Bolen last Saturday night.

She hadn't shown the picture to Bunny; nor had she mentioned it to Vikki when she got home, and she still wasn't quite sure why. Neither was she sure why she had taken the page from the paper and torn it into strips before stuffing it in the bin.

But there was no getting away from the fact that Vikki had lied to them about how she had come by her injuries. And there could be little doubt that the girl was up to something, otherwise why had she sneaked off the boat in the early hours of yesterday morning?

Joanna hadn't seen Vikki leave, but she'd woken to the gentle movement of the boat, and she'd been instantly alert. She thought at first that someone had come aboard, but when she poked her head through the curtain, she could see that Vikki's bunk was empty. She slipped out of bed and went outside, thinking that the girl might have been unable to sleep, but Vikki had disappeared.

Joanna's first reaction was one of disappointment. She liked the girl, and she'd felt sorry for her, but now she felt as if Vikki had been using her until she was well enough to move on. Another lesson learned, she told herself sadly as she made her way back to bed.

She'd been surprised when she heard Vikki come back and creep into her bunk. Perhaps, Joanna thought, she'd misjudged her. Cooped up on the boat all day, it might be that the girl had simply gone for a walk when she thought she would be safe from prying eyes. She decided to say nothing unless Vikki mentioned it herself.

But there was still the matter of the picture in the newspaper.

Joanna sighed. She supposed she should notify the police that Vikki was here, but she couldn't bring herself to do that. At least, not until she had heard Vikki's side of the story.

"HAVE A GOOD SLEEP then, did you, luv?" Joanna asked as Vikki stuck her head through the door and shaded her eyes against the morning sun. "Like some breakfast? Bunny and I have had ours, and she's just gone off to work. How about a fry-up for a change? I've got a lovely bit of bacon, and the eggs are fresh from the farm, and there's a tomato, and a bit of..."

But Vikki was shaking her head violently from side to side. "No, thanks, Joanna," she said, and gulped as if for air. She looked pale and hollow-eyed. "But if you've got some tea...?"

"Of course." Joanna felt the pot. "I'll just make some fresh," she said. "It will only take a tick." She busied herself with the kettle. "But you should eat something, luv. You need a bit of meat on those bones."

Vikki left the shelter of the doorway and slid onto a narrow wooden seat. She was wearing the heavy pullover Joanna had loaned her, and sat hunched over, arms wrapped around herself.

"Just tea, please, Joanna," she said tightly. "I'm not hungry."

Joanna eyed her narrowly. "Not such a good night, then," she said.

Vikki nodded miserably. "Couldn't get to sleep, then when I did I had horrible nightmares."

"Is that why you went for a walk the other night? Couldn't sleep?"

"You were awake? I thought..." Vikki avoided Joanna's eyes.

"I'm glad you decided to come back. Do you want to tell me about it?"

Vikki began to speak, but the words stuck in her throat. Tears trickled down her face, and a deep sob escaped her lips. "Oh, Joanna," she wailed, "I didn't want to lie to you, but I was afraid you wouldn't believe me and you'd throw me out. I thought I'd be safe here, but I keep seeing this horrible face in my dreams…It's…Oh, God, Joanna, I'm so scared, I don't know what to do!"

Joanna sat down beside the girl and put her arm around her shoulders. "Perhaps, then, *Julia*," she said, with emphasis on Vikki's real name, "if you really are sorry and want my help, the best way to start is by telling me the truth about what happened last Saturday night, and why you're running away."

Vikki was hesitant at first, but once she realized that Joanna was taking her story seriously, the words poured out so fast that Joanna was forced to slow her down. "Easy, girl," she chided gently. "Take your time. You're safe here with me."

"You've got to believe me, Joanna," Vikki ended tearfully. "I know it sounds as if I'm making it up, but I'm not. That's what happened, but I daren't go to the police because I know they won't believe me."

She was right about that, Joanna thought. They wouldn't believe her. The girl's story was so bizarre that Joanna had trouble believing it herself. "But surely," she said with a frown, "you can't have gone through all that without remembering *something*, Vikki?"

"But that's just it, Joanna, I don't!" said Vikki. "I've tried and tried, but all I get is this sort of dream where this man is bending over me, holding my face. I know it has something to do with what happened that night, but it won't come clear."

"What man? You didn't say anything about a man holding your face."

"I *told* you, I don't *know!*" Vikki said desperately. "I… Look, I'll show you." Abruptly, the girl took Joanna by the arm and almost dragged her into the cabin. She went straight to her bunk and tossed the pillow aside to reveal several loose pages torn from Joanna's writing pad.

Pencil sketches.

Vikki sorted through them swiftly and handed several to

Joanna. "There! You see? That's the man I'm talking about. I keep seeing him in my dreams, and even sometimes when I'm awake. They're like flashes inside my head, only they never stay long enough for me to see them properly. I'm sure the shape of the head is right, and I think the hair is right, and the mouth, but I can't get the nose and eyes. I'm sorry I used up so much paper, Joanna, but I have to keep on trying until I get it right."

As Vikki had said, the outline of the head was there, the hair and a partial mouth, but the rest of the face was blank. Joanna studied the sketches for a long moment, then handed them back to Vikki. "May I see those?" she asked, and without waiting for a reply, reached over and plucked the remaining drawings from Vikki's hands. She fanned them out. "Did you do all these?" she asked sharply.

Vikki nodded wordlessly. She knew she should have asked Joanna for the paper, but she hadn't wanted her to know what she was doing. She said, "I'm sorry I used so many pages," and wondered miserably if there would ever be a time when she wouldn't have to apologize for living.

But Joanna waved the apology aside. "I think they're terrific!" she said softly. "Where on earth did you learn to draw like that? This one of Bunny, and this one of the swan landing on the water. They're beautiful."

Vikki shrugged. "It's just something I like to do," she said.

"You mean you've never had lessons?"

"Lessons?" Vikki gave a bitter laugh. "As far as my mother was concerned, drawing was a waste of time, so I had to hide anything I did. If I hadn't, she'd have torn them up and thrown them away."

"And that's why you hid them here? You thought I might tear them up? Good God, girl, they're wonderful! You could sell some of these."

Vikki blushed. "They're not *that* good," she said.

Joanna brushed her words aside. "Don't put yourself down, my girl," she said sternly. "These are very, very good. As for those others of the face you keep seeing, all I can suggest is that you relax and stop trying so hard. You can't force something like that. But it will come; you'll see, Julia."

"Just one thing, Joanna, if you don't mind. Please don't call me Julia. I know it's my real name, but I hate it. Please call me Vikki."

THE WOODEN CHAIR was hard, and there were three others exactly like it around the wooden table. But it was the tape recorder and microphone at the end of the table that made Douglas Underwood feel most ill at ease. He'd been asked by Paget—more like *ordered*, he thought resentfully—to come down to Charter Lane this morning to "clarify one or two small points," as Paget had put it, and he hadn't dared refuse.

He'd seen rooms almost identical to this on television and recalled that things rarely turned out well for suspects on those shows. It reminded him that he would have to be very careful and stick to his story about Bolen offering him a job. After all, Bolen wasn't in any position to deny it, was he?

The door opened and Paget entered, followed closely by another man whom Paget introduced as Sergeant Tregalles. Both men were businesslike, but affable. Paget thanked him for coming in, and when he apologized for keeping him waiting, Underwood took heart and began to relax. But when the sergeant sat down beside the tape recorder, pressed a button and began entering the date and time and names of everyone in the room, the feeling of unease returned.

"You have no objection to having this interview recorded, I take it, Mr. Underwood?" inquired Paget pleasantly as he moved the mike to the centre of the table.

"No. No, of course not." Underwood forced a smile and waved a hand around the room. "It's rather like a scene on TV, isn't it?" he said.

"Except that everyone gets to go home after the take on TV," Tregalles said drily.

Underwood laughed, a bit nervous. "Yes, I suppose that's true," he agreed, and wondered what the sergeant had meant by that.

Paget laid a folder on the table in front of him. "What I would like you to do, sir, is run through what you told me last Sunday, for the benefit of my sergeant, and as a record of your statement. All right, Mr. Underwood?''

Underwood nodded and sat forward in his chair. This was going to be easier than he'd thought. "Oh...sorry, yes," he said as Paget pointed to the tape recorder. He settled back in the chair, thought for a few moments, then repeated what he had told Paget on Sunday morning.

"Mr. Bolen must have been getting a bit desperate by the time he rang you," Tregalles observed when Underwood had finished. "I mean, the deadline for the presentation on Monday was approaching fast."

"Oh, he was. Quite desperate," Underwood agreed. "He practically pleaded with me in the end."

"But you wouldn't budge?"

"Absolutely not!"

"So, if you had no intention of accepting Bolen's offer, why didn't you simply hang up?"

Underwood shifted in his seat. "I was curious," he said. "About how far he was prepared to go."

"So you were on the phone for how long? Five minutes? Ten?"

Underwood shrugged and spread his hands. "I don't know exactly. Perhaps close to ten."

Tregalles looked at Paget, then sat back in his chair. The chief inspector opened the folder in front of him. "Do you recognize these?" he asked. He took out a sheaf of papers protected by a clear plastic cover, and turned them for Underwood to see.

Underwood's heart sank as he recognized the papers he had given Bolen. But there was still a chance he could brazen it out. "That looks like a copy of the Ockrington bid," he said.

"That's right," said Paget. "Except there are a couple of pages that are different in this document, aren't there, Mr. Underwood? And please don't try to argue the point because I took the trouble to compare them with the original supplied to me last night by Keith Lambert."

Paget leaned back in his chair. "Do you know what I think, Mr. Underwood? I think you gave these figures to Bolen as you've been doing in the past, but for some reason best known to yourself, you gave him the wrong figures. When Bolen realized that, he rang you. That's why the phone call you say took ten minutes took less than two, because it didn't take long for Bolen to tell you to get over there with the correct figures, did it?''

Paget eyed the man coldly. ''And I think he threatened to expose you if you didn't. But you didn't have the figures at home, and you couldn't get into the office that late at night without having to explain yourself to the night security man, could you? So you went over to the hotel, and when Bolen answered the door—''

''No!'' All colour had drained from Underwood's face as he listened with growing alarm to the chief inspector's words. ''No! It wasn't like that. I had nothing to do with Bolen's death. I didn't even *see* him that night, let alone kill him.''

''But you did go over there,'' Paget insisted. ''As you have been doing on Sunday mornings for quite some time now.''

Oh, God! Underwood felt as if he were shrinking beneath Paget's accusing gaze. He passed a shaking hand across his face, then let out a long breath, and nodded slowly. ''I did go over there,'' he admitted, ''but I didn't see him. I'm telling you the truth. Honest to God, he wasn't there!''

''The same as you told us the truth about Bolen offering you a job?'' Tregalles scoffed.

''No!'' Underwood looked at Paget and spread his hands. ''Look,'' he said earnestly, ''I admit I lied about the reason for the telephone call, but I didn't know what else to say. You caught me by surprise and that was the only thing I could think of at the time. And you're right about the figures being wrong, and about my not being able to go back to the office. But I had nothing to do with Bolen's death. Honest to God. You have to believe me.''

''Why should we?'' said Paget. ''You've done nothing but lie to us up till now.''

''Well, I'm not lying now. I swear!'' Underwood leaned forward across the table to emphasize his words. ''Jim Bolen was in a rage when he phoned. He wanted the figures immediately, but I'd just come out of the shower, so time was getting on by the time I got dressed and sorted through the papers I had at home. So I drove to the hotel. I went up the back stairs and knocked, but Bolen didn't answer the door. I couldn't understand it; the man had insisted on my coming over immediately, and then he'd gone out. I kept knocking on the door, but it was obvious he wasn't there. So, rather than hang about in the corridor, I went back downstairs and waited in the car."

"What time was this?"

Underwood ran his fingers through his thinning hair. "Ten o'clock or just after; something like that; I'm not sure."

"And how long did you wait?"

"I waited about fifteen minutes, then went back up and tried again, but he still didn't answer when I knocked. I didn't know what to do. I didn't dare go home without talking to him, so I went down again and waited. His car was there, so I knew he couldn't have gone far."

"And…?"

"Bolen never did come back. Or if he did, it was too late for me to go back up and see him, because Harry had arrived by that time."

"Harry Bolen?"

"That's right. He and Mrs. Bolen parked a few cars away from me. Harry got out and went into the hotel, and I—"

"By which door?" Paget demanded. "Front or back?"

"The front door. At least he went round the front, so I assumed he was going in the front door."

"How long did you stay after you saw him leave the car?"

"Ten minutes or so. I thought I'd wait to see if Harry came back, and then try once more. But when Mrs. Bolen got out of the car and went up the back stairs, I decided there wasn't much point in staying, so I went home."

"When you say 'Mrs. Bolen,' do you mean Laura Bolen?"

"That's right. Jim's wife."

Paget and Tregalles exchanged glances. "Tell me," said Paget, "why did you give Bolen that false set of figures?"

"It was a mistake. I had to make copies in a hurry, and when I put the folder together I must have put in the preliminary figures by mistake. I didn't mean to, but Bolen seemed to think I was trying to put one over on him. But I wasn't. What would have been the point?''

"How long have you been supplying Bolen with copies of Lambert's bids?" asked Paget.

Underwood moved uncomfortably in his seat. "Close to four years," he said.

Tregalles snorted. "Well, I for one, don't believe you," he said flatly. "I think you did see Bolen. I think you were scared shitless because you thought Bolen might expose you, and you wanted out. So you took your knife, and when Bolen opened the door, you—"

"No! I never saw him that night, and that's God's truth. I swear!"

"Hmmph!"

Underwood's lips trembled as he looked from one to the other. "Does Mr. Lambert have to know?" he ventured. "I mean, it is all over now that Jim Bolen's dead."

Paget scooped up the folder. "What makes you think he doesn't?" he said softly, and nodded for Tregalles to terminate the interview.

TREGALLES HAD GONE home for lunch, but Paget was still in his office when Ormside rang through. "Bad news, I'm afraid, sir," he said. "Simone's flat has been turned over, and no one has seen her since last night. Uniforms are there now, and—"

"I'll be right down," Paget cut in. "You can give me the details then." Two minutes later, Paget entered the Incident Room, and Ormside carried on from where he'd left off.

"A girl by the name of Janice Osborne found the door ajar when she went along to borrow some fresh milk from Simone. She went in and saw that the place had been turned over, but there was no sign of Simone."

There was a cold, hard knot in the pit of Paget's stomach as he drove the short distance to Cresswell Street. He didn't like the sound of it at all, and he liked it even less when he arrived and surveyed the scene. Whatever the intruder had been looking for, he or she had certainly done a thorough job.

There was no sign of a forced entry, so either Simone had

opened the door herself—which seemed unlikely—or the intruder had let himself in. Simone wasn't the sort who would leave a spare key under the mat, so where had the intruder found a key? Unless it was Simone's.

"She always locked her door when she went out, even if it was just to the shops on the corner," Janice told him, "so when I saw it open like that, I thought she must be in, but she wasn't."

'When did you last see her?''

"About half past nine last night. Down by the old bookshop just up the road. See, some of us decided to go down to the Green Man, you know, for…well, for a drink, like, but Simone didn't want to go."

"But she stayed on the street? She was still working?"

The girl hesitated, and Paget shook his head impatiently. "I'm not interested in what she was *doing* there," he assured her. "Just in what might have happened."

"She said she'd give it another hour, then pack it in for the night if there was nothing doing."

"What time did you get home?"

"About two."

"And you noticed nothing untoward? Simone's door was closed?"

"I suppose so. Can't say I noticed."

"Your room is next to hers. Did you hear anything during the night?"

Janice shook her head. "When I put my head down for the night, that's it," she said. "They could've hammered on the wall and I doubt if I'd've heard them. Sorry." She looked at Paget with worried eyes. "It's this business with Vikki, isn't it?" she said. "I saw the kid's picture in the paper, and Simone said you'd had her in. She'll be all right, won't she? Simone, I mean."

Paget could only shrug and shake his head. He thought of what Simone had told them about a man who had called Vikki over to his car, a man who wore dark glasses and drove Jim Bolen's car. It had to have been Bolen's car, taken from the carpark while he was having dinner, because there wasn't another one like it in Broadminster. It was all part of a carefully constructed plan to make it appear that it was Bolen himself who had propositioned Vikki and, once at the hotel, abused her to the point where she had turned on him and killed him.

But the plan had gone awry when the girl managed to get away. Now the killer was searching for her, which meant he must believe either that Julia Rutledge could identify him, or she had something in her possession that would point to him.

And the logical place to start was with the woman who had been with Julia Rutledge when he'd made his approach that night. Simone. It wouldn't be hard. Simone had never seen enough of his face to recognize the man, so all he would have to do was cruise the streets and pick her up. But once she'd seen his face, her chances of survival would be very slim indeed.

The fact that he had found it necessary to search her flat suggested that Simone had been unable—or unwilling, perhaps—to tell him what he wanted to know, so he'd taken her key and searched the place in the hope of finding something that would lead him to Rutledge.

The question was: Had he found what he was looking for? And was he even now on his way to complete the job he'd started?

"WE'VE HAD ONE HIT on the computer under the name of Vikki Lane," Ormside greeted Paget when he returned to Charter Lane. "She was held overnight for soliciting here in Broadminster. No prints were taken, so there was no connection made between Vikki Lane and Julia Rutledge."

"Anything that would give us a clue to her present whereabouts?"

"I'm afraid not, sir. She gave Simone's address, and it was Simone who paid the fine."

Another dead end, thought Paget bitterly. He'd left SOCO dusting for prints in Simone's flat, but he was sure it would prove to be a waste of time. "Is that it, then, Len?" he asked irritably. "Is that the best we can do?"

"About the only good news," said Ormside, undaunted by Paget's sour mood, "is that Reg Starkie has been moved from intensive care to a regular ward. His doctor says he's still pretty groggy, but you're welcome to try to talk to him if you really feel it's urgent.''

Paget thought about it for a moment, then shook his head. "It can wait," he told the sergeant. "Give him a couple more days to mend.''

ELEVEN O'CLOCK. Dee pressed a button on the remote control, and the television screen faded to black. She slid down in the bed and lay there, arms behind her head, staring up at the ceiling. Should she try ringing the office again? She turned her head and looked at the telephone beside the bed as if seeking an answer from the instrument itself. And what if there was no answer? Again. She thought of ringing Laura, but what good would that do? She could ask to speak to Harry, but Laura would probably deny that he was there.

But he *had* to be there. He hadn't answered any of the calls she'd made to the office last night or tonight, and yet that was where he'd said he would be. Dee had hardly seen him since she'd come home to find Laura's earrings in their bedroom.

Since then he'd been out all day at work, and gone again all evening. Midnight last night, and here it was after eleven again tonight. So much to do since Jim died, he'd said by way of explanation.

She wanted to believe him. Dee felt the sting of tears behind her eyes. The thought of Harry straying had never entered her mind before last Monday. She'd always been very proud of their marriage; she'd never so much as looked at another man, and she had never doubted Harry for a moment.

Until now.

Was Harry losing interest? Laura was an attractive woman, and Harry had always said he admired her, but was it something more than admiration now?

Dee slipped out of bed and stood in front of the mirror. She remained there for a long time, turning this way and that, examining her face and every inch of her body with a critical eye. She didn't think she looked so bad, considering she would be fifty in a couple of years. She certainly hadn't let herself go like some women she knew. She swam, she played tennis, and she'd been doing tai chi for years.

On the other hand, Laura *was* three years younger, and she could still turn men's heads.

Dee climbed back into bed. Twenty-five past eleven. She turned out the light and lay there, her body taut as she stared into the darkness.

But the darkness could not blot out the pictures in her mind.

MARK MALONE WAVED goodbye as he watched the twin tail lamps disappear into the darkness. Pru hadn't wanted to go, but he'd insisted. "You shouldn't be here at all," he'd told her gently. "You should be at home, helping your mother. She needs her family around her at a time like this. There must be a great deal to do, and your being there would mean a lot to her."

But Pru had clung to him. "John's there," she told him. "He enjoys that sort of stuff—ploughing through papers and making out lists, sorting out this and that. She doesn't need me."

"But I need her on my side," he told her. "I need to prove to her that I really want you for yourself, not, as your father said, simply for your money."

Pru pulled away. "We don't need her permission to get married," she said, sulking. "Sometimes I wonder if you really want to marry me at all."

Malone put his arms around her and pulled her to him. "How can you say that, Pru? I want us to be married just as soon as you do, but I don't want to be the cause of friction between you and your mother. I could never forgive myself if that happened."

He kissed her. "Be patient, my love. It will all work out, you'll see, and we will be together forever."

"Oh, Mark! I do love you so much," she whispered fiercely. "I do try to be patient, but it's so hard!"

The lights of the car disappeared. Malone shut the door and locked it. He yawned and wondered whether to clean up before going to bed or not. He'd wanted to wash up after they'd eaten, but Pru wouldn't let him; all she'd wanted to do was get into bed. He liked sex as much as anyone, but Pru was insatiable.

He yawned again. Better do the washing up now, he decided. He hated facing dirty pots and pans first thing in the morning.

"I'm not surprised you're tired after spending the evening with that little vixen," someone said. "I thought she'd never leave. I've been out there in the car in the back lane for close to an hour."

"Jealous, are we, Ronnie?" Malone turned to face the speaker. "Of her? You must be joking."

Veronica Beresford moved out of the shadows and into the light. She was tall, sleek, and moved with a feline grace that aroused him even now. "I hope you've left enough for me," she said archly as she took his face in her hands and kissed him. Her tongue darted between his lips, and he pulled her roughly to him, his broad hands tearing at her clothes.

She pulled her head away. "Do be careful with the threads, lover," she warned. "They cost the earth, and even dear old Trevor might notice if they're torn to shreds."

Without a word they moved to the bedroom, stripping off their clothes in frantic haste. Malone pulled her toward the bed, but Veronica held back.

"I'm not getting into a bed where you've just had her," she told him. "The sheets aren't even cold!" She dropped to her knees. "Come down on the floor."

Malone slid down beside her, his mouth seeking hers, when suddenly, embarrassingly, he yawned!

He felt the colour rushing to his face. "I'm sorry, Ronnie…" he began, but Veronica put her fingers against his lips.

"I understand," she said soothingly. "You've had a busy night, haven't you, lover? But don't worry, I'll do all the work. Just lie back and think of England."

NINETEEN

Thursday, 28 September

THE AREA AROUND Cresswell Street had been literally blanketed with uniformed and plain-clothes police going from door to door, working through till almost midnight last night, and back at it again this morning, asking the same questions over and over again. Have you seen this woman? When? Where? What time was that? Did you hear anything? See anyone cruising the street?—which, considering the neighbourhood, was thought by most to be a silly question, but it still had to be asked.

Simone was well known, and apparently well liked by many of the residents of Cresswell Street, because a number of the locals had come forward to say that they had seen her in the street that night. A list of names, together with approximate times, had been compiled on the whiteboards in the Incident Room, but there was nothing later than ten past ten. A woman who lived over one of the shops in the street was returning from walking her dog when she saw Simone standing outside the darkened chip shop at the bottom end of Cresswell Street. Simone had patted the dog, the two women had exchanged a few words, and they'd said good night.

After that, nothing! Simone had simply vanished, and any hope they'd had of finding Rutledge through Simone had vanished with her. That in itself was bag enough, but Paget's immediate concern was the fate of Simone herself. If, as he suspected, she had been picked up by the killer, the chances of finding her alive were, at best, extremely thin.

Grim-faced, Paget stared at the whiteboards and shook his head. More than four days into the investigation and they were no closer now to finding Bolen's killer than they had been on day one. He sighed heavily.

"We don't have any choice," he told Tregalles. "We have to start again from scratch. We go over every bit of evidence again, and we concentrate on the people who had the most to gain from Bolen's death.

"Len," he said to the sergeant who had been listening at his desk, "I want backgrounds on all members of the Bolen family and on Keith Lambert: relationships, personal situations, business connections, financial positions, and anything else you can think of. Dig deep. But most of all let's check and double-check their alibis. Tregalles and I will be talking to the principals themselves, but I want every angle covered. And get a couple of people over to the Tudor Hotel and have them interview the staff again; maybe lean on them a bit if they seem to be holding back at all. Especially Quint. Let's make sure they've told us everything.''

He glanced at the clock. ''And let's hope to God we find something before someone else is killed.''

''SORRY IF I SEEM DISTRACTED, Chief Inspector,'' John Bolen apologized, ''but it's been a bit hectic around here since my father died. Harry and I have spent most of our time working with solicitors, banks, and building societies, trying to come to some sort of agreement with them regarding the mortgages Dad took out. We would like to cancel them, but there are penalties, and no one is willing to negotiate until the will is probated. Unfortunately, while all that is going on, we are faced with some pretty stiff monthly payments we can ill afford.''

Paget and Tregalles were seated in a small glass-walled office in the corner of a larger office in the Bolen Building. They had once again been going over John Bolen's visit with his father the night he died, but had discovered nothing new. Now Bolen looked pointedly at his watch. ''I have an appointment with one of the solicitors in half an hour,'' he told them, ''but I can give you a few minutes.''

''Speaking of your father's will,'' Paget said, ''I believe you told me that your mother is the sole beneficiary as far as the business is concerned, but are there any other bequests or provisions?''

Bolen sat back in his chair and regarded Paget and Tregalles with brooding eyes.

''As I told you,'' he said with exaggerated patience, ''my mother inherits my father's share of the firm, which amounts to fifty-one percent. Harry owns forty-nine percent. I inherit nothing. My sister inherits nothing. Does that make my mother the— what's the term you use?—prime suspect?'' he asked sarcastically.

''Not necessarily,'' Paget said blandly. ''As you mentioned the other day, if your father had gone ahead with the Ockrington project, everyone in your family would have lost, including your uncle, so in that sense, everyone had something to gain by his death.''

Before John Bolen could reply, Tregalles put a question to him. ''As I understand it,'' he said, ''your father was very much in charge of the day-to-day running of the firm when he was alive. Who is in charge now that he is gone? Would that be you, sir?''

Bolen eyed Tregalles for a long moment, then shook his head. ''No, although, because of the family connection, and my familiarity with our financial position here, I have been working with Harry to get things sorted out, but he is nominally in charge.''

Paget raised an eyebrow. ''I was under the impression that your uncle avoided the administrative side of the business,'' he said. ''He told me he prefers to oversee the jobs themselves.''

''He does,'' John agreed. ''But when it comes down to it, Harry is just as capable of running this business as my father was. People tend to underrate Harry because he is less aggressive, but he grew up with the business, and he'd have no trouble running it. Whether he *wants* to do that is another question, but you'd have to talk to Harry about that.'' He looked at his watch again. ''And now, if you'll excuse me, I'm afraid I must prepare for my meeting,'' he said.

''Just one more thing before we leave,'' said Paget as he rose to his feet. ''Can you tell me where you were last Sunday evening between the hours of, say, seven and nine?''

John Bolen frowned. *''Seven?''* he repeated. ''My father was alive when I left him about nine-thirty, so why seven?''

''If you would just answer the question, sir?''

Bolen frowned. ''Very well, but I don't know that it will do you much good. I was at home, by myself, trying to think of some way to stop my father from going through with the Ockrington project. Short of murder, that is—in case you were wondering,'' he added sardonically as he rose to usher them out.

A BEGRIMED ISUZU TROOPER loaded with building materials stood next to Prudence Bolen's bright-red MG outside the front door of Brookside. Paget put his hand on the bonnet of the Isuzu as he passed and found it barely warm.

Laura Bolen answered the door, and standing in the hall behind her was Harry. "I'll be off, then, Laura," he said loudly. He looked at Laura as if expecting her to say something, but she remained silent. "Just popped in for a minute to see if Laura needed a hand with the arrangements for the funeral on Saturday," he said by way of explanation. With a nod to the two detectives, he ran down the steps and got into the Trooper as Laura closed the door.

Paget introduced Tregalles. "Sorry to trouble you again, Mrs. Bolen," he said, "but we would like to ask you one or two more questions."

Laura made no attempt to conceal a sigh of resignation. "In that case, I suppose you'd better come through," she said. She turned and led the way across the entrance hall to a spacious living room overlooking the garden at the side of the house.

"Please sit down," she said stiffly, gesturing to a leather sofa. She took a seat facing them and clasped her hands in front of her. Her cheek was still swollen, and the colour of the bruise could still be seen beneath her make-up. Her face was slightly flushed, and Paget couldn't help wondering what Harry Bolen had been doing there in the middle of a day when there must be so much to do at work.

"I know we've been through all this before," he began, "but sometimes people remember things later, so please bear with me when I ask you to go through everything once more, beginning with when your brother-in-law arrived after his flight back from Canada?"

The expression on Laura's face said clearly that she thought it all a waste of time, but she made no comment. Perhaps she felt it was easier to comply than to argue the point. And perhaps it was a waste of time, thought Paget, for what she told them was essentially the same as she and Harry had told him Sunday morning.

"You said you stayed in the car while your brother-in-law went up to your husband's room," Tregalles observed. "Are you quite sure that's correct, Mrs. Bolen?"

"Yes…?" An unspoken question hung there in the answer, followed by a hesitation and what appeared to be the dawning of a recollection. "Oh, my goodness; I'd quite forgotten, Sergeant. I *did* leave the car. But on the other hand, it's not something one is apt to remember, is it?"

A half-smile touched her lips. "I'm sorry," she said apologetically, "but I did leave the car for a few minutes. It was a chilly night and…well, the fact of the matter is, I had to go to the loo. I knew there was one next to the conference rooms on the first floor, so I left the car and went up the back stairs. I wasn't gone long, and I came straight down again and waited in the car for Harry."

"Did you see anyone on the stairs or in the corridor?"

"Not a soul."

"Have you thought of *anything* no matter how trivial, that seems odd in retrospect?" asked Paget.

Laura Bolen shook her head. "I'm sorry, Chief Inspector," she said with a helpless gesture, "and I have tried."

"In that case, Mrs. Bolen, thank you for being so patient. I wonder if we might have a word with your daughter before we leave?"

"Prudence? I'm afraid she's not in at the moment, but why would you wish to talk to her? She wasn't even here at the time."

Paget frowned. "I thought I saw her car in the drive when we arrived," he said.

Laura Bolen's lips tightened. "You did," she said coldly. "But Prudence has taken my car into town. I'm having an antitheft device fitted, and she offered to take it in for me, and I don't expect her back for some time. Not that she'll be able to help you very much. As I said, she wasn't even here when all this happened. She was in Bristol, where she's attending university. I telephoned her there not long after you left on Sunday morning." Laura sighed. "I didn't relish having to break the news to her over the telephone, but on the other hand, it would have been better coming from me instead of from her friend."

"Her friend…?"

Laura clucked her tongue and shook her head in self-recrimination. "It was my fault," she said. "I should have been more circumspect. Pru's room-mate, Joan Lassiter, answered the phone. She said Pru had gone out early for a bike ride with some friends, but she promised to have her phone me as soon as Pru got back. Unfortunately, I made the mistake of telling Joan why I was calling, and she blurted it out as soon as Pru came in. Pru was devastated. She and her father were very close. She rang me back as soon as she came in, and then came home immediately. Well, late that afternoon, to be more precise. She left straightaway, but she had trouble with her car as she was leaving Bristol, and had a terrible time finding someone to look at it— you know what it's like trying to get service on a Sunday—so she didn't arrive home until about five in the afternoon."

"What was the trouble?" asked Tregalles.

"I think she said it was dirty petrol."

"In that case, Mrs. Bolen," said Paget as he rose to his feet, "thank you for your time and your patience. Please don't get up; we can see ourselves out."

As they made their way to the car, Paget said, "Get on to Bristol and ask them to have a word with this girl, Joan Lassiter. It's not that I don't believe her mother, but let's make sure her story checks out and the girl was actually there. And ask them to find out what Lassiter knows about Malone. Find out if Prudence has talked to her about him. According to Harry, his brother was violently opposed to Prudence marrying Malone, which means they could have had a motive."

"Right. But Mrs. Bolen was right about one thing," Tregalles observed. "There *is* a public loo next to the convention rooms on the first floor of the Tudor. I saw it the other night."

"That may be," said Paget, "but if she knew about the back stairs, Harry must have known about them as well. In fact, didn't Quint tell you that the Bolen Brothers built the place? So why did he go all the way round the front? Unless he *wanted* to be seen."

JOHN BOLEN STOOD UP and stretched his aching muscles. He had been hunched over the figures on his desk for what seemed like hours, and he would have liked nothing better than to dump the lot into the waste-paper basket and be done with it. But he owed it to his mother to make sure that everything was done properly, and he had promised himself he would do that, no matter how long it took.

The ringing of the telephone interrupted his thoughts. He sat down and picked it up. "John Bolen."

"Oh, good! You haven't gone then." The soft Scottish accent was unmistakable. It was Linda McRae, his fiancée, and she sounded out of breath.

"What's wrong?" he asked, immediately concerned.

"Nothing, John. In fact, everything is just fine. Mother and Dad are down from Inverness, and they want to meet you. It's a complete surprise. As I told you the other night, Dad didn't think he could get away until next week, but he and Mum are here now. They can only stay for a few days, so I thought if we could all meet for dinner at Bridge House it would give them a chance to get to know you, and for you to get to know them. I took a chance and booked a table for seven o'clock; I hope that's all right?"

John Bolen tilted back in his chair, lips compressed as he stared at the ceiling. No, it *wasn't* all right; he had too much to do and so little time to do it. But what could he say? He had never met Linda's parents, and although it had never been put into so many words, he knew the main reason for their visit was to take a look at this Englishman who had proposed to their daughter. He hadn't expected them down until next week, but obviously things had changed.

"John? Are you there?"

"Sorry, Linda. I was just trying to think. I had intended going over to my mother's to tidy up a few things before the funeral on Saturday, but I don't think there is anything so pressing that it can't wait. So I'll see you there."

"Seven o'clock." Linda lowered her voice. "You're not worried about meeting them, are you, John? You've no need; I know they'll like you. Just let Dad talk about golf and fishing, and you'll do just fine. As for Mum, she's seen your picture and thinks you have a very nice face."

John Bolen chuckled. "Then I'd better wash it for the occasion," he said. "Love you, darling."

"Love you, too—and don't you dare be late!"

TWENTY

Friday, 29 September

SHE MIGHT HAVE BEEN ASLEEP. She lay on her side, one arm above her head, her face half covered by her hair. And then the doctor turned her over and Paget saw the bloated face.

The body of Simone Giraud was almost hidden beneath a knee-high tangle of grass and weeds, the long-neglected lawn of a vacant cottage in a quiet country lane. A weathered sign beside the gate said the cottage was for sale.

"That's the couple over there," Tregalles told him, pointing to an elderly man and woman who sat in a police car talking to a policewoman. "They say they've been looking for a cottage in this area, saw the sign and decided to take a closer look. Now they wish they hadn't. Rang us on their cell phone just after ten."

The doctor closed his bag and stripped off his latex gloves. "All the signs point to asphyxia due to strangulation," he said. "The ligature marks are plain enough; looks as if a rope was used, but you never know what the PM will turn up. Do you know who will be doing it?"

"Probably the chap we had on loan from Worcester, Dr. Martindale," Paget told him. "He did the one on Bolen."

The doctor nodded. "Right. I'll forward my findings to him, then," he said. "I suppose you will need a copy as well, will you? I'm afraid I'm a bit rusty when it comes to the procedures these days. It's been years since I did any work for the police." He tossed the gloves into a plastic bag. "You can move the body now if you wish. I'm finished here." He paused. "If it's any help, I'd say she's been dead for at least two days, possibly longer, but that's not official, you understand.''

Paget watched as Simone's body was placed inside a bag and zippered shut. He found it hard to equate this lifeless form with the vibrant woman he had interviewed on Monday.

The ligature marks were deep, and there were long scratches on the neck where Simone had clawed desperately at the rope as she struggled for her life. Very little blood. Not like Bolen. Had the killer learned, perhaps? Assuming it was the same man, Paget reminded himself. Prostitutes were prime targets for violence, but this was too much of a coincidence. And if Simone *had* known where Julia Rutledge was hiding, it must be assumed she'd told her killer. It was one thing to withhold such information from the police, but quite another when you were fighting for your life.

The mood in the Incident Room was sombre when Paget returned. Even before the death of Simone, there had been a feeling of frustration among the members of the team. The Bolen case was growing cold. Statements had been taken from well over a hundred people, and yet they were no closer to a solution than they had been on day one. Now they had another killing, and the best that could be hoped for was that the killer had left something at the scene that would give them a fresh start.

''Not much to report, I'm afraid,'' said Ormside in answer to Paget's question, ''although we have had a reply from Bristol that could be interesting. Seems young Prudence Bolen wasn't in Bristol at all when her mother rang on Sunday. She was here, staying with her boy-friend at the nursery. Her friend, Joan Lassiter, said that Prudence had asked her to cover for her if her mother called, but she wasn't prepared to lie to the police for her.

''She said when Mrs. Bolen rang, she told her Prudence was out, but when Mrs. Bolen told her what had happened, she phoned Prudence at her boy-friend's place and gave her the message. Prudence then phoned her mother, pretending she was calling from Bristol, and turned up at home some hours later.''

''Much later,'' Paget said, ''accounting for the delay by saying she'd had car trouble. For someone who was supposed to be very close to her father, she wasn't very concerned about getting home. I think we'd better have a chat with Prudence Bolen and this fellow Malone first thing tomorrow… No, can't do that. It's Saturday, and I'll be busy in the morning, so it will have to be the afternoon.''

''They'll be at the funeral tomorrow afternoon,'' Ormside reminded him.

Paget groaned. ''That's right, I'd forgotten that, and I want to be there. I'll just have to fit it in as best I can. Tregalles is still out at the cottage, and you should be hearing from him soon on any leads that SOCO picks up there. Now, do we have anything new on Rutledge?''

Ormside shook his head. ''Not a word,'' he said. ''We checked again with her parents—not that they seem all that interested—and we've contacted all known relatives and friends. Nothing.''

Paget sat drumming fingers on the desk. ''When was it that Rutledge spent a night in the cells?'' he asked abruptly. ''Using the name of Vikki Lane.''

Ormside reached for his entry-book. ''It was in August,'' he said as he thumbed through the pages. ''Yes, here it is. The fifteenth. Released on the sixteenth.''

''Have a word with the people on duty that night. It's a long shot, I know, but someone might remember something about the girl.''

''Right. I'll get…'' Ormside lowered his voice. ''Super's heading this way,'' he warned as Alcott came through the door.

''Ah, Paget! Thought I might find you here,'' he said as he set a bulging briefcase on Ormside's desk. He opened it and brought out a large, thick envelope.

''I've just this minute been told that I am to attend a seminar tomorrow with Chief Superintendent Brock,'' he said. ''The chief constable was supposed to be there as well, but he's cried off, so there's a seat vacant and Brock wants me to fill it.

''So…'' Alcott paused long enough to find and light a cigarette. ''What it all boils down to is this: I was supposed to be in Worcester tomorrow to give a talk on Community Policing at the close of a course we've been running there all week. Obviously, I can't be in two places at once, so I want you to go in my place."

"Oh, no," said Paget firmly. "Not tomorrow. I'm sorry, sir, but my time is committed tomorrow morning, and there's Bolen's funeral in the afternoon."

Alcott sucked deeply on his cigarette. "I don't think you quite understand," he said. "I'm sorry if it interferes with your plans, but I didn't have a choice, and neither do you. I have everything here; you can take it home tonight and look it over. Anyway, it should be a piece of cake for you. If I remember rightly, you did eighteen months as an instructor while you were with the Met."

"That was ten years ago!"

Alcott dismissed the objection with a wave of his hand. "You can do this with your eyes shut," he said brusquely. "Now, then…"

"That's not the point, sir. I have made a commitment to a friend for tomorrow morning, and I want to keep it. It's very important to me."

Alcott squinted at him through the smoke. "I'm sure your friend can make other arrangements," he said quietly, "so we'll consider the matter closed, shall we? You're on at eleven tomorrow morning, so at least you won't have to go down there tonight." He stood up and handed the envelope to Paget. "You'll find everything you need in there."

BACK IN HIS OFFICE, Paget tilted back in his chair and rubbed his face with his hands. He didn't know what he was going to tell Andrea. It seemed as if every time there was a chance of getting close to her again, some malevolent little god with nothing better to do pushed them farther apart.

But, on the more practical side, if he *had* to go, he might as well get some benefit from it and take a pool car. It would give him the opportunity to have his own car serviced while he was away, something he'd been intending to do for weeks. He picked up the phone and punched in a number. The phone at the other end rang only once before someone picked it up and said, "Mickey's Garage."

"Thought you might still be there, Mickey," he said. "It's Neil Paget."

"Hi, Neil. What's up? Car giving you trouble?"

"Not really. Tell me, do your blokes still work Saturdays?"

"Till one o'clock, yeah."

"Good. Any chance of bringing the car in for an oil change and service check first thing in the morning?"

"Hang on a minute." Paget waited. "Yeah, I can squeeze you in, but it won't be ready till twelve or after. Anything special you want me to look at?"

"No. And I won't be picking it up till Monday," Paget told him. "I have to go out of town, so I'll be using one of our pool cars over the weekend. I'll have one of our lads bring my car in first thing in the morning. All right?"

"Fine. You're booked in. Enjoy the weekend. I wish I could."

Mickey would probably enjoy his weekend more than he would, thought Paget as he made his way downstairs. He stopped at the duty sergeant's desk to make arrangements for his car to be taken in the following morning, then signed for an unmarked pool car.

It was six-thirty by the time he arrived on the doorstep and rang the bell below Andrea's name-plate.

"Yes? Who is it?"

"It's Neil," he said. "May I come up for a moment?"

"Neil?" Andrea sounded surprised. "Yes, yes, of course." The buzzer sounded and Paget opened the door.

He ascended the stairs to the first floor, and found Andrea standing in the open doorway of the flat. She wore an apron and had a tea-towel in her hands. "Hello," he said awkwardly. "Sorry to trouble you like this, but I'm afraid I have some bad news."

Andrea's eyes searched his face. "You'd better come in, then," she told him, and stood aside to let him by before following him inside.

"I hope I'm not interrupting anything," he said hesitantly, but Andrea shook her head. "Just finishing the washing-up," she told him. "What is it, Neil? You look terribly serious. Won't you sit down?"

"Thank you, but I can't stop," he told her. "It's just that...well, something's come up. I had no idea until an hour ago, but I've been told I have to be in Worcestershire tomorrow morning, and I can't get out of it. I really am sorry, Andrea. I know I promised faithfully to be there to help in the parade, and I was really looking forward to it, but now..."

He stopped, baffled by her reaction. "What? What is it?" he demanded. "What's so funny?"

Andrea put a hand over her mouth and tried to smother a laugh. "Oh, Neil," she said, "you should have seen your face! Honestly, I didn't know what to expect; you looked so *serious*." She straightened her face. "I'm sorry you can't make it tomorrow, because I was rather looking forward to having you along. But don't worry, I'm sure I can get someone to fill in. What's the problem at Worcester?"

He felt somewhat deflated. He'd been so worried about letting Andrea down after promising to be there on Saturday, but apparently it hadn't bothered her at all.

"My super was supposed to be giving the closing talk at the end of a police course that's been going on all week," he explained. "But now he can't go, so I have to go down in his place."

"Well, can't be helped," said Andrea, "but it was good of you to come round to tell me. Do you have time for a cup of tea?"

"I'd like to," he said, "but there simply isn't time. I have a lot of swotting to do if I'm to get this talk right and not disgrace the Force tomorrow." He moved toward the door.

"I'm sure you won't do that," Andrea told him as she saw him out. "Pity you didn't come a few minutes earlier; you'd have been able to meet Sarah, but she's gone with Mrs. Ansell to the library. You remember Mrs. Ansell?"

Paget nodded. "Your landlady, as I recall."

"And much, much more," Andrea said with feeling. "She's been wonderful with Sarah."

"Perhaps next time," he said as he paused at the door.

Impulsively, Andrea reached out and squeezed his arm. "Good luck with your speech," she said. "Give me a ring when you get home and let me know how it went, and I can tell you how things went at the parade.''

"I will," he promised. "As soon as I get home."

Andrea watched from the window as Paget left the building and got into his car. He didn't look up. She wandered back into the kitchen and resumed the drying up. She was sorry Neil wouldn't be at the parade tomorrow, but it was good of him to come round to explain. She smiled to herself. He really had looked stricken when he first arrived. So serious. So intense! She wished…

Suddenly impatient with herself, Andrea brushed the thought away. As her ever-practical mother was so fond of saying: "if wishes were horses, beggars would ride. So, if you *really* want something, it's no good wishing. You must *do* something about it.''

TWENTY-ONE

Saturday, 30 September

PAGET ARRIVED AT Hindlip Hall, headquarters of the West Mercia Constabulary, at precisely ten o'clock, and went in search of Tom Baldwin, the course coordinator.

"I thought Alcott was coming down," he told Paget. "At least, that's who I've got on my list to do the 'Go-out-there-and-get-'em' pep talk at the end."

"Alcott couldn't come, so they're stuck with me, I'm afraid," Paget told him.

"I'd better make a note of that," said Baldwin as he stroked Alcott's name from the list. "Still *Chief* Inspector, is it?"

Paget grimaced. "I haven't been reclassified, if that's what you mean. I think they finally gave up on that when someone pointed out they'd spent more money on the study than they could possibly save by dropping the rank of chief inspector. But

I'm still keeping my fingers crossed. Now, which room am I in, and who's on ahead of me?''

"Room twelve, and Lovett's in there now," Baldwin told him. "She was on yesterday as well." Baldwin consulted his schedule. "She did 'The Importance of Accurate Reporting—the Difference Between Looking and Seeing,' and today she's doing 'Contamination of a Crime Scene.'"

"Grave Lovett?"

"That's the one. You know her, then?"

"I do indeed. She works for Charlie Dobbs, and she's a good analyst. She's helped me out more than once."

"Has she, now?" Baldwin twitched his eyebrows. "Good-looking gal. And she knows her job. I listened to part of her lecture yesterday, and she made it so interesting that some of the lads actually stopped looking at her legs and started taking notes." He looked at the clock. "Why don't you slip in the back and sit in on the lecture. You'll be on next, anyway."

"I think I'll do that," said Paget. "I'd like to hear what she has to say."

"Right. And do us all a favour, will you, Paget? Make the closing speech short. Nobody will be listening anyway, because after a week of this, all they want to do is get the hell out of here."

"Suits me. See you later, Tom."

Grace had her back to him when he entered the room and took a seat at the back of the room. Using a projected diagram of a real crime scene, she was pointing out how easily crucial evidence could be destroyed by a single careless movement.

"Use your eyes, ears, and nose before you even move into the critical area," she told them. "Assuming, as in this case, the victim is dead, stop and think before you move. The victim isn't going anywhere, so what's your hurry? Studying the scene from a distance is worthwhile, and it helps you decide how best to approach the body without disturbing the scene any more than necessary."

Grace turned round and faced the class. "It's been my experience," she continued, "that more evidence is contaminated or destroyed in the first five minutes by the investigating officers than at any other time, so stop and think before you move."

She looked out over the class and saw Paget. His presence there surprised her, and she wondered nervously what his reaction would be to the statement she had just made. It was one thing to be preaching to young constables and quite another to be telling senior officers how to conduct an investigation. On the other hand, what she had said was true, so she might as well press on.

"Now, turn to page twelve, diagram seven," she said, and as the students shuffled their papers she felt her confidence returning. "Everyone got it?" she asked. "Now, take a good look at it and tell me what's wrong with it."

Paget sat back and listened—and learned. As Baldwin had said, Grace knew her subject, and she knew how to keep her audience interested. But suddenly it was over, and Paget was surprised at how quickly the last half hour had gone by.

"Now," said Grace, "I want you all back here in ten minutes. Superintendent Alcott will finish up the morning with a talk on Community Policing and the contribution each of you can make to good relations with the general public. And don't try to skip off early, because there will be a roll-call and a head count."

A groan went up around the room.

Paget waited until the room was clear before he approached the podium where Grace was packing up her things. "That was excellent," he told her. "I really enjoyed your lecture, Grace. I'm glad I caught it."

Grace Lovett flushed. "It's very kind of you to say so," she said. "Are you down here with Superintendent Alcott?"

"I *am* Alcott, today," he told her. "I've been stuck with the closing lecture. You're welcome to stay and listen, but I imagine you'll want to be off home straightaway."

"I wouldn't miss it for the world," she said. "How about lunch afterward before we start back? The dining-room is open."

"Sounds good to me," said Paget, "but please don't feel obliged to sit through the lecture. I can meet you afterward."

"I'd like to," she said with such sincerity that he wasn't quite sure what to say.

"FOR AS MUCH AS IT hath pleased Almighty God of his great mercy to take unto himself the soul of our dear brother here departed: we therefore commit his body to the ground; earth to earth, ashes to ashes, dust to dust; in sure and certain hope of the Resurrection to eternal life, through our Lord Jesus Christ..."

The words lingered in the hot and humid air above the open grave like mist above a meadow at the break of day. Laura Bolen stepped closer, stretched out her hand and let the dry earth trickle slowly from her fingers. It fell like the first spatter of rain on the polished wood of the casket below, followed by others as each member of the family cast their small handful of earth into the grave.

Tregalles, watching from a respectful distance, turned his attention to Prudence, the only one of the family who had not been interviewed to date. She was scrubbing at her hands with a tissue, and looking anything but pleased as she began to move away from the grave side. She paused for a moment, and looked to the right of where Tregalles stood, and gave a surreptitious wave before continuing on her way.

Tregalles looked in that direction. A man stood well back, head bowed, hands down and folded as if in silent prayer. Malone? Probably. Nice touch, Tregalles thought, especially for someone who hoped to join the family.

Two people who had been standing apart from the family began to make their way toward one of the cars. Keith Lambert and his mother, Emily.

Leaving the grave side on John's arm, Laura Bolen paused. "Stay here and wait for me," she told him. "There's something I must do." She left the gravel path and moved to intercept Keith and his mother before they reached their car.

Emily Lambert was a tall woman. She walked slowly, hunched slightly forward, troubled by arthritic knees and a crumbling spine, but she shrugged off the proffered arm of her son, preferring to use a sturdy cane instead.

Laura waited, and as they came abreast of her, held out her hand. "I'd like to thank you for coming to Jim's funeral," she said quietly, "and I want you to know that I appreciate the gesture."

Emily Lambert drew herself erect. Her face was gaunt, her eyes deep-set. "He was my nephew," she said in a clear voice. "I owed him that much."

Laura drew in a deep breath and let it out again. "I would like to think that we have done more than simply bury my husband here today," she said. "I would like to think that we have buried old animosities as well. I have no quarrel with you or any member of your family, and I would hope that we could start again."

Emily regarded Laura with stony eyes. "I attended the funeral of my nephew because it was my duty to do so," she said. "But one does not simply shrug off more than thirty years of unfounded accusations. Your husband dedicated his life to destroying my family and the family business—oh, yes, he did," she insisted as Laura opened her mouth to protest, "and you only have to look at the lengths to which he was prepared to go in order to destroy us to know that's true.

"And all because he believed everything his wastrel father told him," the old woman continued bitterly. "Jack was my brother, but he was a slacker and a whiner, and a poor excuse for a man. The only reason he had a job at all was because I pleaded with my husband to give him a chance, but believe me, I've regretted that decision ever since."

"Mother..." Keith Lambert laid a hand on his mother's arm, but she shook it off. She turned to leave, but paused.

'If you really are sincere about burying the past, and if you want to know the truth," she told Laura, "ask Bert Cox. He was there the day Jack died."

Laura stood there, stunned by the reaction of the woman she had once liked very much and had thought of as her future mother-in-law. She watched as Keith helped his mother into the car, then turned and sent a silent message of apology before getting in himself.

Laura walked slowly back to where her family waited. What had Emily Lambert meant when she'd said Bert Cox was there when Jim's father had fallen from the scaffold all those years ago? Jim had never said anything about his uncle being there that day. Albert Cox was Jim's uncle on his mother's side. Laura vaguely remembered meeting him many years ago, but he had moved away, and she had no idea where he might be now.

Perhaps Jim hadn't known his uncle was there that fateful day—or didn't *want* to know.

"I DON'T LIKE THE LOOK of that sky at all," said Grace as they left the building. "I think the sooner we get home, the better."

Paget took one quick glance and agreed. The sun was shining at the moment, but off to the south-east the sky looked dark and brooding. The colours reminded Paget of a monstrous bruise— dark blues and blacks, and yellow around the edges. The air felt warm and clammy against the skin as they made their way to their cars.

"Do you need a hand with anything before I go?" he asked.

Grace shook her head. "Everything's in the boot," she told him. She stuck out her hand. "And thank you very much for lunch. I shouldn't have let you pay, but you did promise to let me buy next time, and I shall hold you to it. Safe journey home."

"It was my pleasure, Grace," he said and meant it. "Drive carefully, and let's hope we both get home before that lot breaks." He nodded toward the darkening sky.

Grace turned to go to her car, then stopped. "That doesn't look good," she said, pointing to a large pool of oil beneath one of the cars. "I think I'd better go inside and let somebody know."

Paget took one look, and his heart sank. "No need," he told her. "That's my car; at least, it's the pool car I came down in this morning."

"Oh, no!" Grace looked horrified. "What are you going to do?"

Paget squatted down beside the car, but all he could see was a steady drip of oil. He unlocked the door and released the latch. "Let's see how bad it is," he said as he raised the bonnet and peered inside. One side of the engine was covered in oil.

Two uniforms came round the corner and stopped to watch. "Looks like you've got trouble, mate," said one cheerfully. He had red hair and a ginger moustache. "They don't run worth a damn without oil."

"I am aware of that, constable," said Paget as he straightened up, "but thank you for your advice. Now, do you happen to know the number of the police garage?"

"Won't do you any good, mate. Nobody there on a Saturday afternoon," the man told him. His partner gave him a prod, but he ignored it. "Besides, they only take police vehicles. You'll have to ring for a tow. What?" he demanded angrily as his partner prodded him hard again.

"It's DCI Paget, isn't it, sir?" the other man said.

"That's right," said Paget. He barely managed to conceal a smile as the first man's neck tried to match the colour of his moustache. "And it *is* a police vehicle. It looks to me like a broken gasket, but whatever it is, it can't be driven."

"In that case it's no problem, sir. But you'll not get it seen to till Monday."

Paget turned to Grace, who had been silent until now. "Any chance of a lift?" he asked. "I live in Ashton Prior, so it would be about five miles out of your way."

"No problem," Grace assured him. "But what about the car?"

"I'll have to leave it and someone will have to come down and pick it up next week," he told her. "If you don't mind waiting, I'll go inside and make arrangements."

"We can take care of it for you, sir," the second man told him. "If you'll leave the keys with me, I'll sign for them and have the car taken in."

"Thank you, Constable, that's very kind of you. I appreciate your help." Paget surveyed the forbidding sky as he handed over the keys and gave the constable his card. "I can be reached at that number if there's any problem."

The man tore a page from his notebook and scribbled a receipt. The name was indecipherable.

"Make a note of when and why that page was torn out," Paget warned. He waited while the man complied, then initialled the entry himself. Missing pages from a policeman's notebook were always suspect.

"And your name is...?"

"PC Quentin, sir."

Paget thanked the man again before joining Grace, who was waiting in her car.

"Henceforth known as Kiss-arse Quentin," ginger moustache muttered as they watched the car leave the car-park.

"I was trying to warn you, you stupid prat! Trying to save your balls! The way you were going on, he could have had you for breakfast."

Ginger moustache pursed his lips and made kissing sounds. "Kiss-arse," he said again as they went back inside.

"Up yours, too, Ginger."

THE FIRST DROPS OF RAIN splashed against the windscreen before they were clear of Fernhill Heath; huge, saucer-size drops that burst like miniature bombs against the glass. Grace switched on the wipers, but within minutes the drops had turned into a downpour, and she had to turn the wipers on full to keep the windscreen clear.

She was a competent driver, and Paget found himself relaxing in the passenger's seat. The rain danced on the bonnet and drummed hard against the roof, making it all but impossible to carry on a conversation without shouting.

He had enjoyed his lunch with Grace. Not surprisingly, the talk had turned to work-related subjects, but he'd finally managed to get Grace to talk about herself.

She was originally from Sheffield, and her parents were still there. Her father was a senior manager with an international cosmetics firm, and her mother was a solicitor. She had two brothers, one older, one younger. Her older brother, Bob, was in genetic research, while her younger brother was mad on golf.

"That's all he thinks about," she said. "He's good, mind you, and he'll probably make a go of it—God knows he lives and breathes the game twenty-four hours a day—but Dad is none too happy about it. Thinks Stan should get himself a real job."

"And your mother? What does she think?"

Grace smiled. "She thinks it's great. She loves golf."

"And what about you? How did you wind up in Broadminster as a forensic analyst?"

"I took two years of law before I realized it wasn't for me,"

Grace told him. "I wanted something more hands-on, something where I could see results. In many respects, my work isn't all that different from yours: probing, sifting through clues, asking questions, and putting the results together. But how about you? Did you always want to be a detective?"

"No, not really. Oddly enough, I started out much the same way you did, except I took only one year of law before I decided to make the change. My father was a dentist, but it was my mother who nudged me in this direction. She was a social worker, and I think it was her stories of all the injustices and results of crime she saw every day that influenced me the most. She died suddenly when I was sixteen, a tumour she didn't know she had until it was too late."

Paget folded his napkin and laid it beside his plate. "So," he concluded, "I changed courses and became a policeman, and I've never regretted it."

"You're from London originally, aren't you?" said Grace. "What brought you to Broadminster?"

"It's a long story," he'd said quietly as he glanced at his watch. "Some other time, perhaps."

A flash of lightning jolted Paget out of his pleasant reverie. It ripped a jagged hole in the curtain of rain, and every tree stood out in stark relief. The crash of thunder followed within seconds, and Grace gripped the wheel harder as wind buffeted the car. "Close," she said as she peered ahead. "I hope there aren't any trees down."

"If you won't take it as a vote of non-confidence, I'd be more than happy to take over for a while," Paget offered, but Grace shook her head.

"Thanks, but we'd have to get out to change over, and we'd be soaked. I'm all right if you are."

Water several inches deep streamed across the road at the bottom of each hill, and Paget could feel the drag on the tyres as Grace ploughed through. Trees and hedges on either side protected them from the wind to some extent, but it was all Grace could do to hold the car steady once they left their shelter. Thankfully, there was little traffic on the road. Others had more sense, thought Paget.

Another flash of lightning lit up the countryside, and thunder rolled down the hills like monstrous bowling balls to crash against the car. "You'll have to tell me where to turn off for Ashton Prior," Grace shouted above the din.

"We still have six or seven miles to go," he shouted back, "but I'll let you know well ahead of time."

They lapsed into grim-lipped silence for the next few miles, eyes glued to the road through the arc of windscreen wipers thumping back and forth with hypnotic regularity.

"It's about half a mile further on," said Paget. "I'll tell you— Look out!"

But even as he yelled the warning, Grace was braking hard, and the car came to rest with its nose buried in a mass of leaves and twisted branches. "Thank God I wasn't going any faster," she breathed, "or it would have hit us coming down."

A huge limb, almost half the tree, blocked the road.

They sat there in silence for a moment. "Are you all right?" he asked.

Grace breathed in deeply. "A bit shaken," she admitted, "but I'll live."

"In that case, there's only one thing for it. I'll get out and shift it before someone else comes along and slams into us. Sit tight."

Before Grace could answer, he was out of the car and fighting his way through rain and wind and broken branches. He managed to get hold of a branch close to the main stem of the limb, and heaved. Nothing moved. He tried again and the branch broke off. He began to strip some of the lesser branches away in order to make the task of moving the limb easier.

He was soaked to the skin and progress was painfully slow. Between the buffeting wind, water pouring over the road, and slithering about on wet leaves, he was having a hard enough time just keeping his feet under him, and an even harder one trying to shift the tree.

The car door slammed, and Grace was suddenly there beside him.

"You'll never do it on your own," she shouted. "But if I can get a good grip on this side, and you pull from where you are, we might move it.''

"Right, but watch your step. Try to avoid stepping on the leaves; they're slippery as hell.''

Grace lifted a hand in acknowledgement and began to pick her way through the twigs and branches. "Got it," she yelled. "On the count of three. One, two, three!"

Paget pulled hard. The limb began to move. He slipped and fell, scrambled to his feet and they tried again. Slowly, inch by inch, they pulled the massive limb far enough to one side to allow the car to get by. Paget grabbed Grace's hand and steadied her as she clambered back through the debris.

"I'll drive," he told her, "then I won't have to direct you. All right?''

Grace nodded and made for the passenger's side of the car. They both fell into their seats and sat there trying to catch their breath. "Thanks, Grace," Paget panted. "I couldn't have shifted that lot without your help, but your clothes will be ruined." He turned to look at her, and started to laugh.

"What?" Grace dabbed at her face with a sodden tissue. "What's so funny?''

"I'm sorry," he said, still grinning, "but it's your hair.''

Grace flicked the rear-view mirror round to look for herself and a low chuckle rumbled in her throat. "Rat-tails," she said ruefully, pushing her long blonde hair back with both hands. "What a mess!" She turned to face him, and began to grin herself. "I wish your colleagues could see *you* now," she chuckled. "Chief Inspector, sir!''

"I can imagine," he said as he did up his seat-belt and set the mirror back in place. "But we'd better get on. The sooner we get to the house, the sooner we can dry ourselves off." He started the car. "And I think it's time we dispensed with this 'Chief Inspector' business, at least away from the job. My name is Neil.''

Grace thrust out her hand. "Pleased to meet you, Neil," she said solemnly. He took her hand and shook it, and they both laughed for no reason at all.

TWENTY-TWO

THE DRIVE FROM THE MAIN road into Ashton Prior was a nightmare. Culverts were plugged, and normally placid streams ran like rivers across the road. Paget eased the car through, praying that the roadbed had not washed out beneath the roiling water, and when he finally turned into the short drive leading to his house, it was with a deep sense of relief. He'd driven in storms before, but nothing quite like this one, and he was more than thankful that the house was close to the top of a hill.

He switched the engine off, leaned his head against the headrest, and sat there listening to the sound of rain drumming on the roof. Jagged forks of lightning slashed their way to earth with stunning regularity, and thunder echoed and re-echoed through the valleys, seemingly without end. Grace, too, sat there in silence, eyes closed as she offered up a silent prayer of thanks.

She turned to Paget. "Thanks," she said simply. "I'm not sure I would have made it if I'd been on my own. I'm glad your car broke down."

He smiled wearily. "So am I," he said, and meant it.

They made a dash for the house and almost fell inside. Paget closed the door, and suddenly it was calm. The storm still raged outside, but they could hear again, talk in normal voices and be heard.

"Better get those wet clothes off," he told Grace briskly. "There's a bathroom upstairs if you'd like to take a hot shower, and in the meantime I'll see if I can find something for you to wear. I can find you a shirt and pullover, but..." He scratched his head. Grace was only a couple of inches shorter than he was, but a pair of his trousers would go twice around her slim figure. "To be honest," he confessed, "I don't know what we can do about the rest of you."

Grace smiled. "If you have a few safety-pins, and you'll let me look through your linen cupboard, I think I can manage to put something together,'' she told him. She turned toward the stairs. ''I'll be as quick as I can, because the sooner you get out of those wet clothes and have a hot shower yourself, the better. Which door is it?''

''First on the right, and the linen cupboard is just down the hall from there. Next to that is the spare bedroom, so I'll put whatever I can find in the way of clothes and safety-pins in there.''

Paget waited until he heard the bathroom door close, then climbed the stairs himself and went into the bedroom, pausing only long enough to pick up a towel along the way. He stripped down completely, and towelled himself vigorously. The house itself was warm, but the combination of rain and wind had chilled him to the bone.

He put on a fleece-lined track suit, something he hadn't worn in years, but it was warm and smelled only faintly of the mahogany-lined drawer in which it had lain since the day he moved into the house. For Grace, he found a clean shirt that was too small for him, and a fisherman's jersey that would probably come down to her knees. The sleeves would be much too long, but they could be turned up, and at least it would keep her warm. He ransacked the drawers, tossing in anything that looked remotely useful, then took everything along to the spare bedroom. He dropped the bundle on the bed, placed half a dozen safety-pins on top, then went downstairs and put the kettle on.

He turned on the radio. Two of the local stations were off the air, but a third was giving sports results. The kettle boiled, and he busied himself making tea.

As he had hoped, there was an update on the weather. The police were warning people to stay off the roads. A bridge was out on the Clunbridge Road. The power was off in parts of Broadminster, and there were other scattered outages affecting Ludlow, Craven Arms, and a number of the surrounding villages. Work crews had been dispatched, but conditions were extremely hazardous, and restoration was expected to be slow.

Trees and power lines were down everywhere, and once again the message was repeated: ''*Please* stay off the roads.''

Grace appeared in the doorway and did a slow pirouette as

she entered the room. "What do you think of the latest in summer fashions?" she asked.

The shirt looked good on her. Her shoulders were surprisingly broad, and the shirt was pulled in and held by a large towel wrapped around her waist. A second towel had been twisted into a turban, revealing her long, slender neck normally masked by her shoulder-length hair. And on her feet, she wore Paget's hiking socks.

"Stunning," he told her, and meant it. "Love the socks. The tea's hot if you'd like some."

"Oh, good! I'm dying for a cup."

"Like anything to eat?" he asked as he poured the tea.

"No, thanks. I'm still full from lunch." She nodded toward the radio. "Any news about the storm?"

"They're warning everyone to stay off the roads," he said. "A lot of trees and power lines down. I think we were very lucky to get through at all." He shivered suddenly.

"I think you had better go and have that hot shower," said Grace. "You'll feel better after it, believe me."

"I think you're right," he agreed. "What did you do with your clothes? We should be getting them dried out. Can they go in the drier?"

"Yes, everything can go in if we're careful with the setting," she told him. "All but the tights. They're a complete write-off after clambering through all those branches, and I'm not sure my shoes will ever be any good again. Still, could have been worse. I'll start the clothes off while you have your shower. Now go on before you catch cold."

He smiled. It had been a long time since a woman had ordered him about, he thought as he made his way up stairs, and it came as a pleasant change to his normally dull routine. Especially when it was done by someone as beautiful and charming as Grace Lovett.

ANDREA MCMILLAN LOOKED at the time. Almost five o'clock and Neil hadn't telephoned. Perhaps he was still stuck in Worcester because of the storm. They were warning people to stay off the roads, so perhaps he had decided to stay over. Still, it wouldn't hurt to ring.

Andrea punched in the number. There was a crackling on the line, but that was all. She tried again. That was better. The phone rang several times, but now there was a loud hum on the line. The ringing stopped. Somewhere close by, lightning struck the ground, and a burst of sound exploded in her head. Andrea snatched the phone away from her ear so fast she dropped it. Stupid thing to do, she admonished herself, phoning in the middle of a lightning storm. Still shaken, she picked up the phone and held it gingerly some distance from her head.

Nothing. Not a sound.

She put the phone down. She wished she had been able to talk to Neil. She didn't care for storms at the best of times, but this one seemed almost malevolent in its fury, and just hearing Neil's voice would have been reassuring. Fortunately, it didn't seem to bother Sarah, who was playing happily with a farm set on the floor, moving cows out to pasture, and sheep into pens.

Andrea moved to within a few feet of the window and stood looking out. It was still chucking it down and showed no signs of stopping. A jagged fork split the skies, and everything in the room stood out in stark relief. Andrea shivered and switched on the lights. At least they were still working, thank goodness. Another crash. The lights flickered but stayed on.

Better put the kettle on while she still had the chance, she decided. She'd long ago set out the candles and the matches, just in case.

"SOMEONE WAS TRYING to phone you," said Grace as Paget came down the stairs, "but I think the storm must have taken the line down, because when I answered there was no one there and it sounded dead."

He thought guiltily of Andrea. He should have tried to call her as soon as he got in. He'd promised her he would. But he'd been so busy drying off and sorting out something for Grace to wear that it had completely slipped his mind.

"Probably a friend," he said. "They said they might call. I'll try to ring them later."

Showered and changed, he looked refreshed, and Grace thought once again of the difference in the man when he was away from work. He was warm and friendly, far more relaxed than she had ever seen him, and she offered up silent thanks for the storm that had brought them so unexpectedly together.

"Any problems with the drier?" he asked.

"No, it's quite similar to mine. I'll need to use your iron, though."

"No problem," he told her, "so long as nothing happens to the electrics."

Grace grimaced at the prospect. "Perhaps we should have something to eat in case we do lose the electricity. Do you have any candles?"

"Top drawer beside the sink," he told her, "together with a box of matches. I haven't looked at them for ages, but that's where they were the last time I saw them, and I'm sure Mrs. Wentworth hasn't moved them."

"I was wondering who Mrs. W. was," Grace said as she checked the drawer. She pointed to the magnet on the fridge, and the note beneath it.

"My daily housekeeper without whom I would be completely lost," he told her. "She used to own this house before my father bought it, and she stayed on as his housekeeper. When Dad died I more or less inherited her. That's the way we communicate; we leave each other notes. I'm gone long before she gets here in the morning, and she's gone by the time I get back at night. She doesn't come in on Saturdays and Sundays, so we sometimes go on for months without seeing each other, but the system works very well."

Grace opened the fridge. "She certainly looks after you," she said as she surveyed the shelves. "What do you fancy for your supper? Fish? Salad? What looks like a cold meat pie?"

"It's chicken and veal," he said. "It's one of Mrs. Wentworth's specialties. She has a number of them, but that's one of the best. It's great warmed up in the oven."

"Sounds good. Why don't we have some of that and salad to go with it, then? No, you sit still," she told him as Paget moved to help her. "Just tell me where things are and I'll get it ready. I enjoy working in the kitchen."

A crash of thunder rocked the house and they both ducked instinctively. "That was close!" breathed Grace. She looked shaken as she returned to what she'd been doing. "I was hoping that the storm would have let up by now, so that once my clothes are dry I can get back home."

"You're not going anywhere," Paget told her firmly. "It would be crazy to even try, with the way the roads are. The storm is bound to be over by the morning and we can try it then. I'll come in with you in case there's a problem. I can either get my own car back from Mickey's Garage, or failing that, get another pool car. Is there anyone who will be worried about you? Anyone expecting you home tonight?"

"No, but…"

"Then it's settled," he told her. "You're staying here tonight."

GRACE ENTERED THE ROOM. She was wearing his dressing-gown, and her feet were bare. The sleeves hung down to her fingertips, and she had pulled the cord tight around her waist to take up the slack. Her hair was dry, and it hung loosely around her shoulders. Her blue eyes shone softly in the light, and she reminded Paget of a little girl, scrubbed and clean and ready for bed.

But Grace was anything but a little girl; she was a very lovely woman, and he had become increasingly conscious of that as the evening progressed. They'd sat in the two big armchairs, Paget with his feet stretched out, Grace with hers tucked under, sipping wine and chatting quietly while music played softly in the background. The sound of thunder slowly faded to a distant grumble and the rain abated.

Paget couldn't remember when he'd spent a more pleasant evening.

Now, as she came toward him, he rose to his feet. Grace touched him lightly on the arm. "I came to say good night, Neil," she said, "and to thank you for everything. I've enjoyed today so very much in spite of the storm."

Their eyes met. She looked so lovely standing there. He

wanted to reach out and draw her to him, to take her in his arms and hold her close, to...

He tore his gaze away, afraid that she might see reflected in his eyes the feelings she had stirred in him.

"I should be thanking you," he said gruffly. "Believe me, I have enjoyed this evening more than I can say, and I'm most grateful for your company." He kept his eyes averted as he moved away. "But it's late," he went on, "and you must be very tired, so I'll let you get to bed. I put clean sheets on the bed earlier this evening and turned them down to air, so I think you should be comfortable."

Grateful! As she lay in the strange bed, the word seemed to be etched against the darkness, and gratitude was *not* what she'd seen in Neil's eyes. In that all too fleeting moment he had let down his guard, and she had sensed a warmth and passion responding to her own.

So why had he drawn back? Grace didn't know the answer, but she confronted herself with the knowledge that beneath the hard exterior was the man she wanted, and nothing would ever change her mind.

Downstairs, Paget went through the house, putting out the lights. It was the charged atmosphere, he told himself. The excitement of the storm; the way the two of them had been thrown together; the wine, the soft music. Grace was a lovely woman. There was bound to be a physical attraction.

But it was more than that, he thought as he made his way to bed. He *liked* her, liked her very much. He'd felt at ease with her, enjoyed her company, and he was sorry she would have to leave tomorrow.

He paused at the top of the stairs and looked down the hall. The guest bedroom door was closed, and he could see no light beneath the door. He remained there for a moment longer, then went into his own bedroom and firmly shut the door.

HE NEEDED AN OLDER MAP, one that showed the canals as they were before so many sections had been abandoned. Parkinson Arm or something like that, Simone had said, and she'd been too scared to lie. She didn't know where it was, but it couldn't be all that far away if the woman who lived on a narrow boat had been in the local jail with Vikki.

Joanna. He felt sure she had given him the woman's right name. Said she'd heard it often enough. She'd been terrified of the knife. Sweat had poured out of her when he had drawn it lightly across her face.

The narrow boat was near a pub. An odd name. She couldn't remember it, said she couldn't think while he had the rope around her neck, twisting it tighter and tighter, the knife point laid against her cheek just below the eye.

Then suddenly she was choking. Her head sagged and she'd gone limp. He thought she was faking, trying to get him to loosen the garrotte. But she was dead.

It should never have come to this, he thought angrily. It wasn't the way he'd planned it at all. He hadn't wanted to kill the woman, but she had seen his face, and there was no other way. It was the same with Vikki; as long as she was alive she could be a threat to him. He didn't want to kill her either, but he couldn't afford not to. Perhaps he was mistaken; perhaps she hadn't seen his face well enough to identify him, but he dared not take that chance.

He folded the map and put it away. He might have better luck trying to track down the pub. The library should have a copy of an AA book listing hotels and pubs. He'd try that; look for pubs in the area with odd names, and find out which ones were close to a canal.

TWENTY-THREE

Sunday, 1 October

GRACE WAS ALREADY BUSY in the kitchen by the time he came downstairs. She was dressed once more in her own clothes, *sans* tights, with one of Mrs. Wentworth's aprons on to protect herself from spitting fat.

"Eggs, bacon, fried tomatoes, toast, the lot!" she told him. "A good Sunday breakfast to start you off."

"Sounds good," he said with an inward sigh of relief as he took his place at the table. He'd lain awake for a long time after going to bed, wondering whether Grace had noticed anything in the way he'd looked at her as they'd said good night, but obviously she hadn't, and he was thankful. He didn't want anything to spoil the camaraderie they'd enjoyed the day before.

Grace contented herself with cereal and tea. "I have to watch my weight or I'd be like a barrel," she'd confessed the night before. Paget doubted that very much; Grace was in great physical condition. She enjoyed exercise, she told him, and mentioned that she belonged to a local walking group.

"It's a loose-knit sort of thing," she explained. "We encourage one another to get out and walk the hills, enjoy the countryside and keep in trim. I noticed you have hiking boots, Neil. Do you get out very much?"

"I haven't been out for years," he said. "Jill and I used to go, but, well, to tell you the truth, I hate hiking alone. Besides, I never seem to have the time."

"You should come out with us one weekend," she told him. She hadn't pressed him, but the thought intrigued him and lingered in his mind.

Surprisingly, considering the condition of the roads, the Sunday papers arrived at their usual time, and Grace and Paget spent the morning going through them and just generally lounging about. At half past ten, Grace made coffee, and they left for town shortly after eleven. Twigs and branches littered the road, but local farmers were out in force, clearing the roads of debris with tractors and front-end loaders, and the run into town was actually quite pleasant. Trees not stripped of leaves looked fresh and clean, the sun was shining and the sky was clear, and it looked as if they might be in for a stretch of nice weather once again.

Mickey's Garage was directly opposite St. Michael's Church, and churchgoers' cars were parked on both sides of the street, leaving barely enough room for Grace to drive onto the apron in front of Mickey's Garage. The garage was supposed to be closed on Sundays, but when Paget knocked on the side door, he wasn't at all surprised when Mickey opened it.

"Thought you might be here," Paget greeted him. "Can't stay away from it, can you?"

The little man shrugged. "Got nothing better to do, to tell you the truth," he said as he stepped outside. "But I wasn't expecting to see you till Monday. Not that it matters. Your car's ready." He glanced across to where Grace was waiting. "Is she with you?" he asked.

"Yes," said Paget, and went on to explain what had happened to the pool car.

"Wouldn't have happened if you'd had your cars done here," Mickey declared. "But you will go with the lowest bidder, and you only get what you pay for."

"You don't have to convince me," Paget told him. "If it were up to me…"

"Yeah, yeah, I know," Mickey sighed. He lowered his voice. "But who's the bird?" he asked. "Looks like you've pulled a nice one there."

"A colleague from work," said Paget, "and she's simply giving me a lift."

"She'd give anybody a lift, she would," said Mickey. "Some colleague! You should see what I've got for colleagues. They don't look like that, I can tell you."

"What do I owe you?" Paget asked to get Mickey off the subject. Grace was sitting in the car with the window down, and he was afraid she might hear Mickey's high-pitched voice.

"Dunno," said Mickey. "I'll look it up tomorrow and let you know."

"Fair enough, and thanks."

Paget went over to where Grace was waiting. "The car is ready, so thanks again for the lift home, and—well, just everything."

"I enjoyed it, Neil." Grace dropped one eyelid in a slow, conspiratorial wink. "Back to 'Chief Inspector Paget' tomorrow," she said with mock solemnity. She started the car. "And don't forget the walking group. I think it would do you good to get out again. Bye." She waved as she drove away.

Across the road, where he was waiting for Audrey and the children to come out of church before meeting friends for lunch, John Tregalles could barely contain himself. He'd maintained for some time that Grace Lovett was after Paget, but he could hardly believe his eyes when he saw her drive up to the garage, and saw Paget get out of the car. The sly old devil! How long had this been going on? he wondered. No wonder Paget had looked so embarrassed when he'd tripped over Grace and grabbed her up there in Bolen's room the other morning.

He glanced at the time, impatient now for the service to be over. He could hardly wait to tell Audrey.

STILL FEELING GUILTY ABOUT not phoning Andrea on his return from Worcester, he tried ringing her from the car. The phone rang several times, then switched to the machine. "It's Neil, Andrea," he said. "Just phoned to let you know I survived the storm and made it back from Worcester despite the miserable weather. Hope your parade went off all right. Talk to you later."

He glanced at the time. Almost twelve. He was close to the hospital, so he might as well do something useful while he was in town.

He made his way up to Starkie's room and found a smartly dressed woman sitting by the doctor's empty bed, thumbing through a magazine. She glanced up and smiled.

"Chief Inspector Paget," she said as she stood up. Her smile broadened. "No, we've never met," she assured him, seeing the question in his eyes, "but Reg pointed you out to me one day, and I've seen your picture in the paper. I'm Ellen Starkie."

In marked contrast to her husband, Ellen Starkie was small, trim, and smartly dressed. She wore a two-piece suit, charcoal-grey with the faintest of pin-stripes, a white tailored blouse, dark stockings, and fashionable shoes. Her face was quite round beneath a fringe of blue-black hair, and there was more than a hint of the Orient in her features.

They shook hands. There was something vaguely familiar...Paget snapped his fingers. "You're on television!" he said. "Something to do with arts and crafts? I'm afraid it's not a programme I normally watch, but I remember seeing you occasionally on Saturday mornings.''

"'Craftswoman' is the name of the show," she told him. "It's not the sort of programme that would appeal to many men, so there's no need to apologize. Won't you sit down? Reg will only be a minute or two. He's in the loo."

"How is he?"

Ellen Starkie compressed her lips and shook her head. "I can only repeat what they keep telling me: 'As well as can be expected, considering his general condition.'" Her eyes were steady on his face, but there was a tremor in her voice as she continued. "But as I'm sure you know, he's not in very good condition."

Paget nodded sympathetically.

"So much is up to Reg," she continued. "If he does everything the doctors say he should, then there's no reason why he can't be back to normal within a few months. But you know Reg."

Indeed he did. Reg Starkie was a stubborn man, and Paget couldn't see him accepting the stringent rules that would ensure his speedy recovery. No smoking, no drinking, and regular exercise? That was *not* a regimen that would go down well with Starkie.

"It's early days," he said soothingly. "This heart attack was a warning, and I'm sure he of all people will recognize the implications, and do what must be done."

"I hope you're right," she said, but her expression was one of doubt. "Still, at least he's up and about again, and of course he's not been able to smoke, so that's a start."

The door in the corner of the room opened, and Starkie came lumbering through, clutching a piece of equipment Paget always thought of as a hat-stand on wheels. One of the wheels caught on the door jamb, and Starkie muttered an oath as he wrenched it free. The whole thing swayed precariously before righting itself. The tube connecting the bag to the needle taped to his hand tightened dangerously, then fell slack once more.

"Bloody contraption," he muttered as he started toward them. "What the hell are you two grinning at?"

Paget straightened his face. "Love your night-shirt, Reg," he said. "Do you need any help?"

Starkie scowled and shook his head. That he was finding it hard going was evident, but he seemed determined to make it on his own. At least his colour was much better than it had been, and Paget was pleased to see the man on his feet again.

Starkie reached the bed and eased himself onto the edge. He lay back against his propped-up pillows, panting hard. His wife stood by the side of the bed and put a soothing hand on his brow. Starkie shot her a grateful glance and put his own hand over hers and patted it.

"I'm all right, now," he told her as his breathing eased. He looked at Paget. "Slit me open from stem to gudgeon," he said proudly, "but they tell me I'll be doing laps around the corridors before I leave, and I should be out of here by next weekend. God! I hope they're right. Do you know what I had for dinner last night? Guess. Go on, guess."

Paget shook his head. "No idea," he said. "What did you have for dinner?"

"A piece of fish you could put in your eye, and six grapes! *And* the fish was over-cooked! Six bloody grapes! Do you know I've lost nearly a stone?"

"That's good at least," said Paget. He turned to Ellen. "But I think six grapes is cutting it a bit fine, don't you? Perhaps you could push it up to eight or ten when he gets home."

"And you can bugger off home any time you please if that's all you've got to say for yourself, Paget," Starkie growled.

"I will," Paget told him, "if you'll bear with me for a few more minutes." He turned to Ellen Starkie. "If you don't mind us talking shop?"

"Not at all. I can leave…"

"No. No need for that," he told her. He turned back to Reg. "The PM on Jim Bolen was delayed until Monday, when we finally got Dr. Martindale in from Worcester," he said. "But by that time it was hard to establish a time of death with any degree of accuracy. On top of that, there was a problem with the tape you recorded, so what I'd like to know is this: Do you recall your own estimate of the time of death? It's not crucial, but it would be useful if you can remember.''

Starkie nodded slowly. "Funny you should bring that up," he said. "I was thinking of that only last night. I mentioned it on the tape, but if the tape's no good…'' He shrugged. "I remember wondering about that myself, because it looked to me as if someone had tried to make it look as if the victim had died later than he actually did. I think he was wrapped in that blanket to keep his body temperature up, and then it was taken off at the last minute and made to look as if he'd dragged it off the bed. See if the stab wounds match the bloodstains. Wrap it around the body if you have to, but that's what it looked like to me.''

Paget didn't like to tell him that the body had been buried the day before.

"What time was it when I examined him?" Starkie asked.

"Roughly three o'clock, but I can verify that from the reports.''

Starkie nodded thoughtfully. "In that case, my gut feeling is that he died around ten—say between nine-thirty and ten-thirty, to be on the safe side. Not that I could swear to it in court, but I think that's pretty close. Is that any help?''

Paget nodded. "It helps a great deal," he said. "Thanks, Reg. I appreciate it.'' He turned to go, but Starkie called him back.

"If you happen to see Charlie, you might tell him it's been a week since I had my last cigarette," he said. "Mind you," he grinned, lowering his voice, "I was unconscious at least half the time, but no need to mention that.''

Paget turned two thumbs up. "Which reminds me," he said. "Charlie was wondering whether you'd throw him out if he came to see you. What should I tell him?''

Starkie scowled. "Tell him he can come if he wants to," he said grudgingly, "but I will personally chuck him out if he turns up here saying 'I told you so' or bearing a bunch of bloody grapes!''

BEFORE RETURNING TO Ashton Prior, Paget went into the office to see if anything new had turned up since Friday. There was nothing. Twenty-two people who had parked in the Tudor car-park the night Bolen was killed had been interviewed without result. Several recalled seeing the red Jaguar, but no one remembered seeing it leave or return. In short, the Bolen case seemed to have ground to a halt. Neither was there anything new on the killing of Simone, and nothing could be expected from Forensic until at least the middle of the week. People in the area had been questioned, but the cottage where Simone's body was found was some distance from its nearest neighbour, and no one had seen or heard anything suspicious.

Paget wondered how the killer had managed to get Simone to go with him to such an isolated spot; there was nothing to indicate that she had been tied up, no traces of sticking-plaster around her mouth. Unless she'd been drugged, but if that was the case, it would show up on the autopsy report.

There was one matter still outstanding, however; Pru Bolen's whereabouts on the night her father died. He picked up the phone and punched in a number. John Bolen answered. Paget identified himself and asked to speak to his sister.

"She's not here, I'm afraid, Chief Inspector," John told him. He sounded tired. "But she should be back later this afternoon. She leaves for Bristol tomorrow morning, and she promised faithfully to spend the evening with Mother. Can I give her a message?"

"Yes. Would you tell her I would like to see her before she returns to Bristol? Perhaps she could come in on her way tomorrow morning."

"I see. Can I tell her what it's about?"

"It's just routine, really," Paget told him. "I doubt if Miss Bolen will be able to tell us anything new, but we would like a statement from her before she leaves. Shall we say nine o'clock tomorrow morning? I shan't keep her long, so there will be plenty of time left for her run to Bristol."

John Bolen put the phone down and sat there frowning as he tried to think why Paget would want to talk to Pru. What did she have to do with the investigation into their father's death? Still, he'd pass on the message and see what sort of reaction he got.

He was annoyed with her himself. Pru never stayed home,

never offered to help, just breezed in and out whenever she pleased. No doubt she would be with Malone again. The man had her hypnotized. If Pru wanted to sleep with him, that was one thing, but he hoped she would have enough sense not to marry him. John and his father hadn't seen eye to eye on many things, but they had agreed on that. He sighed heavily.

"That was a big sigh, John." He looked up. His mother stood in the doorway watching him. "Problems?" she asked. "Anything I can do?"

He shook his head. "No, thank you, Mother. Just thinking. That was Paget; he wants to talk to Pru. Any idea why?"

"No. Didn't he say?"

"No. He's not the sort to give much away."

Laura nodded, but her mind seemed to be on other things as she moved closer to her son. "I want you to know, John, that I do appreciate all the time you've spent helping me through this ghastly business. I don't know what I would have done without you." She stood before him and took his face between her hands. "I do love you, John," she continued in a low voice, "and I would never do anything to hurt you. I truly believe that what I am doing is best for everyone."

John looked puzzled as he took his mother's hands in his. "Only too happy to be here to help," he said, "but I don't understand what—"

But Laura drew away. "It will be all right, John, you'll see," she said soothingly. Her voice changed. "Now, why don't you get off and spend some time with Linda and her parents? The poor girl will be wondering if you're having second thoughts after meeting them."

"But…"

"No 'buts,'" said his mother firmly. "Now, be off with you. I have things to do."

BUNNY HANDED Vikki the mirror and said, "Take a look. Makes a difference, doesn't it?"

Vikki looked into the mirror and could hardly believe that the face looking at her could be her own reflection. The pinched, thin face of a child, framed by long, straggly fair hair of a week ago, had been replaced by that of a young woman with colour in her cheek and a mop of dark curls. The bruises were still there beneath the make-up, but they were no longer obvious.

Her eyes sparkled. "It's great!" she told Bunny. "Did you use to be a hairdresser?"

Bunny began to gather up the curlers and put them in a bag. "There's not all that much to it," she said, avoiding the question. She stood back and surveyed her handiwork with a critical eye. "You do look different," she went on, "and it's not just the hair and make-up. I don't know what it is, but you're not the same girl who came here last week. Go outside and see what Joanna thinks."

Vikki took the towel from around her shoulders. "Thanks, Bunny," she said softly. "I wish I could pay you. But I will one day, you'll see."

Bunny smiled, and wondered if that included the money Vicki had stolen from her the other night. It hadn't amounted to much—a few pennies, that was all—but it meant Vikki couldn't be trusted, and that was a shame because she liked the girl.

Joanna had been sitting on the seat in the stern, reading, but she had nodded off and the book had slipped to the floor. All three of them had spent the morning cleaning up after the storm. Fortunately, the boat was sheltered and had suffered little in the way of damage, but the tow-path and the path to the pub were littered with fallen branches, and it had taken most of the morning to clear them all away.

Vikki picked up the book and put it on the seat beside Joanna. She was very quiet, but Joanna stirred and opened her eyes.

"Now that's an improvement," she declared as she sat up straight. "Turn round." Vikki turned slowly. "Very good," said Joanna. "Now all we need are some new clothes for you."

"I think you and Bunny have done enough already," Vikki told her. "Now that I'm better, I can earn some money and pay you back."

Joanna eyed the girl. "And just how do you propose to do that?" she asked. Her voice had turned cool. "We may not have much out here, but we're not so hard up that you have to go out and earn money by spreading your legs for someone you've never seen before.''

Vikki flushed. "I didn't mean…" She stopped and made a helpless gesture. "It was the only way I could survive," she said weakly. "If there had been any other way…"

Joanna continued to look at the girl, but now with a more critical eye. "How would you like to come work at the pub, say from ten till midnight each night? Give me a hand with the clearing up. It wouldn't give you much, but it would be a start. I'm sure no one is going to recognize you now."

But even as she reassured the girl, Joanna wondered if she had done the right thing in not telling Vikki that her friend Simone was dead. She had seen it in Saturday's paper at the pub, and she'd recognized the name immediately as belonging to the woman who had taken Vikki in. Fortunately, no paper was delivered to the boat, and Joanna had never felt the need to have a radio, let alone a television set. She'd been afraid that Vikki might panic and take off again if she knew, and she didn't want that to happen. She had become attached to the girl and wanted her to stay where she'd be safe.

"What do you say, Vikki?"

Vikki liked the idea, but the thought of venturing very far from the security of the boat triggered a tremor of fear. "I'm still a bit scared that someone will recognize me," she confessed.

"It would be late at night," Joanna pointed out. "We close at ten-thirty, but we start cleaning up at ten because most of the people have gone by then, and I'm sure no one is going to connect you with what happened a week ago in Broadminster. You look completely different."

Vikki hesitated, but it would be nice to get away from the boat, if only for a couple of hours each night. She took in a deep breath and nodded. "Okay," she said. "When would you like me to start?"

"Probably tomorrow. I'll have a word with George tonight, but I'm sure he won't object."

"But won't I be taking money away from you, Joanna?"

"We'll worry about that later," Joanna said soothingly. "Maybe later on we can get you serving behind the bar. Now, what about your sketching? Are you going to do any this afternoon?''

Vikki grinned impishly. "I did one this morning before you were up," she said, "but I'm not sure you'll like it. Hang on a minute and I'll get it." The girl disappeared inside, returning a moment later with a sheet of A4 paper. She handed it to Joanna without comment.

Joanna shook her head slowly from side to side. "Surely to God I don't look like that?" she said as she held up the picture. It showed her lying on her back in her bunk, a couple of curlers in her hair, and mouth wide open. She could almost hear herself snoring.

"It's good," she admitted with a grimace. "It's very good, but I don't think I'll have it framed."

TWENTY-FOUR

Monday, 2 October

ALMOST EVERYONE at work that morning had some dramatic story to tell about the storm that had caused so much destruction over the weekend. Low-lying areas had been flooded; fallen trees had damaged houses and cars; slates had been blown off; and out where Ormside lived, greenhouses and cold frames had been smashed to pieces by hail.

"Much damage out your way, sir?" Ormside asked.

"Quite a few trees down, and a lot of flooded fields, but no damage to the house as far as I can see," Paget told him.

The sergeant picked up a memo and handed it to Paget. "That's the number of the police garage in Worcester," he said. "They want you to call back. It's about the car you had towed in on Saturday. They said the engine block is cracked. It's going to need a complete replacement, and they need authorization and a work order number."

Paget grimaced. "That's going to cost a bit," he commented as he pocketed the memo.

"What happened?" Ormside asked.

"The oil ran out in the car-park, but fortunately I noticed it before I started back, and had it towed in."

"So how did you get back?" asked Tregalles, who had been listening.

"I got a lift with someone who happened to be coming up this way," Paget said off-handedly.

"That was lucky. What was the road like?"

"Wet," said Paget curtly. "Now, can we leave the subject and get on with what we're here to do?" He turned to Ormside. "Anything else?" he asked.

"No, that's it for the moment, sir."

"Right. In that case I'll be in my office. I'm expecting Miss Bolen in at nine, so have someone bring her up when she arrives, will you, Len?"

"Will do, sir."

"I HOPE THIS WON'T take long," said Prudence Bolen as she flopped into a seat in front of Paget's desk. She was dressed in jeans and a baggy sweater at least three sizes too big for her, and trainers. "I have a lunch date with a friend in Bristol at one o'clock."

Paget ignored the remark. The young woman was forty minutes late for their appointment as it was, and he had no intention of hurrying on her account.

"Thank you for coming in, Miss Bolen," he said perfunctorily. "I'll get straight to the point. Can you tell me where you were on the evening of Saturday, September twenty-third?"

Prudence placed a dramatic hand against her chest and widened her eyes in mock surprise. "Me, Guv?" she asked in a hoarse voice. "I ain't done nuffink, Guv, honest!"

Paget's expression didn't change. "If you'll just answer the question, Miss Bolen."

Prudence sighed heavily. "I was in Bristol, which is where I should be going now," she said petulantly.

"Is there someone there who could confirm that?"

"I don't know why you'd want to, but yes, there is, as a matter of fact. I share a room with another girl, Joan Lassiter. She'll tell you I was there all night."

The Lassiter girl had been warned not to let Prudence know that the police had spoken to her, and apparently she had heeded the warning. That should make things easier. Still, he might as well let Prudence hang herself.

"And you were there, presumably, when your mother rang about seven Sunday morning?"

Prudence shifted in her chair. "Well, no, as a matter of fact I had gone out early that morning. I went bike riding with some friends. Joan told me when I came in, and I rang my mother back." She put on a sad face. "That's when she told me about Dad."

Paget frowned. "I was given to understand that Miss Lassiter had already told you what happened before you telephoned your mother," he said. "Is that not right?"

Prudence passed a hand across her forehead and frowned as if trying to recall. "Yes, that's right, now you mention it. Although I'm afraid I don't see the point of any of this."

"You telephoned your mother from where?"

"Bristol, of course."

"Are you sure it wasn't Broadminster, Miss Bolen?"

Prudence became very still. "I don't know what you mean," she said.

"From the Country Garden Nursery?"

Prudence slid down in her chair, hooked one foot over her knee and glowered at him.

"Your friend, Joan Lassiter, was interviewed by the Bristol police," he went on, "and she admitted covering for you while you were here in Broadminster for the weekend." Paget's voice hardened. "Now, shall we stop wasting each other's time and get on with it, Miss Bolen? When did you really arrive in Broadminster?"

Prudence fiddled with the laces of her shoe. "I came up Saturday evening," she said grudgingly. "Got in about nine. I was going to surprise Mark and spend the weekend with him." She looked at him defiantly. "Is that a crime?"

"No, and I'm not interested in how you spend your time as long as it has nothing to do with the events surrounding your father's death. Did you see your father that night?"

Prudence stared at him as if she thought him mad. "He's the last person I wanted to know I was in town," she said. "He didn't approve of Mark. That's why I didn't come up earlier in the day. I didn't want him or anyone else to see me."

"You were with Mr. Malone all that evening?"

Prudence frowned and pressed her lips together. "Mark wasn't there," she said in a low voice. "I should have let him know I was coming, I suppose, but as I said, I wanted to surprise him. He'd gone to Shrewsbury, and he didn't get back until the middle of Sunday morning."

"He stayed there overnight?"

"He said he'd intended to come back that night, but he'd had a few drinks and didn't want to risk getting caught on the road, so he stayed over with them and came back next morning."

"So you stayed where?"

"At Mark's. I've got a key."

"Is there anyone who saw you there? Any way that we can verify what you've just told me?"

Prudence shook her head impatiently. "Of course there isn't," she told him. "Mark and I had to keep a low profile, so I wasn't going to let anyone know I was there, was I?"

"Is it true that you had promised your father you would stop seeing Mr. Malone?"

"I don't see that as any of your business," the girl flared.

"Your father had warned you of the consequences if you continued seeing Mr. Malone, had he not, Miss Bolen? And yet you continued to see him." Prudence remained silent. "Which some might say," he went on, "would be sufficient reason for killing your father."

Blood drained away from Prudence Bolen's face as Paget pressed on. "You admit sneaking back into Broadminster after dark. You undoubtedly knew where your father would be; Mr. Malone was in Shrewsbury—or so you say. But he could just as easily have been at the Tudor Hotel that night, either with or without you. Tell me, do you have a set of keys for your father's car, Miss Bolen? Was it Malone's idea or yours to take the car from the hotel car-park while your father was having dinner?

"And whose idea was it," he ended quietly, "to set things up so that someone else would take the blame for the murder of your father? Yours? Or Malone's?"

Prudence stared. Her mouth moved but no sound came out.

"And where were you last Tuesday evening?"

Prudence blinked rapidly and swallowed hard. "Tuesday? I don't...I was with Mark earlier on, but he had to make a delivery, so I went over to see a school-friend. I can give you her name if you like. But I don't see..."

"And I will want it," said Paget. "How long were you there, Miss Bolen?"

Prudence looked confused. "I don't know. Till maybe ten o'clock. I don't remember exactly."

Paget picked up the phone and punched in a three-digit number. "I need an interview room," he said when someone answered. "And I'll need a WPC to witness a statement."

KEITH LAMBERT PUT DOWN the phone and smiled to himself. He hadn't expected to hear back from London quite so soon. He had banked on their wanting the future of the Ockrington property resolved as soon as possible, but bureaucrats were not known for making swift decisions, and he had anticipated a wait of several weeks before he heard anything.

It was a man named Hutchinson who called. The name didn't mean anything to Keith, but it soon became apparent that Hutchinson was very familiar with the offer he had presented a week ago, and he made it clear from the outset that the offer was not acceptable.

Not acceptable, he hastened to explain, in its present form. The Minister had expressed concern over the fifteen-year time frame, for example, and the amount of money Lambert had offered to put up was, considering the potential of the property, below expectations.

When Lambert asked what would be acceptable, Hutchinson hedged. It was hard to put an exact figure on it until other factors had been worked out, he explained, but if Lambert was still interested, he felt sure that some sort of compromise could be reached. Would it be convenient for Mr. Lambert to come to London? Say, this Thursday? Ten o'clock? Excellent! Hutchinson gave further directions and rang off.

Lambert, hands locked behind his head, rocked gently back and forth in his chair as he re-ran the conversation in his mind. The very fact that they wanted to talk again told him they were eager—more than eager—to make a deal and get Ockrington off their hands.

And what a deal it would be! If Jim Bolen hadn't been so blinded by his obsession, he might have come up with a more innovative approach himself.

With Bolen out of the picture, it had been a piece of cake. But best of all, Laura was now free, and he couldn't see her spending a lot of time mourning her dear departed husband.

It was simply a matter of time, he told himself. Just a matter of time.

PAGET TOOK PRUDENCE BOLEN down to the interview room himself, but once there he left her under the watchful eye of a WPC and went in search of Tregalles. "She's admitted she was in Broadminster the night her father was killed," he told the sergeant, "and what I want you to do is record her statement and take your time doing it. Under no circumstance allow her to get to a phone. I'm on my way to see her boy-friend, Mark Malone, and I don't want her tipping him off before I have a chance to talk to him. I don't know whether either of them had anything to do with the Bolen killing, but the girl certainly hasn't been losing any sleep over her father's death."

Twenty minutes later, Paget pulled into the car-park in front of the nursery, where he could see at a glance that it had suffered a lot of damage from the storm. Boxes of bruised and battered plants had been dragged to one side, and leaves and twigs had been raked into several piles. Tubs of trees had been tipped on their sides, presumably to allow water to drain out, and two girls were pulling down the tattered remnants of a plastic greenhouse covering.

"He's in the office," one of the girls told Paget when he asked for Malone. "Go through the shop to the back, and you'll find him there."

Malone showed no surprise when Paget struck his head through the open door and introduced himself. It was almost as if he had been expecting the chief inspector. "Have a seat," he said, indicating a decrepit wooden chair. "Will this take long? I have a lot on my plate this morning."

"It rather depends on you," Paget said as he sat down. The chair creaked ominously beneath his weight.

It wasn't hard to see why Prudence Bolen was attracted to Malone. He was an extraordinarily good-looking man, bronzed from working outside, and there wasn't a spare ounce of flesh on his body. He wore a T-shirt, shorts and sandals, and looked to be in excellent physical condition. He had a pleasant face, not rugged, exactly, but his features were well-defined, and there were small lines around his dark-blue eyes that made him look as if he were secretly amused.

"Prudence Bolen tells me that you stayed with friends in Shrewsbury last Saturday evening," said Paget. "Is that true, Mr. Malone?"

"Ah! Yes, of course, that was the night Prudence's father died. Yes, that's right, I did. With Peter and Sheila Trowbridge. Known Peter for years. He and Sheila run Lyndwood."

"So you won't have any objection if we ask him for confirmation?"

A flicker of annoyance crossed Malone's face. "I won't *object*," he said. "Although I do question the need. I can't say I like the idea of having the police asking my friends about me."

"What time did you leave Broadminster?"

"Somewhere between one and two o'clock in the afternoon. I got to Lyndwood Farm about three, I suppose, and spent a couple of hours with Peter sorting through stock and making out orders. His is a wholesale business as well as retail, and I get a lot of my three-to-five-year stock from him."

"Which takes us to about five o'clock. What then?"

Malone allowed his annoyance to show more plainly. "I really don't see the point of all this," he said impatiently, "and to be frank, I resent the implication of these questions."

Paget eyed Malone thoughtfully. "Do you?" he said. "Well, let me put it to you this way, Mr. Malone: Jim Bolen was opposed to the idea of your marrying his daughter. He and Prudence had what has been described as a violent argument over it, which resulted in his threatening to disinherit her if she went through with it. She promised not to see you again, but it was an empty promise, wasn't it? She continued meeting you secretly, and she lied about where she was the night her father was murdered. She lied to me, she lied to her family, and even had her room-mate in Bristol lie for her. In addition to that, she received a panic call from her room-mate here shortly after seven o'clock on Sunday morning, telling her that her father had been killed. Yet Miss Bolen couldn't even be bothered to go home until late in the afternoon, lying once again to account for the delay.

"And by an odd coincidence, the same night Prudence Bolen sneaked back into Broadminster, her father was confronted by someone who stabbed him five times. Does that make the situation clearer, Mr. Malone?"

Malone smiled tightly. "Perfectly," he said. "But it is very hard to be in two places at once, and as I told you, I was in Shrewsbury from three o'clock Saturday afternoon until Sunday morning. I had no idea that Prudence was here until I arrived back around ten, so I'm afraid I can't help you."

"Where were you last Tuesday evening?"

"Tuesday? What...? I don't understand."

"It's not exactly complicated," said Paget. "Where were you last Tuesday evening?"

Malone scratched his head. "What time?"

"Let's say from nine o'clock on."

"I'll have to check my book, but I think that was the night I made a delivery to the Spencers in Clunbridge." Malone dug out a tattered book from among a pile of papers on his desk and thumbed through it. "Yes, here it is. Six blue spruce and eight Katsuras." He showed Paget the entry.

"How long were you out there, and what time did you get back?"

"I left here about seven, and I was out there by half past.

Spencer gave me a hand unloading the trees, and we carried them round to where he intends to plant them. We discussed his plans for other parts of his garden, and then we went inside for a drink.''

"And you left there when?''

"Around ten, I should think, but you can check with Spencer if you like.'' Malone was visibly annoyed. "Look,'' he said, rising to his feet, "I've had enough of this, and I have work to do. In case you hadn't noticed, we had a storm the other day, and I've lost almost half my stock.''

"Yes, I did notice.'' Paget remained seated. "Tell me, are you the owner or the manager here?''

Malone hesitated as if searching for some hidden significance to Paget's question. "I'm the manager,'' he said. "This nursery is part of the Beresford chain. I work for Trevor Beresford. He owns Lyndwood Farm as well.''

"Right,'' said Paget. "In that case, if you'll give me the address and telephone number of Mr. Spencer, as well as that of Mr. And Mrs. Trowbridge, I'll be on my way. But let me know if you intend to leave Broadminster, because I feel quite sure I shall need to talk to you again.''

TWENTY-FIVE

"JOHN, I PHONED TO LET you know I'm driving down to Hereford today to see Bert Cox,'' said Laura. "I telephoned, and he's expecting me. As I told you after the funeral, your Great-Aunt Emily Lambert said Bert Cox was there the day your grandfather fell from the scaffold, and she suggested that I talk to him. I know it won't do any good now, but I'd like to know once and for all what really happened. Your father spent his life blaming Keith for it, and I want to know the truth.''

"How did you find out where he lives?''

"I rang Emily, and she told me that he lives with his daughter in Hereford, a Mrs. Leacock. I rang Mrs. Leacock, and she spoke to her father—he's in a wheelchair now—and he's agreed to see me. She sounds like a nice person; she invited me to lunch.''

''Thanks for letting me know, Mother.'' John Bolen looked at the digital clock on his desk. ''When do you expect to be back?''

''Oh, I don't expect to be all that long. Probably by tea-time. Don't worry, I haven't forgotten that you're bringing Linda's parents over here this evening.''

''Actually, I was about to ring you to tell you they won't be coming,'' said John. ''Linda phoned a few minutes ago to tell me that her father found out last night that he'd made a mistake in the date of the golf tournament he's playing in. He thought it was Thursday, but apparently it's tomorrow, so they are going back today. They came down by train, but since Linda had already arranged to have the week off in order to spend more time with her parents, she's going to take them back by car and stay there until the weekend. It will be a bit of a holiday for her as well. You'll just have to meet them some other time.''

''Oh, dear. I am sorry, John. I should have liked to have met them. I've been meaning to ask how you were getting along with them, but I keep forgetting.''

''Her mum's all right, but I'll tell you, I don't want to hear another word about fly-fishing or golf for a long, long time. Her dad's a nut on both.''

Laura laughed. ''Give my love to Linda, if you are talking to her again before she leaves,'' she told him, ''and wish them all a safe journey for me. Bye, John.''

''Goodbye, Mother. Take care.''

''YOU FOUND US ALL RIGHT, then,'' Emma Leacock greeted Laura as she ushered her into the house. ''Do come through. Dad's in the sunroom at the back. Likes the warmth, does Dad.''

Emma Leacock was a buxom woman of about fifty. She had a round face and a double chin that wobbled when she talked. She led the way to the back of the house, where a small, white-haired man sat dozing in a wheelchair.

''It's Mrs. Bolen, Dad,'' the woman said loudly; then to

Laura, "You have to speak up. He's going deaf but he won't have a hearing aid."

"I heard that, Emma," the old man said, opening his eyes. "I hear a lot more than you think." A broad smile took the sting out of his words. He cocked his head to one side as he looked at Laura. "You were just a lass when I saw you last," he said, "but you haven't changed."

"Now that *is* flattery." Laura smiled. "But I'm afraid I can't recall the occasion."

Bert Cox shook his head. "You wouldn't remember," he told her. "You and Jim hadn't long been married. My, but you were a pretty one. Jim was a lucky lad." The smile left his face. "I heard what happened, and I'm sorry. Don't know what things are coming to these days."

"Sit down, Mrs. Bolen," his daughter said, "and I'll put the kettle on. It's just soup and a few sandwiches, if that's all right?"

"That would be lovely," Laura said, "but you needn't have bothered, really."

"It's no trouble," Emma told her. "It's not often anyone comes to see Dad these days, so it's a bit of an occasion." She disappeared inside.

The old man eyed Laura shrewdly. "And what brings you all this way to talk to an old cripple like me?" he asked.

Laura met his gaze. "Accident?" she asked.

"Osteo," he said. "Lifted too many bricks in my time and I'm paying for it now."

Laura nodded sympathetically. "The reason I came down," she said, "was to ask you about the day Jim's father died. Emily Lambert told me at the funeral that you were there that day, and it was she who suggested that I talk to you."

Bert Cox looked off into the distance. "Jack Bolen," he mused. "I thought it might have something to do with that."

"Were you there? Did you see what happened?"

"Oh, I was there all right," Cox said, "and it happened more or less the way they said at the inquest."

"More or less?"

Cox used his elbows to ease himself up in the wheelchair. A

stab of pain made him wince. "Let me help," said Laura, half-rising from her chair.

"No, thanks just the same, but it's best if I do it," he told her, shaking his head. "Ah, that's better." The tense muscles in his face relaxed as he turned his attention once more to Laura.

"It was an accident," he said slowly, "but it was Jack's own fault. He was always playing silly buggers, was Jack, if you'll pardon my French. Always showing off, and the biggest slacker we ever had. If his name hadn't been Jack Bolen, he'd never have got on in the first place."

Laura looked puzzled. "I don't understand," she said. "According to Jim, his father was one of the best workers Lambert ever had. He always claimed that the inquest was a farce, and he was convinced that it was Keith Lambert who was responsible for Jack's death."

Cox waved a dismissive hand. "And who do you think fed Jim that load of rubbish?" he demanded. "Jack himself, that's who. And Jim's mum, my sister Mary. She thought the sun shone out of Jack's backside, and nobody could tell her different."

He shook his head. "No, take it from me, Jack was a no-good layabout who'd run a mile before he'd put in a decent day's work. But talk? By God, he could talk! And it was always about himself. He thought he was cleverer than anyone else, but he wasn't so clever that day, I can tell you, and if you ask me he got what he deserved!"

Laura sat back, shocked at the vehemence of the old man's words. She'd never known Jim's father; everything she'd ever heard about him had come from Jim. Even Harry had never really talked about his father.

Bert Cox leaned forward in his chair, anxious now to have her understand. "See, young Keith was working up there on the scaffold with Jack that day. Old Sam, Keith's dad, wanted the lad to get to know the building trade from the ground up, so he had him labouring. But Keith was deathly scared of heights, and Jack knew it. He was a mean bastard, was Jack. He made that kid's life miserable. But I'll give Keith his due; he could have complained to his father, and Jack would have had his cards. But he didn't. He stuck it out.

"But this particular day, Jack was showing off and daring Keith to do the same. Jack would hold on to one of the metal uprights of the scaffold—like pipes they were—then swing himself out into space, holding on with just one hand, and land back on the platform again. It's not all that hard to do, and some of the lads would do it if they saw some bit of skirt watching them from down below. But Jack would dare Keith to do it, and call him a coward if he didn't.''

The old man sat back in the chair. "But Jack did it once too often. He swung out all right, but lost his grip and that was it. Fell straight down and broke his back on a pile of bricks. Keith was nowhere near him.''

Laura closed her eyes. She found it almost impossible to believe that Bert Cox could be talking about the same man whose memory her husband had revered all his life. Yet what would the old man have to gain by lying? And why had he not said something at the time? She put the question to him.

"It seemed like the best thing to do at the time," he said soberly. "Jack's wife, my sister Mary, wasn't well; we didn't know it at the time but she was dying of leukemia, and she wouldn't have believed it if I had told her how it happened. Neither would young Jim. And then there was Jack's sister, Emily. It was she who persuaded Sam Lambert to take her brother on, and it was mainly due to her that he stayed on. She was there when I told Sam what I saw, but she told me to keep it to myself; she said the family had suffered enough, and there was no need to show Jack up for what he was now that he was dead. So I stayed out of it. I was never called as a witness, so it went down as an accidental death, which it was.''

Bert Cox wheeled his chair forward and put his hand on Laura's arm. "I'm sorry if I've upset you," he said softly. "I didn't mean to, but you did ask me. And my keeping out of it never did any harm. Like I said, it was an accident.''

Never did any harm. Laura didn't know whether to laugh or cry. Never did any harm, indeed! All those years of hatred. All those years...

The only reason I married you was to get my own back on Keith.

Jim had hurt her in so many different ways over the years, but with those words he had killed the last remnants of her love for him. So many wasted years.

"Ah, here we are, then," said Emma Leacock as she came bustling in. "Everybody ready for lunch, then, after your nice chat?"

DRIVING HOME THAT EVENING, Paget couldn't get the image of Simone's distorted features out of his mind. Had she known, he wondered, where Julia Rutledge had gone? Even more importantly, had she told her killer? It was one thing to lie to the police, but it was quite another to remain silent when you were fighting for your life.

The results of the PM had come in that afternoon. Asphyxia by ligature, Martindale had said in his precise way. Her windpipe had been crushed beneath the pressure of a heavy-gauge yellow nylon rope, fibres of which had been found embedded in her neck. There were cuts on her face, and deep scratches on her neck where she'd tried to get her fingers under the rope. Two fingernails were broken, and there were traces of her own skin and blood beneath the rest. There were bruises on her legs, which could have been made as she struggled to free herself, but there was nothing to indicate she had been tied up.

Martindale went on to say he'd found traces of short blue fibres in Simone's hair, neck, and clothing, which suggested to him that Simone had been strangled while sitting in a car, and the fibres were from the upholstery. There were bruises on the back of her head, which could have come from contact with a head-rest, and the bruises on her shins were consistent with what he'd expect to find if someone was thrashing about in the front seat of a car.

With any luck at all, thought Paget, Forensic would be able to identify the fibres, perhaps identify the fabric itself, and if they were *really* lucky, match it to a particular make of car. Charlie's people had found two sets of tyre tracks next to the gate, but neither they nor the upholstery fibre would be of any value unless they found the car itself. As for where the body was found, the location had probably been chosen because of its isolation and proximity to town, but Paget had told Ormside to find out who owned the cottage and whether there was any connection—no matter how remote—to any of the suspects in Jim Bolen's murder.

Estimating the time of death had been tricky, Martindale said, but in his opinion, Simone had died between ten o'clock on Tuesday evening, which was when she was last seen by her friends, and one o'clock Wednesday morning. Tomorrow, Tregalles would be checking on the whereabouts of everyone connected to the case, as well as looking at their cars, but Paget was very much afraid that unless they found Julia Rutledge very soon, she, too, would become a victim.

Dark clouds had been creeping in all afternoon, and it began to rain as he entered Ashton Prior. A sudden gust of wind blew leaves across the windscreen, and it reminded him of the storm on Saturday, and the wild ride home in Grace's car.

He'd enjoyed their time together. It was as if her presence in the house had made it come alive, and even though she had been there such a short time, he was going to remember her cheerful smile and gentle laugh, to say nothing of the pleasant conversation.

He recalled Grace's invitation to join the hiking group, and the more he thought about it the more the idea of exploring the countryside with her group appealed to him. Perhaps Andrea would enjoy it, too. He'd have to ask her.

He arrived at the house and went inside. It sounded hollow and empty again, not at all the way it had sounded when he and Grace had stumbled inside, soaking wet and chilled to the bone. He shrugged off his coat and began to climb the stairs, then abruptly changed his mind and came back down again.

He picked up the phone and punched in Andrea's number.

Andrea answered on the first ring. "Neil. What a nice surprise. I got your message and I've been meaning to ring you back, but we've been rushed off our feet since the storm and I've hardly had a minute to myself. How are you after your horrible trip back?"

"Fine, thanks," he told her, "now that I've had a chance to dry out. How was the parade?"

"It went off very well, but we were lucky the storm didn't hit until after it was all over. Unfortunately, all the afternoon events were washed out, but that's the way it goes some years."

"What are you doing next Saturday?"

The question came out without conscious thought, and it seemed to catch Andrea by surprise. There was a pause, then, "Morning, afternoon, or evening?" she asked.

"Well, depending on your schedule, any of the above, but I was wondering if you would like to go out to dinner?"

"That sounds wonderful, but I'll have to make sure that Mrs. Ansell's free. Can I get back to you?"

"Of course."

"Good. I'll call you, then."

"Fine." Paget was about to say goodbye, when a thought occurred to him. "Tell me," he said, "do you like hiking, Andrea? Tramping the hills? That sort of thing?"

Andrea gave a short laugh. "Much rather go on horseback," she told him. "Why?"

"Oh, no reason," he told her. "Just happened to be thinking about it today, that's all."

"I'M SORRY, BUT WE'LL BE closing in fifteen minutes," the woman warned. The man had been there for more than an hour, studying books and making notes, but now he seemed lost in thought.

He looked at her and smiled. "That's all right," he told her pleasantly, "I think I have all I need." He began to gather up the books around him and was about to pick them up, when the librarian stopped him. "Just leave them there," she told him. "We like to put them back ourselves."

He nodded his thanks and bade the woman good night.

Parkinson Arm, indeed! Had Simone deliberately tried to mislead him? Not that it mattered now. There was no doubt in his mind that he had found what he wanted. And he felt quite sure Simone had given him the woman's right name. She'd had no time to make one up; he'd seen to that.

Joanna.

Tomorrow, he promised himself as he left the library. Now that he was on the right track, the sooner he followed it up, the better.

THE LIBRARIAN BEGAN to pick up the books, pausing for a moment to look at the titles. Waterways of England: A History of Canals; From Horse-drawn Barge to Narrow-boat, Public Houses of Great Britain; Cotswold Country; and one of their older copies of the Ordinance Survey Atlas of Great Britain. It was nice to see someone taking an interest in such subjects. She hoped the man had found what he was looking for.

TWENTY-SIX

Tuesday, 3 October

AS PAGET DROVE NORTH on the A49, there was evidence everywhere of the damage done by Saturday's storm. Gaping white wounds where huge limbs had been torn from trees, water lying in the fields, and the road littered with debris. Work crews, repairing damage to a washed-out culvert, held him up for twenty minutes, so it was after ten by the time he found Lyndwood Farm on the outskirts of Shrewsbury.

Peter Trowbridge was working on a stuck ventilator in one of the greenhouses. He was a small man, slim and wiry, with a weathered face that made it hard to judge his age. He could have been anything from thirty-five to fifty.

"Chief Inspector, eh?" he said when Paget introduced himself. "From Broadminster. Sounds serious," he added with a nervous laugh. "What am I supposed to have done?"

"Nothing, as far as I'm aware," said Paget. "I'm here because Mark Malone gave me your name. You're a friend of his, I understand?"

Trowbridge frowned. "Mark? Yes, I know Mark. Why? Is he in trouble?"

Before Paget could reply, a slim-sharp-featured woman carrying a hanging basket of bedraggled, half-dead flowers, came through the door. "Ah, there you are, Peter," she said, "what do you want doing with these?" She flashed Paget a smile and said, "Sorry to interrupt, but I do need to know. There are six more baskets like this one, and we can't possibly sell them."

"Take them round the back and leave them, Sheila," Trowbridge told her. "I'll see to them later."

The woman began to turn away, but Paget stopped her. "Excuse me, but are you Mrs. Trowbridge?"

She turned back and looked at him, frowning slightly. "Yes?" The answer was a question as she looked from Paget to her husband and back again.

"This is *Chief Inspector* Paget from…Broadminster," said Trowbridge, emphasizing Paget's title. "But there's no need for you to stay, Sheila. I can take care of it."

"No, please stay," said Paget. "I'm going to have to talk to both of you in any case, so this will save time in the long run." He turned back to Peter Trowbridge. "Can you confirm that Mr. Malone stayed with you the night of Saturday, September twenty-third?"

But before the man could answer, his wife spoke up. "What's this all about?" she asked sharply. "What has this got to do with the police?" She set the basket on the ground and folded her arms.

"We are investigating the murder of James Bolen on that night," Paget told her, "and Mr. Malone is helping us with our enquiries."

"Helping you with your enquiries?" The woman's eyes narrowed as she looked past Paget at her husband. "You told me this had to do with Ronnie and some other girl who'd turned up unexpectedly," she said. "But this sounds serious, and I don't intend to lie for him if he's involved in murder, even if he is your friend."

"He's not up for murder," her husband snapped, then looked at Paget. "Is he?"

But Paget avoided the question. "Am I to take it that Mark Malone was *not* here on that night?"

Sheila gave an emphatic shake of her head. "He left here about seven. He said he had to get back to his precious Ronnie. Then he phoned Peter the next day to ask him to back him up if some girl should ring to find out if he'd stayed here overnight. Said he was in a bit of a bind with one of his women, and he'd had to say he'd stayed here with us that night. I didn't want any part of it, but Peter has known Mark for a long time and said he couldn't see the harm." The woman snorted as she gave her husband a withering look. "And now it turns out he's mixed up in murder," she ended. She picked up the basket and was about to leave, but Paget stopped her.

"Just one more question, Mrs. Trowbridge, before you go. Tell me, who is Ronnie?"

"Be with you in a minute," said Malone. "I want to get these trees moved first."

"Leave them," Paget told him brusquely. "I've wasted enough time because of your lies, Malone, and unless I get some straight answers from you now, you could be facing charges of obstruction."

Malone scowled and wiped his hands on a rag. "I'll be in the office if anyone is looking for me," he called to one of the girls. He led the way into the office and closed the door. "All right," he said, "what is it this time?"

"Where were you the night Jim Bolen was killed?" Paget demanded. "And I must warn you I've just come back from Shrewsbury, where your friends state categorically that you did not stay with them that night, but returned to Broadminster in the early evening."

Malone grimaced. "Seems like you can't trust anyone these days," he observed. "Not even your friends."

Paget waited.

Malone sat down behind the desk and leaned back in his chair. "What else could I do?" he asked. "I'd already told Prudence that I was in Shrewsbury, so I couldn't change my story when you came round, now could I?"

Paget grunted. "You could have saved me and yourself a lot of trouble if you'd told the truth," he snapped. "I really don't care what you told Miss Bolen. So, were you with Veronica Beresford, as your friends say?"

"Bastards!" Malone said softly. "I'll bet it was Sheila who told you, wasn't it?" Paget remained silent, and Malone heaved a sigh of resignation. "Yes, I was with Ronnie," he said. "Trevor was away, so I went over there when I got back from Shrewsbury, and stayed the night. I had a hell of a shock when I came back next morning and found Prudence had been in the house all night. I had to think of something, so I told her I'd just driven down from Shrewsbury."

"What time did you get to the Beresford house?"

"Somewhere around nine; I can't be sure exactly."

"And you remained there? You didn't go out again?"

Malone seemed to be amused by the question. "Why should we?" he asked. "We had everything we needed right there."

"And Mrs. Beresford will swear to that, will she?"

"As long as you don't ask her in front of Trevor, she will, yes."

Paget eyed him for a long moment before opening the door. "We'll see," he said grimly, "and if you're lying to me this time, I don't think you'll find it quite so amusing."

"HARRY SHOULD BE HOME any minute now," said Dee nervously as she looked at her watch again. "He told me this morning that he wouldn't be late back. Would you like more tea, Sergeant?"

"Perhaps half a cup," Tregalles told her.

"And a piece more cherry cake?"

"It's very good," Tregalles said as he took another piece. "Is it your own recipe, Mrs. Bolen?"

"Well, no, not exactly, but I do put just a touch of lemon in mine. I think it adds a little something, don't you?"

"It does indeed," Tregalles agreed.

The sound of tyres crunching on the gravel drive announced the arrival of Harry Bolen. Tregalles could see him through the window, getting out of the same Isuzu Trooper he had seen outside Laura Bolen's house the week before. Harry paused to look at Tregalles's car, then disappeared from view.

"He comes in the back," Dee explained. "Takes his boots off and has a bit of a wash before he comes through. He'll only be a couple of minutes. I'll tell him you're here."

Dee hurried from the room, and Tregalles sat back in the chair, enjoying his second generous slice of cake.

Thankfully, this was the last call of the day. He hoped that Harry Bolen was in a better mood than his nephew, John, had been, or, for that matter, Keith Lambert. Both of them had resented the implication that they might have had something to do with the death of a prostitute last Tuesday night. Understandable if both were innocent. Laura Bolen, on the other hand, had shown almost no emotion, seemingly disinterested in why he was asking questions, and answering them with an air of weary resignation.

The trouble was, thought Tregalles, he couldn't see that he was any farther ahead. John Bolen said he'd been at his mother's house until roughly eight o'clock, and then had gone round to see his fiancée. "It had been a long day, and I was tired," he told the sergeant, "so I left Linda's about ten-thirty and went straight home and went to bed."

Keith Lambert said he'd had dinner at home with his mother, after which his mother retired early while he spent the rest of the evening working before going to bed himself around midnight. "So if you're looking for an alibi, Sergeant," he'd concluded, "I'm afraid you're out of luck." As for Laura Bolen, she said she'd gone to bed shortly after John had left the house.

And when he'd checked their cars, none of them had blue upholstery.

Tregalles set his cup aside and stood up as Harry Bolen entered the room.

"Sergeant...Tregalles, is it?" he said. "What brings you here?"

"Just one or two questions, Mr. Bolen. Shouldn't take long."

"Might as well sit down anyway," said Harry hospitably as he dropped into a deep armchair. "Rough day. Too much work and not enough time." He draped one stockinged foot across his other knee, and rested his head against the plump cushioned back of the chair.

"Can you tell me where you were last Tuesday evening?" the sergeant said as he sat down again. "From, say, nine o'clock on?"

Harry frowned and looked up at the ceiling as if searching for an answer there. "Tuesday?" he repeated slowly. "Why the devil do you want to know that?"

"A young woman was picked up that evening and killed later that night, and we believe there may be a connection between her death and that of your brother."

Harry brought his gaze down from the ceiling and regarded Tregalles levelly. "And you think that *I* had something to do with it?" he asked softly. Tregalles didn't answer. Harry shook his head from side to side as if to say he couldn't believe what he was hearing, then gave a sigh of resignation. "All right," he said, "Tuesday. I was down at the office that night, as I was most nights last week."

"How long were you there, sir?"

"Seven till about eleven or twelve." Harry shrugged. "Something like that." His brow creased in concentration. "I think Dee was still awake when I came in; you can ask her if you like."

"Was there anyone in the office with you?"

"No."

"No cleaners who might have seen you? Anything like that?"

"No."

"Do you have any sort of sign-in log when you go in after hours? Any security people?"

"No. I told you, I was alone."

"I see."

"What does that mean—'I see'?"

Tregalles drew in his breath. "Well, it does make it a bit difficult to verify what you've told me, doesn't it, sir? Did you speak to anyone on the telephone? Take any calls while you were there?"

"No."

"Do you have another car, beside the Trooper?"

"The Trooper belongs to the firm," Harry said tersely. "My own car is a Granada, but I don't see what that—"

"The colour, sir? Inside and out?"

The muscles around Harry Bolen's mouth tightened. "Are you trying to wind me up, Sergeant?" he asked bluntly.

"No, sir. There are good reasons for my questions."

"But you don't intend telling me what they are. Is that it, Sergeant?"

"Something like that," Tregalles said. "The colours, sir?"

"The Granada is a creamy brown or beige, whatever you like to call it, and the seats are tan."

"Thank you, sir." Tregalles jotted a note in his book. "Does your wife have a car?"

Harry snorted. "Oh, my God! What the hell has Dee's car got to do with anything?" he demanded.

"If you would just tell me the make and colour of her car, sir, I'll be on my way."

"It's a Fiesta; blue outside and blue inside," Harry said testily. "Now, is that it?" He rose to his feet.

"Just one more thing," said Tregalles as he put away his notebook and stood up. "Could I take a look at your wife's car, sir?"

PAGET WAS STILL IN THE OFFICE when Tregalles reported in. "Run that by me one more time," he said.

"Mrs. Harry Bolen's car has blue seats, and there are several lengths of yellow nylon rope in the boot. Mr. Bolen tells me the rope is in common use around the works yard, and I found more of it in the Trooper he normally drives at work. But he can offer no proof of where he was last Tuesday evening, and when I asked his wife if she could verify what time he came in, and where she was that night, she burst into tears and refused to talk to me. I'd say it's at least worth a look, sir."

"Right. Are they prepared to allow the car to be examined, or will it require a warrant?"

"In Harry Bolen's words, sir, I can do what I bloody well like with the friggin' car if it will get me off his back."

"In that case, stay there until someone comes to bring it in.

Oh, yes, and while I think of it, I checked Malone's car while I was out there. It's a green Escort with vinyl seats.''

"Good. Saves me a trip tomorrow. Thanks. Now, what about Mr. and Mrs. Bolen? Would you like them in for questioning as well?''

"Do you have anything other than the car and the rope?''

"No, not really, but I have the distinct feeling that he's not telling me everything.''

Paget hesitated. "Let's wait until we get the results back from Forensic. Then we'll see.''

It was nine-thirty when he drove into the car-park outside the pub. There were two overhead lights near the entrance, but he made for the far end where trees blocked the light and the shadows were deepest. He got out and walked slowly past the lighted windows, scanning the rooms within. He looked into the lounge, then moved on to where he could see the bar. That was where she'd be, assuming Simone had told him the truth, and he was sure she had. He'd told her he'd cut her face if he thought she was lying.

He took his time, looking at every car to make sure no one was watching before taking a telephone from his pocket and flipping it open. He checked the number he'd taken from the book in the library and dialled. One of the windows was ajar, and he could hear the phone behind the bar ringing above the general murmur of voices. He watched as a stocky, heavy-set man picked it up.

"Invisible Man," he announced brusquely.

"I'd like to speak to Joanna."

"Hold on."

So, Simone hadn't lied to him. Good!

The man moved along the bar to where a woman was serving. She was a big woman, dark, attractive. The man said something to her, and she nodded. She walked to the end of the bar and picked up the phone. "Hello? Who's this?" she said.

He flipped the phone down and slipped it into his pocket. Now that he knew what she looked like, he would wait for her to leave. If his sense of direction was right, the canal should be behind the pub, which meant that Joanna would probably leave by the back door. He looked at his watch again. Plenty of time to have a look round before closing time.

He circled the pub. A path led toward the trees, but he decided against further explanations until later. He returned to the car, where he waited and watched as people began to leave in ones and twos. He checked the time; still a good half hour till closing time. It was starting to rain.

He left the car and took another look through the window to make sure that Joanna was still there. The bar was almost empty, and she was gathering up glasses and emptying ashtrays. A young woman entered through a door at the back, her face hidden by the hood of a plastic mac. She took it off and shook it out, then looked round for somewhere to hang it.

"Over there," he heard Joanna say, pointing to a hook behind the door. She looked at the clock over the bar. "You're early, Vikki," she observed. "Trying to impress George, are you?"

Vikki! He sucked in his breath. He hadn't recognized her at first. She looked different with dark hair. Healthier, too; not at all like the girl he'd approached in Cresswell Street, and nothing like the way she'd looked when he had last seen her, bruised and bloodied by his fists. And unconscious—or so he had believed at the time.

He felt a twinge of regret, but brushed it aside. After all, it was the girl's own fault. If she had played the part he had planned for her, none of this would have happened.

He returned to the car. Time to move to a less conspicuous place; time to get ready. He drove out of the car-park. He didn't want to be the last to leave and have someone remember the car.

TWENTY-SEVEN

Wednesday, 4 October

RUTHERFORD HILL was considered the highest point in Broadminster, although strictly speaking it lay just beyond the southwest boundary of the town. The highest point, not only topographically, but socially, for this was where the people with *real* money lived. Originally owned by the Rutherfords for more than two hundred years, the land had gradually slipped into the public domain as the Rutherford fortunes declined. Now, winding tree-lined streets connected the modern equivalent of country estates, their manicured lawns and floral gardens screened from public view by walls of brick or stone.

Sunlight filtered through an arch of trees, dappling the roads as Paget made his way to Lansdowne Lane. Leaves and small branches brought down by the storm on the weekend had been swept to one side and lay in neat piles ready to be taken away.

Number 700 Lansdowne. Open gates and a wide curving drive that led to the house: mock Tudor, two storeys, gabled roof-line. It was charming in its way, with its leaded windows, beneath which stood white-painted tubs brimming with late-blooming flowers against a background of dark timbers. Even the window-boxes outside the upstairs windows overflowed with flowers and trailing vines.

But it was too set, a bit too much. What was the word Jill used to use? *Twee,* that was it. It reminded Paget of a country pub rather than a country house, and the home of the Beresfords.

Veronica Beresford was expecting him and answered the door herself. She greeted him pleasantly enough, but her manner was somewhat distant and aloof. She was a beautiful woman, elegant, suave, and stylish, and at least twenty years younger than her husband, who, Paget knew, having looked him up, was well over fifty.

"Please come through," she told him, and led the way across a tiled floor to a spacious living-room. "Do sit down." She waved a hand in the general direction of an armchair, then seated herself in a chair facing him and crossed her elegant legs.

"I must say you were rather mysterious on the telephone this morning," she said. "I can't think what I might have done that deserves the attention of a chief inspector."

"I'll try to be brief and not take up too much of your time," he told her. "Do you know a man by the name of Mark Malone?"

"Mark Malone?" Veronica Beresford seemed surprised by the question. "Yes, I do," she said slowly. "He is the manager of the Country Garden Nursery in Broadminster. Why do you ask? Perhaps you should be speaking to my husband."

"No, it is you I have come to see," said Paget, "because it is your name he gave me when I asked him if anyone could vouch for his whereabouts on the night of September twenty-third."

Veronica frowned. "He gave *my* name?" she said in a puzzled voice. "Let's see, when was the twenty-third?"

"A week ago last Saturday." Paget watched the woman closely, but it was impossible to tell whether she was genuinely puzzled or not. "It was the night James Bolen was killed at the Tudor Hotel," he added.

"Oh, yes. That was terrible, wasn't it? We knew the Bolens, well, not *knew* them, exactly, if you know what I mean, but they have done quite a lot of work for my husband, and they came to the house several times when we were thinking of adding a new wing. It was such a shock to read of something like that happening here in Broadminster. Have you caught whoever did it? I'm afraid I don't always keep up with the local news."

Veronica Beresford reached for a small box on the low table beside her and took out a cigarette. She raised a delicate eyebrow in Paget's direction, but he shook his head. "I keep promising myself I'll give it up," she sighed, "but I do enjoy smoking." She lit the cigarette and blew a stream of smoke toward the ceiling. "Now, what's this about Mr. Malone and that Saturday evening?" she asked.

"I don't know that there is any delicate way of putting this," said Paget, "but Mark Malone claims he spent the night here with you. All night."

Veronica Beresford became very still, and her eyes were suddenly cold, like chips of ice. "Is this some sort of joke, Chief Inspector?" she asked. "Because if it is, I fail to see the point, and I am most certainly not amused."

"Believe me, Mrs. Beresford, it is not a joke," said Paget.

"Mark Malone claims that you and he have been having an affair for the past year, and he has stated categorically that he spent the night of September twenty-third here in this house with you. What I would like is a brief statement from you confirming or denying what he told me. I should point out that I am investigating a murder, and I am not the least bit interested in the private lives of anyone, unless directly connected to the investigation, so you won't be compromised in any way."

"Compromised?" Veronica Beresford's eyes glittered. "I've never been so insulted in my life!" she flared. "Mr. Malone said that?" She drew on her cigarette. "I hardly know the man, and I must say I'm surprised at you, Chief Inspector, for giving credence to such a statement."

"In view of what you are telling me, Mrs. Beresford, can you think of any reason why he would invent such a story?"

"I have absolutely no idea," she said. "What's he accused of, anyway? Surely not the murder of this man, Bolen?"

"All I can tell you, Mrs. Beresford, is that he needs an alibi for the time in question, and my impression is that he feels confident you will provide him with that alibi." He paused. "This may sound impertinent in the light of what you've said, but would you mind telling me where *you* were that night?"

Veronica Beresford stubbed out her cigarette in an ashtray. "Yes, it does sound impertinent," she agreed, "and while I can appreciate your position, Chief Inspector, I hope you can appreciate mine. I have no idea what possessed this man to give you my name, but if you must know, I was here with my husband by my side that night, and I can assure you that when he hears of this, Mr. Malone will be facing some very serious charges."

Veronica Beresford rose to her feet, signalling an end to their discussion, and Paget followed suit. As he moved toward the door, he said, "Tell me, Mrs. Beresford, to your knowledge, has Malone ever been inside this house?"

She started to say no, then paused. "Yes, he has," she said. "When he did the flower-boxes outside the windows, I remember him asking if he could plant those outside the upstairs windows from inside the room, rather than going up and down the ladder. I was a bit doubtful about it, but he promised not to make a mess, and I must say he did a very good job. He put plastic sheets down and cleaned up afterward.''

Her voice changed. "But to tell you that he spent..." Words appeared to fail her, and she was grim-faced as she opened the door.

"Thank you, Mrs. Beresford. Sorry to have troubled you," said Paget, "but I must warn you that unless Mr. Malone withdraws his statement, I shall need a statement from you."

"I don't see why I should have to become involved at all," she said indignantly.

"I can understand your reluctance, but I'm afraid it will be necessary. Someone will ring you to arrange a time. Good day, and thank you again."

When Paget had gone, Veronica Beresford turned and leaned against the door and closed her eyes. She heard a sound and opened them to see her husband standing there.

"Ten out of ten, my dear," said Trevor Beresford. "One of your best performances. But I did warn you that Malone could be trouble."

Veronica went to her husband and kissed him. "Sorry," she said softly, "but I had no idea he was going to become mixed up with anything so sordid as murder." She sighed. "If only he hadn't been so set on marrying into a family with money. I wonder what he will do now?"

Trevor Beresford slipped his arm around his wife. "I've no idea," he said, "but if he knows what's good for him, he will have to change his story."

"You don't think he will do anything foolish, do you, Trevor?"

Her husband shook his head. "I'll get on to our solicitor and ask him to have a quiet word. I think Malone will see reason." He frowned and pursed his lips. "Unless, of course, they charge him with the murder," he said thoughtfully. "I suppose you're quite sure there is nothing at his place to show that you were ever there?"

Veronica smiled and shook her head. "Nothing," she said. "There never is, is there? You know that."

He returned her smile. "Pity we have to lose him, though,"

he said wistfully. "He is so wonderfully photogenic, and so ath-
letic."

Veronica Beresford stepped back a pace and looked at her
husband. "But no gentleman," she said. "I think I shall have
to do something about that. An anonymous gift to his girl-friend,
perhaps? What do you think, Trevor?"

He nodded. "The very thing," he agreed with mock serious-
ness. "It will be your good deed for the day."

"FORENSIC SAYS ALL RESULTS are negative on Mrs. Bolen's car,
with the possible exception of the rope," said Sergeant Ormside.
"The fibres from the upholstery are not the same as those found
on Simone's clothing and in her hair, and the tyres do not match
the impressions taken at the scene. There is nothing to indicate
that a struggle took place in the car, and the rope matches only
in the sense that it comes from the same manufacturer. As well,
there are no finger- or palm prints matching those of the de-
ceased. As far as they are concerned, the car can be returned to
its owner.

"The only good news, if you can call it that, is that the fibres
taken from Simone's hair and clothing have been identified.
They come from a blended fabric that was used extensively by
car manufacturers five to eight years ago, and they've attached
a list. Unfortunately, it's a very long list, and most likely incom-
plete. It's probably a waste of time, but since we've got bugger
all else to go on, I'm having a couple of people go over the list
to see if they can find anything that might tie in with one of the
suspects."

Still puzzled over the disparity between the stories of Malone
and Mrs. Beresford, Paget nodded distractedly. He simply could
not understand why Malone would name Veronica Beresford as
his bed partner if he knew she would deny it. And deny it she
had! In spades.

"I want Malone brought in for further questioning," he said
abruptly. "Someone has a hell of a lot of explaining to do."

Ormside looked hard at Paget, but the chief inspector appeared
to be lost in thought. "Right," he said, and wondered if Paget
had heard anything he'd just told him.

"WHY DIDN'T YOU TELL us this before?" Ormside demanded of the uniformed constable before him. "You must have known we were looking for information on Vikki Lane?"

"Nobody told me, Sarge," the man protested. "See, me and Steve Roper did a switch that night, so his name was still on the roster. I just happened to hear that one of your blokes had been asking."

"You were on duty the night the girl was brought in?"

"That's right. And I checked on her by the book throughout the night."

"That's not what I'm after," Ormside said impatiently. "What I want to know is: Did she talk to you? Did she say anything that might help us find her? Mention a name, a place, anything? Was she friendly with anyone in there? Do you remember her saying anything at all that might give us a clue to where she's gone?"

The man scratched his head. "She didn't talk to me," he said. "She was sort of scared, like she'd never been in before. But I remember her and this older woman talking half the night. Every time I looked in, they were nattering away nineteen to the dozen."

"What woman was this? A regular?"

"No. She was in on suspicion of attempting to steal a horse, but the charge was dropped in the morning."

"A horse...?" Ormside echoed, then waved the question aside. He didn't want to know. "Did you hear any of their conversation?"

The constable shrugged. "You know how it is, Sarge. You go in, check, and leave again. I don't spend any more time in there than I have to. Too many other things to do."

"You have this woman's name? The one Vikki was talking to?"

"Not with me, Sarge, but I could get it, if that's what you want."

"It's what I want," said Ormside, "and while you're at it, I want her address, and anything else you have on file about her. And I want it now!"

TWENTY-EIGHT

PAGET AND TREGALLES spent more than two hours in the inter-
rogation room with Malone, but they couldn't shake him; he
insisted that he and Veronica Beresford had been seeing each
other regularly for more than a year. He said she had been to
his place on two or three occasions, but she preferred him to
come to her when her husband was away overnight, which, according to Malone, was quite often.

When challenged to produce evidence of the liaison, he
couldn't. He insisted that in all that time they had never once
appeared together in public. He claimed they had never gone out
for a meal together, even in a distant town or city where neither
of them were known.

"If what you say is true," Tregalles said, "and Mrs. Beresford
did visit your house from time to time, there must be some
evidence: clothing, toiletries, make-up. Can you show us anything like that?"

Malone ran his hands through his hair in frustration. "There's
nothing!" he insisted. "I told you, Ronnie was only in my place
a few times, and she never stayed long. There was no need for
her to leave anything behind."

"So you're saying she lied to me?" said Paget. "Why would
she do that if the two of you were as close as you claim?"

Malone shook his head. "She must be afraid that Trevor will
find out. That's all I can think of. Let me talk to her. Let me
explain how important it is."

"How do you explain the fact that Mrs. Beresford says her
husband was at home that night? And why would she say she
had every intention of telling her husband about your allega-
tions? She even suggested that she would urge him to take legal
action against you."

"No. She wouldn't do that to me," Malone declared. "She

must have panicked when you went to see her. Said the first thing that came into her head. Let me talk to her. Please.''

''And all this time you say you were sleeping with Mrs. Beresford, you were preparing to marry Prudence Bolen,'' said Tregalles. ''Were you sleeping with her as well?''

''So what if I was?''

''And lying to her about where you'd been?''

Malone remained silent.

''As you're lying now.''

''No! I'm telling you the truth!''

''The hell you are!'' Tregalles snorted. ''Jim Bolen stood in the way of your marrying into a rich family. Whose idea was it to kill him? Yours or his daughter's? Was it she who supplied you with the keys to the Jag? Was it she who told you about her father having prostitutes up to his room? Was it your idea to pick up that young kid off the street and make it look as if she killed Bolen in a bedroom brawl?''

''I don't know what you're talking about,'' Malone said desperately. ''I've told you the truth! Look, I can describe the bedroom. I can tell you the colour of the duvet, the sheets, the pictures on the wall. I know Ronnie's bedroom like the back of my hand.''

''Which you saw when you did the window-boxes,'' said Paget.

''Not in detail,'' Malone shot back. ''I can tell you things I couldn't possibly have seen in the short time I was in there doing the flowers. I'll write them down, and you can check it out.''

''Tuesday night,'' said Paget. ''September twenty-sixth. You told me you left the Spencer house at ten o'clock, after delivering a load of trees. Mrs. Spencer swears it wasn't any later than half past nine.''

Malone shrugged wearily. ''So?''

''So Simone was picked up sometime after ten. Where were you from ten o'clock on?''

''I went straight home and went to bed, and I don't know anybody called Simone.''

''Who was with you that night, Malone? Prudence Bolen or Mrs. Beresford?''

Malone's glare was malignant. "I was alone," he grated.

"Whose car did you use that night?"

"I wasn't using the car. I had the truck, remember."

And so it went on, with Malone clinging stubbornly to his story. He insisted on being allowed to write down everything he could remember, including Ronnie Beresford's tastes in night attire and lingerie.

They left him exhausted in the interview room, watched over by a uniformed constable. "What do you think?" asked Paget as he and Tregalles made their way back to the Incident Room.

Tregalles scratched his head. "The thing that bothers me the most is why he would invent such a story. It seems to me that he must have had *something* going with Mrs. Beresford, if not lately, possibly in the past. Maybe she *is* scared her husband will find out, and she lied to you."

"If she did, she did a damned good job of it," said Paget. "She seemed shocked by the suggestion that she and Malone were having an affair; she gave every indication that she would tell her husband, and she couldn't seem to understand what possessed Malone to tell such a story."

"So one of them has to be lying," Tregalles concluded, "but which one?"

LAURA BOLEN WAS tight-lipped as she put the phone down. So, the police had returned Dee's car without a word of explanation. What had they hoped to find?

"They didn't give me any reason," Harry told her on the phone, "but the sergeant made it plain he didn't believe I was at the office last Tuesday evening, and I'm sure it's only a matter of time before they question me again. It's no good, Laura. I'm going to have to tell them where I was, and the reason for keeping quiet. I know I promised not to, but I don't have any choice. I'm going to talk to that man, Paget, in the morning. He seems like a decent chap; I'm sure he'll understand."

Laura wasn't so sure about that. "In that case, I want to go with you," she said firmly. "What about Dee? Are you going to tell her?"

"I don't see that I have much choice. She hasn't said anything, but I know she suspects that something is going on. I'll have to tell her, but I know she won't be happy.''

"In that case, promise me you won't tell her until after you have talked to the police,'' said Laura.

"Well... All right. I'll phone Paget's office first thing tomorrow morning, and I'll let you know when he can see us.''

He'd hung up quickly, perhaps fearing that Laura might try to dissuade him.

Laura picked up the phone again and punched in a number. It rang twice and a female voice answered. "Mr. Lambert's office.''

"I'd like to speak to Mr. Lambert, please, Myrtle.''

"Oh, it's you, Mrs. Bolen. I'm sorry, but Mr. Lambert won't be back until Friday. He left for London an hour ago. He has a meeting there tomorrow.''

"Oh, yes. I forgot. Do you know where he's staying? Perhaps I can reach him there.''

"I'll give you the number. Is there anything I can do for you?''

"No, I'm afraid not; thanks just the same, Myrtle.''

"Very well, Mrs. Bolen. Ah, here it is. Do you have a pencil?''

WHICH ONE WAS LYING? That was the question that kept gnawing away at the back of Paget's mind as he drove home that night. Malone or Veronica Beresford? Pressure would have to be brought to bear on Mrs. Beresford, but that wasn't going to be easy, especially if her husband backed up her story. Which wouldn't necessarily mean she hadn't been lying, but they would have to be very sure of their ground before taking that argument into court.

But his first priority tomorrow morning would be to visit the woman who had spent the night in the local nick with Julia Rutledge. The chances of her knowing where Rutledge might be were slim, but for the moment, at least, it looked like the only chance they had of tracing her.

HE PARKED THE CAR on the grass verge beneath a stand of trees. It was the same place he had parked the night before, just down *the road from the pub. He switched off the lights and listened to the sound of rain. He could have done without that, but he'd come prepared. He pulled up the hood of the dark plastic raincoat, and stepped out of the car, pausing to listen, but all he could hear was the soft patter of rain.*

He walked the short distance to the pub. There weren't as many cars there tonight, and as he drew close to the window he could see that the place was half empty. The man who had answered the phone last night was there behind the bar, and so was Joanna, laughing at something one of the patrons had said. He looked around the room but there was no sign of the girl. Since it seemed that she worked there, he felt reasonably sure that she would come again at the same time tonight. If not, he would have no choice but to go after her on the boat.

A VW mini-bus clattered into the car-park and pulled into a vacant space. He drew back into the shadows as four men piled out and ran toward the door of the pub, hopping and skipping to avoid the puddles. "Ten minutes, mind, no more," said one of them. "It's half nine already."

"Yeah, yeah, we know, but there's time for a quick one."

Half nine. Time to be going.

It was comparatively dry beneath the arch of trees that overhung the path behind the pub. He needed the torch, although he used it sparingly just in case there was anyone else about. Not that it was likely, but there was no point in taking chances. Not when he was so close to eliminating the only person who might be able to identify him. He still wasn't sure that Vikki had seen his face, but why take a chance? After tonight, there would be no way anyone could connect him to the murders. No way at all.

He reached the tow-path, and there ahead of him was the boat, its low black shape made visible only by the pale glow coming from the cabin window and a small light above the cabin door.

He drew back along the path to the place he'd picked out the night before, after following Joanna and Vikki from the pub. From beneath his coat he took out the short length of yellow rope with a wooden handle on each end and slipped the torch

*into his pocket. His eyes were becoming used to the darkness,
and he could make out the boat more clearly now.*

He waited.

*The rain made brittle splashing noises as it hit the water of
the canal, and a restless bird above him flapped its wings as
if trying to dry them out. Faint sounds drifted through the
trees—voices, muffled but distinct enough to tell they were calling out good-nights down at the pub. And then a sharp, insistent sound, someone who'd had a bit too much to drink, no
doubt, playing silly buggers on the car-horn.*

*He thought he saw a movement aboard the boat. Yes! He
gripped the home-made garrotte tightly and watched as the
figure of a girl crossed the plank and stepped onto the path.
She pulled up the hood of her mac and ducked her head against
the rain, then started down the path. She was carrying something, but he couldn't make out what it was.*

*He allowed her to pass his hiding place, then stepped out
behind her. He heard her gasp as the rope went round her
neck, heard her gag and choke as she dropped whatever it was
she was carrying to claw desperately at her throat. He
wrenched her head back and pulled, but she twisted round and
rammed an elbow into his stomach. Hard! It caught him by
surprise, and he lost his grip on the garrotte. He fumbled for
it, but the girl wrenched it from his fingers and it flew into the
darkness.*

*She almost slipped away, but he got an arm around her neck
and dragged her toward the water. She struggled, but she was
no match for him in a test of strength. He dragged her to the
bank, pushed her to the ground, and slammed a fist into the
side of her head. She went limp. He grabbed her legs and
shoved her down the muddy bank, forcing her head under water. He held here there, counting...*

*He heard a noise behind him. Someone was coming along
the path. He could see the light bobbing through the trees. He
crouched down, using all his strength to keep the girl down.
He must make sure this time. Make sure that she was dead!*

*"Hey!" someone shouted, and he realized that there was
more than one person on the path, and they were almost on
him. "What the hell...?"*

He let go of the girl's legs and scrambled to his feet. She slid down the bank and disappeared beneath the rain-swept water as he turned and ran.

Damn those two men! Where had they come from, and why just then? Another minute and he could have made certain that the girl was dead. But she had to be dead. She hadn't struggled when he held her down, and they would have to find her first. Even if they did manage to find her and get her out, she couldn't possibly be alive. No one could live with their head under that muck.

But he wished he'd had a minute longer to be sure.

He cursed them roundly as he pounded along the sodden path, splashing through puddles, slipping and sliding on the wet grass and mud. His feet and legs were soaked, and he hated to think what his trousers looked like.

He must have gone half a mile before he saw the hump-backed bridge over the canal and the path leading from the bank up to the road. It hadn't been used for years, and brambles tore at his clothes as he scrambled up the steep slope. He didn't think anyone had followed him, but he didn't dare slow down.

He reached the road and turned to the left. It should take him back to the road that ran past the pub, and to where he'd left the car. Thank God he'd parked it this side of the pub. But he'd have to hurry; someone had probably phoned the police by now.

The road was narrow, little more than a country lane winding between high grass banks, and the sooner he was off it, the better. But it was farther to the junction than he'd thought it would be; instead of running parallel to the Raddington Road, the canal must have veered to the north, and it was a good ten minutes before he saw the junction. He approached it cautiously and was about to round the corner when the distant wail of sirens stopped him. He drew back into the lane and crouched down beside the hedge. The sounds grew louder and burst upon him as two vehicles flashed by the end of the lane— a police car and an ambulance. Both stopped within seconds, which meant that the pub must be just down the road. He listened, but could hear nothing heralding the arrival of more police cars.

He stepped out into the road and ran the rest of the way.

There were precious few places in which to hide, and he didn't want to be trapped in someone's headlights. He reached his car, and scrambled in, then sat there shaking. He could see the flashing lights outside the pub farther down the road, but all the activity would be directed toward the canal, not back this way.

He had to get away before more police arrived. He started the car and moved out cautiously from beneath the trees. Steady, he told himself as he made a three-point turn in the road. Easy does it. The last thing he needed was to be stopped by the police and asked why his clothes were torn and covered in mud.

TWENTY-NINE

PAGET WAS ON THE POINT of going to bed when he received the call. Not many details, but two stood out clearly. A young woman was the victim, and Raddington Arm was where she had been attacked.

He was on his way within minutes, silently berating himself for not having followed up the information he'd been given that afternoon instead of postponing it until morning. There had to be a connection. How many people lived on a narrow boat on Raddington Arm?

He cut across country and arrived at the Invisible Man in twenty minutes flat. Police cars blocked the road, and people were milling about in the car-park. Paget abandoned his car and identified himself to the nearest PC.

"There aren't any lights on the path, yet, sir," the man warned him. "You'll need a torch." Paget returned to his car and took out the big square-battery job and locked the car again. Other vehicles were arriving, including a couple of SOCO's white vans.

The PC directed him to the path behind the pub. The distance of the canal was less than a hundred yards, and he was challenged by another uniformed constable as he emerged from the trees. "If you wouldn't mind stepping to one side, sir," he said deferentially when he saw Paget's card, "we're trying to avoid contamination of the crime scene, and the ground's a bit churned up hereabouts."

Paget was impressed. It seemed that one man, at least, had taken the lectures to heart.

"It's a bit cramped," the constable went on, "but I've asked all concerned to stay on the boat. There's the two men who dragged the girl out of the canal, and the woman who owns the boat, as well as WPC Jackson. She's been taking preliminary statements from each of them."

"You said 'dragged the girl,' not 'the body.' Are you telling me she's not dead?"

"She would have been if it hadn't been for one of the blokes inside," the PC said, indicating the boat. "He got her breathing again, and the ambulance men reckon she's got a fifty-fifty chance. But it was a near thing from the look of her. Bastard!" He spat the word.

"And the man responsible?"

"Took off down the tow-path." The man pointed into the darkness with his torch.

"Very good, Constable. SOCO should be here any minute, so if you'll stay here and help them get started, I'll go aboard."

As the constable had said, it was cramped inside. Two men wrapped in blankets sat on the edge of a bunk, while a woman sat at a small table across from the young policewoman. WPC Jackson greeted Paget smartly, and gave him the names of the three people there. Todd Elman, Justin Banks, and Joanna Freeborn.

"You've probably told Constable Jackson what happened," said Paget, "but I'm going to have to ask you to go over it again. Who was first on the scene, and what brought you here?"

It was Todd Elman who spoke up first. "We were down at the pub," he said, "waiting for Bunny, but she didn't come and time was getting on. We had a gig in town, see, and we needed to be there by ten to set up. We were cutting it fine as it was, so I said to Justin that I was going to see what the hold-up was, and he said he'd come with me."

"Hold on a second," Paget told him. "Who is Bunny?"

"The girl we pulled out of the canal," said Todd. "That's the only name she has as far as we know, and Joanna gave her that."

Paget turned to face Joanna Freeborn. Her face was deathly pale and her dark eyes looked haunted. "But you know who she is, don't you?" he said. "Because you spent a night in the cells with her in Broadminster."

Joanna stared at him. "That wasn't Bunny," she said. "That was Vikki. And I think it was Vikki he was after. He must have mistaken Bunny for Vikki in the dark."

"So where is Vikki now?"

Joanna shook her head. "That's just it," she said. "I don't know. She's disappeared, and I'm worried sick about her."

Paget groaned and shook his head in disbelief. Would they never find this girl?

"All right," he said resignedly, "now that we know who's who, let's begin again." He looked at Todd. "Carry on from where you left off."

"Right. Well, as I said, we came to see what was holding Bunny up, and we heard these sounds like somebody was thrashing about, and when we got closer, we could see this man trying to drown Bunny. I shouted, and we both went for him, but it's muddy, see, and I slipped and fell. By the time we got to Bunny, the bastard had gone and all we could see of Bunny was her feet sticking out of the water. I jumped in and tried to get her head above water while Justin grabbed her legs and pulled her out."

Justin took up the story. "I thought she was dead, but Todd started mouth-to-mouth, and suddenly she choked and spewed up. That's when this other girl came out. I didn't know who she was; I'd never seen her before, but she ran back in here and got some blankets and helped us get Bunny wrapped up. I told her to get down to the pub, tell Joanna what had happened, and ring for an ambulance. That's the last I saw of her."

"Vikki came down to the pub," Joanna exclaimed. "She was in a terrible state. I could hardly make out what she was saying. She looked awful. Once I got her to calm down and she told me what had happened, I asked George to ring for an ambulance and call the police. Then I came back to the boat as fast as I could. Vikki had disappeared, and I assumed she had come back here, but when I got here there was no sign of her.

"The police and the ambulance arrived, and one of the policemen went with Bunny to the hospital. They wouldn't let me go with her because they said someone would want to talk to all of us. Anyway, Todd and Justin were soaking wet and filthy with mud, so I brought them in here and had them strip down and get cleaned off."

Paget turned to the two men. "I don't suppose you got a look at the person who did this?" he said.

They both shook their heads. "Too dark," Todd said. "All we had was a torch between us and we lost that when I jumped into the canal." He grimaced. "God, it was cold! But at least we got Bunny out in time, poor kid. I hope she's going to be all right."

Paget turned back to Joanna. "Have you any idea where Vikki might have gone?" he asked. He looked round. "Did she take anything with her, do you know?"

"I'm sure she didn't," Joanna said, "and I haven't got a clue where she might be. She came here in the first place because she had nowhere else to go, and all she has with her are the clothes she has on. I'm sure she has no money."

"In that case, tell me what she was wearing and we'll get a description out and start scouring the countryside for her. I'm going to leave you my card, and I want you to let me know if Vikki gets in touch with you, because it's imperative that we talk to her." He saw the look of doubt on her face. "It's all right," he assured her, "she is not in any serious trouble, but we must find her for her own sake before this man gets to her. What happened here tonight gives you some idea of how desperate he is, so please let me know at once."

"She won't be charged with killing that man, Bolen?" Joanna said.

Paget shook his head. "She was set up," he told her. "But we do need to talk to her."

Joanna gnawed at her lip, then abruptly stood up. She reached into the upper bunk and pulled out a sheaf of papers. "Then this might help," she said, handing Paget a single sheet. "Vikki's a bit of an artist, and this is a self-portrait. That's how she looks today."

"THERE'S NOT MUCH we can do till morning," Charlie said. "We found the victim's guitar, and we'll check the case for prints in case your man touched it during the struggle. What about this other girl, Rutledge? Is it worthwhile going through the boat to see if she left anything behind that might give us a clue to where she might have gone?"

"From what Ms. Freeborn tells us, I doubt if you'll find much," said Paget. "The girl arrived with nothing of her own."

"I'll have Grace give it the once-over, anyway," said Charlie. "If there's anything to be found, she'll find it." He began to walk away, then stopped. "And speaking of Grace, when I asked her how the roads were when she came back from Worcester in that storm last week, she told me you came back with her. She said she might not have made it through without your help in pulling a tree off the road."

"It's Grace who deserves the credit," said Paget tersely, very much aware that Tregalles had pricked up his ears. "She drove most of the way. I was just a passenger."

"All the same, it was a bit of luck, her being down there when your car broke down," Charlie observed, casting a side-long glance at Tregalles. "Sort of like fate, you might say."

"Fate," Tregalles agreed solemnly.

"What did happen to the car?" asked Charlie. "Grace said there was oil all over the ground, and you thought it might be a broken gasket."

"Cracked engine block," said Paget tightly. "Now, are we going to stand round here all night, or can we get on? We still have a lot to do, so what are you waiting for, Tregalles?"

"Nothing, sir," said Tregalles. "I'm on my way."

Later, as he was on his way home, Tregalles thought about what he had heard. So Paget had come back from Worcester in Grace's car. They'd come back through the storm on Saturday, and yet he had seen Paget getting out of Grace's car on Sunday morning. And since Paget lived in Ashton Prior, which was closer to Worcester, it would make more sense for them to have stopped there rather than come on to Broadminster.

The storm hadn't abated until well into Saturday evening, so it wouldn't have made much sense for Grace to drive into Broadminster on her own in the dark with trees all over the road.

Which meant she must have stayed out there in Paget's house all night!

"The crafty old bugger!" Tregalles said beneath his breath. So he'd finally noticed Grace, though God knew it had taken him long enough. She'd certainly tried hard enough to get Paget to notice her in the past, but even Tregalles couldn't see her going so far as to crack his engine. Perhaps it had been fate, as Charlie said, even if he had said it with his tongue firmly in his cheek. On the other hand, maybe it was Paget who had engineered the whole thing. Now, there was an interesting thought.

"Got a lift back with someone," he'd said. Never mentioned that it just happened to be Grace Lovett. Or that she'd stayed the night. Tregalles rubbed his hands. He'd have that fiver off Ormside yet.

IT WAS ONE O'CLOCK by the time Paget reached the hospital and spoke to the constable who had accompanied the girl in the ambulance.

"She's just been taken up to ICU," he told the chief inspector. "Dr. Marshall is the one you want. He's the one who worked on her when she first came in."

Dr. Marshall was a slight, sandy-haired man of about thirty. "All I can tell you at the moment is that the young woman is relatively stable, but in cases such as these where someone has been immersed in stagnant water and was not breathing when taken out, the next twenty-four hours are critical. A massive influx of water like that can affect the heart, lungs, kidneys, blood—you name it. All sorts of complications can arise, which is why she will be monitored closely. People have been known to die many hours after they were thought to be stable, so we don't take chances."

"Was she injured in any other way?" Paget asked.

Marshall nodded. "Severe bruising around the throat, and she had received a blow to the side of the head. That doesn't seem to have caused any serious damage, but only time will tell. She was conscious throughout most of the examination.''

"Did she say anything? Anything that might help us find who did this to her?"

"No. She was still somewhat disoriented, and it was hard for her to talk at all after being half strangled, as she was, so I'm afraid I can't help you there. However, perhaps you can help me. All I have on my record is the name 'Bunny.' She gave me that herself, but I couldn't get a surname from her. Do you know her full name?"

"No. I'm afraid I don't know any more than you do."

Marshall sighed. "In that case we'll have to give her one or the computer won't accept it," he said. "Let's see, now, is it going to be Smith, Jones, or Brown? Ah, yes," he said, answering his own question, "it has to be Brown, doesn't it? Bunny Brown—Brown Bunny. Do you think she'll like that?"

THIRTY

Thursday, 5 October

"*...DOCTOR WOULD ONLY say that the young woman who was attacked and almost drowned in a canal last night is in serious but stable condition, and will remain under close supervision for the next twenty-four hours. The identity of the young woman is still unknown.*

"*The police are still looking for Julia Rutledge, also known as Vikki Lane. Rutledge is seventeen years of age, and when last seen, had altered her appearance, and is now believed to have short dark hair...*"

He switched the television off. Not Vikki? The young woman he had almost killed was not Vikki? No! It wasn't possible; they must have it wrong. Unless... He closed his eyes and tried to think. Just suppose for a moment that the girl in the hospital really was Vikki, but the police wanted him to think she was still at large. What would be the point?

He smiled grimly to himself. It was obvious, wasn't it? They wanted him to think that Vikki was still on the run and have him chasing all over the countryside looking for her, while she was safely tucked away in hospital.

The question was: How much did she know? And how much had she told them already? One thing was certain: After last night's botched attempt, they would be much more likely to believe her story about being set up for the Bolen murder.

On the other hand, without her they had nothing. He got up and began to pace.

On the plus side, the very fact that she had remained hidden on the boat suggested that she had been afraid to go to the police for fear they wouldn't believe her story. And why should they, with all that evidence against her? Perhaps he was mistaken in thinking that she had seen his face. Perhaps she had been unconscious all the time and he had nothing to fear.

But he couldn't afford to take that chance.

He sat down and bent forward, elbows on his knees, head in his hands. That damned girl! She had ruined a perfect plan. If it hadn't been for her... He stared at the floor with unseeing eyes, thinking hard.

"Yes!" he whispered fiercely as he raised his head. It could still be done. And this time he'd make absolutely sure there was no one there to save her life.

VIKKI SNIFFED and wiped her nose on her sleeve. She had spent a miserable night huddled between bales of hay stacked high in an open-sided shed. She'd made a bed of loose hay and burrowed into it, but it was no match for wet clothes and the chill of an October morning, and she was cold and stiff and hungry when she awoke.

The hay shed was in the middle of an open hillside, overlooked by a farmhouse at the top of the hill, and bordered by fences on two sides and the road below. Vikki heard the sound of voices and cautiously raised her head above the bales. A man and a woman chatted in desultory fashion as they crossed the yard and entered a stone shed. A large black dog sat on the farmhouse steps, yawning and surveying the world. She ducked down again. The last thing she needed was a dog sniffing around.

Vikki groaned aloud. The sun had yet to show itself above the eastern horizon, but the sky was crystal-clear. She'd planned to be on her way before daylight, but if she moved now she was almost bound to be seen. And the police would be looking for her, so she daren't venture out on the road.

She couldn't stop shivering. She reached out to pull more hay around herself, and uncovered the wheel of the bike she had borrowed last night.

Stolen, a small voice said inside her head. Vikki drew her knees up to her chin and rested her head on them. She hadn't meant to *steal* the bike, but she had to put as much distance between herself and her pursuers, so when she saw it sitting there along with several others in a builder's yard in Longford Marsh, it had seemed like a gift from heaven.

Like Joanna's horse.

She heard the sound of a car. Vikki raised her head and watched the bend in the road, waiting for it to appear…and drew back when it did.

Police! And they were looking for her. Why else would they be on a small country road at this time in the morning? The car drifted by and disappeared around the next bend. Vikki flopped back in the hay and stared up at the sky.

She was trapped…and she couldn't stop shivering.

MARK MALONE SLID DOWN in his seat as the blue Mercedes came out of the driveway and turned toward town. Good. Trevor was driving and he was alone. He glanced at the time. Twenty past nine.

He'd been waiting there in the tree-lined street for more than an hour, waiting for Trevor to go so he could have it out with Ronnie. What the hell she thought she was playing at he didn't know, but the one thing he did know was that she had better change her story or he would personally make sure that Trevor found out what sort of wife he had. See how she liked that!

He started the car and drove slowly along the street. No one was about as he turned in and drove up the curving drive and stopped in front of the house.

A woman answered the door. She was short and dumpy and wore brown tweeds. A pair of glasses hung from a chain around her neck, and she put them on as she looked him up and down. Malone hesitated. He hadn't considered the possibility that someone else might be in the house. "Who are you?" he blurted.

"Ms. Gage," the woman answered brusquely, "Mrs. Beresford's private secretary, and I was about to ask you the same question."

He remembered now. Ronnie had said she'd engaged someone to deal with her charity work. "Never mind who I am," he told her; "I'm here to see Mrs. Beresford."

"Is she expecting you?"

He smiled mirthlessly. "I doubt it," he said and pushed the woman aside as he entered the house. "Where is she?" he demanded.

"You can't force your way in here just like that," the woman shrilled. "Besides, Mrs. Beresford isn't up yet. She's still upstairs, and... No!" she screamed as he made for the stairs. "You can't go up there. I'll call the police!"

"You'd better not," he warned as he started up the stairs. "Not if you know what's good for you! Now shut up and mind your own damned business!"

"What the devil is going on here?" Veronica Beresford appeared at the top of the stairs, clad in a shimmering wrap-around negligé. "What are you doing here?" she demanded. "Get out of my house!"

She looked magnificent, eyes ablaze, hair spilling round her shoulders, and suddenly all he could think of was the wonderful times they had enjoyed together, and how much he wanted her. He'd known many women in his time, but none like Ronnie. His anger evaporated.

"Ronnie, please!" he pleaded. "We have to talk. What have you been telling the police? They think that Prudence and I planned to kill her father, and you know that's not true. I was here with you. You have to tell the police."

Veronica Beresford started down the stairs. "I don't know

what you are talking about," she said angrily, "and if you are not out of this house in thirty seconds, I shall call the police myself. Now, get out!"

She went to push past him, but he grabbed her wrists and held her. "You don't mean that, Ronnie," he said earnestly. "Not after all the great times we've had together, you can't just..."

The woman tried to free herself but he held her firm. "Jane! Ring the police!" she called to the woman standing transfixed at the bottom of the stairs. "Now!"

She wrenched one hand free and swung it hard.

The open-handed slap sounded like shot. Malone blinked and staggered back, releasing her other hand. "You bitch!" he breathed, and struck her with his fist.

It caught her on the side of the chin. Veronica's head snapped back. Her feet left the step and she fell, tumbling over and over down the long staircase to land with a bone-crunching thud on the tiles below. She lay there like a discarded doll, face down, her hair a golden halo round her head.

"KEITH! I'VE BEEN TRYING to reach you ever since yesterday afternoon. I finally gave up at midnight. The hotel kept telling me there was no answer from your room."

"Sorry, Laura, but I went out with some friends and it was late when I got back." He stifled a yawn. "And I slept in this morning, so I'll have to leave in a minute. Is anything wrong?"

"Harry thinks the police suspect him of being involved with the murder of that girl last week—you know, the prostitute— and perhaps of killing Jim as well. They took Dee's car in for some sort of tests, and he's convinced the police know he's been lying to them. He wants to tell them the truth about where he was last Tuesday evening."

Keith Lambert was silent for a moment. "Has he told anyone else?"

"I'm sure he hasn't, but he is going to tell Dee, and you know what that means. She's going to be very upset, but I don't think she'll do anything rash—at least, not right away. Harry and I will have to make sure she doesn't, that's all. As far as his going

to the police is concerned, I made him promise to let me go with
him. I want to make sure they understand the situation."

Lambert gnawed his lip. He didn't need this. Not now, but he
didn't see how he could stop Harry from going to the police. If
Laura couldn't stop him, there was nothing he could say that
would change Harry's mind.

"Are you still there, Keith?"

"Yes. Yes, of course. I was just thinking."

Laura sighed. "God! I'll be glad when this is over," she burst
out. "Did you watch TV this morning? They're broadcasting the
picture of that girl again. Remember the one they were looking
for after Jim died? Julia Rutledge. The police aren't saying much,
but there was an attack on another young woman last night, and
the implication is that there could be a connection."

"No, I haven't seen it. Who's this other girl? Did they say?"

"If they know, they're not saying. I don't understand what's
going on."

"Look, Laura, sorry, but I have to go. This meeting is crucial.
If this goes well, I think we may have an agreement in principle
by tomorrow. Do your best with Harry. Got to rush. Bye."

RUTHERFORD HILL was one of the prettiest areas in Broadminster, but its beauty was lost on Paget, preoccupied as he was
with his forthcoming interview. Veronica Beresford was hardly
likely to welcome him, especially when he explained to her exactly why he was there.

*Do you mind if I take a look round your bedroom, Mrs. Be-
resford? This employee of your husband's insists he spent a night
in bed with you, and I'd like to verify his description of the
room—oh, yes, and would you mind showing me your night attire?*

Number 700. Paget entered the driveway and drove up to the
house. A car blocked the drive beside the steps leading up to the
front door, and Paget pulled in behind it. The car was old, the
body rusted, and the driver's door was open, giving the impression that the car had been abandoned rather than parked.

A green Escort. Malone!

Paget swore softly under his breath as he got out and mounted the steps. He rang the bell.

Suddenly, the door was flung open and Malone charged out. Bent low, he rammed a shoulder into Paget's chest and sent him sprawling. He ran down the steps and jumped into his car. The engine roared into life, and gravel sprayed in all directions as he slammed the car into gear and took off down the drive and rocketed into the street.

Shaken, Paget struggled to his feet. It was too late to follow Malone, but at least he could call in and have the man picked up. Limping slightly, he moved toward his car, but stopped abruptly when someone screamed inside the house.

THE POLICE WERE OUT in force, talking to everyone who had been within a mile of the Invisible Man the night before. George had given them a list of everyone he could remember being in the pub the previous evening, and they were all being sought out and interviewed.

Scene-of-crime officers had been over the path inch by inch. They found the home-made garrotte in the long grass, and it was quickly bagged and sent off to be examined by Forensic. Men in wet suits searched the waters where Bunny had been pushed in, but between the reeds and two feet of mud on the bottom of the canal, it was hardly surprising that they found nothing of consequence. With Joanna's help, Grace Lovett searched the narrow boat from stem to stern, but there was so little that had belonged to Vikki that it wasn't worth the effort.

The guitar and case yielded three sets of fingerprints— Bunny's, Joanna's, and those of Julia Rutledge—which was hardly surprising considering the cramped quarters aboard the boat. The guitar itself was undamaged.

''Thank God for that, at least,'' Joanna said when she was told. ''That guitar means everything to Bunny.''

Too late for the morning papers, pictures of Julia Rutledge had been on the telly since early morning, together with a description of what she was wearing when last seen. The Incident Room was swamped with calls from people who were convinced that they had seen Rutledge, some as far afield as Leicester in one direction and Alderly Edge in another. Unlikely as they might seem, they all had to be carefully logged and submitted for follow-up. Meanwhile, in an ever-widening circle around the crime scene, half a dozen constables went from door to door asking the same questions over and over again. It was a thankless task, but it had to be done, and notebooks filled up quickly.

Closer to home, a man's bicycle was reported stolen from a builder's yard in Longford Marsh. According to its owner, it had been there around nine o'clock last night, but it was gone when he went to get it at seven-thirty this morning. There were other things there worth stealing, but nothing else had been touched. Ormside jotted down the details.

Longford Marsh wasn't any more than a mile from the Invisible Man. If the Rutledge girl had taken it, chances were she'd be well away by now, but at least it might indicate in which direction she had gone. He motioned to one of the constables as the phone on his desk began to ring once more. "Add 'may be riding a man's bicycle' to the Rutledge information," he told him.

He swallowed a mouthful of coffee and reached for the phone. The thought flashed through his mind that perhaps—just perhaps—this would be the call that brought good news for a change. "God knows we've had more than our share of the other," he muttered as he snatched the phone from its cradle. "Sergeant Ormside."

But it was not to be. Paget was on the line, reporting yet another murder.

TREGALLES WAS HALF-WAY up Rutherford Hill on his way to the Beresford house when he saw the flashing lights ahead. An ambulance and a police car blocked the road, and a uniformed PC stepped out to wave him down.

"You'll have to go back down and round..." he began, then recognized Tregalles. "Oh, sorry, Sergeant," he said. "Didn't realize it was you. You got here fast. It can't be more than ten minutes since we reported in. Malone's alive, but we've had to send for the cutters to get him out. The other poor devil's in shock, and no wonder when you see what was done to his car.

Alfa Romeo, it was. Not much more than scrap metal now. That's him over there being looked after by the ambulance men.''

"Malone? You're sure it's him?"

"It's his car, according to the description."

"What happened?" Tregalles turned off the engine and got out of the car.

"Seems like the other driver was proceeding along Oakview Drive when the Escort came screaming past the stop sign on Tanglewood, couldn't make the turn, and smashed into the side of the Alfa. If there'd been a passenger he'd've been mincemeat, but the driver was dead lucky. Got away with hardly a scratch. God knows how, but he did. Shaken up pretty badly, though."

"And Malone?"

"Like I said, still trapped inside. Unconscious but still breathing. Engine was pushed back and his legs are trapped. Gashed his head as well."

Tregalles moved closer. "It's Malone all right," he said. Malone's head had been forced back by the steering wheel, and his hair was matted with blood. The ambulance men had managed to get an oxygen mask on him, but there was little else they could do until help arrived and Malone could be cut free.

"Better call in and tell them that Malone's identity has been confirmed," he told the constable, "and have them cancel the alert."

It was mid-morning when an elderly man by the name of Moss was brought in to look at pictures of cars after telling the police that he had seen a car parked about a hundred yards down the road from the Invisible Man on two successive nights—last night and the night before. He'd thought it odd that someone would park there when the pub car-park was half empty and there were no houses in the immediate vicinity.

It wasn't much, but it was worth pursuing, Ormside decided, and arranged to have the area cordoned off for further examination.

It was clear from the beginning that Moss was trying to please, but after more than half an hour of looking at pictures of cars, he shook his head. "They all look the same these days, don't they?" he said to the young policewoman who was with him. "Sorry, miss, but I can't tell one from the other."

"What was it that drew your attention to the car in the first place, Mr. Moss?"

"It didn't look right—not parked on the grass verge under the trees like they were trying to hide it. It's not as if anybody lives there, you see, so I wondered why it had been left there." He chuckled. "I didn't give it much mind the first night; I thought it was probably some courting couple who'd stopped there for a bit of you-know-what, but when I saw it there the second night and I couldn't see no one in it, I took a closer look. Shone me torch inside, but I couldn't see nothing."

"You told the police at the site that it was a light-coloured car. Was it actually white? Or was it a light shade of some other colour? And what can you tell me about the seats and the colour of the upholstery? Were there two separate seats in the front, or was it a bench seat?"

"Two separate seats. I remember that, and there was this case, a briefcase, on the seat. As for the colour, well… See, I'm what you might call a bit colour-blind, so it's difficult. I *think* the seats were darkish—well, sort of—and they were leather or some such. Could've been that other stuff that looks like leather, I suppose. Hard to tell these days. Sorry, miss, but that's the best I can do."

"And you didn't see anyone about who might have been the driver?"

"No, there was no one about, and that was what got me thinking when one of your lot called round and asked if I'd seen anything suspicious."

"What time was it when you saw the car?"

"About five past ten both nights. See, I always leave the pub at ten, so that's how I know."

The policewoman thanked him for coming in. "If you should think of anything about the car that might help," she told him, "please ring us immediately even if it doesn't seem very important to you. Now, if you'll come with me, I'll have someone take you home."

A few minutes later, Ormside glanced through the police-woman's notes and grunted. "Not a hell of a lot we can do with that," he muttered. "Pity he didn't think to look at the number plate. Still, it's all grist for the mill, I suppose. Depends on what Charlie's people find."

THIRTY-ONE

"IF YOU THINK I'M PAYING up on the grounds that a ride in a car together means there's something going on between them, you've got another think coming," Ormside growled. "I'll need more than a bit of gossip from Charlie before I believe it. Circumstantial evidence based on hearsay? No, you'll have to do better than that, Tregalles."

"It's more than that," Tregalles protested. "You should have seen Paget's face. You know that look he gets when he's annoyed? I mean *really* annoyed. Sort of a set to the mouth and eyes like flint. Well, that's the way he looked last night, and he wasn't too pleased with Charlie for mentioning it, either. I'm sure there's something going on between them. See," he went on earnestly, "if she gave him a lift back from Worcester and stopped at his house, she wouldn't have come on to Broadminster by herself in that storm. She'd have stopped there. Stopped the night. Stands to reason, doesn't it? And I saw them with my own eyes the next morning when she dropped him at Mickey's Garage to pick up his car."

"Look," said Ormside patiently, "all we *really* know is that she was already down there giving lectures long before Paget even knew he was going down. I was here, remember, when Alcott told him he was going. It's only natural she'd offer him a lift when his car broke down. Even assuming they did stop at Paget's house, she'd driven all that way from Worcester in the storm, and she probably wanted to get home. Then, on Sunday, she went back out and drove him into town to pick up his car. It's not that far."

"I dunno," said Tregalles doubtfully. "I'll bet I'm right. I know I wouldn't miss a chance like that."

"You?" Ormside scoffed. "You're all talk, Tregalles. If somebody like Grace Lovett so much as smiled at you, you wouldn't know what to do with yourself. Besides, Audrey would kill you. Now, can we get off the subject of Paget's sex life and get on with what happened on Rutherford Hill this morning?"

It had taken more than two hours to free Malone from the wreckage and get him to hospital, and the doctors were still assessing the damage. At the house, Jane Gage described in graphic detail the chain of events from the time Malone pushed past her at the door to the moment when Paget appeared on the scene. The police doctor confirmed what had been obvious to anyone who'd viewed the body—that Veronica Beresford's neck was broken, and cautiously offered the opinion that this was the probable cause of death.

Trevor Beresford, who was on his way to Birmingham in the car, was contacted on his mobile telephone. Stunned by the news, he said he would return immediately.

At the house, Paget took the opportunity to examine the bedrooms and found, contrary to Malone's assertion that Trevor and Veronica Beresford had separate bedrooms, that there was every indication that the main bedroom was shared by both of them. The massive bed was still unmade, and it was apparent that two people had slept there recently. Paget poked his head inside two other bedrooms, neither of which matched Malone's description.

"They're guest bedrooms," Jane Gage told him. "Mr. Beresford's son and daughter-in-law and their two children used them just last week. His son by his first wife," she explained.

"What about these other two rooms?" asked Paget. "The ones that are locked. Are they bedrooms also?"

"No. One is Mr. Beresford's office, and the other is his dark-room. He's quite an accomplished photographer, you know."

"No, I didn't know," said Paget absently, still puzzled by Malone's insistence that he'd been having an affair with Veronica Beresford. Perhaps they had had an affair at one time, and he'd hoped that she would give him the alibi he needed. It had been a vain hope at best, and now the only person who might have cleared him was dead, and he had killed her.

It would be nice to think that Bolen's killer was now in hospital under guard, but apart from the fact that he had no alibi for that time, there was no real evidence to connect Malone to that killing. Neither was there any evidence that it was Malone who had attacked and almost drowned the girl last night, so again their only real hope was to find Julia Rutledge. She had to be the key. Why else would Bolen's killer pursue her so relentlessly?

When Paget returned to Charter Lane, Ormside greeted him with a report from the hospital. "Malone is on the critical list," he said. "Besides both legs being broken, he has a cracked pelvis, dislocated hip, head and facial cuts, and as yet undetermined internal injuries. He's still in the operating room, and the prognosis is not encouraging.

"The good news is that Bunny Brown is doing better than expected, although she has some congestion in her lungs, so they're keeping her in a special observation unit for a couple of days. And we have nothing back from Forensic yet."

The sergeant tilted back in his chair and clasped his hands behind his head. "And that, sir, is it, I'm afraid. Apart from knowing that it was Malone who killed Mrs. Beresford, we're no further ahead than we were ten days ago. And if you ask me, this whole damned case is going cold; I can feel it in my bones."

"I'M ENQUIRING ABOUT THE GIRL who was brought in last night. The one who was almost drowned in the canal. Can you tell me how she is? I'm one of the people who rescued her, and I'd like to know if she can have visitors yet."

A moment of hesitation, then, "Oh! You must mean Bunny Brown. I'll transfer you to ICU."

He waited. "ICU." A young voice. He repeated what he had said before. "I'm not a relative or anything, but I am concerned," he said worriedly.

The voice softened. "She's a very lucky girl," said the nurse, "and I'm sure she must be very grateful to you, but I'm not allowed to give out any information on a patient. Besides, she's not here now. She's been moved to SOU on three. You'll have to talk to them.''

"SOU?"

"Special Observation Unit,'' the nurse explained. "We put people in there who can be moved from ICU, but who are not quite ready for a general ward. It's a monitored room, and we—''

"Nurse!'' He heard the sharp command in the background, and the nurse dropped her voice to a whisper. "Sorry, sir, got to go.''

"Right. Thank you.''

He hung up the phone and stepped out of the call-box. Bunny Brown? Bunny/Vikki; Vikki/Bunny. Not the most imaginative pseudonym he'd ever heard. Clearly he'd been right; there never was another girl. He certainly hadn't seen any sign of one when he'd followed Vikki and Joanna back to the boat that first night, and he'd stayed there until they'd turned the lights out.

So, now that he knew where she was, it was simply a matter of getting to her, and this time there would be no mistake. The girl would be in bed, so the rope would be no good. Better to use the knife. Hand over her mouth, throw the bedclothes back— one quick thrust should do it—then cover her again to make it look as if she were sleeping.

HARRY AND LAURA BOLEN had been waiting for half an hour when Paget and Tregalles joined them in the interview room. "Sorry to keep you waiting,'' said Paget as Tregalles switched on the tape recorder and entered in the details.

"First,'' said Paget, "let me ask you, Mrs. Bolen, and you, Mr. Bolen: Did you come here of your own free will to correct an earlier statement you made to the police?''

"I did,'' said Harry, "but I don't think Laura has anything to correct. She is here primarily to corroborate what I'm about to tell you.''

"Very well, then. Please go on, Mr. Bolen.''

"First, let me say it was never my intention to mislead,'' said Harry, "but I had promised not to tell anyone where I was or what I was doing almost every evening last week. But I knew

Sergeant Tregalles didn't believe me, and when my wife's car was taken in for examination, I realized I had to set the record straight.

"Last week, on the Monday when I returned from Manchester with my wife, I had a call from Laura asking me to go over to her house immediately. When I got there I found Keith Lambert there as well." He looked at Laura again. "I think it might be best if you told them how he happened to be there, Laura."

Laura Bolen picked up the story. "If you recall, Chief Inspector, I told you that Keith Lambert had proposed sharing the cost of the Ockrington venture between the two firms. That was before Jim died, of course, but the more I thought about Keith's proposal, the more convinced I was that there was merit in the idea. But time was running out. So, when he rang on Monday morning to say how sorry he was about Jim's death, I brought the matter up again."

Laura leaned forward across the table. "I know how this must sound," she went on. "My husband had been killed less than two days before, and I was discussing business with the man he hated most, but there was a reason for that. Keith and I had spent a lot of time talking about the Ockrington project prior to his coming to the house the Friday before Jim died, and I believed—and still do—that a joint venture would be a sound business proposition. Combine the assets of the two companies to provide the capital that would be needed, especially in the early stages of development, and halve the risk.

"Of course, as we all know, Jim would have none of it, but that didn't really change anything. The problem was, Keith was already into negotiations with the M.o.D., and while he felt that, assuming they accepted his proposal, his company could manage the financing required, it would still be a heavy drain and he would feel much more comfortable if he knew he had some outside backing.

"But that in itself posed another problem. So long as the M.o.D. believed they had only one bidder on the Ockrington property, they either had to lower their expectations or abandon their attempts to sell the land. If they got wind of a joint venture, where more capital would be available, they might be inclined to sit back and rethink their position.

"Up to that point, Harry hadn't been involved in any of these discussions with Keith, but now it was vital that he should be. So I arranged for Keith to come to the house after John had left on Monday night, and Harry came over as soon as he got back from Manchester. We began by talking about Ockrington as a joint venture, but the discussion took another turn when Harry announced that he was thinking seriously of retiring."

Laura took a deep breath and looked at her brother-in-law. "And that prompted me to put my own cards on the table. Until then, my life had been so governed by the business that I'd never really thought about what *I* wanted. But when Harry spoke of getting out, I realized that I wanted to get out as well. I was sick of it. It has dominated our lives, as has Jim's obsession to drive Keith out of business, and I wanted nothing more to do with it."

Harry was nodding agreement. "It's as if we'd all been carried along on Jim's energy, Jim's dream, Jim's goal," he said quietly, "and now Jim's gone, there is no reason to continue. So we found ourselves talking, not only about a joint venture, but a phased-in amalgamation of the two companies over the next few years. Laura and I will still be part owners, but the idea is that Keith will have the option to buy us out over a period of time. I'm prepared to stay on for another year or two to ensure a smooth transition, but after that I'm leaving. And that's what Keith and I have been working on every evening for the past week or so."

"You weren't there?" Paget asked Laura.

"No." Laura glanced briefly at Harry. "I had other things to do, and John's been coming over in the evenings to help me sort through Jim's papers and things like that."

Paget looked surprised. "I should have thought he would be involved in your negotiations with Mr. Lambert," he said.

Harry looked uncomfortable as he exchanged glances with Laura, and it was she who answered. "John hasn't been involved because I wanted it that way," she said, "and to be honest, this is where it gets a bit difficult. You see, John has always idolized his father, and I'm very much afraid he would see this move as a betrayal. We have, of course, made it clear to Keith that John is to keep his position, and no doubt he will continue onward and upward in the new company, but for the moment, and especially, while Keith is in the middle of negotiations with the M.o.D., I decided it would be best to say nothing to John. I hate to be working behind his back, but I feel I must until this Ockrington business is settled. We simply can't afford to have *anyone* making waves until that is done.''

Harry nodded. ''Neither of us *wanted* to exclude John, but as Laura said, we felt it was a necessary precaution until the Ockrington deal is signed and sealed.'' He grimaced. ''And that meant not telling my wife as well, and she's not going to be very happy when I do. You see, Dee thinks the world of John, and I don't think she would approve of keeping him in the dark. She's my wife and I love her dearly, but she doesn't understand business, and, well…to be honest, she can't keep a secret worth a damn.''

Harry stopped speaking, and they both looked at Paget.

''I see,'' he said. ''I take it that Mr. Lambert will confirm what you've just told us?''

Laura nodded. ''I spoke to him in London this morning,'' she said. ''He's meeting with the M.o.D. today, and hopes to have an agreement in principle by tomorrow at the latest.''

''Anything else you wish to tell me?'' asked Paget. They both shook their heads. ''Please answer for the tape,'' he said. ''Mrs. Bolen?''

''No. Except to ask you not to tell John what we have told you here today.''

''I see no need for it to go any further,'' said Paget. ''Mr. Bolen? Anything to add or change?''

''No.''

''Any questions, Sergeant?''

''No, sir.''

''Good. In that case, this interview is terminated at four thirty-three P.M.'' He nodded to Tregalles, who switched off the tape recorder.

After they had gone, the two men made their way upstairs. ''I wonder if they realize what they've done?'' Tregalles said.

"We know they were both there at the hotel about the time Bolen was killed, and we know they had a motive, so this makes their motive even stronger."

"They've also strengthened someone else's motive," Paget observed. Tregalles gave him a sidelong glance. "I'm thinking of Keith Lambert," Paget continued. "Laura Bolen told us that it wasn't until they met after Jim Bolen's death that they talked of a complete merger with Lambert. But what if she and Lambert had talked this through earlier? With Jim Bolen out of the way, Lambert would not only rid himself of the man who had spent his life trying to destroy him, but he could have the whole package. I wonder…" he ended thoughtfully.

"Wonder what?"

"I was wondering if the package includes Laura Bolen."

THIRTY-TWO

THE SUN DROPPED behind the hills, and thick, dark clouds were moving in. It was time to go, if for no other reason than to find some water and something to eat. The dust from the hay seemed to have drawn every last ounce of moisture from Vikki's body, and she felt as if she hadn't eaten for a week.

But go where?

It was a question she had wrestled with throughout the day. Self-preservation was urging her to continue on, to get as far away from Broadminster as she could, but her conscience was telling her something entirely different. It was telling her to go back.

The trouble was, she doubted very much if Joanna would want anything to do with her after the way she had run off at the first sign of trouble, deserting Bunny the way she had.

Vikki's eyes became moist as she thought of the kind and gentle woman who had cared for her those first few days. Bunny had even given her some of her own clothes and a pair of shoes when she had barely enough to clothe herself. As had Joanna.

And she'd repaid them by stealing from them and running away when she should have stayed to make sure that Bunny was all right.

Thank God those two men had been there to pull Bunny out and get her breathing again. She'd looked terrible. And no wonder, with all that filthy water inside her. She might still be deathly ill.

Or dead!

She could still see Bunny's chalk-white face, still hear her laboured breathing and the awful sounds of retching as Bunny tried to rid herself of all the muck she'd swallowed. The sights, the sounds were all still there in Vikki's head, and no matter how far or how fast she ran, they would always be there.

There was no choice. She must go back.

Vikki wiped her eyes with the back of a grimy hand. The thought of returning terrified her. Whoever had attacked Bunny could still be looking for her; he'd tracked her down once, so why not again? Yet she knew she had no choice. She *owed* it to Bunny. She *owed* it to Joanna. And she owed it to herself. She could not go on without making sure that Bunny was all right. Perhaps then the only choice she would have left would be to give herself up to the police and pray that they'd believe her. They just might, now that Bunny had been attacked.

And she couldn't run forever.

Vikki stood up and poked her head above the hay. No sign of movement at the house; no sign of the dog. She stood there, motionless, for several minutes, then pulled the bike from beneath the hay. She mounted it, breathed in deeply several times, then left the cover of the shed, head down, pedalling as fast as her legs would move over the rough ground to the road below.

No one shouted. No one saw her leave.

Vikki's mouth was dry and her stomach rumbled noisily, but she felt a surge of exhilaration at being on the move again. So far, so good, she told herself—and tried not to think of what might lie ahead.

THE SMELL OF RAIN was in the air as Vikki trudged slowly up the hill. She'd lost track of time, lost track of everything except the pain and the knowledge that she dare not stop to rest.

Of all the rotten luck! She hadn't seen the pot-hole in the road until the front wheel dropped in it, twisted sharply, and threw her and the bike into a tangled heap. She was shaken up, but apart from a bleeding hand and elbow she seemed to have escaped serious injury.

Or so she'd thought until she tried to stand.

She felt her ankle swelling, and gasped with pain when she put her foot to the ground. She winced and prayed it wasn't broken. Gingerly, she tried again. It was painful but she thought that she could manage. Besides, what choice did she have?

Fearfully, she'd examined the bike. A few spokes were bent, and a bit of paint was gone, but it was otherwise undamaged. Vikki heaved a sigh of relief as she mounted it and set off again. But she couldn't put enough pressure on her injured foot to make it up the hill. Painful as it was, she'd had to dismount and walk. Her foot throbbed with every step as she plodded toward the top.

She lifted her head; only a few more yards to go.

The road was narrow, and Vikki moved closer to the high grass verge as she heard a car approaching from behind. She didn't bother to look up as it went by, so intent was she on counting every step. It was only when she heard it slow, then stop, that she raised her head and saw it wasn't a car at all, but a half-ton truck, and the driver was getting out.

"Looks to me like you need a lift, girl." The driver was a grey-haired woman with a lean and weathered face. She walked back down the road and took the bike from Vikki. "Come off and hurt your foot, did you?" she asked as she laid it down.

Vikki nodded.

"Sit down," the woman ordered, pointing to the high bank. Vikki did as she was told, too tired to do anything else. The woman bent to examine the foot, and clucked her tongue. "I don't know if it's broken or not, but I do know you shouldn't be walking on it. Come on, I'll give you a lift. The bike can go in the back. Don't know what you were doing on the road without lights in any case. You're lucky I didn't run you over." She picked up the bike and walked back to the truck, with Vikki hobbling along beside her. "Get in," the woman ordered. "I'm going into Broadminster anyway, and that foot needs attention, so I'll drop you at the hospital. All right?"

Vikki could have kissed her. "Thank you very much," she said gratefully as she climbed into the passenger's seat.

"Put the seat-belt on," the woman commanded as she got in and started the engine.

It felt so good to sit down. Vikki clipped the belt in place and leaned back and closed her eyes. She just wanted to go to sleep and forget that any of this had happened.

"How old are you?" the woman asked.

"Seventeen—eighteen in November."

The woman eyed her shrewdly. "Left home, have you?" she asked.

Vikki pressed her lips together. She was grateful—more than grateful—for the lift, but there were some things she was not prepared to share with this woman.

The woman nodded slowly. "All right," she conceded, "so I'm a nosy old woman, and perhaps I don't have a right to pry into your affairs, but I can see that you've been sleeping rough. You've got hay in your hair, and it's all over the back of your clothes, and it seems to me that you might be running away from more than home."

The truck hit a rough patch of road, and Vikki gasped as her foot bounced against the floor. She gritted her teeth against the pain, unable to speak.

The woman gave Vikki a searching look. "What have you had to eat today?" she asked. "Not much, I'll be bound. Look in that glove box, child. Go on, open it. There's a packet of biscuits in there. Always carry a few with me; never know when you might need a bite when you're diabetic like me. Go on, eat them. There's more where they came from."

"But…"

"Never mind buts, girl, get 'em down you. Do you good. Do you have any money?"

Vikki's mouth was full. They were plain biscuits, but they tasted so good it was hard not to wolf them down. She swallowed. "Not much," she said. Then, "Well, to be honest, no, I haven't." It was hard to lie to this woman.

"Soon be there," the woman observed as they came to the top of Strathe Hill. "We'll have you down to the hospital in no time. What's your name, girl?"

"Vikki."

"Right, then, Vikki. I'm going to take you to Casualty and drop you there. I should stop, but I have to get on. I'm going to visit my mother, and I'm late as it is. She's ninety-two and she'll worry herself silly if I'm late."

They crossed the bridge and turned into Broad Lane. The headlights swept across the broken walls of the minster ruins, stark and forbidding against the darkening sky, and Vikki shivered. The massive ruins gave her an uneasy feeling, and in the short time she'd been in Broadminster she'd avoided them. Now, in the full glare of the headlights, the walls seemed even higher, and the shadows darker and more menacing.

The truck swung in through the hospital gates and came to a halt outside the Casualty entrance.

"I'll get your bike out of the back and put it over there in the bike rack," the woman told her. "I don't suppose you've got a lock and chain?" She saw the look on Vikki's face. "No, I didn't think so. In that case, I'm afraid you'll just have to take your chances on its being pinched. Perhaps someone inside can tell you where you might put it, because I have a feeling they'll want to keep you in once they see that foot."

Before Vikki could say anything, the woman was out of the truck and lifting the bike out of the back. She wheeled it across to the bike rack, then came back as Vikki eased herself out of the truck.

"Thank you every so much," Vikki said gratefully. "It was very kind of you to—"

"No need to go on about it," the woman said gruffly as she took Vikki by the shoulders and began to brush her down. "There, that's better," she declared. "Don't want them to think you've been sleeping in a barn, do we? And you'd better take this." She held out two five-pound notes. "They have a cafeteria in the basement. It will probably be a while before they get round to treating you, so go down and get yourself a hot meal. Go on, take it," she said roughly as Vikki hesitated. "I may not look as if I have two pennies to rub together, but I'm not so badly off that I'll miss it, and you need it more than I do."

"I don't know what to say," Vikki stammered. "Thank you ever so much"—she glanced at the worn ring on the woman's left hand—"Mrs...?"

"Meadows." The woman prepared to get back in the truck, then paused and looked around. "The last time I was here was when they brought my Len in after the tractor rolled and he was pinned underneath it," she said softly. "Been gone now a good many years, and it still seems like yesterday."

Mrs. Meadows got back in the truck and closed the door. "Now, you take care of yourself, young Vikki," she said through the open window, "and get that foot seen to straight-away. Good luck, girl."

Vikki watched with tears in her eyes as the truck left the car-park. Mrs. Meadows didn't look back, but a rough brown hand waved as she went out into the street and disappeared into the darkness.

Vikki looked at the money in her hand. She needed change, so she would do as Mrs. Meadows had suggested and have something to eat. The biscuits had disappeared, and she was ravenous. She entered the hospital and made her way to the basement. Her foot throbbed with every step, but she wasn't going to chance having a doctor keeping her in until she had done what she'd set out to do.

She looked at everything on the glass shelves and chose a ham-cheese-and-lettuce sandwich and a bowl of vegetable soup, because other than sweets and muffins, they were the cheapest things on offer.

It took Vikki only a few minutes to finish the soup and devour the sandwich, and moments later she found a public phone at the entrance to the cafeteria. The telephone book beneath it was in tatters, but the page she wanted was still intact. She punched in the number and waited.

"Invisible Man. George speaking."

Vikki lowered her normal speaking voice and mimicked the

local dialect as best she could. "I'm a friend of Bunny's," she said, "and I only just heard about her being in hospital. Is she very bad?"

"She was, but they say she's much better today."

"Can you tell me what room she's in?"

"Hang on a minute." He cupped a hand over the transmitter and called, "Joanna? Do you know what room Bunny's in?"

He took his hand away from the phone. "Joanna says she's in the Special Observation Unit on the third floor, and she wants to know if you're—"

Vikki put the phone down quickly and let out a sigh of relief. So Bunny was all right! Great! Perhaps she should be satisfied with that and go and have her foot seen to now. But it was still her fault that Bunny had been almost killed, so the least she could do was find her and tell her how sorry she was for all the trouble she'd caused. But not yet. Bunny might have visitors, and she'd rather see Bunny alone.

Vikki went back upstairs to look for a place where no one would notice her. The waiting room in Casualty seemed to be as good a place as any. People there were too preoccupied with their own troubles to pay any attention to her. She chose a seat farthest from the desk, leaned her head back against the wall and closed her eyes. It was such a relief just to sit and rest, and even the police wouldn't think of looking for her here.

She'd wait an hour, she decided, and then go down and have another bowl of soup. That was something to look forward to. Visiting hours would be over by then, and she could go upstairs and look for Bunny.

THIRTY-THREE

THE INCIDENT ROOM was quiet. The day shift had gone home, but Paget sat at a desk, going slowly through the log and the mass of reports and notes that had accumulated over the past two weeks.

Tregalles had spent some time at the hospital earlier in the day, talking to the young woman they called Bunny Brown, but she remembered little of what had happened on Wednesday night. She recalled leaving the boat and setting out on the path. She remembered being choked and fighting back, but from then on it was all a blur. It was raining and it was dark. She hadn't seen the man who had tried to kill her.

It was frustrating. So close, and yet it seemed that they were blocked at every turn. By six o'clock, Tregalles had been ready to call it a day, but Paget was not prepared to give up so easily. "We'll go through every statement, every scrap of evidence again," he said. "There has to be *something* that will give us a lead."

Which was why the sergeant was working his way through statements instead of spending a quiet evening at home as he had planned. It was a tedious job, and he was having trouble keeping his eyes open. "Anyone want coffee?" he asked as he poured a mug for himself.

Paget, immersed in the middle of a report, grunted something unintelligible, which Tregalles took to mean no, but Ormside, who had volunteered to stay behind as well, and was talking on the phone, raised his hand.

Tregalles poured another mug and popped two sugars in, then set it down on Ormside's desk. "Anything new?" he asked idly as Ormside put the phone down.

Len Ormside leaned back in his chair and stretched. "Not much," he said. "We had this old chap in earlier on today. Name of Moss. He said he saw a strange car parked just down the road from the Invisible Man the night before last, and it was there again about the same time that the girl was attacked. We showed him pictures, but all he could tell us about the car was that it was light-coloured, fairly new, and there was a briefcase on the seat. We sent him on his way and told him to give us a call if he thought of anything. That was him." Ormside picked up his coffee and sipped it slowly. "He rang to say he'd remembered something else. The car had a sun-roof.

"Funny what makes some people remember things," he observed. "This old chap said he was clearing out his tomato boxes in his greenhouse when he got a splinter in his finger, and it reminded him of the sun-roof because he cut his finger on the car. Said he was leaning down, trying to see inside, with his hand on the roof to steady himself, when he nicked his finger. He never thought anything of it until he got home and saw the blood on his hand. He's on blood thinner, and he says even the smallest cut bleeds like a bugger. He reckons there must have been a sharp bit of metal on the edge of the sun-roof. If it hadn't been for that, he never would have remembered it."

"A *sun-roof*, Len?" said Paget sharply as he pushed his chair back. He came round the desk. "Let me see that report." He scanned it quickly. "And split seats!" he said softly. "By God, Len, this could be the very thing we've been looking for!" He dropped the report back on the desk and grabbed his mac. "Come on," he told Tregalles, "we've got work to do."

HE WAS PARKED ON THE STREET. The exit from the hospital car-park was narrow, and he didn't want to risk being held up when it was time to leave. He watched from his car as visitors came down the steps and went their separate ways. Anxious as he was to be going, it might be best to wait a few more minutes; there were always a few stragglers who lingered after the bell had gone.

He had telephoned the hospital less than an hour ago and asked to be connected to the nursing station on the third floor. "Was it permitted to visit someone who was in SOU?" he'd asked.

He was assured it was.

He'd pretended to be hesitant. It was just that he didn't want to disturb other patients in there who might be in serious condition, he explained.

No fear of that, he was told. There was only one patient in there at the moment.

It was better than he'd hoped for, and the sooner it was done, the better.

There were only a few cars left in the car-park, and no one had come down the steps in the last five minutes. It was time to go.

He picked up the box of flowers, got out of the car and locked it. There was a chill in the air, and mist rising from the river in the valley drifted through the trees. He entered the hospital and walked purposefully to a door beside the lift, opened it, and began to climb the stairs.

He paused on the first landing, where he put on the latex gloves, then took the knife from his pocket and thrust it in his belt where it would be instantly to hand.

His biggest fear was that Vikki might scream. He must get to her before she had a chance to utter a sound, which meant hiding his face when he entered the room. He opened the box and removed the flowers. The box could stay here in the stairwell. Nothing could be traced back to him.

He went up the stairs to the third floor and looked through the window in the door. The corridor was empty. He eased the door open and held the bouquet of flowers in front of his face as he moved toward the door beneath the sign that said SOU.

A nurse appeared at the far end of the corridor and began walking toward him.

He kept on walking. The nurse drew nearer then veered off to one side and opened a door marked STAFF ONLY and disappeared inside. The door beneath the sign was open, and fifteen feet away was the high counter behind which he could hear the nurses talking. He slipped inside the door.

The girl lay on her side, face toward the wall. Still holding the flowers in front of his face, he moved swiftly toward the bed, eyes fixed on the bedclothes he would have to pull away before the thrust directly to the heart. The girl stirred and turned her head to see who it was.

He froze! He couldn't believe his eyes. He'd never seen this girl before!

She rolled over and squinted at him as if a light were shining in her eyes, and he realized she'd been asleep.

He turned away. "Sorry, must have the wrong room," he said gruffly as he retreated, almost running from the room. To his left a nurse, still talking to someone behind the desk, came out into the corridor. He walked rapidly away and had almost

*reached the door when she called out behind him, "Sir...?
Sir...?"*

*The stairwell door closed behind him, shutting out the sound.
He dropped the flowers and ran down the stairs. The sooner he
put some distance between himself and the hospital, the better.*

*He was at the top of the last flight of steps when the door to
the ground floor opened. He put his head down and a hand up
to his face as he continued on down, then stopped, slack-jawed,
as the person below looked up.*

Vikki!

*At the same time he recognized her, she recognized him. He
could see it in her eyes, see the shock on her face as she stood
there, paralysed with fear as all her nightmares suddenly came
true.*

He ran down the steps, knife glinting in his hand.

"NO ONE HOME," said Tregalles. "No sign of the car, either."

Paget looked at his watch. They could sit here for the rest of
the evening and wait for their man to come home, or they could
return in the morning. Julia Rutledge was probably half-way
across the country by now, so it wasn't as if there was any
immediate danger, and he couldn't see their man leaving town.

Assuming he *was* their man.

He yawned and stretched, and heard the rustle of paper in his
shirt pocket. It was the note he'd made to remind himself to ring
Andrea. He'd tried to reach her earlier, but Mrs. Ansell had
answered and told him that Andrea was working late at the hospital.

"We'll come back first thing tomorrow morning," he told
Tregalles, much to the sergeant's relief. "But stop in at the hospital on the way back. I'll only be a couple of minutes."

"The hospital it is," Tregalles said. "Something to do with
the girl, is it?"

"No."

Tregalles waited, but as the silence between them lengthened,
it became obvious that no further explanation was forthcoming.
Five minutes later, he swung the car into an empty space close
to the hospital steps, then settled back in his seat as Paget got

out and went inside. A couple of minutes, Paget had said. That probably meant ten or fifteen.

Inside, Paget identified himself to the elderly head porter who sat behind the reception desk, walked over to the open door of the lift, and pressed the button for the fourth floor.

Andrea was in her office, and she looked pleased to see him when he knocked and poked his head inside. "What brings you here?" she asked. "I hope it isn't anything serious this time."

"Oh, but it is," he assured her. "I happened to be passing, so I thought I'd drop in and make sure everything is set for Saturday. It seems that every time we make plans, something gets in the way. We're still on, are we not?"

"As far as I'm concerned, we are," said Andrea.

"Good. What time would you like to go for dinner? Seven? Eight?"

"I think seven," she said. "I don't like keeping Mrs. Ansell up too late if I can help it. Where are we going?"

"I thought the Tudor. What do you think?"

"I should have thought you'd had enough of the Tudor after that murder there last week, but yes, that would be very nice. The food is always good there. You haven't booked, then?"

Paget hesitated. "I suppose I should have," he said, "but to tell you the truth, it slipped my mind. Could I use your phone?"

"I'll do it," Andrea told him. She flipped a Rolodex and punched in the number.

"Very efficient," Paget commented. "I'm impressed."

"Put me through to the dining-room, please," Andrea said into the phone. "Yes, good evening. I'd like to make a reservation for two for dinner tomorrow night, and...I see. Completely booked? That is unfortunate. I'm sure Chief Inspector Paget will be most disappointed when I tell him...Oh! Yes, I can hold on."

Andrea put her hand over the phone and raised an eyebrow in mock surprise. "It seems he may have made a mistake," she said softly. "Yes? Oh, there is? A cancellation. Wonderful. Yes, at seven. Thank you so much."

She put the phone down and grinned. "I thought it might be

worth a try," she said, "and it seems to have worked. They're familiar with your name."

Paget returned the grin. "They should be," he said, "but I doubt if I'm on their list of favourite people. There's probably a note against my name saying: 'Don't upset this man, whatever you do!'"

"Now it's my turn to be impressed."

"I have to go," he told her. "Tregalles is waiting in the car. Quarter to seven all right? It's not as if we have far to go."

"That would be lovely. I'll see you then, Neil. Take care."

VIKKI WRENCHED OPEN the heavy door at the bottom of the stairs and ran. The lobby was deserted except for the elderly night porter on duty at the desk, and he wouldn't stand much chance against the man who was after her. Where were all the people when you needed them? She made a dash for the door, the instinct for survival overriding the pain.

"Oi!" the porter yelled as he scrambled out from behind his newspaper. "Oi! You, there! Where do you think you're going?"

But Vikki was through the door and down the steps before he could so much as come out from behind the desk. His back was turned toward the man who hurried past, a hand to the side of his face. "Good night," the man said as he, too, left the building.

"Good night, sir." The porter didn't even look at the man as he made his way back to the desk. "Bloody kids!" he muttered as the door closed behind the man. "Need their arses tanned, the bloody lot of 'em!"

Tregalles saw the girl come flying down the steps. She was running awkwardly, and she kept glancing back over her shoulder as she cut off to the right towards the trees. He lost sight of her as she plunged into the shadows. A man was standing at the top of the steps, framed in silhouette against the light. Tregalles couldn't see his face.

But he'd seen the face of the girl, and she'd been terrified. She'd looked familiar, and yet her features had been so distorted that it took a few seconds for it to register that she was the girl whose picture had been taped to a board in the Incident Room for more than a week.

Julia Rutledge.

Tregalles paused only long enough to snatch something from the glove box before leaping out of the car. The girl had disappeared, but the sergeant caught a glimpse of the man as he passed beneath a light, running hard. Tregalles was half-way across the car-park when Paget appeared on the hospital steps.

"It's him!" Tregalles yelled. "He's after the girl. Come on."

Vikki heard the shouts, but they only served to spur her on as she tried to find an opening in a chain-link fence that surrounded the hospital grounds. She hadn't realized it was there when she'd made for the shelter of the trees, and found out too late that the trees were on the far side. The fence was high, impossible to climb, and she could hear the man behind her as she followed the fence toward the road. There had to be a break somewhere. There *had* to be!

She found it. A small gate exiting to the street. She darted through. There wasn't a soul to be seen in either direction. *Oh, God,* she screamed inside her head. *Help me. Please help me.*

Across the street, the crumbling towers of the ancient minster rose against the sky. Beyond the perimeter lay a maze of broken walls and tumbled stone and shadows darker than the night itself. It was her only hope. There was nowhere else to hide.

With every step a piercing stab of pain, Vikki plunged across the road and reached the shelter of the ruins. She blundered on, seeking ever deeper darkness, spurred on by the thud of feet behind her, twisting, turning, bumping into walls until she didn't know where she was. She staggered on, her whole body now a blinding sheet of pain.

She tripped and fell, but was up on her hands and knees in an instant, scrambling sideways like a crab into the deepest shadow she could find. She lay there panting, trying to still the pounding of her heart so she could listen.

Nothing. No sound at all. But then there wouldn't be, not here on the grass. Perhaps the man would give up and leave. She'd heard someone shout back there. Perhaps he'd been scared off—but it was far more likely that he was listening, too, waiting for her to make a move. All right, she wouldn't move. She would simply lie here close to the wall and wait for him to go away.

But it was hard to lie still. What if he didn't go away—or worse! What if he knew that she was there and was creeping closer?

She held her breath. Was that another footstep or her own imagination? She dare not take a chance; she had to move. The man with the knife had tracked her down, and he was not going to leave until he'd found her.

Her only hope was to work her way out of the ruins on the Bridge Street side where it was well lighted and she'd find more people. But which way was Bridge Street?

Vikki attempted to stand up, but as soon as she touched her swollen foot to the ground she knew it wouldn't hold her. If she was to get out of there, it would have to be on hands and knees. She dropped back down. The grass was wet beneath her hands, and her jeans were soaked.

She used her hand to probe the darkness ahead of her and found an opening. She paused, listening. Nothing. Within these walls she couldn't even hear the sound of traffic. Vikki crawled through, gritting her teeth to prevent herself from crying out against the pain, inching forward, careful not to make a sound.

A shoe scraped on stone, and Vikki froze. The sound came from the other side of the wall. She could hear him *breathing!* She held her own breath and crouched low, covering her face and hugging the ground.

Suddenly there was a movement, a thud, and someone swore. Vikki had a sudden urge to laugh hysterically. Serve the bastard right! She hoped he'd turned *his* ankle. Better still if he'd broken his bloody neck!

But she had to move while she had the chance. Still on hands and knees, she inched forward—and ran head-first into a wall. Dazed, she was forced to turn to her left again. Another wall! She bit back a groan. She'd boxed herself in.

She turned too quickly; her hand slid on the grass and she toppled over. Her foot shot out and hit the wall. She screamed and rolled around in agony. A blinding light exploded in her face and pinned her there. She saw the upraised arm; saw something glint...

She closed her eyes and waited for the blow to fall.

HE PRESSED HIMSELF into the niche of darkness, panting hard and shaking. He'd managed to get rid of the knife, stuffing it and the gloves under one of the many fallen stones that lay scattered among the ruins, and he'd eluded his pursuer. But he dare not stop for long. Reinforcements might well be on the way, and he had to get away before anyone else arrived. He could see the car from where he stood. The street was quiet; nothing stirred. No sign of movement anywhere.

He stepped out of the shadows, forcing himself to keep to a normal walking pace, eyes darting everywhere. His keys were ready in his hand as he approached the car. The air was cool, but his face was damp with sweat.

He pressed the remote button on the key chain and heard the quiet click as the door unlocked. He glanced up and down the street as he grasped the handle, then froze as he heard the voice behind him.

"That's far enough," said Paget quietly. "Don't turn round. Let's have your hands on top of the car where I can see them."

His legs began to shake. It wasn't supposed to end like this. How could everything have gone so wrong? Tears of sheer frustration streamed down his face as he sagged against the car.

SHE HEARD THE WORDS but she couldn't comprehend. Why didn't he have done with it? Put her out of her misery. But he kept on talking, talking...

"Look at it, please," the voice insisted.

She opened her eyes, squinting against the light. He was holding out a card, and the words slowly filtered into her brain.

"I'm a policeman, Julia," he said, "and you're safe. You don't have to run any more. Look at the card. That's me, Sergeant Tregalles." He flipped the torch so the light shone on his face.

It was all too much for Vikki. There was a roaring in her ears, the light began to spin, then everything went black.

THIRTY-FOUR

Friday, 6 October

THE WARRANT DIDN'T arrive until eight o'clock in the morning, but John Bolen was talking long before the team went in to search his flat. He admitted freely to the killing of his father and seemed more concerned with the fact that his carefully thought-out plan had failed so miserably than he was with the consequences of his act.

"You have to understand," he said earnestly. "It wasn't supposed to be like this at all. I didn't *want* to kill the girl. But she shouldn't have run away. If she had stayed there in the room, it would have worked, I know it would. The courts wouldn't have gone hard on her. I mean, everyone would have seen how badly she'd been beaten by my father, and that would be taken into consideration. She might even have got off completely."

"But she wasn't beaten by your father, was she?" said Tregalles. "That was done by you!"

Bolen merely shrugged. "The courts wouldn't have known that, would they?" he countered.

"I must remind you once again that you are still under caution, Mr. Bolen," said Paget. "And I ask you again: Do you wish to have legal counsel or anyone else present during this interview?"

John Bolen shook his head impatiently. Now that it was over, all he wanted to do was make them understand, and the last thing he needed was some solicitor telling him what he could or could not say. He was sick and tired of having someone else tell him what to do. He didn't *need* advice; didn't need *anyone* telling him what to say. For as long as he could remember he had done whatever his father wanted him to do, said whatever his father wanted him to say. But that was finished now. It had ended when he thrust the knife deep into his father's heart, time and time again.

"Please answer for the record," said Paget.

"No!" John Bolen turned his head toward the tape recorder and spoke loudly and distinctly: "I told you before, *I do not wish to have anyone else present!* I don't *need* anyone else. I'm perfectly capable of taking care of myself, thank you." He sat back in his chair and met Paget's gaze across the table. "I had everything worked out, you know," he insisted. "Absolutely everything!"

"Even so, something went wrong, didn't it, Mr. Bolen?"

"But that wasn't my fault," Bolen objected. "It was the girl. She..." He looked baffled. "I simply don't understand how she could have got away before someone came up to the room."

"The receptionist was delayed by a gang of hooligans who wouldn't let her off the lift," Paget told him, "which is why no one found your father until much later."

Bolen stared at him. "Well, there you are then," he said flatly. "I couldn't possible have known that, could I?" He hunched forward, brow furrowed as he continued. "You see, not knowing that, I couldn't understand why there was no mention of her being taken into custody and charged with the murder. That's why I asked you to come out to the house. That was my idea, not my mother's, as I told you. I told you about the prostitutes, expecting you to tell me that you had Vikki in custody, but you made no mention of finding her in the room."

The man leaned back in his chair, lips pursed as he stared off into the distance. "Mind you," he said pensively, "I suppose things *really* began to go wrong when Dad told me that Underwood would be along in half an hour. He'd just finished talking to him when I arrived, and that forced my hand. You see, I hadn't planned on killing him until just before the regular prostitute was due to arrive at eleven, but I couldn't afford to let Underwood see me there, so I had to do it before Underwood came round."

"So you arrived in your father's room *after* he'd phoned Underwood," said Paget. "Not before, as you told me. And you must have known it was Underwood who was supplying your father with Lambert's figures.''

"Of course I knew!'' said Bolen contemptuously. "Although I didn't let on to Dad that I knew until recently. He thought he was being so bloody clever, but I knew he must be getting figures from somewhere, and it didn't take long to find out it was Underwood who was supplying them. I used to sit in the carpark of the Tudor and watch him arrive on Sunday mornings, then I'd try to look surprised when Dad came along on Monday to tell me that the estimates I'd worked on for the past month were useless, and I was to use the figures he gave me. Finally, I'd had enough and I tackled him about it, and do you know what he said?'' His voice rose. "Do you?'' Paget shook his head. "He said, 'Go and play with your calculator, John, and leave me to run the business.'''

His face grew dark with anger. "I could have been at Wimbledon long before now if it hadn't been for my father; everybody said I had the talent. My tennis coach even came to the house and pleaded with my father, but, no, I had to go into the firm because that's what *he* wanted. It didn't matter what *I* wanted. To him, tennis was a waste of time, and no son of his was going to pursue something like that as a career.''

Bolen shook his head sadly. "I was only sixteen at the time, so I had little choice, but I thought: All right! If that was the way it had to be, I'd show him. So I went to university, got my degree and went into the firm. All those years I'd worked my guts out for him, and that was all he thought of me.''

He turned moist eyes on Paget. "I'm twenty-seven years old and he still treated me like a child,'' he ended bitterly.

"So you were in the room when Underwood arrived?'' Tregalles prompted.

"That's right, although I'd been downstairs in the meantime to tell them that my father wished to be called at seven-thirty, because I wanted to make sure they saw me leave. Then I nipped around to the back stairs and returned to the room. I knew I had the time, because Dad told me that Underwood wouldn't be there for half an hour.

"I had taken his key with me, so I let myself in and set to

work. Underwood knocked on the door for a few minutes later, but he soon went away and I was able to get on with arranging things for when Vikki arrived."

Bolen frowned into the distance. "The trouble was," he continued, "I hadn't counted on there being so much blood. I wanted it to look as if he and the girl had been having it off when things turned ugly and she'd killed him in self-defence. But he had to be undressed for that to work, and his clothes were soaked in blood. I thought that when the heart stopped, it would stop pumping blood, but it kept on pouring out, so I had to get rid of the clothes."

"And you wrapped him in a blanket to keep the body warm so that it would look as if he had been killed at a later time."

"Oh, yes. Mind you, I'd planned on that in any case," he said. "I knew I'd have to kill him before the regular prostitute arrived at eleven, so the body would have to be kept warm until Vikki arrived. Killing him an hour earlier simply meant keeping the body warm for a bit longer, that's all."

"How did you know about the prostitute?"

"I used to hear my father making the arrangements with Quint. He always called from the office. Everybody knew why he spent weekends at the Tudor. And he always arranged for the girls to come at eleven. But what I hadn't counted on was Harry turning up. He kept knocking and calling out, and I thought he'd never go away. Then this woman came—Stella, she said her name was—but I was ready for her. I imitated my father's voice and shouted at her through the door."

Bolen turned to Paget. "You see, I wanted her to be able to testify that Dad was alive at that time."

"And then you settled down to wait for Vikki to arrive."

"That's right." Bolen leaned forward and spoke earnestly. "Turned out the lights and left the door ajar, then waited for her. I had the dark glasses on and kept my face turned away when she came in, so I *know* she only had a glimpse of me before I knocked her out. It must have been later..." He fell silent.

"But her fingerprints and hair were everywhere," Paget prompted.

"Oh, yes." Bolen sounded almost pleased that Paget had brought it up. "And that was a job, I can tell you," he went on. "She's not very big, but when you're carrying her around, trying to get her prints on things in the right places, it's hard work, harder than you'd think."

He paused and pursed his lips, avoiding Paget's eyes.

"I didn't *like* beating the girl up," he said, "but she had to *look* beaten up, I mean, *really* beaten up, or they might not believe that she'd killed my father in self-defence. But I didn't enjoy it; in fact I found it quite distasteful, especially when I had to drag her nails across Dad's face."

Tregalles found it hard to hold his tongue. There wasn't even a trace of pity or remorse in Bolen's voice as he continued.

"After that, all that remained to be done was to phone down to the desk, pretending to be my father calling for help. I took a quick look at the girl to make sure she was completely out, and then left by the back stairs. I left the door ajar deliberately so they were bound to go in.

"The first time I knew for certain that Vikki had got away was when I heard your broadcast, and that made me wonder if she'd been faking when I last looked at her. I didn't *think* she would be able to identify me, but I couldn't afford to take the chance. And the one thing your broadcast did tell me was that she must be afraid to go to the police because she feared they wouldn't believe her story, so if I could get to her first, everything would be all right."

"So you went after Simone," Tregalles put in harshly.

Bolen shrugged. "I'd seen her with Vikki," he said. "It was the logical place to start." He might have been discussing the weather for all the emotion he displayed.

Tregalles could contain himself no longer. "And once she'd told you what you wanted to know, you killed her," he said angrily.

"Well, yes. I had to; she'd seen my face."

Paget was feeling no less repelled by the man, but he kept his own voice under control.

"You killed her in a car," he said. It wasn't a question. "But it wasn't your car, was it, Mr. Bolen?"

Bolen shot a baleful glance at Tregalles. "You rang Linda in Inverness, didn't you?" he accused. "You must have done, because she's the only one who knew I'd borrowed her car that night. What was it? Something to do with the colour of the upholstery?"

Tregalles remained silent. John Bolen, lips pursed, stared into the distance. "I really didn't want her dragged into this," he said. "I was afraid she might mention that I'd borrowed her car if you asked her about that night. But I thought with her being away in Scotland, there was a good chance no one would think to question her when she got back."

Bolen drew in his breath and sighed heavily. "But you're right, of course; I did use Linda's car. As I told you, I went over to her flat after leaving Mother, and pretended that my car wouldn't start when it came time to leave. I asked Linda if I could borrow her car till morning, then went round to Cresswell Street and picked up Simone. Trouble was, Simone knew where Vikki had gone, and the name of the woman she was with, but she couldn't remember the name of the canal or the pub where she worked, so I had to do a bit of digging. That's why it took so long to find the boat, that and the fact that I had to spend so much time with Linda's parents, so that set me back a bit."

He frowned as a thought occurred to him. "But how did you know I killed Simone in a car?" he asked Paget.

"Never mind that for the moment," Paget told him brusquely, "but I am curious about one thing: How did you manage to get behind Simone to do it? She was a street-wise woman. I can't see her allowing that to happen."

"Ah!" Bolen slid forward on his chair, eager to explain. "That took a bit of thinking about, but it was simple, really. I put a package on the back seat, all tied up with ribbon as if it were a gift for someone, and I told Simone I had to deliver it before going on to a motel. When I got to the house, I got out of the car, went round and opened the back door as if to take the gift out, but instead I slipped into the back seat and had the rope around her neck just like that! Then all I had to do was keep twisting until she told me what I wanted to now. You see," he continued earnestly, "that's why I used Linda's car. It has four doors; mine only has two."

"And you still got it wrong in spite of all your so-called planning," Tregalles burst out. "And damned near killed another innocent girl."

"You can hardly blame me for that," Bolen shot back. "How was I to know there was another girl on the boat?"

The sergeant opened his mouth to speak, then clamped it shut as Paget gave him a warning glance.

"This plan of yours," said Paget, "stealing your father's car, arranging for a girl to come to his room so that she could be set up to take the blame, knowing ahead of time what time Stella Green would be coming to the room—all that took planning. How did you do that in such a short space of time? I mean, you must have thought there was still a chance that your father could be persuaded to drop the Ockrington project."

John Bolen stared at the chief inspector. "This had nothing to do with the Ockrington project," he said scornfully. "You don't understand at all, do you? *I've been planning this since the day my father forced me into the firm when I was sixteen years old!* I hated my father, hated him for making me do what *he* wanted instead of letting me do what *I* wanted. But I couldn't fight him, not then, so I pretended to fall in with his wishes. I became the dutiful son, and he never once suspected that I was just biding my time. As for the Ockrington deal, that was just the catalyst. I could see that Dad was going to destroy everything if he went through with it, and we would all be left with nothing. But the final straw was when we hit my mother. When I saw her at the hospital that day, and she told me what had happened, I knew the time had come. My father had to die; it was the only way, and I knew exactly how to do it."

And Laura Bolen had been afraid that John would be upset because she wanted to sell the firm, thought Paget. How little she had known about her son.

"WE FOUND BLOODSTAINS on the rim of the sun-roof of the car where Moss said he cut his hand," said Paget. "There's a nick in the chrome, and blood has soaked into the seal. Forensic will check it out, but I don't think there's the slightest doubt that the blood came from Moss's finger. The car is also being checked for mud, grasses, tyre impressions and the like for a match with samples taken from the area where Moss says he saw the car.

"And speaking of cars, we've been on to the Inverness police and asked them to impound Linda McRae's car and hold it for a forensic examination."

Paget, Tregalles, and Sergeant Ormside sat in Superintendent Alcott's office. Len Ormside had been roused at four o'clock by Paget, and had been at his desk by five. He, in turn, had called others out, and the Incident Room was fully staffed by seven.

The hospital stairway had been searched, the flowers and the box had been found, and members of the staff who had been on duty the previous evening were being questioned.

"A length of yellow rope and a piece of wood found on a bench in Bolen's lock-up garage appear to match the rope and home-made handles of the garrotte found where Bunny Brown was attacked," Paget continued. "We also checked his belts, all of which are of exactly the same length, and creased in the same places as the one found on Jim Bolen's body, the belt John was forced to substitute for Bolen's own when it became soaked with blood. And, of course, we have Julia Rutledge's testimony as well."

Alcott butted out a cigarette and lit another. "How is the girl?" he asked.

Ormside spoke up. "When I spoke to the doctor this morning, he said her ankle was badly sprained but nothing's broken. But there is a hairline fracture in the skull where Bolen hit her, so he wants to make sure there's no hidden damage before he releases her from hospital.

"And speaking of Rutledge," Ormside continued on, "I checked her record with Northampton, and they confirmed that her case is under review. She was convicted for stealing from the motel rooms where she was employed as a cleaner, but just last month the owner's son was caught stealing from the rooms, and among the things recovered were several items young Rutledge was supposed to have stolen. The lad admitted that he was responsible for the thefts and said his mother knew about it when she testified against Rutledge. So she faces a charge of perjury. Which," Ormside concluded, "leaves only the theft of a bicycle in Northampton, and the one she took from Longford Marsh."

"It's about time that kid had a break after what she's been through," Tregalles observed. He could still see the terror on the girl's face as he shone the light on her in the minster ruins.

"And Bolen still refuses to talk to a solicitor?"

"That's right, sir."

Alcott swung his chair around to face the window and the playing fields beyond. "Do you think he's sane?" he asked.

"I'm sure he understood what he was doing," said Paget. "But I'm no psychiatrist."

Alcott grunted. "You can be sure the family will want one brought in," he said, "and Bolen could still retract his statement. Let's make sure we have every scrap of evidence there is. I don't want him wriggling out of this through some technicality."

He swung back to face Tregalles. "You're to be commended, Sergeant, for saving that girl's life," he said warmly. "If you hadn't gone in when you did, we could have had another murder on our hands. Good work, Tregalles."

"Thank you, sir."

Alcott turned to Paget. "But what puzzles me," he said, "is how you happened to be at Bolen's car when he came out of there?"

"Bit of luck, really," Paget told him. "Tregalles had the only torch, and it was pitch-black in there, so I couldn't see that I would be much help blundering about in the dark. But I spotted Bolen's car as I crossed the road—I remembered it from the first time I went to see him at his mother's house—and I knew he'd have to come back to it. So I called for back-up and waited by the car."

There was a light tap on the partly open door, and Alcott's secretary, Fiona, stuck her head inside. "Excuse me, sir, but I thought you would like to know they've found the weapon and a pair of latex gloves hidden under a stone in the minster ruins."

"WHEN *CAN* WE SEE HIM?" Harry Bolen paced the floor, hands clasped behind his back. He and Dee had come to the house as soon as Laura telephoned earlier that morning. Prudence was there as well, numb with shock, although she was more concerned with the fate of Mark Malone than that of her brother, John. She had raced up from Bristol the day before when a close friend had phoned to tell her she'd heard that Mark Malone had been injured in a car crash. She'd spent a tearful hour beside his bed before a doctor managed to persuade her that there was little point in staying while Malone was still unconscious.

First her father, then Mark. Now John had been arrested. It seemed to Prudence that the world around her was falling apart.

"They said they'd ring," said Laura. She rose from her chair and moved restlessly around the room. "I rang our solicitor as soon as I heard the news," she continued, "but he rang back a short time ago and said that John refused to talk to him and told him to get out. Perhaps you could ring them to see what's..." Laura clamped her lips together. Her eyes filled with tears.

Harry picked up the telephone. "Do you have the number?" he asked.

"Here, I wrote it down." Laura picked up a bright-pink envelope from a side table and read the number off to Harry. She was about to put it back, then handed the envelope to Prudence. "I'm sorry, Prudence," she said, "but this was delivered yesterday while you were out, and it completely slipped my mind."

It was a large envelope. The name and address were typewritten, and there was no return address. Probably some promotional material. Prudence thought idly as she slit the top with her nail. She'd had all sorts of things like that come through the post since she'd entered university. But why had it come here?

"Yes, I'm his uncle," she heard Harry say as she pulled out the contents. "I'm calling on behalf of John Bolen's mother. She..."

Prudence didn't hear any more as she stared at the pictures. Pictures of Mark, naked and entwined in the arms of a woman. The woman's face had been blotted out, but the rest of her body... Prudence didn't want to look but she couldn't help herself. There were seven of them in all, each more revealing than the last.

She began to shake. No one noticed; all eyes were fixed on

Harry. Her long, thin fingers curled around the prints and began to tear them into strips. Her mother heard the sound and looked at her. "What is it, Pru...? You're shaking."

Prudence rose unsteadily to her feet. The torn pieces fluttered to the floor. Without a word to anyone, she walked stiffly to the door and left the room.

TREVOR BERESFORD SAT in front of the console, staring blankly at the row of screens mounted above it. The room was sound-proof, and one wall was lined with shelves, three quarters of which were packed with tapes, all carefully indexed and labelled. Next door was the bedroom Malone had described in so much detail; a room covered from virtually every angle by concealed video cameras.

It was a pity about Malone, thought Beresford, but then studs like him were two-a-penny. Not that they would be much use to him until he could find a replacement for Ronnie. And that wasn't going to be easy, especially as he would have to play the part of the grieving widower for a while. She'd been a delight to work with, very professional, and very much in demand by the clientele on the net.

He sighed. He was going to miss her very much.

THIRTY-FIVE

Saturday, 7 October

THE NURSE SMILED encouragingly. "I should think they'll let you go home tomorrow, or Monday at the very latest," she told Vikki.

Home! There was a hollow ring to the word in Vikki's ears. It was a word that should mean warmth and safety and comfort. It should not be a place where you were scared to death of being left alone with your stepfather, where your mother accused you of lies and worse when you tried to tell her what he was doing to you.

Vikki lay there, staring at the ceiling. She didn't have a home. The police had said they would be talking to her again, which probably meant that her next home would be a cell somewhere. After that she'd be on the streets again.

They had given her something to ease the pain, and she was half asleep when someone sat down beside the bed and took her hand. Vikki opened her eyes.

"Joanna!"

Joanna smiled. "Feeling a bit better, now, are you, luv?" she asked. "You certainly look better than you did yesterday."

"You were here yesterday?" Vikki struggled to sit up in bed. "How...? I didn't now you were here."

"You didn't know because you were still out of it when I was here. You'd had a pretty rough time, so I let you sleep. And as for how I knew you were in the hospital, Chief Inspector Paget telephoned George at the pub and asked him to let me know that you'd been found and were in safe hands."

Vikki's fingers closed tightly on Joanna's. "Bunny *is* all right, isn't she?" she asked anxiously. "The police said she was, but..."

"She's fine," Joanna assured the girl. "She's coming out on Monday."

Vikki's eyes were moist. "I'm sorry I ran off like that..." she began, but Joanna reached over and put a finger to the girl's lips.

"Now that will be enough of that!" she said severely. "And don't you worry about what will happen when you're released from here. I've talked to Bunny about it, and she's agreed: You're coming back with us, and you can stay as long as you like on one condition."

Vikki swallowed hard. "Condition?" she echoed fearfully.

Joanna looked stern. "You have a talent, Vikki, and it would be a shame to waste it, so I want you to promise me you'll keep working on your sketching. Later, perhaps, who knows, it could lead to something you can do for a living, and we'll help you as much as we can."

"Oh, Joanna!" The light in Vikki's eyes was answer enough. But suddenly the light went out. "But what about the police?"

"No doubt they'll want to talk to you," Joanna told her, "and you may be needed as a witness later, but for now they are prepared to release you into my custody. So, at least you'll have a home to go to when they let you out of here."

A home to go to! Vikki blinked back the tears.

Joanna rose to leave. "I have to go," she said. "Being Saturday, George will be needing me. Sorry I didn't bring you anything, but with all the dashing about I've been doing, I'm afraid…"

"Oh, but you *did* bring me something, Joanna. You did!"

Vikki reached out and clutched Joanna's hand. "You couldn't have brought me anything better," she whispered as the tears rolled down her cheeks.

THE LIGHTS WERE LOW, the music soft, and Andrea McMillan looked ravishing, thought Paget as he looked at her across the table. Leonardo himself had escorted them from the door, and the table was one of the finest in the room.

Andrea looked around. "It's been a long time," she observed quietly, and Paget knew exactly what she meant. It seemed like an eternity since their last evening here together, and even now he had trouble believing that this was actually happening. He took a deep breath. Forget the past, he told himself sternly. Look to a new beginning.

"You're not on call, I hope?" he said. He hadn't told a soul where he would be, and he'd left his pager at home.

Andrea smiled. "Not tonight," she assured him. "But that reminds me; I meant to tell you earlier. Dr. Starkie went home today, and I must say he looks one hundred percent better than he did. He's still not smoking, which is a good sign. Unfortunately, now that *he's* stopped, he's making life miserable for everyone who does smoke."

"Sounds like Reg," said Paget. "But his wife will be pleased. I know she's been very worried about him, so I hope he keeps it up." Paget liked the crusty and sometimes cantankerous pathologist and wished him well. But tonight he intended to leave work and everything related to it behind. He looked out across the room...and froze!

Threading their way through the tables were Tregalles and his wife, Audrey.

"Why, Chief Inspector, what a lovely surprise!" Audrey beamed at Paget. Behind her stood Tregalles—looking somewhat confused.

Paget rose to his feet. "Dr. McMillan, I'd like to introduce Mrs. Tregalles," he said formally. "You know Sergeant Tregalles of course." The two women exchanged smiles and unintelligible murmurs, while Paget prayed that no one would suggest they sit together.

Something of his thoughts must have conveyed itself to Tregalles, because he took his wife firmly by the arm. "They're waiting to show us to our table," he said quietly.

"In just a minute, John," she said, and went on to explain that tomorrow would be their wedding anniversary. "We're having the family round for Sunday dinner," she told them, "but John thought it would be nice if we had this dinner together, just the two of us tonight. He had to book ever such a long time ago to get in. I expect you had to do the same, didn't you, Mr. Paget?"

"It is very popular," said Andrea before Paget could reply. "So nice to have met you, Mrs. Tregalles. I hope you have a lovely evening, and a happy anniversary tomorrow."

"Thank you, Doctor." Tregalles tapped his wife's arm again, and Audrey rolled her eyes expressively.

"Got to go," she said in a stage whisper. "Can't keep John away from his dinner for too long or he'll be grumpy all night. Nice meeting you, Doctor."

As they moved away, Audrey tugged at her husband's arm. "I thought you told me that Mr. Paget was going with..."

The rest of her words were lost, and not a moment too soon, thought Paget as he turned once more to Andrea.

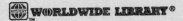

A TORY TRAVERS/DAVID ALVAREZ MYSTERY

ROSEWOOD'S ASHES

by
AILEEN SCHUMACHER

New Mexico engineer Tory Travers is
summoned home to Gainesville, Florida,
where her estranged father lies in a coma
after a hit-and-run accident. While preparing
to face the demons of her past, Tory finds
herself unwittingly embroiled in a complex,
emotionally charged and deadly conspiracy
connected to a 1923 racial massacre—the
torching of a town called Rosewood.

*Available May 2002
at your favorite retail outlet.*

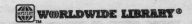